Lemonade

Lemonade

Nina Pennacchi

Translated by Scott P. Sheridan

This is a work of fiction. Names, characters, organizations, places, events, and incidents are either products of the author's imagination or are used fictitiously.

Previously published as *Lemonade* by the author via the Kindle Direct Publishing Platform in Italy in 2014. Translated from Italian by Scott P. Sheridan. First published in English by AmazonCrossing in 2015.

Published by AmazonCrossing, Seattle.

www.apub.com

ISBN-13: 9781503944404

ISBN-10: 1503944409

Cover design by Scott Barrie

Printed in the United States of America.

Prologue

This is the only reason we cannot complain about life: it holds no one against his will.

—Seneca

London, March 18, 1806

Someone had taken a light object—a pillow?—off his face and grabbed his hands violently. *Let me sleep, Mrs. Taylor,* he said to himself. *Please. Just a bit longer.*

"He's alive!" shouted a woman's distressed voice. "He's alive, thank God!"

Who had been shaking his shoulders so abruptly? He breathed through his mouth, gulping air, and a painful coughing fit suddenly came over him. "Mrs. Taylor?" he murmured, opening his eyes.

He was lying on an unmade bed between light gray sheets. Around him he heard hurried steps and screams, but they sounded far-off and muffled. The light of a lamp, although weak, hurt his eyes. The fog that had blurred his vision slowly cleared, and he saw an unknown, frightened girl standing over his bed. She had a beautiful face and wore an odd hat decorated with an enormous white feather that seemed to curve down toward him like a dead bird.

The walls, which were covered in ochre and beige wallpaper with heavy floral designs, were unfamiliar to him. It was not the room he usually slept in, and moreover he was alone in the bed, and Martin and Ronnie weren't with him.

Where am I? he asked himself.

After a few moments he remembered. His mother had gone to fetch him at the Widow Taylor's that night—and she never usually went to get him at night, and especially not at this late hour. His mother had asked him with a bright smile, "Would you like to come away with me, ducky?" For a moment his heart—and the world—stopped. To him it seemed that the room was spinning, and he had thought that happiness could make him fly like the birds in the sky. He had held back the outburst of joy that was ripping him in two, and with the seasoned maturity of his five years (and a half, almost) he had answered calmly, "Yes, Mummy, I want to come."

"Mummy?" he now asked.

"He's alive," repeated the girl who had awakened him, as she stopped shaking him. "Who are you, child?"

Christopher didn't answer. The tense tone in her excited voice frightened him. Instead, he turned over on his left side. His neck hurt, as if he had slept on it wrong. *This is my mummy's house,* he reasoned. But where was she? What was all this noise? And all this yelling?

"Are you Martha's son?" the girl with the dead feather asked him. Her hands were on his shoulders, blocking the room from view.

From his right came nervous male voices. "I will pick her up. You take off the rope. Go ahead, do it now. Bloody hell! There's shit everywhere."

Why were they all speaking so loudly?

"Yeah," said another voice, high-pitched like a boy's, "the stench makes me want to throw up."

"Mummy?" Christopher asked again. What was happening? He tried to get a glimpse behind the young lady, but he couldn't see around her.

"Don't look," she ordered him suddenly. She held him down on the bed, her head bent over him, the feather coming ever closer. "Francesca!" she shouted toward the door. "Come help me!"

Christopher wriggled and, since he was used to freeing himself from the grips of the older kids in the common dormitory, slipped easily out of her delicate fingers. He sat up on the bed and leaned over to see around her.

"No," she said, and she put her arm around him to pull him toward her. She wanted to spare him the sight, but it was too late.

There was a rope tied to the ceiling, the end of the rope knotted around the neck of a woman. Her face was swollen and blue. The woman wasn't moving, and two men were pulling her down. One man had her by the legs to hold her up and take pressure off the noose, while the other stood on a chair as he removed the rope from her neck. For a moment it seemed to Christopher that she was looking at him. Her two purple, bulging eyes turned toward him, and her tongue, which stuck out like a grim joke, seemed to say, *It's not all that bad up here, Christopher.*

"Mummy!" he screamed, trying to get out of the girl's hold. "Mummy!"

Why did he call her Mummy? That wasn't her. His mother's eyes were blue and not at all red, like those were. And his mummy didn't have a swollen face but tiny, pale, fine features.

The two men freed the woman from the noose, then laid her down flat on a blanket on the floor. A piece of paper fell out of her right hand.

"Mummy!"

Why did he call her Mummy? It couldn't be her. His mother was so beautiful. When she took him to the park, everyone turned to look at her, even the gentlemen.

It wasn't his mother, even if she had the flower that Mummy had been wearing when she had come to fetch him at Mrs. Taylor's. She had promised him so many times that she would take him away from there, and in the end she kept her word, because that's what mothers do.

"Mummy!" he cried madly. "Mummy!"

But it really wasn't her, was it? It meant nothing that she had dark hair or the flower or the elegant dress—stained with feces and urine, but it was his mother's blue dress.

"Elise," called a woman's voice at the door. "Elise, oh my God!"

"Come help me!" begged the girl with the feather, desperately holding Christopher, who was kicking and scratching to get away. "Let's get him out of here!"

The two men hastily wrapped the lady up in the colorful blanket. "C'mon, to the river," said the younger man, and he lifted her up like a rolled-up carpet.

It wasn't his mother inside of the blanket, hidden between folds of multicolored fabric. Christopher continued to scream and scream, until another girl joined the first, and then yet another, and they dragged him from the room as he kicked and screamed madly over and over, "Mummy! Mummy! Mummy!"

1

I do not know if it was by will, or fate, or chance . . .
—Dante Alighieri

Coxton, July 7, 1826

"Well, what do you think?"

Sitting on a settee nearby, Lucy wrinkled her brow and examined her as if she were a new type of insect. "Anna, this dress does not suit you at all. It's dreadful!"

Dreadful, dreadful. Anna repeated the word to herself in Lucy's tone and began to giggle, looking at the mirror in front of her. Dreadful? Bah. The dress was simple, with an empire waist and a round, high neckline. "Come off it," Anna responded. "It's not that bad."

Lucy rolled her eyes without deigning to reply.

"Don't you find that it matches the color of my eyes?" Anna insisted.

Her friend took a pillow and pressed it against her face. "Well, yes, but . . . brown . . ." She pronounced the last word with emphasis, as if it were a vulgar term absolutely unworthy of her.

"It's not really brown. It's . . . brownish."

Anna knew it was hardly wise of her to provoke Lucy, because there was the definite risk that she would begin again to explain the importance of pastel colors in highlighting a rosy complexion. However, she didn't manage to avoid it—and to be honest, she didn't even try—and she stifled another laugh under the critical gaze of Lucy's striking blue eyes. *Who knows if today she will talk about pink or white?* she thought, expecting the worst.

If there was one thing she loved about balls it was those moments just before leaving when her friend would give her advice on manners and attempt to make her elegant. She would have liked to have drawn out those little talks forever, because evening dance parties always ended up being rather disappointing. That night in particular she was in no hurry to leave: Daniel would not even be there, and—

"Would you like to take me seriously or not? Look how cross I'm becoming," Lucy said, and she threw the pillow at Anna as physical confirmation of her anger.

Anna dodged it with a jump, then picked it up and tossed it back at Lucy. "I wouldn't even dream of it," she responded with a scowl. "You should know that the rules that apply for petite blond girls do not apply for fat girls with brown hair."

"You're not fat. You're plump, and it's not a bad thing."

"Do you really think so?" Anna said, and gave her a spiteful grin. "Then it should be about the dress. Like I told you, it doesn't look so bad on me."

She turned toward the mirror and stared at the dress, then her face. It was nothing special: her features had a few irregularities, and the only thing that she liked, to be honest, was the natural dark-pink color of her lips, which that evening were almost purple in the summer sun. What a shame that a chipped tooth—her left incisor—made her smile permanently crooked.

Lucy shook her head. "Anna, listen and don't get angry. I would like to give you a dress, if not—"

"We have already discussed it, it seems," Anna replied. She sounded a bit too abrupt, and Lucy made an upset face. "I'm sorry," she quickly added. "You know that I don't want your gifts. But I can promise you that I will follow your instructions the next time I redesign one of my mother's dresses, all right?"

Returning to being in a good mood, Lucy nodded. "Even the dark-green one?"

"Whichever you'd like. It doesn't matter what I put on, after all. In any case, nothing will stop me from looking disturbingly like an artichoke."

Lucy laughed tenderly with the affection of their twelve-year friendship, which had completely overcome obstacles of many fabrics, even brown ones. "Come here, little artichoke," she said, inviting her to sit down by tapping on the settee. "Many boys could find you to their liking if you weren't so surly," she suggested as Anna sat beside her. "Like on Wednesday morning when Mr. Clarke came to pay you a visit. Tell me, why weren't you at home?"

"You got Nora to squeal?" *Oh, what a traitor!* Anna thought. She had asked her not to tell anyone. "How did you get her to talk?"

Anna already knew how. Lucy, all sweetness and smiles, could get a horse to talk. Good heavens, she could get the saddle to speak!

"I didn't torture her—don't look at me like that," Lucy chuckled. "All I had to do was compliment her on her biscuits. And anyway, I believe she could hardly wait to tell me—she wants you to find a husband. And she is quite anxious about it, because it has already been six months since you made your debut in society, and you've shown interest in no one. *Almost* no one," she added, smiling.

Lucy delivered this correction with a sneer—a slight one—which made Anna blush. Anxiety grew in the pit of her stomach.

"About tonight," Anna said, prudently changing the subject. "Explain to me how you managed to get even me invited."

"How *I* did?"

Clueless astonishment filled Lucy's eyes. It was an expression Anna knew all too well—a look that told her not to believe her friend, not even for a moment.

"Of course, you! Who else?" Anna retorted. "Without your assistance, Mrs. Mortimer would have never sent an invitation to my family. Come, tell me the truth: Did you threaten to burn down her house, or did you promise to marry her firstborn?"

Giving in, Lucy chortled. "Perhaps I promised to burn her firstborn, now that I think about it."

"Lucy Edwards, of all the sneaky . . ." Anna laughed, then said with a playful fear in her eyes that perhaps wasn't so playful, "It's better if we go now, or your mother will burn us alive! She must be waiting impatiently for us."

Yes, very impatiently, as they could tell when they went downstairs. When she saw them, Mrs. Edwards popped up like a fountain. "You're finally here," she exclaimed gruffly. It was always an odd sight to see her next to Lucy, because in comparison Mrs. Edwards seemed like a pale, less joyful copy of her daughter.

Anna's father also got up from his armchair, but with extreme difficulty. "Enjoy yourself, darling," he said, wheezing heavily. He had a distorted face, paralyzed on the left side.

"Are you staying awake a little longer, Daddy?"

"No. I'm waiting for Nora. Then . . ." He stopped speaking for a moment to catch his breath. "Then I'm going to bed."

And here they came, the heavy footsteps of the old cook. As if conjured by these words, Nora appeared at the side door of the drawing room.

"Oh, you're here," Anna said to her, looking sweetly at her short, round shape. "I came to say good night."

"Go. You'll be late." The words came out of Nora's mouth quickly, like falling pebbles. "Don't worry. I'll see to your father."

"Thank you," Anna replied.

"Humph," was all the response Nora could muster.

"Yes, be off, dear," repeated Mr. Champion. He was leaning on the back of the armchair, and Anna noticed the unfortunate trembling of his hands.

(They shake more and more, don't they, Anna?)

Of course, after his stroke two years before, her father lost his mind and his strength, and it seemed to her that the situation was getting worse day after day. This man who had once been mentally sharp and physically strapping now could hardly walk or talk—the very same man who would lift her when she was a child as if she were a twig, who would twirl her around effortlessly as she stretched out her arms and closed her eyes and dreamed of flying.

***

The Mortimers' ball was in full swing when Christopher stepped into the brightly lit room. Overhead were enormous, luxurious chandeliers, which stood out in an otherwise drab country village. *Quite different from the brothel where I grew up,* he thought to himself, taking secret pleasure in the idea, as he usually did. *What would these people say if they knew whose son I am and where I come from?*

To be precise, one could not say that he really "grew up" in the brothel in Covent Garden, because after the death of his mother he stayed there only six months. Nevertheless, fragmented memories of that place came to mind in the most unthinkable moments. He remembered Elise's room, always messy, and the big vertical mirror on the side of the bed—the one with a crack across it on the side that gave a reflection split in two. He remembered the noisy footsteps of gentlemen on the stairs as they came and went, and the forced, loud laughter of the girls of the house, who accompanied them to the rooms, and the hiding place under the staircase behind the cluster of old clothes and newspapers, where he and Simon would hide as soon as any visitor arrived. In truth, Simon was so ugly that he wouldn't have needed to hide: with his big head, his long, dark, forever-filthy hair, and the violet birthmark that nearly covered his entire right cheek, there was certainly no danger that any gentleman would be interested in him. If he went into the hiding place, it was only to keep Christopher company. It was in this cranny, which smelled of rags and humidity, that he taught Christopher how to shine shoes, how to beg for money, and how to pick pockets for handkerchiefs and wallets. And Christopher always asked him before going to sleep, "Will we beat up kids in the street tomorrow?"

Simon appeared pensive, and his face seemed adult at only nine years of age. "Once we are sure we can beat them up, we stop; if not, we run away," he would say. "That way we can get them some other time."

But Simon was dead now—he had died more than twenty years ago from measles contracted from a mattress thrown on the ground. And Christopher was in a sumptuous room, welcomed with open arms at an elegant ball and—oh, sirs!—how many lights there were, how much expensive clothing, and how neat and tidy everything around him was. *I would like to jump up and say, "Hey, people! I am a landowner now," but the fact is that I am the bastard son of a whore.*

***

Heavens, what am I doing here? thought Anna for the twenty-first—no, the twenty-second—time. The noise of the music and of people chattering made her dizzy. It seemed as if everyone was at the Mortimers' ball. And not only was everyone there, but they were trying to make their presence known as loudly as possible.

Left alone while Lucy was dancing, Anna roamed uncomfortably around the drink table, trying not to be noticed—and, in particular, not to be noticed by Mr. Pembrooke. It wasn't just because of her usual surly nature, either. All the young women avoided him like the plague, whether due to his slightly too audacious way of handling his dancing partners, or due to his breath, which smelled of liquor. What liquor exactly it was impossible to say; perhaps one that he himself brewed right in his stomach, because he reminded one vaguely of a barrel. Anna picked up a glass of lemonade as she moved along his line of sight, hoping all the while that she could manage to avoid him until the end of the evening.

Out of the corner of her eye, she noticed that Lucy—who had finished her dance with Mr. Rossington—was heading toward her. She immediately began to think of a topic of conversation before her friend could ask her . . .

"How did your dance with Mr. Hickson go?" Lucy said, her voice a bit breathy from the dance.

Oh, damn. She wasn't fast enough. It wasn't easy to talk faster than Lucy. "You don't want to know," she ended up answering.

"Oh, yes. On the contrary."

Anna gave her a guilty look. "Well, let's say that I may have stepped on his feet two or three times."

"Or maybe two or three hundred?"

"The exact number escapes me," she admitted. "But it could be close to that."

"And you want me to believe that you didn't do it on purpose?"

"Come now, Lucy, everyone knows that I'm a horrible dancer, and . . . Oh, very well!" she acknowledged. "Perhaps once or twice I did it on purpose, but I assure you, when he began to speak to me about carriage racing I couldn't hold myself back. You, on the other hand," she added quickly, to prevent her nagging, "what do you have to say about Mr. Rossington? The last time I talked with him, he seemed very taken by you."

Her friend pursed her lips. "I don't know. I believe I could tolerate his red hair if not . . ." She stopped speaking suddenly, her attention drawn elsewhere. "Oh, look who's here," she whispered, and then she called out "Daniel!"

Anna tensed up and her heart skipped a beat, and then another. *What is he doing here?* she wondered nervously. Lucy had said that he would be out of town, and Anna now found herself absolutely not ready to see him. She wasn't prepared, and she hadn't even thought about what to say to him! What if she stammered? Or if she stumbled? Or if . . . She did her best to not show her confusion, and she turned toward him, perfectly composed—or at least that's what she hoped.

Daniel DeMercy was incredibly dashing that evening—he was incredibly dashing every evening. Tonight he wore a dark-blue coat that outlined his slender, athletic build. He smiled, and the bright flecks in his dark-green eyes sparkled.

"Lucy. Miss Champion," he greeted them, bowing and kissing them each on the hand. "You are both very lovely this evening."

Lucy thanked him in her adorable way, and a pair of gentlemen passing nearby stumbled, as they were too busy looking at her face to watch where they were walking. It was wasted attention, since she didn't even look at them. "You came back in time for the ball, then," she said to Daniel. "You do realize you cast the young ladies of Coxton into despair when you announced that you could not come."

"I managed to get out of my commitments," he responded, smiling with a certain cheekiness. And Daniel had such a nice smile, which showed not only how charming he could be but how unfair. He was devoted to Lucy—but why did it eat at Anna's heart?

"I must therefore deduce that I have cast you into despair," Daniel said, again smiling at Anna's friend.

"Perhaps," Lucy responded spitefully. "How do you propose to atone for this inexcusable conduct?"

"Atone?" he asked, and ran his finger between his neck and his neckerchief, as if it were too tight—dramatically, of course, but judging by his worried look, he probably felt the need to loosen the knot. "Lucy, when you say that word, I can't help but think of that afternoon—how many years ago? Eleven almost—when you made me run back and forth on the staircase in your house with two buckets full of water. Ten times! And all because I accidentally stepped on your tomcat's tail."

Despite Daniel's charm and its unwitting cruelty, Lucy continually showed indifference toward him. Anna held back a sigh and hid behind an expression of polite playfulness.

"It was a female cat," corrected Lucy resentfully. "And I believe that now you've earned a new punishment."

"And to think I came over here with the hope of a dance," he muttered. "I am truly a deluded wretch. But listen, before you decide to cut me off at the knees again—"

"I may not cut you off at *both* knees—this time!"

"Before your unrelenting judgment befalls me, won't you grant me one last dance? Certainly," Daniel said, touching the right side of his head and grinning, "certainly I will not be able to go out in public for a very, very long time if this time you decide to cut me off . . . even at only one knee."

They laughed, and Anna seemed to see them as friends from ten years before. *Sometimes,* thought Anna, *the only thing that separates adulthood from childhood may be found in laughter.*

"I accept your invitation, Daniel," answered Lucy with ostentatious condescension. "This way you can't possibly doubt the goodness of my heart."

"That I could not do in any case—not aloud, at least," he assured her. And then the dreaded moment arrived—the moment Anna longed for, both ghastly and marvelous: Daniel turned his eyes toward her. The heavens moved and the earth quaked and . . . and . . . well? Of course, all of this was only in her mind. (If one really wanted to be precise.) Daniel didn't show any particular emotion when he looked upon Anna, and she didn't swoon at the sight of him, which all in all wasn't such a bad thing. "Miss Champion," he said to her. "Lucy and I aren't bothering you with our childhood memories, are we?"

Oh no. It just gives me a slight stabbing pain in my heart, Daniel, nothing more. "No, not at all," she responded with heroic nonchalance. The stuttering remained in her stomach. "When we were young, Lucy would speak to me of her male friend who went to boarding school—the one she would plan tricks to play on months before he would return home on vacation."

"It's not true. Don't believe her, Daniel," Lucy protested. "Two or three weeks was more than enough time for the likes of you."

"A few times we all even played together, Mr. DeMercy," added Anna, blushing. "But perhaps you don't recall."

"Two little girls eight and nine years old against a young lad of thirteen—of course I recall. After having passed that test and living to tell the tale, I could never again be afraid of anything—except little eight- and nine-year-old girls, obviously."

"Oh, stop it," Anna said to him, scolding. "We weren't all that bad."

He raised an eyebrow.

"Were we?" Anna asked, a grin spreading across her face.

He gazed back at her, saying nothing.

"Oh, very well, perhaps we were a bit."

Daniel laughed. "And as for now?" he asked after a moment. "Are you enjoying yourself this evening, Miss Champion? If I'm not mistaken, you're not that fond of dancing parties."

She shrugged her shoulders. "There are few worse ways to spend one's time."

"Such as?"

"I don't know . . . listening to my little sister playing the flute, perhaps."

Daniel let out a laugh that was musical and contagious, and Lucy said, "Please don't listen to her, Daniel. Anna finds these evenings to her liking, even if she would never admit it."

"I agree with you," he declared, though his eyes shined in a way that did not bode well. "All the more so," he added matter-of-factly, "as it seemed to me that she was enjoying herself quite a lot with Mr. Hickson." Anna reacted with her usual imperturbable nonchalance, although this time perhaps slightly less heroic. "It's a pity that he had to leave right in the middle of your dance, Miss Champion," the rascal continued mercilessly with the greatest of speed. "Did he leave the dance floor limping, or am I mistaken?"

Scoundrel! she thought, sipping her lemonade in order to stall. "I believe he had a problem with his ankle. Something happened while he was on a walk," she finally affirmed. If not absolutely credible, she was absolutely crimson.

"I understand." He nodded his head, as if reflecting deeply. "Walking is becoming a more and more dangerous sport every day, don't you think? Parliament should do something about it."

Anna chuckled without bothering to cover her mouth with her fan in order to hide her chipped tooth. "Mr. DeMercy, I could be mistaken—I'm not perfect, even if I imagine that may surprise you—but I could swear that you are teasing me. Are you insinuating ever so slightly that it was my fault?"

"Not hardly. Although perhaps I can make it up to you afterward if you do me the honor of a dance. May I count on it?"

Anna feared her heart would burst into pieces from emotion; after all, that would not at all be acceptable. "You like to live dangerously, I see," she responded, mustering the last bit of indifference she had within her. "And yes, obviously. It will be a great pleasure for me to dance with you."

"Thank you, Miss Champion," Daniel replied. *Clearly it is wrong to allow a boy with a smile like that to walk around freely,* Anna thought. *Perhaps it isn't even legal.*

"But now we must go, Lucy," he continued after a moment. "The music is about to begin."

"Certainly, Daniel. And Anna," she whispered as she came closer, "stay out of trouble and keep away from the buffet."

"Yes, don't worry."

Quite uncertain of what could happen—and moreover, she had good reason to be, as she knew Anna all too well—Lucy walked away with her dancing partner.

Lucy took Daniel's arm as the pair made their way to the dance floor. Anna watched them go, and as she did, Lucy turned to her with a strange, knowing look on her face. With that, Anna was alone again.

(And now you'll begin to daydream about Daniel, won't you, Anna?)

Staring off into the distance, she thought about his words, his looks, and the warm, tender tone of his voice. As she touched the glass to her lips, it met a wistful smile—and she spilled lemonade on herself, because a man who was striding briskly across the room bumped into her suddenly.

"Oh, dear heavens!" she exclaimed, dismayed.

She looked at the spot getting bigger and bigger on her dress as if she didn't believe her eyes, but it was definitely there. Anna could not deny it once the fabric was soaked—sticky, even—the blotches caused by her spilled drink transforming the brown of her dress into something uglier altogether. After she got over her moment of grief—and another moment dutifully doubting the fair and rational order of things—she looked up in a huff at the guilty man. He was a tall and elegant stranger, and he wore a mortified look on his face. His clothing showed no signs of the incident that had just occurred. (Of course.) In fact, his waistcoat and white tie stood out all too immaculately against his black tailcoat. His build was unusually muscular, but his considerable height and upright posture gave him a certain lightness, and he looked imposing but not displeasing. His dark hair was swept across his forehead and touched his eyes; he moved his hair with a little flip of his head as he gazed at her. He suddenly seemed to be appraising her, his blue eyes shifting about her, staring at her modest dress, noticing her simple gloves and her fan, which lacked all decoration. In a manner as abrupt as it was odd, his expression changed. He became arrogant, and giving her a contemptuous glance, he turned around and left quickly without saying a word.

2

I could easily forgive his pride, if he had not mortified mine.
—Jane Austen

Christopher was quite satisfied with himself as he walked away from the girl dressed in brown. He had a real gift for recognizing social climbers—after all, he was one, wasn't he?—and a single look was all he needed to understand that this young lady was out of place in the dazzling great hall of the Mortimers. *Good,* he said to himself. *She will not go far on this night with her shabby frock all stained.* He smiled as he thought again about the helpless and hurt look she gave him, and then he put her out of his mind.

He went quickly toward Michael Mortimer, who was in a corner of the hall talking with a fetching blond lady and a man in his thirties with flushed cheeks and rather bulky ears.

"Davenport," said the master of the house, greeting him. "I am happy that you could come."

And he truly was happy to see him, Christopher realized. He could hear cheerfulness and hope in his voice. Mortimer owed him several thousand pounds, and he probably wanted to ask him for another loan that evening. *Well, you will earn it,* he thought. *After all, you will introduce me to whomever I like.*

"It's an honor for me," Christopher politely replied.

Mortimer turned toward the people who were with him. "Allow me to introduce to you a dear friend, Mr. Christopher Davenport. Mr. Davenport, Mrs. Edwards, and Sir Colin . . ." The introductions done, Mortimer continued: "Everyone knows that Mr. Davenport bought Rockfield Park a few months ago, and today he is all settled in."

"We've been anxiously awaiting you, Mr. Davenport," Mrs. Edwards said melodically. "How did your trip go?"

"Very well, thank you. Only three hours on smooth roads without accidents. The weather was splendid the entire time."

"And tell me, did you like the village?" Mrs. Edwards asked.

"Certainly, it's truly agreeable and well cared for. Kent is, after all, one of the most beautiful counties in England."

They showered him with other inquisitive questions, and Christopher answered them all with perfect courteousness. He always kept a polite and respectful tone. He paid Mrs. Edwards the proper compliments and praised the gentlemen at the right moment. The right words, the right laughter. He knew the script perfectly. My God, it was so easy to fool these people. Then, turning toward the center of the hall, he saw Daniel DeMercy.

He recognized him immediately. He had studied images of DeMercy down to the finest details, but having him right here in person made Christopher almost giddy. The blood rushing through his veins felt hotter. *So there he is.* He watched him while he danced with a sophisticated blond girl, who seemed to hang on his every word. *A refined dandy who twirls on the dance floor.*

(Leopold's son, Christopher.)

Daniel's light-brown hair was perfectly tidy, his coat fit with exact precision, and even his lady seemed to suit him. Daniel DeMercy, who had grown up in cotton wool, destined since he was little to lead a life of prosperity and privilege. And of perfection, naturally.

"Who is that girl?" Christopher asked Sir Colin, a dull baronet who, judging from the things he had said a moment ago, would not be able to count to ten without using his fingers.

"That's Miss Lucy Edwards. Very beautiful, don't you find?" Sir Colin responded.

"Exquisite."

"As her mother," interrupted Mrs. Edwards, "I can only be proud of her."

Christopher smiled gentlemanly at her. "Of course, how stupid of me. I should have seen the resemblance. But I would have said that you were sisters."

Was that too much? *Obviously not,* he thought sarcastically. Smiling, Mrs. Edwards was indeed flattered. Was she also blushing a little? Yes, absolutely. *Oh, come on!*

He turned again toward Daniel. Both he and his lady moved so lightly that it seemed as if their feet didn't touch the floor. Lucy was stunning. Her flushed, lovely face, her gaze fixed on Daniel, the flowers in her hair—everything came together to make of her a perfect vision of loveliness. Christopher knew before his arrival there that the Edwards family was one of the wealthiest in Coxton, and he also knew that Leopold was pushing intently for a marriage between his son and Lucy. *Well,* he thought, *if dear Daniel is thinking of her as his future wife, it will be a real pleasure to take her from him.* He eyed this girl who seemed to fly like an angel dancing. *Foolish girl, you'll be mine before you're aware of what's happening.*

***

Anna remained so shocked by the behavior of this stranger that for several minutes she couldn't even manage to move. *It didn't really happen,* she thought. On the contrary, though, it had. Pompous and arrogant, the infamous lemonade spiller had crossed the room like a god come down from Olympus, moving away from her with all the regard of a lion toward an ant.

(You are a nobody, Anna.)

Well, she wasn't the most important person in the room—she knew that—and he wasn't the first little lord to slight her, either. But to not even apologize? No, the more she thought about it, the more it seemed incredible. A nagging anger rose within her and went from her stomach to her chest and finally to her eyes, which began to see the world in shades of delicate reds. The thing that sent her most into a rage was the vague feeling of humiliation that penetrated her. *What does it matter what these people think of me?* she asked herself bitterly. *I constantly grumble about how shallow they are, and then I fret when they consider me to be a poor girl. Ignore him—that's what I should do. Ignore him.* But he was a few steps away, speaking pleasantly with the man of the house and Lucy's mother. Her eyes were drawn to him like a magnet, and she kept glaring at him, forgetting that in a short while she would have to dance with Daniel, forgetting about the disaster with her dress, forgetting about everything with the exception of this smug, rude, contemptuous—

Stop it at once. Take a deep breath to calm down. There is certainly something I could do to punish this bully, she thought. *Maybe I'll go up to him and make a scene.* She shook her head. She would do nothing, she finally concluded. Even to address him without having first been introduced would be improper. The people around him would look at her with bewilderment, and she did not want to look ridiculous—if anything, she wanted to make him look ridiculous, this conceited, cocky, contemptuous, presumptuous—

"Miss Champion?" an elderly gentleman nearby called to her. "Miss?"

Not far away, Mrs. Edwards was laughing, lightly tapping the stranger's hand with her fan because of something he had said to her with a suave look. *Heavens,* thought Anna. She absolutely had to find a way to let this man know what she thought of him, or she would burst.

"Miss Champion?" repeated Mr. Gutman.

Anna, startled, looked at him, astonished. How long had he been standing there? She made an effort to smile, and Mr. Gutman handed her a clean handkerchief. "Use it to clean up your dress, Miss Champion," he politely suggested.

Depressed, she looked down at the ugly brown of her dress. "Thank you, you are very kind. I believe I will leave for a moment to straighten myself up calmly."

He nodded. "This man was very rude not to offer you his assistance," he stated regretfully, shaking his white, exceptionally thick head of hair.

Anna turned red. "Oh, it's nothing," she muttered, attempting to force a light tone out of her voice. "He was in a hurry, apparently. He did not notice. Surely . . . If you would please excuse me," she added quickly, "I'll now withdraw to tidy up my dress."

And in fact she would have to hurry if she wanted to make herself presentable before the next dance. Goodness! She had thought so much about this nasty creature that she completely forgot that soon she would be dancing with Daniel. Daniel-Sound-the-Trumpets-DeMercy! She freshened up as best she could, and when she went back into the ball, the second dance had barely finished. She looked for Lucy and Daniel and spotted them in a corner not far away.

"Anna!" Lucy exclaimed just as she reached them. "What happened to your dress?"

"Never mind that," she replied. "You told me that I needed to make it better, didn't you?"

Mercifully, Daniel did not comment on the disaster, for which Anna was rather grateful. She already felt uneasy at the thought of dancing. Her worst fear was, in fact, that she was so excited she would not be able to take a step. Instead, when Daniel took her under his arm, she was able to follow him with commendable coolheadedness: she only stumbled one time. And when she got back in step, she found herself facing him, and she thought that life could have beautiful moments in store for her, even while she wore an old, brown, stained dress.

Her contentment was short-lived.

Lucy was moving toward her, and she was not alone. Anna was extremely displeased to see that Lucy was with *him*, the destroyer of her dress. Evidently she had accepted to be his partner for this dance. Why shouldn't she, after all? He was a rather attractive man. Accursedly attractive, to tell the truth—one of the most handsome men in the entire room. He possessed elegant bearing and had strong but regular facial features.

No, she corrected herself. *It isn't so. First, it's not elegance he possesses, it's arrogance. And he's too tall. And too muscular. And that dark hair of his makes him look like a crow. And those locks hanging in his eyes need to be trimmed. Yes, he has long legs, but they look ridiculous in such tight trousers, and someone needs to tell him that for his own good. Oh damn!* She sighed with resignation. *All right, I'm chubby, I have a patched-up dress, I haven't a penny to my name, and I expect to make this wicked man pay for pushing me. I don't see why I shouldn't be able to.*

This thought bothered her so much that when she began the dance she was off step a bit. She awkwardly resumed her place and tried to pay attention to Daniel, who had asked her about the health of her family members. Anna responded politely to him, but she couldn't help glancing over at the couple dancing nearby. Lucy's blond head and her white dress stood out against the dark coat of the unpunished stranger. He was smiling seductively at Lucy, and Anna noticed that his face no longer had any traces of the pride it was full of only a half hour before, when he was looking at her.

Anna felt the rage in her rise, hot and bubbly like milk on the stove.

"Miss Champion?" Daniel asked.

"Hmm?" she responded, distracted. She was watching Lucy, who was laughing, amused by something he had said. *Good heavens, how cheeky!*

"I was asking you how your little brothers and sister are getting along," repeated Daniel, slightly annoyed. "I am sure that without your loving care they would have set fire to the village by now, if I'm not mistaken."

Anna managed to look back at him. "Oh, to all of England, I believe," she replied. "But, as you say, my care is truly loving. I don't attempt to kill them more than once every half hour as a matter of fact."

He giggled. "I believe they are fortunate to have a sister like you." His face darkened, as if he was taken by some thought, and he added, "I have always felt burdened as an only child."

An expected dance movement split them up and put them in a row with another pair of dancers. Anna took Daniel's hand on one side and Mr. Pembrooke's on the other, being very careful not to get too close to the latter. He had indeed found a companion for the ball, which did happen at times, despite all logic. She was a thin girl with a nice look about her, and she had probably never refused anyone a dance, but Anna was certain the girl would begin to refuse from now on. Finally the dance step ended, and she and Daniel again found themselves face-to-face.

"I could pretend to be your sister for the remainder of this ball if you'd like," she proposed warmly to lighten the serious mood that still showed on his face. "But I must warn you that this will involve a few of my demands: first, I must ask you to memorize your multiplication tables; second, I must check your ears to see if you've cleaned them; and third, I must mess up your hair every five minutes for the simple joy of bothering you. And obviously I will do all of this while endlessly yelling and blaming you."

Daniel laughed loudly, causing a few heads to turn and embarrassing Anna a bit, but at the same time giving her a warm pleasure. "If we could skip the part about the multiplication tables and the ears and go directly to the hair, for me it's a done deal, Miss Champion."

Anna blushed, astonished, and lowered her gaze, feeling a horrible agitation all the way up to her bosom. Even Daniel seemed to become aware that their conversation did not really respect all the standards of convention, and he cleared his throat. She thought he would speak again, but nothing came. They remained silent, dancing in discomfort. It had been decided beforehand that they would dance together, and it wasn't the first time that they spoke face-to-face. It wasn't even the first time Anna felt moved by his presence, but it was definitely the first time she risked falling apart completely, like an overcooked lentil.

She thanked her lucky stars when the moment came to dance with another couple; this would ease the tension a bit. Maybe she might even manage to regain a bit of composure, or the appearance of composure, at least. She was scrambling for something—anything that would prevent her from melting on the dance floor.

The couple that was waiting for them, however, was not the one best suited to calm her down. It was Lucy and . . .

Oh no, she moaned to herself. *Him.*

The stranger looked her up and down rudely while he drew nearer, and Anna stiffened with anger. Heavens, how she would have loved to wipe the smug sneer off his face! Turning, she locked eyes with Mr. Hickson, who, from the other side of the room, quickly looked away.

But of course, she laughed to herself. She got herself in line, with Daniel on her right and the stranger on her left. Her calm was admirable as she waited, and she didn't even give a dirty look at the arrogant man, pretending to feel neither his gloved hand in her own, nor his graceful dancing. No. She waited imperturbably, like a strategist, without making him suspicious, and when the dance step neared the end, she took action.

"Ow!" said the man, spluttering, when Anna gave his ankle a firm kick.

She innocently looked up and saw two furious blue eyes staring at her.

"You did that on purpose," he hissed at her.

"So the cat's no longer got your tongue," she responded.

As the music stopped, she walked away. The dance step was over.

***

Few things surprised Christopher, but the reaction from this insignificant, ridiculous girl was one of them. Shouldn't a young girl of this sort keep a low, submissive profile? At heart she was searching to gain access to a world that was not her own, one that belonged to that category of people who were usually fawning and flattering. It was a world full of people who didn't kick wealthy gentlemen.

He moved again opposite of Lucy, shaking his head and trying to forget the attack he had just suffered. *I must not let myself be distracted,* he thought, eyeing the beautiful Miss Edwards. *I must strike at the heart of this girl here and now.* His face took on an extremely charming expression with a sweet smile, but in spite of himself he had one last look at the stupid girl dancing with DeMercy.

Lucy followed his gaze. "That is Anna Champion," she informed him.

"Beg your pardon?"

"The girl you are staring at. Her name is Anna Champion."

Bewildered, Christopher wrinkled his brow as a doubt crossed his mind. *Miss Edwards couldn't possibly be implying . . . She can't possibly believe that I find this girl attractive!*

"I was just thinking," he responded in a hurry, "that some girls sadly lack grace. The fact is, when one is lucky enough to be in your company, one can't help but notice faults in all other women."

His companion's face dropped unexpectedly. "She's my dearest friend, I'll have you know."

This surprise rendered him momentarily incapable of a response. Perhaps there were many things that were still able to surprise him, after all. *Tonight it seems that I really can't manage to do anything right. Anna Champion could represent a problem,* he reflected while watching her furtively. *A disturbingly unexpected problem. But what does a poor girl like this have to do with the beautiful and sophisticated creature in front of my eyes? Maybe Lucy is fond of surrounding herself with people of decidedly inferior looks and social standing to make herself stand out even more.*

He couldn't wonder about it for very long, because his companion said the exact words he hoped she would not utter: "I would like to introduce you to her, Mr. Davenport." She added, "I have the impression that you two might get along well."

Was there a way to refuse? All he could do was nod. *In any case,* he said to himself, rationalizing, *knowing Miss Champion could have a silver lining.* If he could manage to gain her trust—and make her forget about the insignificant incident a little while ago, which he didn't doubt he could—he would gain access more quickly to Lucy's heart. One good word from her best friend—that's all it would take. Wasn't that how the female mind worked, after all? And after a couple of kind words, this drab girl would be eating out of his hand—he was sure of it. It wouldn't be enjoyable to win over her affections—he admitted that much to himself dryly. He was absolutely certain she was a social climber. She had probably sought out Lucy's friendship precisely to push her way in among people in high places.

Hiding his irritation, he performed the last dance movement together with his partner, and as he bowed the music finished.

***

Satisfaction is something impalpable, but it brings a shine to one's eyes and even one's appearance. Or at least that's what Anna believed, and after she had taken her revenge she felt thinner and more graceful. The music ended, regrettably, but the dance had gone very well. She had stepped on Daniel's feet only one time, and very lightly—so lightly that maybe he didn't even notice. To tempt fate any more would not have been wise, because sometimes fate gives you "more."

In the excitement of the kick she gave the stranger, Anna had completely forgotten about her moment of awkwardness with Daniel as they left the dance floor, and she began to babble about Napoleon and his military prowess. Unfortunately, Mr. Pembrooke was making his exit at the same time and, in the most unsavory of coincidences, came in their direction. "DeMercy," he said while crossing in front of Daniel—or perhaps he said something else because, in fact, his voice didn't sound very sober. He didn't look sober, either, when he settled in next to Anna like a slimy slug. "Miss Chapman, you look ravishing tonight."

She made a grimace. *I'm leaving you to the devil, Daniel,* she told him with her eyes, and his slight sneer indicated he had received the message. "If you would please excuse me," she said hastily, "I really must see to Miss . . . *Champion*."

In her full strategic retreat, she reached the couch for the chaperones. While she was looking for a little space to sit down, she realized that it was really quite silly to have considered not coming to this ball. Good gracious, she hadn't had so much fun in years.

"Anna," Lucy said, calling her.

She turned happily toward her friend, ready to ask her all about the stranger who had danced with her. Much to her disappointment—no, "disappointment" wasn't quite the right word, because she felt like a bucket of cold water left outside in midwinter—she discovered instead that she would have to find out on her own what she wanted to know about the man.

That unbearable snob was at Lucy's side.

Oh damn it all. She gave him a defiant look, but he remained without emotion; in fact, he unexpectedly gave her a polite, completely innocent smile.

What? Anna thought.

For a few moments she was dumbfounded. This man was pretending to be cordial. Worse yet, he was pretending to have not ever seen a glass of lemonade in his life—nor her, apparently. Why? Amazed, she watched him smile at Lucy. Then smile some more. And more—always more delighted, always more gallant.

It was all clear now.

He wants my acceptance. This is why he appears so amiable with me. The anger from earlier, which had been appeased by the kick she had given him, came back even stronger. *He believes he can make a fool out of me with his fraudulent smile and blue eyes, his elegant clothing and all of his other things. Well, he is about to find out that he is very sadly mistaken.*

"Anna, dear," Lucy said to her jauntily, "I would like to introduce you to a new acquaintance, who has hardly arrived in town. Mr. Christopher Davenport. Mr. Davenport, Miss Anna Champion."

Anna tensed up indecisively. What should she do? Point fingers at him and denounce him as the reason for her miserably sticky state? That would most definitely be the worst punishment for him, but . . .

(But there is always the little matter of private insults and those made in public. Isn't that so, Anna?)

It was not that she would be going too far if she told Lucy how he had treated her. She didn't want her friend to defend her. And even if she really wanted to, did the reason really matter?

"Very honored to make your acquaintance," he said to her. He had a low, deep voice that had a bit of a raspy undertone. No, not raspy: haughty. Genteel and melodious, yes, but undeniably with a haughty undertone. He bent over to kiss her hand, and this gesture—repeated hundreds of times by hundreds of people—struck her quite differently. Perhaps it was the slow way he did it. Or the elegant way his lips lingered on her glove. Or perhaps, quite simply, because he was the most hateful man she had ever happened to meet.

"Mr. Davenport comes from London," Lucy informed her. "He is a financier, even if now he intends to devote himself completely to his estate at Rockfield Park."

"Oh, really?" Anna asked, glaring coldly at him. Indeed, she had decided to keep quiet, though the prideful part of her still surged. She had to be careful to keep from kicking him again. "It would be a good thing if you stayed out of finance, Mr. Davenport," she commented with just a hint of bitterness. "One can't be sure there may not be other collapses in the stocks to avoid."

Lucy looked at her without understanding. "Collapses in the stocks?"

Mr. Davenport, on the other hand, understood her perfectly, and his eyes showed surprise for a moment. But he showed not a single sign of antagonism, Anna noticed regretfully. Absolutely stone-faced, absolutely polite. On the contrary, he looked rather relieved that she was keeping quiet about the incident. "Yes, Miss Edwards," he said calmly. "There was quite a substantial breakdown in the financial markets last December. It's truly remarkable that you are aware of it, Miss Champion."

Anna did not respond—she could not, not while the word "remarkable" spun in her head. Lucy, on the other hand, had no trouble speaking up at all. "What did I tell you, Mr. Davenport?" she said. "I knew that you two would get along well."

Unflappable, he smiled. And Anna, gracefully and behind the fluttering of her fan, actually let out a couple of coughs.

"It's exciting to have a new face in the neighborhood, isn't it, Anna?" Lucy said.

She cleared her throat. "I wouldn't know," she responded flatly. "You know what they say about new faces: they hide old tricks."

"Oh really?" Lucy frowned angrily. "That's the first time I have heard that proverb, Anna. Are you sure it really exists?"

Hardly, given that I just invented it. "Of course," she said, lying.

"Humph." Lucy seemed doubtful. "Mr. Davenport, you'll have to excuse my friend," she muttered. "Anyway, don't be frightened. Speaking of *actual* sayings, you could say that her bark is worse than her bite."

Not so. My bite is quite bad, and Mr. Davenport—to be specific, his ankle—knows it.

"Don't fret, Miss Edwards. I appreciate mental acuity, and Miss Champion is apparently very gifted in that regard," he replied. His tone was a perfect combination of sugar and molasses, smeared on a slice of sponge cake.

Was he attempting subtle irony? Anna wondered incredulously. No. No, not at all. He seemed sincerely convinced that a couple of flowery, sweet words would be enough to erase the memory of his rudeness. And maybe it would be enough, she admitted to herself, if he hadn't said it only for Lucy's benefit.

But look at him, she thought while he was talking with Lucy. *Artificial from his feet to his unreachable head. When he smiles, his eyes don't create wrinkles, and every time he speaks, his niceties are coated in platitudes.* What an insufferable flatterer. What an intolerable third-rate actor. He even looked down at her stain, and this hypocrite didn't even pretend to make a contrite face! But to dwell on it was pointless, unless she decided to give him away . . .

Perhaps dwelling on it wasn't all *that* pointless, after all, Anna realized. This gentleman was very keen on making a good impression on Lucy, wasn't he? It was quite obvious, even if he would have to resort to less pathetic compliments to succeed. He certainly would never show his true face nor reveal the incident from before. And that which went unsaid could work to her advantage in the end. Anna smiled while a plan began to take shape in her mind. Nothing complicated (nor anything, to be quite honest, *remarkable*) but its simplicity was truly divine.

"It's a bit warm in this room, don't you think?" Anna said, taking advantage of a pause in the conversation.

"Ah, quite," responded Mr. Davenport, not yet understanding. "Temperatures typical for the beginning of July. As for that, last year—"

"Certainly," Anna interjected, "it makes one incredibly *thirsty*. Don't you agree, Lucy?"

"Oh . . . yes indeed," said Lucy, caught a bit unawares, but without suspicion.

The same could not be said for Mr. Davenport. His eyes showed a glimmer of tentative comprehension. "Would you care for something to drink, ladies?" he asked politely.

Lucy lit up. "That would be wonderful."

"It would be absolutely sublime," Anna confirmed, looking at him defiantly. "A lemonade is the only thing that will do right now."

Oh, he understood now! For a lengthy while it seemed that he couldn't move. Surprised, he examined Anna through half-closed eyes. Perhaps he was trying to intimidate her. *This might be his first true facial expression,* Anna thought, satisfied to have finally cut through his veneer. Finally he made off, inevitable as it was. And when he came back, he had two glasses in his hands.

Here we go, thought Anna. Mr. Davenport handed a glass to Lucy.

"Thank you, you are very kind," Lucy said, quickly taking a drink. "Oh, it's delicious."

"My pleasure, Miss Edwards. Miss Champion," he said to her calmly, although his eyes narrowed as he squinted. "Here is the relief you ordered." He stretched his arm out to her, holding the glass between his fingers.

(Are you certain, Anna? Are you certain you want to do it?)

"You are so extraordinarily kind," she muttered. "Good manners are always rarer among gentlemen, don't you think?"

Mr. Davenport stared at her seriously but did not respond. Anna did not look away, but the duel with their eyes was not as amusing as she had imagined—it didn't amuse her at all, in fact. *How does he manage to darken those angelic eyes?* she wondered, alarmed she felt something like fear in her chest and stomach, because she seemed to detect an actual threat in these shadows and flashes of blue. It was undoubtedly only an impression she got, because Christopher Davenport could not be more than a dandy who made trite remarks and silly laughter. He was absolutely not a ferocious and relentlessly determined man, as suggested by the panic that had made its way into her belly.

(Don't do it, Anna.)

Her hand shook with uncertainty, and the already meager desire to put her plan into action lessened. She wondered if this wasn't a reason against it, and all of a sudden she decided to forget it, not out of fear—no, absolutely not—but because such a childish game of getting even would make her look ridiculous, not him. And besides, she had given him a kick first, hadn't she? He could say that she had evened the score . . .

She lowered her head with a resigned sigh and took the glass. She felt herself being carefully watched, and she couldn't help but look up. Unexpectedly, she saw a look of triumph on Mr. Davenport's face. There was a smile on his traitorous lips, and his blue eyes sparkled in mockery. This gentleman had accepted her challenge—he had considered her important, his equal—and he had won.

No. Not yet, Anna thought.

With a mixture of horror and primitive joy, she flipped her wrist, and the contents of the glass glistened as they spilled down his immaculate clothing. Lucy gave a little mortified cry, and someone nearby let out a chuckle. Fascinated, Anna watched the spot grow larger on the coat and waistcoat of this gentleman, then raised her eyes toward his face. There she discovered that she had started something that perhaps she would not be able to control.

3

There is a woman in every case; as soon as they bring me a report, I say, "Look for the woman."
—Alexandre Dumas, père

When Matthew joined him at the long, dark table, Christopher was spreading marmalade on a piece of bread. They were in the dining room—one of the dining rooms—of the stately mansion of Rockfield Park. Blinding morning light was streaming in from the window left wide open in the sultry weather. The room was immense and majestic, with arabesques and tapestries decorating the walls. Plaster wisteria and grapes ran prominently around the room's ceiling.

The opulence of all this was wasted, since Christopher sullenly did not look up from his plate. Matthew filled a cup with hot chocolate and then, with an exaggerated sigh, said, "Judging by your sour look, I would say that things did not go well last night. Did you manage to get introduced to your half . . ." he said, barely stopping himself in time. Referring to Daniel DeMercy as Christopher's half brother would have gotten him a slap on the head. "Did you manage to get introduced to Daniel?"

"No, damn it all." Having lost his appetite, Christopher tossed the piece of bread on his plate.

The night had gone all awry. When it seemed that he had nearly succeeded in making contact with the DeMercy family—someone would have definitely introduced Daniel to him in the course of the evening—that damned Anna Champion came along and completely ruined his plan. And his clothing, of course. Worst yet, she had done it all on purpose. She had spilled the glass on purpose! Christopher heard laughter coming from nearby and, turning his head, saw an old gentleman sneering. He had exceptionally thick white hair, like a lion's mane. For a moment Christopher nearly lost his temper and threw years of work and preparation into the air. My God, how he hated when people laughed at him. Distant memories quickly crossed his mind, memories of a child with dirty, bushy, jet-black hair. A child who ran, chased by other children his age; a child who was spat upon and had rocks cast at him; a child who was taunted, who was called a bastard and the son of a whore. This laughing—children laughing in his face and calling him names—still haunted his dreams today. So he ran and ran.

"Well, what happened?" Matthew asked him.

Nothing important, he thought, brooding. *I was only ridiculed during my first public appearance in this wretched place.* He didn't answer, seething bitterly. *I hope at least that this girl is satisfied, and she says nothing to her friend.*

Miss Edwards had not suspected a thing, fortunately, and she had exclaimed in dismay, "Anna! You are dreadfully clumsy this evening! Mr. Davenport, what a shame. Your elegant attire . . ."

With an air of defiance, Miss Champion had looked up at him. *Expose me if you dare,* she said with her eyes.

Christopher was silent; there was not much else he could do, after all, even if he wanted to. (And he wanted to. He *really* wanted to.) This treacherous girl had then said to him, "I am *so* very sorry, Mr. Davenport. Do you see this?" She pointed at the spot on her own dress.

"This is already the second glass that I have spilled this evening. Thus, it's likely"—and she grew pensive—"that if this hadn't happened first, it wouldn't have happened the second time, either, because bad habits happen in haste, don't you think so?" She hadn't lowered her eyes, despite the fear that appeared prudently on her face. Instead, she just smiled.

She smiled!

He barely managed to maintain his calm and not wring her neck, and he walked away, making the excuse that he had to clean his clothing.

And he left in a cloud of laughter.

("Bastard! Son of a whore!")

For him to flee like that from the ball, as if he were a frightened dog leaving with his tail between his legs, was humiliating, but he knew that he couldn't have met Daniel in that condition. He couldn't have met Daniel in *any* condition in which he was inferior.

Irritated, he put his hand to his forehead and changed the subject. "Did you find anything at all out about Leopold's debtors?" Christopher asked.

"Oh no, don't think you're going to get out of it that easy," Matthew protested. "You must tell me everything that happened last evening."

Christopher looked at him grimly. "Well?"

"Well what?"

"Leopold DeMercy's debtors, you stupid cousin of mine."

"Oh, very well," he sighed. "This afternoon I will try again to prod my contacts at the bank."

Christopher raised an eyebrow. "This afternoon?"

"Fine, fine. I'll go straight away. If there is anything else I could do for you, let me know—shine your boots, iron your shirts."

"That would be nice, but I believe that would require more intelligence on your part, so I won't bother you with that."

Matthew looked at him sideways. "Are you sure that being intelligent means having that apelike expression on your face?" he asked him doubtfully.

He took a piece of bread and marmalade and ate it slowly, almost absentmindedly, as Christopher had seen him do since he was a child. Matthew had not changed much growing up: he still had the same big eyes, the same thin build, the same damned short hair. "Long hair brings lice," Barbara Davenport would say, and by God, Matthew still listened to her, even though she was dead. And this was only one of thousands of rules that the aunt had impressed upon her son—and on Christopher, after the Davenports had taken him in.

"Don't climb on the wardrobes," said Mrs. Davenport. "Don't run; you'll sweat too much."

"One mustn't fight, one mustn't jump, one mustn't . . ."

Although Christopher often and quite gladly refused to obey these rules, Matthew did. Most of the time, at least. "Don't play with strange children; you'll catch something," she nagged. And even so, Matthew had come near him one September afternoon some twenty years ago, and he had offered him a sandwich, and they had played in secret for a good five minutes before his mother noticed his absence and called him loudly—for five minutes that day, and then five minutes every day for nearly a month, every afternoon. It was the first rebellion of a child who seemed so emaciated that he could be carried off by the first gust of wind.

Fortunately there was no wind on September 2, 1806. It had been a hot day—good and hot—the kind of heat that gets in your bones like a healing balm. Christopher was shining boots for gentlemen between Piccadilly and Green Park, and he had seen Matthew arrive with a thin, nervous lady and a fat nanny, who was a bit out of breath. It wasn't the first time he had seen the three of them; before his mother killed herself, she had taken him to the park from time to time, and once she put her veil down on her face and walked quickly away with him after having seen the thin woman. His mother, who never ran away. Why? She committed suicide a few days later. Maybe it was this lady's fault.

Maybe it wasn't my fault.

With this thought in his head, Christopher had followed the three of them. He spied on them from behind a tree, without making a sound. After a while Matthew had noticed him and had given him a timid smile.

***

With a sigh, Anna turned toward her brother, who was fiddling with the nib of his pen. "Anthony, come back to do your lessons," she said.

"I finished them," he replied.

She was seated at the kitchen table, where her siblings were doing their exercises. Anthony was doing a difficult assignment for mathematics, which he loved. (A worrisome thing at almost eleven years of age. "Where did I go wrong with you?" Anna would sometimes ask him, laughing.) Dennis, struggling with the mysteries of handwriting, was writing the sentence "I am trying to write the sentence," and guiding the pen with little precision and quite a lot of yawning. Grace, the baby of the house, was drawing different kinds of flowers in her notebook with the red cover. She had decided to color them all yellow and brown.

"How is it possible that you've already finished?" Anna looked at the tidy notebook of her brother, checking the sums. "It's right," she admitted, "and it's all correct. Very good!"

She messed up his bushy brown hair, which he hated.

"Oh, Anna!" he grumbled. He tried to put his hair back in order, and under his hands it went from messy to even messier. "If I'm so good," he said, his voice dead serious, "why couldn't I help you with the accounts?" He pointed to the black registry in front of him. "You seem so tired."

"Anthony, my dear little man, you do know that one should never tell a young lady that she looks tired. If Lucy heard you, she would beat you for sure."

But she truly was exhausted, Anna admitted to herself. Last evening she had come back late, and in the morning the routine of the Champion household had kept her from resting. Nevertheless, it was worth it; Daniel had danced with her twice, and everything had gone splendidly.

Or *almost* everything.

A slight uneasiness came over her as she thought again about Mr. Davenport and his angry face after the revenge she had taken on him. *Come on, it was fun, wasn't it?* she thought, trying to convince herself. It was just a little joke, and there certainly would not be consequences. Since when had she become so fainthearted?

And yet this morning she felt dissatisfied and considered the possibility that she had not behaved properly. *Oh, please!* His abominable manners certainly deserved to be punished. She shook her head to rid herself of the thought of that snooty man. She knew she was in the right, although the inexplicable feeling of guilt never left her. It seemed to her—for a brief, imperceptible moment—that behind the anger of those blue eyes was some distant sorrow.

Ridiculous, she said to herself. *I'm only imagining it.*

From now on she would have to avoid Christopher Davenport—which shouldn't be terribly difficult, as it wasn't as if she had much of a social life. If she could manage that, then everything would be taken care of. Deciding to put the ball out of her mind, she rubbed her forehead as she turned her attention to the account registry. After her father's illness, managing the estate gave her anxiety. There was relief in sight, though. The rent from her family's land holdings would cover their debts, and in just a few more years they would be free and clear.

I can do it, Anna thought.

She didn't say this aloud. Never aloud.

I can do it. In five or six years the debts will be discharged. To hell with marriages of convenience.

Anna was all too well aware that it was for that reason that Lucy dragged her to parties and balls. Her friend worried about her and wanted to procure an advantageous marriage for her. *Is it so selfish to want to marry for love?* she wondered again. She knew the answer: yes, it was selfish. Refusing a good match would mean leaving her own family in the relative poverty they were currently mired in. They had done away with all unnecessary spending, and for three years most of the house had been closed up, and they no longer had horses or servants. The only help that remained was Nora, who stayed on even when they could no longer pay her, as she was part of the family to all intents and purposes.

And that missing shilling—where did it go? she wondered, racking her brain as she recalculated the sum for the third time. Well now, the cost of sewing thread, plus father's doctor, plus—

"Ugly toad!" a familiar voice cried out, shaking Anna from her thoughts.

Anna turned toward Dennis, who was fighting with Anthony for the umpteenth time.

Dennis tossed his notebook, and Anthony got up suddenly from his chair, tipping it over. "Horseradish!" he replied, vexed.

Horseradish? Anna said to herself, perplexed. "Children, please," she begged, holding her head in her hands. *Gracious, I'm not getting anything done this morning.* She gave up on the accounts registry and grabbed her secret diary. She opened it. Inside there were indecipherable scribbles that seemed to have been made by someone left-handed who had only his right arm and was drunk besides. Only Lucy could have made any sense out of those marks, because there were only words written in LuAnGraphy, the modified stenography they both used to exchange encrypted notes. For Anna, writing in LuAnGraphy had become as automatic as writing things out completely, and even now the nib of her pen moved quickly while she noted in her diary the happenings of the night before.

She couldn't wait until afternoon to meet Lucy. She wanted to discuss the ball together with her, and, in spite of herself, she was curious to know something more about this Christopher Davenport. After the incident he had strutted away quite humiliated—or so it seemed to her—and this thought stirred a new pang of guilt.

***

"Hey, what's wrong with you? You seem more daft than usual today, and I thought that was impossible."

Christopher got up from the table. "Thank your lucky stars that you're my cousin, Matt, because otherwise I would have clocked you a long time ago." He paused, then added distractedly, "Uh, listen. Find out about a certain family named Champion. They have an estate to the east of the village and I want to know everything about them. Everything. How much they earn, if they have debts. Leave no stone unturned."

Matthew wrinkled his brow. "Champion? Never heard of them. Are they an important family that slipped by me?"

"Not exactly. I believe they are rather poor, actually." He thought again about the night before and clenched his jaw. "In particular, I want you to uncover every possible piece of information regarding Miss Anna Champion."

His nonchalant tone did not fool his cousin, who whistled softly. "Anna Champion? Are you in love just a little bit, Chris?" He laughed mockingly. "Now I understand why you were so dressed up this morning! You were so starched up that I wondered how you were going to bend your knees to walk."

Sulking, Christopher didn't respond, and he went toward the door. He had too many things to do, all equally bothersome, and he had to get going.

"Should I advise this Anna Champion to leave town, Chris?" yelled Matthew worriedly. "I don't like it at all when you have that look on your face—not that I ever find your face that attractive, but . . . Hey, come back here!"

Without another word for his cousin, Christopher departed.

4

After the sweetness comes the sorrow.
—Proverb

If he asks me again for information on horse exhibitions, I will break his neck. The intended recipient of this unspoken, albeit disturbing, threat made by Christopher was Joseph, the stable boy at Rockfield, who was unaware of the danger he had happily attracted.

"Are you going on a ride, Mr. Davenport?"

"Yes."

"I will bring this beauty right out for you." Joseph was sixteen years old and had a fatiguing exuberance. He loved his own work and, what was even more unforgivable, he loved to talk about it. "I already gave him a good grooming."

Christopher gave a cold nod, hoping to dampen the boy's enthusiasm. He did not succeed.

"At the estate of Upperfield, they just bought a new colt, Mr. Davenport, and right after they noticed that its gums—"

"Fine."

He mounted the horse and rode off in a hurry. He went down the lane at a gallop, but then, without realizing it, slowed down and turned back to look. His estate loomed brightly in the morning sun; its beautiful location, its well-kept garden, and the expansive grounds boasting spectacular views made it the dream of every gentleman. "But don't get too attached to it, Matt," he had advised his cousin the day before. "When our work here is finished, we will sell it all—you know that." It wasn't his intention to stay in the country nor to be a landowner. He had been living there for hardly a day and already he missed the noise and grit of London. It was all so quiet at Rockfield Park.

He set out slowly on the road that led to Coxton. It had taken him more than twelve years to get here; there was no reason to be in a hurry now. A few farmers were working in the distance, and they were perhaps singing some song, but the sound did not reach his ears.

What bloody oppressive silence.

He had determined he would establish himself in Coxton as soon as he managed to figure out, in general terms, his mother's past. If he hadn't taken this as a goal, he would have probably become a lawyer, like Matthew's father, and not a rich financier and new landowner. Or he would have left for some faraway place—America, Europe, India. Maybe he would have let the wind take him where it might, floating about without being tied down to any place or person.

In front of him a wagon filled with straw blocked the road. He went around it and kept on, increasing his speed.

He hadn't needed to choose what to do in life. His mother hanging in the room—with the smell of her excrement and her hideously swollen face—had chosen for him.

He began to gallop, spurring the horse to go faster than the wind. "Come on, beauty, giddyup," he prompted him, leaning forward.

He didn't remember much about Martha from when she was alive. A few unforgettable images popped into his head. He remembered the time that an old lady had insulted her at a baked-apple stand. Back then a young Christopher tried to take her away by the hand. "No, Chris," she told him. "Let's stay here." He also remembered when she had shouted, while doing a little spin on a chilly but sunny day, "It's almost spring, Ducky! Things will be better in no time."

These fragile memories only called to mind a pitiful part of what his mother was. She had childlike gentleness, and her unapproachable beauty attracted admiring looks from men and women. It was a beauty that vanished in a moment. It disappeared with a sudden jump in a filthy room in a brothel, a beauty that left Chris asking the same question again and again: *Why? Why, Mummy?*

As a child, he had no way to find out about her. He didn't even know what his real family name was—Smith, she said—and he didn't know a single relative or friend. He remained at the brothel because he was alone in the world, and even this arrangement seemed like a luxury to him. "You can't stay here . . . you mustn't stay here," Elise had told him at first. "And I certainly can't pay to keep you somewhere else. There's no other choice: either go live in the streets or at the orphanage. And as frail as you are, you won't last a month." Hearing these words, Christopher fell silent. He almost never talked, in fact, after seeing his mother's cold, lifeless body. Then Elise had stood up, sat down, and stood up again. She swore, cursing against Martha, and finally gave in. "All right"—and her tone changed from rage to resignation—"for now you can stay. You're still little, and they will leave you alone. But listen: you should never ever let yourself be seen by the gentlemen who come here. And stay away from Madam. Be noticed as little as possible."

And that's what he did. He did everything to not be noticed; up until his very last night at the brothel, he had burrowed under the staircase. There he slept alone, like he was used to. There were two other children in the house, George and Catherine, but at ages nine and ten they were already accompanying gentlemen to the rooms. He, on the other hand, curled up behind a stack of old rags, worrying about a few papers he held in his hands. *I would like to learn to read,* he thought.

Maybe I would learn new things in these letters. In fact, the correspondence belonged to his mother, and Elise had read it and given it to him a few days after Martha's suicide. It didn't say much. There were seven letters in all, and all of them from a certain "L."—his mother's lover—who signed with only his first initial. There was no family name, no city, nor mention of schools or stores, or any other piece of information that could at least help understand *where* Martha was from. There was even a notebook—with a black cover, a bit damaged, that Christopher held tight sometimes before falling asleep—a type of diary full of notes, sayings, poetry excerpts, and stories. It was written in his mother's handwriting, but it revealed nothing about her origins. Better yet, it revealed only what was important for her: her soul, her outlook on the world. Certainly not her past, which she had erased even on paper.

Christopher had wanted to ask Elise to reread the letters to him, or at least the diary. Oh, he wished that more than any other thing. But she definitely would have neither the patience nor the desire to do that for him. *And she has been so sad for quite some time . . . She doesn't want me around anymore, she said.* In truth, she had never been affectionate toward him, and she often scolded him, because Madam made her pay to allow him to live there. Sometimes, though, she gave him a little pat—like when Christopher brought her an additional penny or gave her a stolen apple from the Covent Garden market. *Maybe she will be happier when those red things that showed up on her face go away, he hoped. The lotion that she puts on hasn't cured them yet, and so she covers them with a lot of false beauty marks and then cries.* A sound of footsteps made him raise his head: someone was coming down the stairs. He was well hidden under his old clothing.

"Chris?" he heard. Elise was calling him. "Christopher? He must be here, Mr. Jones. You'll see. He's a beautiful child, well mannered, and docile."

An unfamiliar, sheepish giggle followed. "Good," responded a man's tiny voice. And after a brief pause the voice said anxiously, "He is . . . he is pretty, you said? And he hasn't . . . he has never . . ."

"Never," Elise responded determinedly—reassuringly even. "I have guarded him well. Chris!" she called. "Christopher, are you here?"

What did Elise want from him? Maybe she wanted him to polish this gentleman's boots. Chris hid the letters and notebook under his shirt, and he came out from his hiding place.

"Elise? Are you looking for me?"

He stared curiously at the short man at her side. He had a large belly, despite the fact that the rest of his body was thin. He practically had no shoulders or bottom, only a belly. He seemed like a child, too, because he was trembling, and his tongue kept licking his lower lip.

"Oh . . . perfect," the man exclaimed when he saw him. "He's perfect."

He seemed very happy, Chris thought.

Elise held her hands in her lap, wringing them like wet cloths. "Chris, I want to introduce you to someone," she said with a bit of a high-pitched voice, but for once without any hint of unkindness.

Mr. Jones stooped toward him. "Hi . . . Christopher. I am Bernard."

Christopher looked questioningly at Elise. "Is he here for me to shine his boots?"

"Oh . . . yes. Yes, that's it." Her hesitation lasted only a moment. "However, not here. Mr. Jones wants you to go with him someplace."

"What place?"

"A nice place. You'll see. You're going there now."

"Now?" Christopher was tired that night, and he was hoping to sleep for a bit. "But . . . no . . ."

"Mr. Jones is very nice with children," Elise said, interrupting him. "You'll be glad you went with him."

"It's true, Christopher," the man confirmed with an excited voice. He took a little sack out of his pocket and held out a praline to him.

Christopher watched him without accepting it and took a step backward. Mr. Jones suddenly straightened up to his full height—which wasn't much—and looked at Elise. Outraged, he said, "You told me he was docile! I am not—"

"Oh, he is, he is," she said quickly, as if desperate. "You'll see, sir. Christopher, don't make me look bad. Go with him. He has a beautiful carriage outside. You haven't been in a carriage for a long time. Isn't that so?"

"Yes, but . . ." Christopher began.

"Take the sweet," Elise told him with a voice that sounded . . . like she was begging? "And say thank you to the gentleman."

If Elise said it, it must be the right thing. Wasn't she the one who kept him far from Madam and who paid his lodgings here? Christopher stretched out his hand and took the sweet. "Thank you, sir." He ate it, and it was good: a caramel-covered almond, a flavor that he would never forget from then on.

Mr. Jones seemed very relieved.

"Bernard, call me Bernard," he repeated. Beads of sweat had formed above his mouth, and he wiped them off with his hand. "So we can go, can't we, Christopher?"

He seemed very anxious to leave. His eyes were bright and open wide, his face flushed and his breathing a bit irregular. *Maybe he has a fever,* Christopher thought.

"Come now, Chris. Go with the gentleman."

"All right, but . . ." But he felt sad, and he didn't understand why. Perhaps it was because Elise seemed sad, too. "But after I can come back here?"

Elise put a hand on her face, brushing against a false beauty mark that looked like a large fly. "Of course," she responded. Her eyes moved nervously, looking first at the walls, then the floor, then the stairs. She looked everywhere around the room, everywhere but at him.

"Come, Christopher," said Bernard. "Give me your hand."

He couldn't. He couldn't hold the tense grip of this man. He didn't understand why, but he kept thinking of George, the other boy in the house, who said that the men did odd things when they went into the room with him, and they weren't nice. Christopher didn't know what "things" exactly, because he only heard these words in passing. In fact, he avoided talking with George, who was bad and beat him every time he saw him. "If we are sure we can beat them, we stop; if not, we run away," said Simon before he died—and Christopher always ran away from George, without a doubt.

"Come on, Chris, give your hand to the gentleman," Elise prodded.

Such a sweet tone coming from Elise made him want to cry, and that wasn't a good thing, because Elise couldn't stand his tears. He raised his arms and took Bernard's hand. The older man's sweaty palm seemed like a mouse to him, but without hair, and again an incomprehensible fear gripped him.

"Go ahead, walk," Bernard said, pulling him.

Why be afraid? Why was he always such a coward? Elise didn't send him in rooms with gentlemen. Elise told him to hide from them. If she asked him to follow this man, it meant there was nothing to worry about. He should stop acting like a little girl!

With weak legs, he walked toward Mr. Jones. He pissed a little, his tummy hurt, and he didn't want to go, and yet he was at the door, together with Mr. Jones.

"Chris!"

Frightened by Elise's scream, he turned around, and even Bernard gave a jump.

"What is it, Elise? What's wrong?"

Maybe she wasn't feeling well. She looked with wide eyes at Christopher and put her hands over her mouth, one over the other. He had never seen that expression on her face before. To him it seemed that she wanted to throw herself on him, maybe to gobble him up or squeeze him until he suffocated.

"What's wrong, Elise?" he asked.

There was only silence for a long while. "Nothing," she answered finally, covering her eyes with a hand. "Nothing, Chris."

Then, as if she thought more about it, she ran up to him and, bending her head toward his, gave him a little kiss on his forehead. Shocked, Christopher bit his lip to keep from crying.

"You're such a good little boy, Chris," she whispered in a husky voice that she had never used before. Even her eyes seemed different. "Chris . . ."

Mr. Jones snorted. "Can we go now?"

She nodded without looking at him. Her gaze was fixed on Christopher, while her lips still quivered. Shaking, he felt afraid like never before. "We'll see each other afterward, won't we?" he asked her impulsively.

She closed her eyes. "Yes. Afterward."

***

"And so Mr. Davenport came to see you this morning!" Anna exclaimed while sipping her tea. *But of course he went to Lucy's house,* she thought. *Really, all one had to do was look at her. Beautiful, rich, intelligent. Lucy, the proof of the existence of angels.*

"Yes, he was very nice," Anna's friend replied.

Anna couldn't manage to hold herself back. "But don't you think that this gentleman may be a bit—how to put it?—haughty?"

Puzzled, Lucy looked at her. *"Really?"* she said. "What gives you that impression? To me he seems quite nice, besides being very charming." She took a sip of tea. "You talked to us for barely five minutes, and he seemed to me to be very friendly toward you. Perhaps he seemed a bit cooler toward the end, but I would say that it was understandable, seeing that you spilled a pint of lemonade on him." She stopped for a moment to frown. Her eyes gave a nervous flash. "You didn't do it on purpose, hmm, Anna?"

She lowered her head down to the cup. "No, of course not," she answered with a shrill giggle.

Too shrill perhaps, because Lucy looked at her suspiciously. "Well, do you want to tell me what happened this morning?" she asked her hastily to divert attention from herself. "How did Mr. Davenport behave?"

A bit of mischievous doubt still shined in her friend's eyes. Then it went out, and Anna breathed a sigh of relief. "He brought me a big bundle of flowers," Lucy responded, "and he didn't stop paying compliments to my mother and I the entire time."

Anna laughed. "To your mother?"

"Absolutely. In fact, I wasn't sure if he was trying to impress me or her."

"Oh, stop playing modest. You know that no one can resist you."

Lucy shook her head skeptically. "I doubt that. He said nothing particularly interesting. In fact," she added with a sideways look at Anna, "he only livened up when I mentioned your name."

Anna nearly choked on her tea. Putting the cup down, she tried not to let her anxiety show. "You spoke about me?"

"Well, not much. At any rate, it seemed to me that he listened with great interest to everything I told him about you. I believe you impressed him."

Or something like that. "Impossible," Anna responded. "I ruined his waistcoat! Probably, if at first he thought that I was dowdy, now he will avoid me like the plague, thinking that I am also excessively clumsy."

"Oh, Anna! You underestimate yourself incredibly."

"Miss . . . Miss Edwards is right," muttered Anna's father, sitting nearby. It was rare for him to take his tea with them, and the few times that it happened, he practically never spoke, blending into a cozy armchair almost as worn out as he was. "You are very beautiful . . . like . . . like your mother was."

Anna felt a lump growing dangerously in her throat, and she hurriedly changed the subject. "Why don't we speak about someone more interesting to *you* instead?" she asked Lucy. "You seemed to be the favorite topic of Mr. DeMercy when I met him on the road this morning."

"You met Daniel? Today?"

"Yes, while my brothers were bringing me back from running an errand at the Tuckers' farm. I saw him there. He got off his horse and accompanied us for a bit."

"What a strange coincidence. That place is a bit far from his house, isn't it? How did he explain his presence there?"

"He didn't have to explain it," Anna pointed out. "He said that he was roaming about aimlessly."

Lucy took a sip of tea. "I see."

"As I told you, he asked me about you." *It was true,* she admitted to herself unwillingly. *And Lucy didn't even find him the least bit interesting!* she thought to herself. In fact, she barely listened to Anna as she was speaking, and she looked around, distracted. "And obviously," Anna added, "he had to undergo Anthony's interrogation."

Finally Lucy leveled her eyes at her. "No!" she said, laughing. "What did that little devil say to him?"

Her cheeks flushed just thinking about it. "You must know that my brother has it in his head that I will be getting married soon. The thought seems to terrify him. Perhaps it's the idea of becoming the brother-in-law of a horrible man like Mr. Pembrooke."

"And what did he ask Daniel?"

"He asked him," she said, covering her eyes with her hand, still disbelieving, "if he intended to marry me."

The look on Anthony's face—"Sir, do you intend to marry my sister?"—was terribly serious, and Anna was speechless. She didn't know whether to laugh or play it down, but all the blood from her brain rushed to her face, making it impossible to think rationally. She stood there like that, her mouth open in the middle of the countryside, her face peeking out, all red under her little white parasol.

"And how did Daniel react?"

"Oh, you know—nothing ever ruffles him." This was true. Daniel was perfectly pink and completely calm. The young man's complexion showed no sign of betraying his emotions when the question was put to him. "Daniel asked him, 'Would you like to have me as a brother-in-law, Anthony?' And my brother . . ." Anna gasped again, as if mortified, and added, "My brother looked at him askew and responded, 'No, sir.'"

Lucy laughed. "That child is ruthless!" However, she seemed to be thinking about something else, and in fact she soon said, "Listen, Anna, as you know, Monday evening there will be a dinner party at my house, and . . . No, don't make that face. You can't miss it."

"Oh, Lucy, I beg you—"

"You must come," Lucy said firmly. "The Rotherham sisters will be there, and you positively cannot leave me alone with them. I'm not sure if I could manage to survive. Either that or I shall have to kill the both of them, and you know that my mother would not approve if I dirtied the carpets in the drawing room. Besides," she added, giving Anna a knowing look, "Daniel will most certainly be there."

Anna blushed and pretended to examine her teacup.

"And you can apologize correctly to Mr. Davenport," Lucy continued. "He has assured me that he wouldn't miss it."

And that, dear Lucy, is the only reason I need to not come. To see Daniel would be pleasant, true, but he was interested in Lucy, not in her, and meeting Christopher Davenport was not exactly on her to-do list. There were at least sixty-two other things she would prefer to do instead, including dance with Mr. Pembrooke, go to the dentist's, and have a tête-à-tête with the elder of the two Rotherham sisters.

Oh my, sooner or later I will have to see him again—it's inevitable, she thought. Her stomach was already turning at the thought of his dreadful eyes. Let a little time pass and hope that he had a short memory—that was the only surefire solution. "Lucy," she said, "couldn't you spare me this time?"

Her friend returned the question with a relentless stare. A response wasn't needed. She wouldn't even dignify Anna by giving her an answer.

An excuse—Anna needed to find an excuse quickly. *But what? Come on, it's not that difficult, any excuse, any . . .* "Regrettably, I have nothing to wear," she finally mumbled. "I could never get a dress ready in time. It is only two days away, and with all of my commitments . . ." Her sentence trailed off in sadness—or so it seemed, because in reality she was quite happy with herself. Lucy would certainly have to accept *this* reason to allow her to pass on this society event.

Against all odds, however, Lucy didn't bat an eyelid. "That's why I am here," she affirmed.

What? "What?" Anna asked, only to confirm her worst fears.

Lucy picked up the large wicker basket that she had carried with her and opened it. Inside there was a cake for the children. Craning her neck, Anna realized with disappointment that it also contained sewing fabric. "Lucy?"

"You said that you would give me permission to help you with your mother's dark-green gown."

"Lucy . . ."

"You promised. This evening I will stay here, and we will alter it together."

"But—"

"Mr. Champion, will you allow me to stay here as your guest?"

My, what an unfair trick!

"Oh. It would be a great, great pleasure, Miss Edwards," Anna's father responded.

Mortified, Anna searched for words to explain to her that the dinner would not at all be suitable for her. But heavens! Those words did not come to her. "Lucy," she began, putting her hand to her forehead, "we're only having potato soup this evening, and—"

Suddenly leaning toward her, her friend snapped back at her in a low voice so Mr. Champion wouldn't hear, "Trust me, Anna, for once! I might be better at this than you think. You know that?"

Beaten, Anna said nothing. She gave in.

And in spite of everything, it was a splendid evening. The children were happy because of Lucy's presence, Nora was flattered by Lucy's compliments on her modest cooking, and for Anna, staying up until the wee hours of the morning altering her mother's old dress seemed to be one of the most enjoyable things she had ever done. Lucy had the eye and Anna had the skills, and so the end result was better than they had hoped, but it wouldn't make a single bit of difference, because the dress—already embellished with their laughter—seemed wonderful, anyway. And when they finally went to bed—both in Anna's bed, since the guest rooms were unfit for use—they continued to chat for a long while, despite the incredible tiredness that overtook them.

5

I know very well what I am running from, but not what I am looking for.

—Michel de Montaigne

When he entered the imposing drawing room, coyly welcomed by Mrs. Edwards, Christopher looked around, searching for Daniel's face. *He has not yet arrived,* he thought as he relaxed.

(But you have no fear. Isn't that so, Christopher?)

It was normal for him to take stock at moments that weighed heavily on him. For God's sake, he had been preparing for this for twelve years, and he had been waiting for it for twenty.

He breathed in, then out. He did this again and again until he calmed down. He then went to pay his respects to Miss Edwards, who was in a nearby corner. That evening she was even more beautiful than he remembered, and it left him completely unmoved. Oh, he loved women, and yes, he was even willing to admit that if he could have his way with Lucy Edwards for a half hour, it would be a very enjoyable experience. That was impossible now, however—but he had no regrets about it. For sex was a physical need, it was true, and his desires definitely needed to be satisfied, but sex did not come without complications. Therefore he dismissed all girls like Lucy—those who were searching for husbands. He knew enough about brothels and the suffering hidden behind the smiles of prostitutes to reject that idea as well. He had to find another, more pragmatic solution. He could instead choose his lovers from among the wives of high-ranking well-to-do men. A rather easy thing to do, usually. And these cold women, bound to social etiquette and expected smiles, suited the purpose perfectly. It was a real pleasure for him to take them in the oddest nooks in their houses, and at the same time he felt a deep satisfaction in humiliating the husbands.

Not far away Mrs. Edwards glanced over at him and smiled. She was a bit beyond his age limit, but she was still passable, he thought with generous condescension. *And after all, there's no denying anyone a little favor, is there?*

He smiled at Lucy and graciously greeted his host—Mr. Edwards.

***

"Anna, what a *wonderful* dress," said Miss Rotherham in a shrill voice. "Green suits you *so* very well. This sash, *so* high up, is *so* wonderful. I envy you *so* much, you know, but my mother says that it's out of fashion—not that you are out of fashion, *dear*—and she wouldn't like me to wear something similar, because . . ."

Anna continued to smile but stopped listening, her face frozen. Whoever looked at her must have thought she had taken leave of her senses. She quickly looked around. *Lucy, you traitor, where are you?*

". . . and then she said to me that little *white* hats will be *all the rage* next winter, but pink lace . . ."

It wasn't easy to escape from Rosemary's high-pitched voice. *Dear God, have mercy!* What excuse could she use to get away? It seemed she had already used the one about the upset stomach . . .

". . . like Miss Howe, she had a bit of a *wilting* flower on her dress, but I do say it was so *pretty . . .*"

Could she pretend to faint in the middle of the room? *Good heavens,* she thought desperately, *doesn't this girl ever take a breath?* And she hoped that it was Miss Rotherham who would faint, due to lack of oxygen.

***

Lucy smiled graciously. "You are really very kind, Mr. Davenport, but now, however, I must leave you."

"You are breaking my heart. Could I accompany you?" he replied.

"I'm afraid that this requires courage beyond your strength. I absolutely must run to help my friend over there." She indicated Anna and Rosemary. "If I don't save her now, I risk her getting even with me in the future in some atrocious and original way."

"You are very selfless," he responded, trying to hide his disappointment. He looked at the insufferable social climber, the detestable Miss Champion, smiling artificially at Miss Rotherham. *Damned hypocrite!* Not able to hold his tongue, he said sourly, "So your friend doesn't know how to defend herself when she's alone."

Lucy's charming forehead wrinkled up in an expression that was far from approving—far from even half-approving. *Bloody hell,* Christopher said to himself. What the hell had gotten into him? Making missteps because of an insignificant girl across the room—even if she was damned irritating.

"Anna defends herself very well when alone," Lucy responded dryly, "and that's exactly what I would like to avoid. She could set fire to the curtains in order to create a diversion to escape from Rosemary." It was Lucy's eyes, not the curtains, that flared up, though, and Christopher saw something genuinely interesting in her for the first time since he had met her. He was struck by how much she truly cared for her friend and how very fond of her she was.

And clever Anna Champion, he thought in disgust. This flatterer knew how to do it—he had to admit. However, she could fool Lucy but not him. He stared scornfully at her. She was looking up in the air as Miss Rotherham continued to talk without stopping. This evening she was wearing a vulgar and badly refashioned dress, and yet Christopher noticed that she wore it with the same pride as if she were wearing a dress fit for a queen. She held her head high, and her thick brown hair was gathered in a simple hairstyle; a few ribbons the same color as her dress were woven into her curly tresses. The dress fit well, he admitted reluctantly, and all things considered it suited her, but perhaps it wasn't the dress—perhaps it was her contradictory, proud look that made her seem so beautiful.

Beautiful? The thought was so unexpected that it left him dumbstruck. *Beautiful? That wretch? Dear God, I must be going mad.* Beside himself with this ridiculous worry, he continued to stare at her. She looked lost in her thoughts and raised a hand to arrange a lock of hair that had escaped from the prison of hairpins and fallen onto her face.

"Well, then, would you like to accompany me, Mr. Davenport?"

Miss Champion turned her head, and when her eyes met his, she became pale.

"Mr. Davenport?" Lucy repeated.

Christopher turned slowly toward her, and for a moment his mind went completely blank as he looked at her. "Pardon me?"

A look of playful delight sparkled in Lucy's eyes. "Miss Rotherham would be very pleased to speak with you."

"Oh." *Absolutely not. Out of the question.* He had to avoid Anna Champion until he came back to his senses. "I believe that I will pay my respects to Mr. and Mrs. Mortimer if you think you can do without me," he answered.

"You are a coward," Lucy said, laughing. "You're leaving a damsel in distress. But this time I will excuse you." And saying this, she went to leave, but she noticed someone on her left and stopped short. "Daniel!"

Christopher tightened up, Anna Champion and every other thought except one disappearing quickly from his mind. He clenched his jaw enough to hurt, and his heart began to beat furiously in his chest.

He swallowed, and slowly he turned around.

He hoped he wouldn't stagger, because coming face-to-face with Daniel DeMercy made him feel as if he were drunk or in front of a distorting mirror. They did not look like each other at all—Christopher had darker hair, harder features, and was taller and more muscular; Daniel's eyes were dark green, while his were blue. It was only the shape of their eyes that was strangely similar. For a very brief moment—so infinitesimal that Christopher later thought he had only imagined it—Daniel's pupils opened wide, as if in acknowledgement.

"Daniel, allow me to introduce to you Mr. Christopher Davenport," said Lucy. "Mr. Davenport, Daniel DeMercy."

***

Waiting desperately for someone to help her get away from Miss Rotherham—*Lucy, you'll pay for this. You know that, don't you?*—Anna decided to find a way to get out of it by herself.

The plan that she had worked out first seemed so crude that she doubted she had the nerve to carry it out completely, but the alternative—another half hour with Rosemary—made her fully understand the meaning of the saying, "all's fair in love and war."

All's fair in love, war, and when it comes to Miss *Rotherham*.

Sir Colin passed by. Sighing and feeling impish, Anna took a step back and stuck out a foot. Sir Colin fell down flat (the sound that he made seemed eerily loud to her), and she barely had time to say "I'm sorry, Sir Colin." Miss Rotherham was on it. She helped him to get back up while she explained to him that falls "can be *very* serious, don't you know? Georgia told me once that . . ."

Free! thought Anna with a slight sense of guilt in seeing that Sir Colin was listening to the story about Georgia and her right hip. *I'll seek your forgiveness in the future, Sir Colin.*

She looked around and saw Lucy standing near Daniel. Anna would have liked very much to join them, but they were together with Mr. Davenport.

No. It's not that she was afraid. On the contrary, she was sure that he didn't at all hate her. The look he had given her a few minutes before was not all that terrifying . . . was it? And perhaps it wasn't meant for her. Perhaps he had only eaten some tart that didn't agree with him and now he was in the middle of having dreadful pains in his stomach.

A tart, she thought. Yes, nothing more than a tart. No one would ever have a look like that because of a person, not at all. *Exactly*, she decided, convinced. *Tonight I will not eat a single tart.*

Because the look that Christopher Davenport had was *really* terrifying.

In a corner of the room, they had begun playing music. She saw Mr. Rossington coming in her direction, but she did not feel like dancing; in truth, she wanted to be alone for a bit. She felt like a fish out of water, and the tedium of having been subjected to Miss Rotherham rang again and again in her mind.

Just five minutes alone, she thought. She made for the drawing room door to find a little corner in the house where she could rest her ears and her weary spirit. *Definitely love, war, and Rotherham,* she repeated to herself.

***

Christopher felt incredibly worn out. His meeting with Daniel was exhausting. He had listened to his deep, melodious voice. He had noticed his elegance, and his fine, polite manners, as well as his relaxed face.

And in his chest he felt an old hatred, with all of its primitive force—a hatred that had festered during many long nights spent crying in his bed, holding back sobs so as not to wake up his cousin in the room next to his.

He had to let it out, to unburden himself from the rage that could explode. He caught sight of a green spot—an out-of-date dress—and a brown head discreetly making its way to the door. He had no idea what she was doing, but he followed her.

***

Anna slipped into the library and closed the door behind her. She liked very much the library in the Edwardses' house. Actually, she *loved* the library in the Edwardses' house.

The lights were low, with only four or five candles burning in the room, but nevertheless she could see well enough to be able to appreciate the books and their welcoming presence. Someone had left an open book on the large ebony table at the far end of the room. Curious, Anna went to peek at the title. *It couldn't have been anyone but Lucy,* she thought, smiling and flipping a few pages. It was a romance novel.

She turned toward the shelves of books behind her. The dim lighting magnified the charm of the expansive rows of elegant books of all different sizes. She went closer and delicately touched one with a red and gilded cover.

A noise in the hallway startled her; someone stopped in front of the library. What a shame—she would have liked to stay alone in this immense place, which was timeless and almost magical in the candlelight. She saw the door handle turn slowly, and the door cracked opened.

"Mr. Davenport," called out Mrs. Edwards in the hallway.

Anna jumped. She jumped so high that she almost feared landing on the highest shelf in a single leap. *Not that name. Dear God, anything but that name,* she begged. Her reaction was a tiny bit exaggerated, she knew, but how could she explain that to her heart, which was beating as if she were running from a band of thieves?

"Oh, you're here, Mrs. Edwards," answered Mr. Davenport, his voice perfectly audible behind the partly closed door. It was very raspy, as Anna remembered.

"Are you looking for a book?" Mrs. Edwards spoke with a low, slightly sweet tone. It seemed a bit like the purring of Nightshade, Lucy's cat. For no clear reason, Anna grew tense.

"Not at all," responded Mr. Davenport, now emotionless.

Her very girlish laugh rang in the hallway. "Not at all, you say? I could help you find what you are looking for, then."

The words made sense—they were all appropriate and polite—but it was as if there was a hidden allusion, as if—

Anna held her breath.

Even Mr. Davenport seemed troubled. "They will perhaps notice your absence very soon, Mrs. Edwards," he said in a hurry.

"Please, call me Louise."

What in the world is happening? Anna clenched the pages of the book she had in her hand, crumpling them. For a few moments she heard nothing; then another burst of laughter struck her ears.

"Christopher," said Mrs. Edwards, breathing heavily.

"Mrs. . . . Louise."

"Come on, let's go in the library," Mrs. Edwards said as she grabbed the door handle.

"No!" he said tensely, holding her back.

Anna quickly crouched down, hiding behind the table, terrified.

"Come now, silly. You don't want to kiss me here in the hallway," said Mrs. Edwards. And she threw the door wide open.

They entered, closing the door behind them. And, worst of all, Anna was hidden behind the table. Trapped in this room with two lovers. (And what's more, unfaithful cheaters. But given the situation, that seemed the least of Anna's worries.)

A soft moan, and then another, and then another, and then gasping for air, and then . . . kisses maybe? They were still near the door. *But are they really going to . . . ? No. Of course not. There is a ball going on in the drawing room, for heaven's sake!* Anna put her hands over her ears, trying not to listen.

"Oh, Christopher . . ."

Anna thought she was having a bad dream.

"Louise, they must be looking for you," he said, trying to reason with her. "Perhaps it would be better if—"

"Christopher, I beg you . . ."

This couldn't be happening. No.

Was this perhaps the punishment for the cruel trick she has played on Sir Colin? *I won't do it again,* Anna silently swore. *Dear God, please, please make all of this stop right now.*

"Louise, now isn't the right time really, it's not . . ."

Anna heard the sound of a hand rubbing against fabric, and she pushed her hands against her ears harder. *Oh God, God . . .*

"No, Louise, don't do that . . ."

(How did that nursery rhyme go, the one her mother used to sing? Couldn't she think of that? Couldn't she . . . ?)

Louise let out a low laugh that seemed to echo in the entire library. "I only wanted to give you a taste, Christopher," she said. "That should be enough until . . . tomorrow night?"

"Yes, of course," he assured her with some difficulty. "Tomorrow night."

Are they stopping? So that is it: they are stopping. Oh dear God in heaven, thank you! She let out a deep sigh of relief and began to breathe again. They wouldn't be going any further than that—"until tomorrow night" of course, but that wasn't important to Anna. The worst experience of her life was over. Thankfully she heard the sound of the door opening again. She waited with her eyes closed.

Then Mr. Davenport said, "If it's all right with you, I will rejoin the ball in a few minutes, Louise. I believe I need to collect myself."

Anna didn't open her eyes. With her arms wrapped around her knees, she didn't move. She didn't move at all, even to breathe, but her heart raced ever more wildly inside her chest.

Mrs. Edwards laughed. "I believe so as well," she replied, and left the room, closing the door behind her.

Some time passed without a single noise; then Christopher Davenport cleared his throat.

Please, God, make him leave. Please, please, please—

"Show yourself, Anna Champion."

His voice reverberated high off the massive bookcases.

Anna opened her eyes. She didn't move.

He knows I'm here, she thought, shocked.

6

A man must know how to fly in the face of opinion; a woman how to submit to it.
—Madame de Staël

"Anna, don't make me search for you," continued Mr. Davenport, his voice low enough to make her blood run cold. "I will count to five and then I will come to get you. But I advise you"—his voice was barely more than a whisper—"I advise you to come out on your own."

Intimidation, without a doubt. In her fear, Anna's organs twisted, giving her the sensation she might lose control of her bodily functions. But why was he so angry? Because of the lemonade?

"One."

Or maybe he wanted her to keep quiet about Louise Edwards. Her temples were soaked in an icy sweat. She had to stand up if she wanted to avoid the humiliation of being discovered under the table, like a thief. She knew that she would have to stand up, but her legs would not obey. They were planted underneath her like dried branches.

"Two."

She tried to prevent her heart from bursting—she breathed deeply two or three times, her chest heaving frantically. But what was there to be afraid of? He was a gentleman, after all, and he certainly would not . . .

"Three."

Attempting to control her fear, she placed her hands on the edge of the table, and with a strong pull she raised herself up. My God, how *gigantic* he was. He seemed even more so to her than earlier in the drawing room. She felt again as though she might lose control of her bladder, but somehow she managed not to.

"I hope that you enjoyed the spectacle, Anna," he said to her calmly and—although absurdly—without the slightest embarrassment.

(You must look back at him, Anna.)

It was imperative that she maintain eye contact, but it wasn't easy. His eyes seemed to undress her. It was impossible to describe them any other way. They lingered on every visible inch of her. Her face, her shoulders, her breasts. Repeatedly on her breasts, and Anna raised her arms, as if to cover herself. Mr. Davenport smiled, content. That was what he was really hoping for: the admission of discomfort.

She felt something well up inside her, something between panic and embarrassment. That something was anger. Hoping to hide her agitation, she put her arms down at her sides and raised her chin. She would not give him the satisfaction of seeing her tremble with fear. Did he wish to frighten her? Well, he succeeded. But she would be damned if she would let him know that.

Christopher stared at her in silence and seemed to nod, as if he had recognized her just at that moment. "Finally we are talking, just the two of us, Anna," he whispered, moving toward her.

Anna stepped back all of the sudden without thinking. And she inevitably hit her back against the library bookshelves. She bumped it hard, and it was painful. And humiliating. Christopher was sneering and, much to her horror, she could feel tears welling up in her eyes.

She fought them back while gritting her teeth and clenching her fists. "Don't you dare use my first name," she said coldly. Her voice came out perhaps a bit weak, but all that was important was that she said something.

He smiled bemusedly. "Oh, really?" he mocked, stopping in front of the table. "And tell me, *Anna*, how do you intend to stop me?" He put his hands on the wood of the table and began to make his way around it to the side, as if avoiding an obstacle.

No, he should not come closer to her. He would not limit himself to just talking to her—Anna was suddenly very sure of that. She didn't know how, but she needed to rush out of there immediately. She looked toward the door, judging her chances of reaching it. Pretty slim, she realized with lucid fright, comparing the length of her legs to his.

Christopher seemed to read her thoughts, and he stopped. "I have every right to call you whatever I like, Anna Champion." His voice was harsh and insulting. "*You*, on the other hand, have no right whatsoever to be in this house, except as a servant."

These words—the words of a ridiculous snob—were so predictable that under other circumstances Anna may have considered them to be a sad attempt at humor. "I would have no problem whatsoever if I were a servant, here or anywhere else," she replied queasily. Her heart was beating in her throat, but that didn't prevent her vocal cords from working—not much, at least. "I would remain myself, no matter what. But what would remain of you without your elegant clothing? Nothing, like the man that you are."

Christopher stared at her silently for a few moments, stunned. "A worthless man, I understand," he muttered finally. He lowered his head and looked at his hands placed on the table; then he looked up again at her, and Anna knew that her instinct was not wrong: this man was *truly* dangerous.

(You're starting to pee, aren't you, Anna?)

War: that was the promise that she read in his eyes. War. Deliberate, rational, and, most of all, terrifying war. The war of a soldier who had already seen thousands of battles.

(Run away, Anna. Run away.)

With astounding speed for such a large person, Christopher leaned on one hand, raised both legs in the air, and leaped over the table. He was next to Anna before she realized it, and driven by panic she fled. He chased after her along the bookshelves and pushed her as she ran, sending her bumping into the shelves. Anna struck her right side and nearly fell; she managed to keep her balance and turned toward him, raising a hand in front of her.

"You are mad!" she screamed, distraught. Her body barely felt any pain, since her fear was so great. "Stay away from me!"

They were very close to each other: if he had stretched out his hand, he would have touched her, and if Anna had tried to leave, he would have caught her. She was nearly completely blinded by fear. *Dear God, this man is a brute; he really is a brute!* "Keep far away from me, or I scream for help!"

The calm that she saw on his face shocked her, and she was holding on to the shelves for support. *But who in the hell are you, Christopher Davenport?*

"No one will hear you, Anna," he responded. His voice was soft and reasonable. "We are quite far from the drawing room, don't you think? And the music seems to be so loud there."

She tried to breathe. She could not think straight because she was overcome with distress. *I must not faint! Not here, not in his hands!* She bit her lip, and the pain helped her regain her composure. With a voice broken by crying, she tried again: "Someone could come in here at any moment!"

"Oh, I don't believe so. No one goes into a library during a party, do they? With the exception of very, very silly girls, apparently." He smiled. "Besides, dear Louise—such a lovely lady, don't you think?—will see to it that no one pays the slightest attention to this part of the house. And at any rate," he added, taking a little step closer to her, "I enjoy a little risk. Very much. And judging by how you have challenged me so far, I think you like it as well. Isn't that so?" The distance between the two of them was minimal, and his impressive size made him tower, dark and enormous, above her. Anna turned her head desperately, looking for a way out.

"Don't even think about it," he warned her flatly. "You could do much worse." He had a calm look on his face, as mundane as if he were having a perfectly pleasant conversation. He stepped back ever so slightly, giving her a bit of breathing room.

Trying to forget about the pain in her side and the throbbing in her temples, Anna asked him in a whisper, "What do you want from me?"

Her voice was trembling so violently that she was able to blurt out only an unintelligible sound, but somehow he understood her words. "That is an odd question," he answered with feigned surprise. "I only want to finish our interesting chat, obviously. Besides that, you couldn't possibly hope that I might want . . . *something else* . . . from you." He paused, sizing her up with his look. "I am sorry if I have hurt your feelings," he added with a contrite expression, "but ugly girls do not interest me."

Anna felt overcome with indignation. What an odd emotion. It appears even in the most appalling situations, when someone strikes you where it hurts most. And it makes you find your voice even when common sense tells you not to speak out.

"I would never want to have a man like you fancy me!" she screamed, disgusted, using her own real voice for the first time since Christopher had surprised her in the library.

He wasn't particularly impressed, however. "I thought as much," he said, mocking her.

Anna shook with repressed anger, and her eyes filled with tears. She didn't even try to hide them. "You are nothing more than a little filthy scoundrel, Christopher Davenport! Go ahead and strike me if you like, but I will tell everyone. Everyone will know—"

"They will know what, Anna?" His tone was hushed and sweet. "Hmm? Do you want to tell your friend that her mother was here to let me . . . on this table?"

She felt her heart fall. She could not hurt Lucy, it was true. She simply could not. "I . . . I . . ."

"If you speak of the episode from earlier, a scandal will break out, and you know it. And you could no longer play the little puppy, the little bitch"—he pronounced this last word slowly, as if chanting—"for Miss Edwards, don't you think? She would hate you. Try to use your head, Anna. Besides, someone like you should know very well how to figure the gains and losses."

Anna wiped the tears with the back of her hand. *Damn him.* "Then I will tell what you did to someone like me," she whispered.

These words seemed to amuse him. "But I did nothing to you, silly girl," he replied condescendingly. "Do you want to talk about our little exchange of opinions? I will deny it. Or I might even say that you were waiting for me here," he said, staring again at her breasts, "and then you offered yourself to me."

Anna was so stunned that the tears stopped running down her cheeks. "No one . . . no one would believe—"

"Really?" His gazed shifted back to her face. He wore the smug look of one who is feasting at another's expense. "I think so, actually. You see, I don't have much to lose, staying here alone with you. But for you it is different, isn't it? You are a woman—well, more or less—and not much more is necessary to ruin a woman's reputation." He sighed emphatically. "It's cruel, don't you think?"

I don't care! Oh, Anna would have screamed. She would have liked to tell him that whatever he thought about her world was irrelevant and that his lies didn't scare her. But she heard a few cheerful children's voices in her head—those of her siblings; and her father, if he had known . . .

"I . . . I . . . will make you pay for this," was all she could say, loudly, using words that had been stuck in her throat, as if it was swollen from powerlessness.

"No, I don't believe so," Christopher replied. And suddenly his face became serious. Almost displeased. "I believe rather that you will become very nice with me now."

He took a step forward, shortening the distance between them. Anna shouted and pushed him back with her hands. He grabbed her by the wrists and threw her shoulders up against the bookcases.

"Don't touch me!"

Christopher was on her. Causing a feeling of terror like she had never before experienced, his body leaned into hers. He was taller than her by almost ten inches, and she was made completely captive by his size and strength—and by his body heat, which wrapped around her like a blanket in winter.

"No!" Anna tried furiously to break free, while her heart beat faster than a fly against a windowpane. "Let me go!"

She couldn't move. Christopher seemed to not even notice her desperate motions. "Shh," he whispered to her. She was shackled to him, and his strength held her up despite her weakness. "Don't make any noise, silly girl. You wouldn't want anyone to find us in this position."

Never had she had a man so close to her, and never had she felt the muscles beneath a man's clothing, or his hot breath, or breathed in his smell. Freshly cut grass, mint, and something similar to cinnamon—that was his soft aroma, and unexpectedly it mixed with her delicate scent. Weakened, Anna began to sob uncontrollably, lowering her head, leaning her forehead on his coat.

"Do you know what would happen if someone came in now?" Christopher's question was like a warm whisper against her head. "No one would ever marry you, Anna, and you would have to . . . you would have to give up . . ." He stopped himself, taking a big breath; then he began again, speaking in a voice that was slightly unsteady: "You would have to give up on finding a rich husband, which is what you want so badly. Isn't that so?"

She managed to shake her head.

"No?" he asked her softly.

His body was pushing fervently and arrogantly against her. Anna felt it against her breasts, against her stomach, and lower, between her legs, where it was touching her indecently and deliberately. "You know nothing about me," she sobbed. "Let me go."

Christopher crushed her harder against the bookshelves. "These men will never marry you," he mumbled, his voice sounding surprisingly hoarse. "They . . . they will take everything from you. Everything. And they will leave you."

He breathed down on her, the contact with his body hot and intrusive. He was gripping her wrists, which hurt her, but Anna was too frightened to find it seductive, and this fear had nothing to do with pain. It was a new fear, one that stirred her loins and made her legs go weak, like mashed potatoes. It was a more undefinable fear than she had ever known, a mixture of torment and listlessness.

"Let me go," she asked, crying shamelessly. "I beg you. Please, Mr. Davenport, let me go!" She spoke the words painfully in an outburst.

"You're *begging* me, Anna?" he said tenderly in a hushed tone. He kissed her head, startling her. "I didn't think you were capable of that." He dropped his head into her hair, breathing in the scent. She closed her eyes. That is what this man wanted—to defeat her. And so she did not react. She did not move, she did not try to push him away, and he remained in that position for what seemed like a very long time. The silence of the room was punctuated with their irregular breathing and the agitated beating of their hearts.

(Do you hear his heart, Anna? It's beating almost as fast as yours, isn't it?)

It was beating, yes. It was beating, and Christopher let up on his grip of her wrists. Then he let them go. They dropped down to her sides, but she didn't put them back up to fight. No, she stood still, just as he wanted. And when she felt him put one hand on her side and the other on her head, she let him. In silence. She allowed him to run his finger through her curls and softly tousle them. Never ever was there such cruel tenderness . . .

"Good girl," Christopher finally whispered to her, and he lifted his head. "I see that you understand." He moved back far enough to see her face, hanging low and in tears. "I will let you go, then. For now."

He suddenly took a step back.

Dazed, Anna didn't know what to do. Could she really leave? Shaking, she wasn't even able to raise her head.

"You can go," he repeated.

Was it over? Was the nightmare over? She collected herself, turning quickly. *Get out of there quickly! Quickly, before he changes his mind, before—*

His hand grasped her left wrist, and Anna stopped without struggling, drained. She understood that he was only playing with her, like a cat plays with a mouse. "You said that I could go!" she protested in a crackling voice.

"That's true," Christopher confirmed with a smile that seemed almost nice. "First, however, you must offer me your apologies." He let go of her wrist, and her arm fell heavily to the side of her body.

For a long moment Anna could not manage to grasp the sense of these words. Then she understood. *It's still not enough for him,* she realized clearly. It then dawned on her that in a crazy way there was a logic—an absurd logic—in what he was doing. *He wants to humiliate me, completely and totally.*

"You want apologies," she repeated flatly. Apologies. She, to him. He wanted her to know that the world rotated around Christopher Davenport.

He nodded, with derision in his eyes. "Oh, just a few words," he explained nicely, "and then you can leave here."

The door was so close. Her freedom was so close. *Just a few words.*

"And then I can leave," she said flatly. It seemed to her that she could do nothing more than repeat his words; she felt incapable of thought.

"I give you my word," he assured her. "It won't be difficult, Anna, you'll see—even for someone like you."

Someone like me.

"Just a few words," he repeated. "I'm not even asking you to kneel. All you have to do is look me in the eyes and say, 'I am sorry that I disrespected you, Mr. Davenport.'"

I am sorry that I disrespected you, Mr. Davenport. How difficult could that be, after all?

The combative nature that she seemed always to have was gone, extinguished in the first real defeat of her life. In the dim light of the room—while the flames of the candles flickered strangely, and the shadows of the books moved with them—there was only a beaten girl with wet cheeks, a runny nose, and a humiliated face.

Christopher stood facing her, tall and arrogant. His strength was too dominating; it was impossible even to think of resistance. His dark hair gave off blue reflections in the candlelight; his face was a mocking sneer.

"You see, Anna, perhaps I could do without your apologies," he admitted, displeased. "However," he added in a patient tone he would have used for a small, stupid child, "people like you must be put back in their place every once in a while."

My place.

And suddenly, like a ray of sunlight in the nighttime sky, Anna understood that he was right. Completely right. Her place was not here. Ah, no—heavens, no! No, her place was in the home of those who loved her, those who lit up just at the sight of her, those who considered her perfect, those who even at this moment were waiting for her.

What was she doing here? What was she doing in this dimly lit library with this madman? What was she doing among these crazy, absurd, pompous—?

"Anna, I'm waiting."

She nodded, closing her eyes. There was so little left before the end of her nightmare. In no time she would be out of this dark room, in the light, and then she could hurry home to her siblings, to her father, forgetting . . .

I am sorry that I disrespected you, Mr. Davenport.

"Go to hell, Mr. Davenport," she said, opening her eyes again.

7

A kiss may ruin a human life.
—Oscar Wilde

"Go to hell, Mr. Davenport."

And she ran away, as if she were running for her life. She ran fast, lightly, with her dress that floated like a cloud of color. She reached the door and grabbed the handle, which slipped out of her trembling hand. She grabbed it again, turned it, opened the door. She had nearly done it; she was almost outside!

"You have three little siblings and an idiotic father you must look after."

His words left her frozen in the doorway. Christopher hadn't chased her, and the tone of his voice was relaxed. If she had been punched right in the stomach, the pain would have felt less sharp. She turned toward him, distraught.

"Your family has quite a lot of debt, it seems." He watched her calmly. Fear made her legs buckle. Weak, she clung to the door. He continued, unmoved: "You see? I do know something about you, after all."

How could she have thought that this man had a tortured soul? How could she have seen any type of suffering in his eyes? "Coward! Don't you dare . . . don't you dare mention my family!"

His face hardened. "Anna, don't persist in defying me. For your own good, don't do it."

The sharp pangs in her stomach did not let up and, nauseated, she was afraid she might vomit. Who was this man in front of her? How could he harm her family? She didn't know, because she knew nothing about him. No, that wasn't so, she corrected herself desperately. *I do know something, don't I? I know that he betrays his friends, and he has no remorse in frightening and striking women.* She felt her heart in an icy grip, as if squeezed by sheets of ice in the middle of summer. Her brothers and sister were probably in bed at this hour, she thought, and the grip grabbed her tighter. (Unless they had gotten it into their heads to play some scary nighttime game, like they sometimes did . . .)

She let out a sob of anguish. "Are you threatening my family?"

Christopher opened his arms. "If I'm forced to," he responded with a sort of resigned displeasure. "But if you want, you can end this story here and now, without consequences."

She couldn't look at him; disgust overwhelmed her. "You are a scoundrel," she murmured. "A treacherous, miserable scoundrel."

He didn't react angrily. If anything, it was with a thoughtful seriousness. "I am treacherous, it's true," he admitted. No, he didn't "admit"—he "noted," rather. Because in his voice there was nothing left to imply that he considered it in any way to be a disgraceful thing. "At times it is necessary to be treacherous, don't you see? To win. And I win, Anna. Always."

For a few moments she wasn't able to respond. "Win? Over me?" she finally asked, and she gave a smile, because it was all too absurd. Perhaps she was merely dreaming. "You're speaking as if I were your worst enemy, Mr. Davenport. But my offense against you is so small, so very small. Heavens, how could you possibly not realize that?"

"It was small, and it will remain small if we end it here. You're the one who is drawing it out, aren't you?"

She fell silent as she leaned on the door without energy.

"You do *not* want to continue this game, Anna."

He began to walk toward her slowly. Only fifteen or twenty feet at most separated them. Anna turned her head to look outside the door, surprised at how the hallway could still be deserted, lit with bright candles.

(You can't escape, Anna.)

Twelve feet, nine feet.

She listened to the noise that came from the drawing room nearby. *The world, she suddenly understood, is not a single place that is clearly governed by logical laws. There are also other worlds, distorted and senseless, like this one that I've fallen into by chance.*

Six feet.

The reality that reigned in this room was awful and had its own inscrutable laws, and while Christopher was drawing nearer and nearer to her, the moving flames of the candles deformed his face. He was less than three feet from her.

"Now I will tell you what you must do. And I will be *clear*."

Anna closed her eyes without moving, and he stood next to her. He put his left hand on hers—still leaning on the door handle, from an eternity before, when she thought she was safe—and he again closed the door without making a sound.

***

In principle, everyone rants, yells, and curses, thought Christopher, *but in the end everyone ends up always at this point, don't they? At the moment of surrender.* And Anna had surrendered, but—with her body shaken with sobbing as she stood in front of him—she seemed as if she would collapse at any given moment. Her simple hairstyle was ruined, and the curls fell on her face messily; the green ribbons looked ridiculous as they poked out of her hair. The dress that she had altered—to look like a queen, Christopher remembered having thought—seemed to fall about her like a pile of old rags. With her face exhausted, her nose swollen from crying, and her eyes red, this girl was anything but arrogant and proud.

And yet she still made him furious, capable of a rage so excessive that it had inexplicable results. Given the women Christopher had dealt with who were mostly brothel keepers or moneylenders, it wasn't the first time he had frightened a female—but it certainly was the first time he had acted like a villain against a defenseless young woman. It was also the first time he had used sexual contact as a weapon. Because that was the case, wasn't it? Sexual threats against a naive girl. One way among others to scare her, obviously—perhaps hardly honorable, but only that, only that . . .

Naive girl. Yes, Anna was that. Naive and scared. Christopher knew it, damn it. He would have liked to let her be and he had considered it even, but when she ran off in a hurry—proud and as light as air—fury overcame him, and to defeat her, he used what Matthew had reported to him that morning. *Threatening children—oh how refined,* he thought sarcastically. *Who knows if she will support me as a candidate for hero of the year.*

Oh, the look of disgust she had . . .

She was breathing heavily. She needed a little lesson; she had deliberately defied him, after all.

"Let's begin again," he said calmly. "The sentence didn't come out quite right the first time, did it?"

Anna lowered her head. The tears slid slowly down her dress, soaking it, making dark spots on her chest.

"Come, Anna," he urged her softly. "Let's do it quickly. I will help you, all right? Repeat after me: 'I am sorry . . .'"

Oh, that was cruel. Even more cruel. Shaking, she swallowed unsuccessfully. Christopher couldn't see her face, but he imagined that she was making quite an effort to manage to say a few words.

"I am . . . sorry . . ." Her voice was faint, like a child's, as if she were grieving and prostrate.

That's not enough, little girl, thought Christopher. The rhythm of his breathing matched hers. Listening to her. *Not yet.* "We're almost there," he conceded. "However, you must say it while looking me in the eyes."

Anna couldn't look up; he put a hand on the nape of her neck and, pulling her hair, raised her head. He wanted to see the humiliation in her eyes. He wanted her to see mocking in his. She would no longer defy him, never again.

"Let's begin again," he said to her.

Anna's face was red, swollen, and her eyes were closed. A tear quickly slid down her face and stopped on the side of her mouth, closed out of helplessness.

"Open your eyes."

For a moment—the flash of a light—she did it. But she closed them again immediately when her eyes met his. Christopher pulled her hair tighter, making her groan.

"Open your eyes. *Now.*"

Anna opened her eyelids slowly and maintained her gaze. Her breathing was agitated, irregular, and her chest followed the rhythm, going up and down in a haphazard fashion. There was a tear that shined against the whiteness of the bare skin at her neckline, and Christopher suddenly felt thirsty. A horrible thirst.

"Very good," he said, clearing his voice. "Let's begin, then. Say 'I am sorry.'"

She quivered violently. She opened her mouth a bit, but not a single sound came out. She tried again, while her face contracted in a painful spasm. "I-I am . . . I am sorry . . ."

(You won, Christopher.)

Triumph appeared on his face, together with a smile. He looked at her in silence for a few moments, enjoying her defeat. "But what a good girl," he murmured, getting closer to her. He perceived her soft hair beneath his fingers and the warmth of her skin, marked by suffering. He saw her eyes laden with fear and hate—and behind that, perhaps, still a trace of pride. He felt the need for air, a dangerous and spasmodic need. He took in a deep breath, and the sweet smell of Anna—a delicate and tender odor, like bread and apples—filled him. Every fiber in his being responded. Every fiber wanted the same thing, and that was not good, damn it—not good at all. Ignoring his beating heart and cursing his own unstable voice, he took up the torture again: "'That I disrespected you' . . ."

"That . . . I . . ." Her muttering was hardly more than a breath, barely audible in the perfect silence of the room.

It was almost over. Christopher put his hand on her wet cheek and wiped away a tear from her flushed, exhausted face. Her eyes were filled with fear, and he slowly rubbed his thumb across her skin, feeling its softness through his gloves. "'Disrespected you,'" he finished softly.

Defeated, she closed her eyes. For a moment—only for a moment. Then she reopened them. "Disrespected . . . you," she muttered. She made a painful grimace and added weakly, "Please let me go now, Mr. Davenport."

He couldn't have let her go even if it would cost him his life. "You were such a good little girl," he said softly. "It wasn't so difficult, was it?"

Anna looked away, staring at a point beyond his shoulder. "Let me go now, as you promised. Please." She closed her eyes and stayed in his hands, inert.

She was so warm, so close; their breathing blended together. Her faced seemed very beautiful, and the candlelight, and the delicate scent of her skin. Her lips were full and red.

God help me, thought Christopher. He bent down over her and kissed her.

8

My friend, the wisest among us is much happier never having met the woman—whether beautiful or ugly, clever or foolish—who is able to drive him mad enough for the insane asylum.

—Denis Diderot

My God, what a headache. The room was only half-lit, and it seemed to him to be spinning. Still drawn shut, the curtains gave him no indication of how late he had slept. *But what time is it?* Someone was knocking at the door, and to Christopher it seemed like a thousand cannons firing.

"Hey, cousin, did you have a drinking spree last night?"

It was Matthew's voice—but when *exactly* did it become so high? It must have happened overnight. The day before it seemed normal, but it seemed shrill in the darkness of the room.

Christopher buried his head in the pillows. "Matt, go away," he mumbled, half-asleep. It was impossible to speak louder; every word seemed to strike his brain like a hammer.

His petulant cousin did not give in. "Come on, get up. I have some news for you," he said.

"No," Christopher yelled back from the other side of the door. He opened his mouth to say "*Later, Matt*" and felt vomit suddenly rise up into his throat. He pulled the bedpan out from under his bed and vomited straight into it. This was hardly an elegant experience, as he had often remarked. And, as always, with the experience came both the relentless feeling that he was a piece of human garbage and the even more relentless—and unmistakable—sound.

Matthew quickly recognized this sound. "Hey, Chris, what's wrong?" he asked him. He now seemed worried, like a mother hen—the worst thing possible. "Don't you feel well?"

"I'm absolutely fine," he answered, and he vomited again into the pan. Another clumpy bunch of an undefinable color—a mixture of every shade between brown and white—splattered on the floor and stained the sheets. *Perfect,* he thought. After a few minutes he was better and said weakly, "I'm fine. Leave me alone for a bit."

"Someone drank a bit too much last night, eh? I told you, you don't have the stomach for it, old chap."

"Matt, if you don't go away I will have to murder you."

"Oh." It seemed that Matthew took this possibility seriously. "I think I'll be going, then. We'll see each other later . . . maybe even have a scotch." He laughed and went off down the hallway.

Christopher lay on his back in bed with an arm over his eyes. His mouth tasted horrible. He felt a sour burning sensation in his throat, and his head was so dizzy it prevented him from getting up. *Ladies and gentlemen, I give to you a man of integrity.*

The smell of vomit and alcohol in the room made him nauseated. He began to shudder and tried to contain it. He struggled to sit up, the room continued to spin, and his mind drifted as if in a daze. He reached out his hand to the night table and picked up a glass that was on top of it. He drank a sip of water, trying to breathe normally and regain control of himself. Then he finished off the rest of the glass in a gulp.

I'm in bad shape, he thought. Damn it, he shouldn't have drunk so much last night. After returning from the Edwardses', he had poured an entire bottle of whisky straight down his throat almost all at once, spilling some of it on his shirt. Then he had thrown the bottle against the wall and thrown himself onto the bed, hoping to collapse unconscious.

He gave a sigh and got up carefully, making sure his own legs were solid. He walked to the curtains and opened them slightly; the light hurt his eyes. His drunkenness was gone, though his hangover would no doubt last until the afternoon. If there was anyone who needed to stay sharp, it was him.

By God, he was not there to play games.

He walked to the water basin and washed his face.

His meeting with his half brother must have shaken him more than he expected if he risked ruining everything—or, at least, of causing an embarrassing showdown—by getting even with this girl. Things had gotten *a bit* out of hand, he admitted. In the dim light of the library he had thought about frightening Miss Champion, about scaring her to tears, about humiliating her as necessary—and up to a *certain point* everything had gone perfectly according to his plans.

He ran his hand through his hair, shocked. Anna had tried to give a frightened "No!" when he kissed her, and the word was muffled as their mouths met. She had let out a distressed groan, but he dismissed it. It would have been difficult for her to give more than that as a reaction—he had threatened to exterminate her family and all future generations, or something of the sort—and Christopher had taken advantage of that. With his hand on the nape of her neck, he had pulled her face toward his, exploring her mouth greedily, ravenously taking it over, delighting in her taste, sweet and salty and something undefinable—daffodil? Hawthorn? He hadn't any idea what to call it.

"No!" she had repeated, but Christopher wouldn't listen to her, and he continued to kiss her mouth, then her face wet with tears, then again her lips, then her very pale neck. He had put his hand on her back, drawing her closer to him. He bit her lips, and his tongue ran over her crooked tooth—that ridiculous tooth that gave her smile a peculiar unique quality. Anna did not return his kisses, but she let him kiss her and, frightened, her rapid breathing caressed his skin and his lips, and her taste consumed him. Her warmth made him feel at home. With timid courage she had finally put her hands on his chest to push him away, but Christopher leaned into her harder, crushing her against the closed door. Their bodies were joined together perfectly, and fearful moans combined with panting. Dear God, how soft, supple, and warm she was, and Christopher felt himself lose control. He felt things getting out of hand, and he felt himself wanting things to get out of hand, so—damn it—he continued . . .

"Stop, sir!" she had begged him, with her cheek against his head, while he was kissing her neck. "Please . . . !"

As if stunned, he wasn't listening to her. His heart raced faster, and inside him a cursed need grew and grew. He had kissed her while shaking with urgency, ignoring her feeble attempts to break free. He had put his face down on her chest, which rose and fell frantically, and put his lips on her open cleavage, licking her tears at last, and with one hand had begun to make room to touch her breast.

"Let me go, I beg you!"

But he couldn't. He had followed the outline of her cleavage with his tongue, tasting her skin, breathing in her scent, listening to her madly beating heart . . . God, the taste of her—that mixture of sweet and salty—could have driven him mad.

"No, Mr. Davenport! Sir!"

What was that scent? Freshly baked bread, red apples—and what else? His hand had managed to reach her right breast, and he had caressed it, then squeezed it. He had been driven nearly completely by instinct.

"No, Christopher! Mr. Davenport, no!" Grasping his hair in her hands, she had managed to raise up his head, and she had begged him brokenly, "Please . . . please, Christopher . . . Let me go . . ."

Maybe it was the sweetness of that voice that broke the evil spell that seemed to have taken possession of him. With blurry eyes, he had looked at her, panting hard. He had to blink his eyes several times to see sharply again; with great difficulty, he finally managed to. Anna was in agony, like a caged animal. Her eyes were staring blankly in panic, and her lips were swollen from the kisses that he had given her.

But what the hell?

As if someone poured boiling oil on him, he jumped backward and continued to move away from her. Disturbed, he stared at her. Then he turned his back to her.

"Leave, Miss Champion."

His voice was so different from his usual voice that even he had problems recognizing it. There was no sound coming from behind him, so he spun around, and he saw her standing still, as if paralyzed by fear. But right in front of him she opened her eyes wide, grabbed the door handle, opened the door, and fled the room.

Thrown off by this completely unexpected disruption, Christopher had remained motionless, listening to the noise of her frantically running down the hallway. His unsatisfied desire would not leave him for a long time (a goddamned long time, bloody hell!), and he had breathed in deeply, opening and closing his fists, counting to ten—or was it ten thousand? He didn't remember. Finally it seemed to him that his excited state was over, and when the fog cleared from his mind—a decidedly small mind, he was convinced—his sense of reason began to come back.

How could he have been so crazy? *What* exactly did he think he would do to this girl? She had stopped him—and he still wasn't sure how—but in any case, he had stolen her first kiss, or at least he believed he had. He waved his hand as if to ward off that thought, still quite dumbfounded for even considering such an idiotic thing. *If anything I did her a favor,* he said to himself, ignoring the throbbing pain that had taken over his guts. *Girls like that are not often kissed by men like me.* And he certainly did not feel guilty for having humiliated her, or for taking advantage of his own superior physical might and social power. As a matter of fact, this would be a lesson for her: never go looking to enter into an environment different from your own, because you may get burned. In fact, she should thank him twice. *Maybe tomorrow I will send her the bill,* he thought angrily. *Damn you, Anna Champion!*

The real problem was not that, and he was astounded he hadn't thought of it first. What had this girl done when she ran from the room? She certainly had no intention of saying anything—she knew all too well what she was risking if a scandal broke out, and his threats had definitely frightened her—but she was in a pathetic state. The fact that something . . . unusual . . . had happened to her was bloody obvious. And if someone had seen her . . . *Stop worrying about it, stupid, and get back in there right away,* he thought to himself. He couldn't stay in this library forever; that's how he would get burned, all by himself, like a fool. It was definitely worth finding out quickly what had happened so he could then decide what to do.

Taking deliberate breaths, he slowly went back into the drawing room and looked around. Relieved, he noticed that she was not there. Miss Champion was not there.

In a corner stood Lucy Edwards, looking a bit sullen. He walked up to her and, with a nod, greeted Miss Rotherham, who was still in the company of Sir Colin.

"You've let your friend go?" he asked her casually. His cordial tone came out without any emphasis. He had been practicing speaking for years, after all.

Lucy tittered and waggled her head. "She left on her own, as I predicted," was her response. "She removed herself from Rosemary's attention and went away. She didn't even come to say good-bye to me, so I imagine I have offended her." She became sad. "She is probably already thinking about a terrible way to make me pay for it."

"She went home, then?"

"Yes. She asked for the coachman to take her back, complaining of an unexpected stomach ailment. She blithered something about a tart that had gone bad, but I must say that I expected a more original excuse on her part," she said with a disappointed smile.

Oh, the excuse isn't all that bad, Christopher thought. Very pleasant words to his ears, matching the very pleasant feeling he had of avoiding a risk.

But now, while still half-drunk in front of the washbasin, he looked in the mirror and saw the dark circles under his eyes and had to admit that he had truly been a fool to risk everything like that. *From now on I will avoid Anna Champion at all costs,* he decided. It wasn't that he feared that seeing this ridiculous girl could again drive him to behave rashly, since it was only the stress of the evening that made him lose his senses.

He plunged his head in the basin, submerging it underwater for a few moments, then lifted his head up, trying to rid himself of the stupor.

***

"Anna, you can't be serious."

Lucy looked at her with such disappointment that for a moment Anna almost changed her mind. But she couldn't reconsider it, not even for her friend. That morning she felt torn to pieces. Her face was taut and dry, her eyes swollen, her skin chapped. Lucy had gone over to see her very early to ask her how she was, and to find out why she hadn't said good-bye the night before—but no sooner had Lucy seen her than she was convinced about the truth regarding her upset stomach. After all, she did like to eat! But accepting her decision was a completely different story.

"Anna, please don't abandon me."

(What a hard heart one has to have sometimes.)

"Dear Lucy, you know how much I adore you," she said again, moved, prevented from making Lucy happy. "And you know that I always like to see you. You are the one person in the world I get the most pleasure out of seeing. But I will no longer participate in the social life of Coxton. I don't feel at ease among these people and . . ." She stopped suddenly, while a sentence echoed in her head.

I am sorry that I disrespected you.

She tried to rid herself of the distressing memory. All morning long she had kept busy in order to not think about it.

Lucy looked at her like a whipped pup. "You can't punish me so much for leaving you with Rosemary! I swear it won't happen again."

Oh, Lucy. "It's not because of that, really," she replied. In the depths of her being she heard the echo of the humiliated voice that she didn't recognize as her own: *I am sorry . . .*

She slowly took a breath and put a hand up to her eyes, which were closed for a moment. "I think I need just a bit of time," she finally said, lying.

I am sorry . . .

"It may be that now is not the right time for me," she continued, her cheeks on fire.

To have . . .

She swallowed hard and closed her hands into fists, until her short fingernails dug into her skin. "We will continue to see each other in the afternoon," she said encouragingly. "We always have, haven't we?"

A spark of pain gleamed in Lucy's eyes, and Anna wanted to cheer her up. But she could not change her mind; no, how could she? That man who had moved to Coxton so recently—how long ago was it? Five days?—had already turned her into a coward, and . . .

Disrespected you.

She didn't want to think about it. She *couldn't* think about it. One thing was certain: she would not be frequenting any places where there was the slightest chance of running into *him*.

Talking about everything publicly, and asking someone to avenge the offense she had undergone, was out of the question: she definitely would be putting her family in danger. "Do not continue to challenge me," Christopher had said to her. "I will hurt you."

And she couldn't say a word, even to Lucy. Even if she left out the part about Mrs. Edwards—who that very night would be giving herself to that man, Anna remembered with a shiver—she lacked the courage to reveal to Lucy how much she had gone through. And anyhow, it would have not been enough for Lucy to know. No. She would have wanted—and sought out—revenge for Anna. And that was too dangerous. *Christopher Davenport* was too dangerous.

She reflected on how many times the two of them, as children, had spoken about their first kiss, and how many times they had discussed men and women kissing. She smiled to herself, remembering how at the beginning they swore that they would never kiss anyone. "It must be a disgusting thing," a tiny, very blond Lucy had proclaimed one day ten years earlier while she drew designs with a stick in the dry dirt in a far corner of their secret garden. Convinced, Anna had nodded, sitting on a large rock under her favorite mulberry tree, warming herself in the rare autumn sun. With the passing of time, however, the subject had come to acquire an odd fascination for them. Little by little they had found something positive in this mysterious act; they had discussed it and debated the how and the why. Toward the age of thirteen, they stopped speaking of it, as they were taken by an unusual, unknown shyness, but Anna was sure that Lucy still had in her head a fanciful plan for her first kiss. Perhaps she had already thought about the place, the words, and the whispers of that long-awaited moment, full of anxiety and fear. Perhaps in her daydreams she lacked only the face of that man who would finally remove the delicate modesty from her lips.

Anna also had had a foolish dream—*at least until last night,* she thought, trying to hold back the tears that she felt forming dangerously in her eyes, and in her own vision the man's face was there, and it was a pleasant face, with dark-green eyes and thick light-brown hair.

But instead . . .

But instead it was Christopher Davenport's lips that had kissed her; it was his heat that had warmed her. It was he who, violently but without harming her, had made his way into her mouth, terrifying her in new ways, provoking shudders of fright. It seemed like fear . . . it had to be fear . . . Although perhaps confusing and a bit titillating . . . it was still fear. Of course he had come just to humiliate her, to show his strength, and, in fear, she let herself be kissed, clenching. When he had touched her, when he put his hand on her breast . . . She lowered her head. Dear God, she couldn't think about it. But this man's burning passion—his tongue, which had licked her skin; his fingers, which caressed her with strong but sweet strokes—was still with Anna, and she still felt his teasing bites, his breath, which smelled of mint and cinnamon, his body that shook hers.

Her first kiss.

A vile kiss, a kiss to be forgotten, a kiss to silence her. And, apparently, a kiss to be hidden, especially now, especially in front of Lucy. She needed to find out instead what feelings her friend had toward this villain. For, if Lucy liked him—the very thought turned her stomach—Anna would have to confess it all to her. She hoped not. No, dear God, no.

"Why don't you tell me what happened after I left?" she asked her, sounding light. Sounding light? She tried, at least. "I saw you talking with the newcomer, that D-Davenport." What a coincidence that she stuttered when saying his name. Lucy looked at her for a moment.

Was there suspicion in her eyes? Anna added quickly, "So, what do you think of him?"

"Oh, he's very handsome. And polite, also." Revolting words for Anna to hear for sure, but Lucy said them with a great lack of enthusiasm, and better yet, with a grimace—a real, authentic grimace. An excellent, excellent sign that got even better when Lucy added, "It's a pity that he's so incredibly boring."

Boring? Anna let out a giggle that was positively impossible to hold back and stifled it with her hand. *Of all the insults that I could give this man, this would certainly not be one of them.*

"Don't look at me like that, Anna, I assure you! Even Mr. Rossington uses more original compliments than his—and that's saying a lot, given that he could have been Adam in Eden. Or maybe even the apple!" She shook her head in disbelief, and Anna tried to imagine an apple that could talk and give compliments. Not bad, she concluded, concerning Mr. Rossington.

"Really, Anna," Lucy continued, "I have thought about it and I've come to the conclusion that the sayings used by Mr. Davenport date *at least* from when the Allens' biscuits were baked—those that we ate last Monday."

Anna had nearly broken a tooth on those biscuits. "That's impossible. Nothing could be that old!" she exclaimed, shaking as she snickered. It was the first real laugh she had let out since the night before, and she felt relieved.

"Try to spend a half hour with Mr. Davenport"—Anna startled—"and then we will talk about it again. You know, I must tell him that it's truly a pity that he's so banal. With his dark hair and his straight nose, I was expecting a strong personality." She had an offended tone. Certainly this accusation was serious. "When I was introduced to him for the first time, for a few marvelous moments I thought that he might be a real cad. Can you imagine how exciting that would have been?"

More or less. Memories flooded her mind—and her cheeks—and she felt like she was soaked in boiling water. She coughed and quickly changed the subject.

"And what of Sir Colin? What can you tell me?" she asked with exaggerated liveliness. "Since I tripped him to get away from Rosemary, I feel terribly guilty."

Lucy would have made a less stunned face if Anna had said she could fly. "Oh, come, you don't believe that, Anna. That man is such a complete loss that worrying about him is an absolute waste of time."

"Now, now, don't be mean. He's really not so bad."

Lucy looked at her with her mouth gaping open, speechless. Such an occurrence was more than rare, given that it had happened at most only a couple of times in her entire life, and for the rest of her visit she stopped harassing Anna to persuade her to go along with her to social events: the fact that Anna had defended Sir Colin was such a testament to the truly difficult time her friend was going through.

9

Who doesn't wish for his father's death?
—Fyodor Dostoyevsky

After he arranged his handkerchief in front of the mirror without the valet's help, he was ready to go out. He lifted his head and pursed his lips tightly. *There's not much more left to do.* His heart beat faster; his blood raced through his temples. *Just a few more months and it will all be over.* God, he felt saturated with anger and fatigue. He put a hand to his forehead and rubbed it slowly, trying to rid himself of his restlessness. For God's sake, it was ridiculous to fear a worm like Leopold DeMercy. He took a deep breath, stepped toward the wall, and leaned his back against it. He needed to calm down.

He let his thoughts flow. His fears. Then he remembered the words of his mother's death sentence. Word for word, syllable for syllable.

I don't believe that the bastard you are carrying in your belly of a whore is mine . . . A faded, short sentence.

I want to know nothing more, neither of you nor of this matter . . .

This letter was the one that he held on to when he lacked courage, the one that saw him through the endless years in which, without letting himself be distracted by compassion or love, he had stolen, cheated, intimidated, and beaten—but not killed, not yet. A rumpled pretext of three sentences written in firm handwriting that perfectly summed up their author.

I'm sending you money. Get rid of it.

Martha did not get rid of him, however, and Christopher was not a bastard—at least not in the eyes of society.

"Chris?" asked Matthew, at the door.

He suddenly lifted up his head and stepped away from the wall. "What, Matt?"

"I have those two names, of DeMercy's creditors. With a bit of persistence we could manage to acquire their promissory notes."

"Good," he responded, distracted. One couldn't say that Leopold led a life of moderation; he had just come back the day before from London, where he had stayed for nearly a month. His continual commitments—or rather, the ladies who welcomed him into their beds and the clubs where he stopped to get drunk and gamble—made him careless and easy to attack. He had simplified Christopher's work in an embarrassing way. *If I don't hurry, he will ruin himself,* Christopher thought ironically. There was not even much left upon closer inspection: Riverstone Manor, his father's estate, was already completely mortgaged. *It would be quite irritating if I didn't have that pleasure after all the trouble I took to get here.*

"Chris, are you all right?"

Christopher didn't answer as he made for the door. He had no need for a mother hen—not tonight, damn it.

But the damned mother hen would not move to let him pass. "Do you want me to go with you, Chris? It won't be easy for you to see him again."

"You'd like to fight my battles for me?" he asked, mocking him. He was nearly eight inches taller than his cousin, and he was twice his size. Hard but necessary training, because it was tied to certain secondary aspects of his job. For this reason, the last few years he had gotten used to delegating tasks that were primarily *physical.* Even so, he preferred to keep himself ready for action: breaking someone's legs required more force than one might think, and it was not something that one could improvise on the spot if one needed to.

Matthew didn't respond, and Christopher, exhaling slowly, tried to control himself. "Don't worry about me," he said, adjusting his tone. "I know how to manage on my own."

"I know." Matthew gave a worried look, and his words did not sound particularly believable.

Christopher ignored him and made to step around him.

"Ah, Chris . . ."

"What now?"

"That Champion family."

Her soft red mouth and the scent of fruit. And flowers perhaps. Christopher looked silently at Matthew.

"You told me to check on their debts."

"Make it quick, Matt."

"Are you still interested in buying their debts? One of their creditors would be receptive to selling you his, and perhaps we could lay our hands on their mortgage." He bit his lip. There was doubt in his eyes. "Chris, they are a respectable family. I don't know what this girl may have done to you, but for once, could you let it be?"

"Don't start again with your bloody scruples, all right, Matt?" blurted Christopher. Dear God in heaven and all the saints, did he really want to preach to him tonight? "I am sure that if it hadn't been for you I would have gotten here a couple of years ago—*at least* a couple of years ago. I don't know why I continue to drag you along with me, like a ball and chain."

"I wouldn't know." Matthew thought about it, preoccupied. "Maybe it's because of my 'bloody scruples.'"

Not bloody likely, thought Christopher. *Far less likely, anyway, than a punch in your ugly mug if you don't shut up.*

But Matthew continued. "You need someone who can patch up the messes you make, and you know it."

Of course: patch up. "Of course, patch up! First I ruin a few arse-holes, and then I end up helping their families. You even make me pay for Fortescue's sons' schooling." He looked sullenly at him. "Oh, did you believe I wasn't aware?"

Matthew shrugged his shoulders; nonchalance was his middle name. "Did you want to let them live in the streets?"

Hit him and be done with it. But where? In the mouth or on his nose? "Of course, by God, let them deal with it on their own!" he said, exploding. "You know very well that my priorities are elsewhere."

"Oh, really?" Matthew wrinkled his brow. Or he was imitating someone with the mental capacity to remember, thought Christopher, or he was straining—without pretending—to do something else. Since there was no chamber pot in sight, he was inclined to believe it was the former.

"Naturally. You had mentioned something like that," Matthew finally admitted, meditating. "The vendetta against someone in Coxton, it seems to me, and if I concentrate the name will come to me. You should repeat it to me more often, Chris, because a few hundred times a day isn't enough, as you can see."

(You do know why he's trying to rattle you, don't you?)

I'm not afraid, Matt. I'm not afraid of that pig. Don't worry about me. "Matthew, listen," Christopher said, tired. "Do whatever you like. Manage the funds as you see fit—I don't care about it. All I need is for you to stop nagging me. If to keep you quiet I have to pay for the children of someone whose life I ruined, so be it."

Matthew smiled, as if distracted. "Chris, you do know what it means if I stay with you even if you don't like how I work."

"You haven't been listening to a word that I have been saying, have you?"

"It means that you love me."

"No," he snapped, "it means that if you don't move your feet, you'll find yourself spitting your teeth into a glass."

"Oh. That doesn't seem like fun." Matthew carefully moved out of the way.

"So they say." Christopher went by him and made quickly for the stairs.

"Hey, wait! Do you or don't you want these promissory notes?"

The promissory notes. Anna's debts. Christopher stopped and turned toward his cousin with a certain exasperation. He noticed the usual signs of worry on Matthew's forehead. Very typical, for Matthew, to have that expression with parallel wrinkles. Typical and tiresome. *Cheer up, you pain in the neck. For once you have no reason to nag.* In fact, he had decided to let go of the game with this girl, as he had promised. He had no idea what he would do with her lousy mortgage, nor did he want a hand in purchasing her debts. He hadn't thought of Anna Champion a single time in five days; he wanted nothing more to do with her.

"Offer the creditor whatever he wants and buy the mortgage," he answered.

***

There he is.

In front of him, Leopold DeMercy was dancing with a rather elderly woman, who looked at him, enchanted, and laughed like a little girl. At fifty-two years old, Leopold kept his proud bearing. His black hair, streaked with gray, was still full, and his lean physique showed no signs of the excesses Christopher knew him to be capable of. Daniel resembled him a great deal, especially in the subtle profile of his nose and the slightly elongated shape of his eyes—the characteristic he had also passed on to Christopher. Leopold's face still showed all the signs of angelic beauty—absurdly angelic—that had charmed Martha.

My father.

Christopher had decided a little more than thirteen years ago—when he had discovered who L. was—that he would never call Leopold DeMercy "Father," not even in his mind. And the first time that they had been introduced to one another, in a club in London nearly four years before—a brief and random encounter, because Christopher was not yet ready for his vengeance, but he was getting there; he was getting there in long strides, climbing the social hierarchy higher each month—Christopher was left stunned that the episode had not provoked a single emotion. *So it's true. I don't have a father,* he had thought to himself. He had already been convinced, but finally he was able to confirm it. And a year and a half later, when he came into contact with one of Leopold's lovers—the very ravishing Susan—he had no qualms in using all of his charm to win her over to him. Even before he met her, he had decided that he would seduce her, and then he would direct her right where he wanted her—against Leopold.

Everything was going perfectly, he remembered: Susan had accepted his flowers, his chocolates, his expensive gifts, and laughed at all of his jokes—even the most tiring—and finally she had invited him to her house. Christopher showed up at her home with the bravado and quiet confidence he would have needed for a common administrative matter. Well, a common and *pleasant* administrative matter.

Susan greeted him wearing a shiny scarlet dressing gown. She was a vision: long blond hair, soft white skin, gray eyes tinged with blue. When she let the dressing gown fall, Christopher was forced to recognize that she was one of the most beautiful and perfect women he had ever seen. She took him by the hand. "Your hand is cold," she commented, placing it on her breast. Then she led him gently to a large bed with immaculately white sheets, and they stood there facing each other.

Susan had kissed him passionately and knowingly, he had returned her kiss, and when she lowered her hand to the fly of his pants, he let her do it, happy he wasn't directing her actions. With a light and sensual touch, Susan searched for his manhood and gently touched it. Then slowly she got down on her knees in front of him and began to caress it with her mouth, tasting it with her tongue.

After a few minutes she stopped. "We have a problem."

"Hmm?" Looking down, Christopher had to note that the problem was indeed small—well, it had shrunk. Disoriented, he had noticed his body's betrayal while Susan, naked and lovely, was getting back on her feet with a look of pity on her face. He didn't know what to say; he didn't even know what to think. He didn't know how he was able to get to the door to leave that house as quickly as possible, and he bumped into the edge of the door and knocked over a little figurine while dashing—followed by laughter that wasn't at all understanding.

From that day on Leopold had become "my father" for him. That epiphany took place when he, alone and dazed, realized that his hatred had grown, not diminished, from this observation that he *did have* a father, after all. With a perverse pleasure he realized that it was his own father who he would have to first destroy, then kill. Matthew knew nothing about this last part of the plan, but Christopher had always known that this would be Leopold's end: death at the hands of his son.

He looked at the man dancing in front of him. *I found you, Daddy. And soon I will take your place.*

Daniel. Daniel was the key to getting close to him. Where was his damned half brother? He saw him not far away, and he walked up to him, without any particular emotion this time. And Daniel welcomed him with the same enthusiasm.

"Mr. Davenport," he said, greeting him flatly. "How are you getting along in town?"

"Very well, thank you," he responded pleasantly. Daniel seemed in a bad mood that evening. Even better. He would not have to put up with his inane sense of humor. "The people here in Coxton are incredibly friendly." He pointed toward Miss Edwards, who was dancing with a young man with red hair. "What a beautiful girl," he said. He wanted to test his half brother's feelings toward her, but Daniel only gave a nod in agreement. *A man of few words, eh?* "These beauties in the country resemble wildflowers in bloom, don't you think?" he said to rouse him a bit.

He succeeded in doing so, even if it wasn't perhaps in the way he had expected. Not even in the way that he had hoped, in actuality. In fact, Daniel burst out laughing quite uproariously. "'Wildflowers that . . .'" He couldn't finish. Perhaps he feared that he couldn't manage. He cleared his throat, trying to regain his dignity. "'Wildflowers in bloom' certainly, my good man," he said, pointing a finger to the corner of his eye, where there was a twinkle of suspicion. "But where on earth do you get these sayings?"

Perhaps the possibility that he was vaguely impolite flashed in his little brain—if he had one, which Christopher seriously doubted. Uncivil. Unbearable and obnoxious. The fact was Daniel was able to become serious again and recompose his face so that it reflected the appropriate society expectations. Not that Christopher had protested or grumbled in any way: on the contrary, he was the epitome of perfect congeniality.

"Excuse me if I have offended you, Mr. Davenport," he said contritely. "My behavior was inexcusable."

Inexcusable? Daniel, you don't know what that means. "You didn't offend me," he assured him with a smile and a grim wish to chop his heart to bits.

"Really, you must excuse me. I don't know what came over me," he begged his brother again. "It's just that I thought what Lucy would do if she heard you say something like that. She would turn up her nose, wrinkle her mouth . . . and then she would take on the delicate coloring of a lemon that's not yet quite ripe. At any rate, she would be green," he said in an apologetic tone that was a bit more credible. "Even if it is often used, it is certainly a metaphor that suits her. She is a very beautiful girl, intelligent, and keen," he concluded warmly. He looked at Christopher with a knowing expression. "Do not underestimate her if you want to possess her."

This very polished boy has definitely crossed the limits of the ridiculous, thought Christopher. What did Daniel think? That he knew more than he about women? Lucy had in fact not turned lemon-green earlier when he had said she seemed like a flower or a rose, or whatever the hell he had said—he didn't remember. He would have noticed, because he had been watching her carefully. He wanted to understand, in fact, if she was still respectful toward him; in other words, he wanted to know if Anna Champion had told her anything. Her perfectly bland behavior gave him the answer he was hoping for, thank God.

He looked at Daniel, who continued to giggle to himself. Christopher teetered between feeling a need to punch him and, in spite of himself, not finding him so hateful. But, in short, did his half brother intend to marry this girl or not? He talked about her enthusiastically, but right after he gave advice to *him* on how to have her, so the question remained unanswered. Christopher would probably have to win her over no matter what to avoid the problem at its core. *And to give you a lesson that you will not forget, little brother.*

Daniel's cheerful mood was suddenly dampened as an odd seriousness came over him. Christopher followed the direction of his eyes.

(It's Leopold, Christopher. Breathe.)

But he didn't breathe while the man who had given him life joined them.

Finally, Daddy.

Here he was, his father, three feet from him.

Here it was, his hatred, which swelled up and burst forth from his soul. But Christopher felt it deep down, hidden and cold. That cold that covered his emotions. Only perhaps his heart felt like joking a bit.

Leopold gave Daniel a slap on the shoulder and said his first words: "Sonny"—vague frustration mixed with a desire to embarrass him, in a voice that rolled like pebbles on a walkway—"perhaps I must inform you that we are in a ballroom and the object is to dance and not just stand here with an idiotic look on your face, like you are."

This single sentence, coming from his father's mouth, was better than a piece of rubbish in a trash bin. It was a lucky thing, thought Christopher, that Leopold was such a blatant arsehole. It made his task easier, since for many years he had gotten used to swallowing the sense of guilt that his victims' tears, sweetness, and sympathy provoked in him. Certainly Leopold's harshness—and what's more, flaunting of his pride—made everything simpler.

Clenching his jaw, Daniel took a step back. "Father," he said coldly, "allow me to introduce you to—"

"Oh, hush." Leopold looked toward Christopher. Incredibly bright, his eyes were a lighter shade of green than Daniel's. A few red capillaries wound around the yellowed whites of his eyes, but it was the clear color of his irises that captured Christopher's attention. He was almost as tall as Christopher, who was rarely in a position to not have to look down to exchange looks with another. "Mr. Davenport," said his father to him, "what a pleasure to see you again."

(He remembers you, Christopher.)

A moment of bewilderment. A meeting in the smoky drunkenness of a club, a meeting that at times Christopher thought he had only dreamt. But instead, here he was. His father had not forgotten it.

"Mr. DeMercy," he said, greeting him politely. His voice was sure, decisive. He had never doubted it, at any rate. "It is an honor that you recall me after so much time."

(How much do you hate him, Christopher?)

"Well, perhaps it is only the relief of seeing a city dweller in this dreadful countryside," responded Leopold. *I hate him enormously, immensely.* "Daniel, you know Mr. Davenport and I met in a club in

London a few years back." He lowered his voice and winked at his son, who looked as if he were swallowing a toad. A pondful of toads. "A gentleman's club, obviously."

And Daniel, the dandy, became very angry. A bonfire burned in his eyes, a bonfire in a green valley with lights and smoke, rage and bitterness. It was heavy and almost unbearable. He said nothing for a few moments, tensing up. "If you will excuse me, Father," he said finally, "I promised someone I would dance. Mr. Davenport." He gave a nod and walked away, hatred in his every movement, with rapid steps that lacked elegance.

Watching his son go, Leopold sighed. "You young men, Mr. Davenport, you absolutely do not know how to enjoy life."

Christopher felt the thoughts empty from his head, too dumbfounded to understand what was happening. "Perhaps your son has misunderstood, Mr. DeMercy. It seemed almost that he had understood—"

"It's obvious that he understood the word 'bordello,'" he said.

(Breathe, Christopher.)

"Come, Mr. Davenport, don't make that face." There was slight annoyance in his voice, mixed with delusion maybe. "Don't tell me that even with you certain terms can't be used. Sometimes I wonder . . ." He looked around, irritated, leaving the sentence unfinished. "Mr. Davenport, how does a man of the world like you manage to stay in this godforsaken hole? It seems inconceivable."

Christopher had regained his composure. After all, he knew even more about brothels than his father, didn't he? "Oh, I hardly arrived a few days ago, sir. But I believe that there may be something interesting in these parts."

"Really? You are a damned optimist, then. I assure you that here the boredom is fatal, the women are ugly as a donkey's arse, and gambling is rare and poor. If it weren't for a few out-of-the-way places, I would have already run to drown myself in the river. Do you gamble, Mr. Davenport?"

"Of course, sir."

"I will call on you for a few games of dice or cards in that case."

"I would be very appreciative."

Leopold nodded but seemed distracted. "Now, if you will excuse me, I must join a few friends in the back of the room."

(He's getting away, Christopher. He's getting away from you after barely two minutes.)

No, you can't go like that. "Just a moment, sir, if you will permit me," he said. "I wanted to ask you . . . seeing that you are not afraid of speaking frankly, in fact . . ." He lowered his voice and looked him in the eyes. "I wanted to ask you if you could suggest to me some—how shall I put it?—particular place where the ladies do not look like . . ." He paused, smiling. "The backside of a quadruped."

Even Leopold smiled, finally pleased. Christopher knew very well that a smile could wound as much as a dagger; he didn't know, however, that daggers sometimes don't cut but make you swell up on the inside.

"Well, a man with blood in his veins," said his father, rejoicing. "Good, this means that I will accompany you myself if you want, Davenport. Let's go in a couple of days."

He felt a thud inside himself. Maybe his heart or maybe his soul—Christopher couldn't tell. Only one thing scared him even more than having to go to a brothel with his father: the observation that Leopold considered him to be truly equal to him.

10

What the fable has invented, history sometimes reproduces.
—Victor Hugo

"Miss Edwards!"

Lucy raised her hand in a greeting and stopped outside the entrance of her house while Christopher rode on horseback toward her.

"Miss Edwards, where are you going off to like this?" he asked her, getting off his horse. "If I may be allowed to inquire, of course."

That afternoon Lucy was wearing a little yellow muslin dress and carrying a parasol of the same color, with her blond hair and the glow of her skin all combining to make her a dazzling spot against the green of the countryside. Christopher thought that any man could fall in love with this lady; at this moment she shined with her own light.

"Mr. Davenport, what a pleasure to see you," she said cheerfully. "What are you doing in these parts?"

"I was coming to pay you a visit, Miss Edwards. Today you are . . ." He bit his tongue before he could let out a sentence with the words "gold," "blond hair," and "sun"—and probably in that order. Not that he was following the advice of his stupid half brother, obviously. After all, he didn't need to. In fact, it was obvious to him that Miss Edwards was already mad about him. "You are positively luminous," he finally said.

"Thank you, you are too kind," Lucy responded with her sunny disposition. "As for your gracious social call, I'm afraid I must inform you that I have a prior engagement this afternoon."

"Oh, I'm so very sorry. May I join you?"

Lucy shook her head apologetically. "It's a tiresome little thing, I assure you. One of those afternoons spent with women who chat about gowns and lace doilies. Another day perhaps."

"Certainly," Christopher responded, with a sigh of relief. He did not wish to remain in Miss Edwards's company; mind you, he found her adorable, and he knew he had to charm her, but so far he had done a very poor job of it. His half brother was absolutely right, and, even worse, he truly had too many things to attend to that afternoon and could not spend it with her.

"Allow me to accompany you to your destination at least," he proposed politely. "A young lady such as you should always be escorted."

"Don't worry. Clement is following me at a distance. Do you see him?" She pointed behind her toward one of the Edwardses' domestics. He was about fifty feet away, pretending he just happened to be there. "My mother thinks the same as you, and I rarely manage to escape from her infernal watchful eyes." She snorted. "And to think that I walked this way nearly every day when I was a child."

"I see. But allow me nevertheless to accompany you."

She nodded with a smile, and they began to walk slowly. The July countryside was warm and fragrant. Heat rose from the ground, and the tall stalks of the wheat fields, nearly ready for harvesting, had their own strange and mysterious language. After twelve days Christopher had almost gotten used to the silence of this place. It wasn't really silence, to be honest; it was rather a combination of secret messages between the insects and the birds in the sky and the animals of the earth. Light verse, joyful chants, unusual rustlings, and unexpected sounds all combined, as if in an infinite whispered conversation.

They walked in front of a large, rusty gate, which seemed out of place among the gold and green of the farm fields, between hop vines and wheat. A long stone path covered with dead branches led to a broken-down house, now abandoned and victim to old ghosts. Its walls had been blackened by a fire that had left it in a horrible condition but not defeated it, as it still stood proud and ominous.

"That is the old haunted house of the village," Lucy informed him as she noticed the direction of his eyes. "All the children are terrified of it, and many say that they hear horrible screams coming from there."

"And you walk along this path every day without ever being afraid?"

"Of course I am afraid, like everyone," she responded with a faint smile. "I always keep my distance from it, you know."

They continued to walk in silence for a little longer while the crickets flirted with each other among the wheat, which itself produced its own tiring and relentless melodies.

"Here we are, almost there," said Lucy, pointing to a redbrick house. It was rather small and was at the end of a short path bordered by thick linden trees, which were neglected. The house's walls were flaking badly, as if it had needed repairs for years.

"So, we are now in front of the house of your friend"—as he was saying it, he realized he didn't need to—"Miss Champion." He bit his tongue, but by then the sentence had slipped out, and the fact that he knew *exactly* where the Champion family lived was amply evident.

Lucy smiled but let it go. "Yes, Anna and I live less than a half mile from each other. And as I said, we love to spend our afternoons speaking about things that are absolutely incomprehensible to everyone, except to us." She laughed and lowered her head, as though she were remembering one of those things.

"It doesn't sound so tiresome."

"Pardon me?" said Lucy, looking dismayed.

"I said that doesn't sound so tiresome. You had called it that earlier, I believe."

"Well, perhaps not tiresome, but surely an unbearable torture for anyone who hopes to hold on to his mental sanity."

"Nothing could be a torture with you there."

Well, the words had slipped out, and it was fine, for it was only an expression, wasn't it? It certainly was not a request to enter. However, it seemed an awful lot like it, damn it. *I must pay attention to the words that I use,* he said to himself. *I absolutely do not want to enter into that house, and I will not.* To see Miss Champion again would definitely be stupid, and it would be provoking the young lady beyond all limits. Besides, paying her a visit after having insisted that she discontinue all social outings—he knew very well that if she was absent from recent parties it was because of him—was so illogical that it bordered on the unthinkable.

Fortunately Lucy was not swayed to invite him in. In fact, she seemed more apt to do anything but that.

"If I wished harm on you," she said, amused, "I would ask you to go in with me, Mr. Davenport." Pretending to reflect on it, she then shook her head. "And today, at any rate, I don't remember any offense on your behalf that was so serious that I feel compelled to such cruelty."

Christopher laughed, sincerely for once, because the relief he felt was certain. He could return home, drink something, and study his latest moves against his father.

"I thank you very much, miss, for your kind concern," he responded. Then out of nowhere he added, "I do believe, however, that I would miss your company too much."

Why the devil had he said something like that? Was he mad? Perhaps, and his condition seemed serious, because he cleared his voice and said again, "Please let me go in with you."

***

Frightened, the children were watching Anna. They could not do otherwise. The sorcerer was about to kill the sweet princess, and the prince was still in the forest, fighting against the seven evil cabbages and four bread trees, which were burying him under countless hot loaves.

"And the prince knew that he could not help the princess," continued Anna as Grace let out a shriek.

They were sitting on a carpet on the floor, among pillows they used as chairs, turned toward the window. Grace was sitting in Anna's lap, and the brothers were on each side. Nora was sitting in a chair nearby, sewing. Even she listened to the story with a faint smile, pretending to think about other things while muttering a "humph" every now and then.

"And so the prince knew that he could do only one thing for the princess. He gave his sword to the gray dragon and said to him, 'Take this to the sweet Penelope, dear Grigo, as fast as the wind.' Grigo flew away, opening his great gray wings striped with green," said Anna, imitating the dragon flying by flapping her arms, "and in a moment he reached the castle tower of the wicked sorcerer."

Was she perhaps subjecting her siblings to an emotional tension that was too intense, she wondered? The very dramatic moment tormented their little hearts.

"How will the prince survive without a sword?" Dennis protested. "He won't be able to cut the loaves open anymore and fill them with evil cabbages. He will be flattened by bread!"

"The prince knows what he's risking, but sometimes love means making sacrifices," Anna explained. What a sloppy bit of philosophy meant to quiet her little brother with all the might of an irrefutable platitude. She continued: "Grigo the Dragon took the sword to the princess, who managed to peel the giant potato. She cut it up in pieces and threw it in boiling oil, and the smell that spread throughout the castle was oh so very good that that sorcerer could not resist. He ran to the kitchen, and on the table he found twenty-five pounds of hot and crispy chips. He dived right into them and began stuffing himself without being able to stop, and the more he ate, the more swollen he became, and he got bigger," she said, opening her arms wide, "and bigger"—her arms were even wider—"and then he got so big that he finally burst with a poof." With her hands, she mimed the explosion.

"Poof," Grace repeated.

"The princess flew on Grigo the Dragon and rejoined her beloved prince, who was completely entombed in a mountain of bread and evil cabbages, and she saved him. And they had bread and cabbage to eat for the rest of their lives."

"Like us!" Grace shouted.

"Exactly!" Anna said, laughing.

"I would not at all like to meet an angry cabbage," came an affectionate voice over her shoulders.

Lucy!

Anna got up quickly, along with her brothers and sister. She ran her hands over her dress to smooth it out and turned around, with the beaming smile she always had for her friend.

And then she saw him.

Him.

A kick to the head. Someone must have given her a kick to the head, because the shock was so strong that her legs gave out, and she was able to hold herself up only by putting her hands on Grace's shoulders, nearly making her fall as well.

"Ow!" the child whined.

Anna looked at her, terrified, and Grace misunderstood her frightened expression.

"You didn't hurt me, you know," she said, calming her while hugging her legs.

Nora looked up and, seeing the new guest, jumped up from her chair. "Oh, dear heavens, Miss Lucy. We didn't see you arrive. You had to let yourself in. And your companion."

The children's eyes all turned toward this tall gentleman.

"The sorcerer!" burst out Grace, pointing her little finger at him without hesitation. She recognized him immediately, on account of the description her sister had given in the fairy tale.

"Grace!" exclaimed Lucy. She let a little laugh slip out that was altogether noticeable despite Lucy's attempt to muffle it with her hand.

Anna, on the other hand, was not laughing. Nor could she speak or breathe or move or even blink. Her mind went totally blank, and it showed in the complete motionless state of her body.

(It's Christopher Davenport, Anna. Do you remember him? He kissed you a little more than a week ago. He humiliated you. He laughed at you, and he threatened your family.)

Her family. Her family—dear God, it was true—her family was here with her right now! Anna was scared, certainly; she was even silly, but she was still the oldest sister to three small children! She stood up tall and moved in front of them to protect them with a fierceness she didn't believe she possessed. *How* could he have been allowed into her house, this scoundrel?

Since she couldn't make a scene, she said, "Nora, please take the children into the kitchen and give them a bit of bread."

"Who is that man, Anna?" asked Anthony.

"Anthony, go to the kitchen right now."

Noticing her sharp tone and the abrupt bobbing of her head, her brother decided it was better to not ask any questions, and he followed Nora, together with the other children, although he was a bit hesitant.

"Don't worry, Anthony," Grace said, comforting him as they made for the kitchen. "Soon he will go 'poof.'"

But despite the optimism of these words, the sorcerer was fine. There he stood in the doorway, unfazed and calm. Maybe peaceful, even. Anna, on the other hand, felt like she was fading away, and she stood in the middle of the room, looking at him with a hatred that she had never felt before, for no one. A harmless hatred, sadly, and in fact he merely returned her look with his perfectly blue, relaxed gaze.

"Anna, are you feeling well?" asked Lucy, entering the room.

"Well" was perhaps not the most appropriate term. Anna barely managed to turn toward her, diverting her eyes from that . . . from that . . .

"I know that you don't care for him, but really, it wasn't my fault," Lucy whispered to her when she drew near. "He wanted to accompany me here at all costs."

Her friend was so sorry, and what could Anna do? Throw him out of her house in front of her? Scratch his face until she wiped the smug look off it? Or ask him to have tea with them and offer him a few biscuits and smile cordially at him?

Oh, damn it!

But she had no smile for him, to say the least. She breathed in deeply. "It doesn't matter, Lucy," she finally responded. Her tone was more lifeless than a snuffed-out candle. "I'll have to kill you, of course, but I hope that doesn't ruin our friendship."

Lucy laughed quietly. "We'll be here only five minutes, I swear," she murmured. "Then I will come back secretly. I'll have to fly away on a gray dragon."

"May I enter, or will you make me stay in the doorway, Miss Champion?" asked Christopher with perfect composure.

He was amusing himself.

(Like he amused himself eight days ago. Isn't that right, Anna? You cried and begged, but he was amusing himself oh so very much.)

She stared at him with anger. And fear. And shame. That damned shame that she didn't deserve to feel. She didn't even know how to answer him. Then she saw the quizzical look on Lucy's face, and she said what she would have never wanted to say: "Please, have a seat. Here." Her voice sounded terribly pitiful and agitated. *She* was terribly pitiful and agitated.

Christopher came into the room. His size was impressive, just as she remembered. He sat down, and even the broken-down sofa, which generally swallowed guests up, did no such thing to him. Even seated he remained incredibly big. And incredibly threatening. But why was he here? Was it simply unlucky coincidence? Or else . . . or else was he still vexed at her? The prospect ate at her heart and her gut. God in heaven, her siblings were in the kitchen and her father in the vegetable garden.

Oh, *why* was this gentleman here?

Lucy cleared her throat and tried to initiate a polite conversation. The tension was so thick that it seemed as if they were looking at each other through a dense, black smoke.

"So, Anna," she began cheerily. "I came for a very important reason today, one that could not be delayed."

"Oh." And his kisses, and that fear in the pit of her stomach, and those words that still mocked her again and again, and the tears and the weakness, and his might, which had crushed her and taken every bit of dignity from her, and—perhaps the worst thing—he had fondled her . . .

Nora came in, carrying a tray with teacups. "Anna. I made tea. For your guests."

Painfully, she stood. "Thanks very much, Nora."

She took the tray from her, and the teapot shook dangerously. She nevertheless managed not to tip it over, and she put it down on the parlor table. Lucy helped her pour the tea, perhaps because she noticed she was having a few problems. Really quite a few problems. What a fine euphemism to say that she was shaking like dandelion fluff in the wind. And she was right in front of Christopher, who was enjoying the scene and had his lips turned up into a slight smile.

But why was he here? And what if he had realized he was a horrible, shameful person and he sought to beg her forgiveness?

(Anna . . .)

But of course! That must be it! Not that it was possible for her to forget his attack, obviously, but the thought calmed her down. That was it, no doubt about it!

"How is your mother, Miss Edwards?"

Christopher had spoken to Lucy, but Anna felt his gaze upon her. *Definitely not. He doesn't want to apologize,* she thought lividly, squeezing the handle of the teacup.

"Oh, to tell the truth, she has been incredibly unhappy for quite some time."

Christopher coughed, spitting a sip of tea into his cup; apparently, he had not thought that type of response possible.

"It must be the weather," Lucy continued. "I try to stay far from her as much as possible, because when she is like this, nothing good comes of it." She stopped and suddenly changed the subject. "But Anna, as I was saying, I have a very important bit of news to give you."

Christopher listened carefully, and Anna responded, trying to put a thought out of her mind that she couldn't get rid of. "Do tell."

"I know that you still feel guilty for having *accidentally* tripped Sir Colin," she said with a knowing look that only the two of them would understand.

"Mmm-hmm," Anna said, nodding distractedly.

"You should know," Lucy explained to Christopher, who looked at her without understanding, "that Anna was the unintentional cause"—she glanced at Anna—"of Rosemary's captivity of Sir Colin during the party at my house about a week ago."

Hearing that evening mentioned took Anna's breath away, and she tried to calm down. It wasn't difficult to breathe in and out, she recalled. She had been doing it for nearly nineteen years, and she couldn't possibly forget now.

Christopher, on the other hand, had no reaction whatsoever that could possibly indicate any kind of emotion, as if for him that evening had been something he had already experienced a thousand times. And maybe, Anna thought, feeling her stomach tighten, that was exactly it.

"Really?" he asked politely.

Lucy nodded. "Exactly, and she hadn't the foggiest idea how to apologize."

How excessively cruel this all was, even for destiny. Anna lowered her head toward her teacup and closed her eyes. She started to feel her cheeks blush. *Lucy, I will truly have to kill you, after all.*

The gentleman said nothing in return and leaned over to take a sip of tea. But on his lips the slight smile from a little earlier returned, and Anna wished intensely that a gaping pit would open up and swallow him whole. *A big pit, a little pit—dear God, what would be the problem with that?* However, in spite of the legitimacy of her prayer, it went unanswered.

"Well, Anna, you can stop feeling guilty."

Her friend's tone piqued her curiosity, regardless of the absurd situation Anna found herself in, and she looked at Lucy questioningly.

"Can't you guess?" Lucy gave her a look as if she were about to announce she had just discovered the elixir of life. After a theatrical pause, she said, "They just announced their engagement. Sir Colin and Rosemary Rotherham will marry immediately."

"No!" Anna slammed the teacup down on her saucer, and once she understood, for a moment—which was over all too quickly but was still a blessing—she forgot this man and his presence there, and she shouted happily, "Oh, but that's fantastic, Lucy!" And as if it were the most important thing in the world, she added, "And it's all only thanks to me!" Her face lit up radiantly, her cheeks flushed with delight, and her eyes shined brightly.

Then her eyes met his.

Her smile withered on her lips, and her thoughts scattered like sparrows after a gunshot. *Why? Why is he looking at me like that?* She didn't want to cry, and she didn't want to feel that agony in her stomach, but my God, there it was—right there—and a fog clouded her vision. Christopher had wanted that same look—that damned look, as if he could devour her—even in the Edwardses' library, and Anna felt something tremble inside of her. The teacup and saucer slipped out of her hands and fell to the floor, and the noise they made seemed impossible for dishes that were so small. Tea splattered everywhere—on the floor, on her dress, on Lucy's dress.

She jumped to her feet.

"Oh, Anna, leave it. I'll help you," Lucy offered.

Both she and Christopher stood up quickly, eyeing the disaster.

Anthony chose this exact moment to enter the room. He was probably just outside the door the entire time. He was brandishing a wooden sword in his left hand, a tangible demonstration of his courage as a manly brother.

"Sir," he said to Christopher, "stop frightening my sister." His tone sounded threatening, admittedly, but he was still a child and not even five feet tall, and, facing this giant man, seemed to be helping stage a biblical farce.

Aghast, Anna couldn't even wonder how Anthony was able to read her mind. The only thought that came to mind was that she absolutely had to get him out of Christopher's sight. Immediately. "Anthony," she said, dead serious, "the gentleman is not here to play."

"Is this man frightening you, Anna?" Anthony asked.

"Anthony, get out of here."

Her brother did not listen to her, and he turned again toward Christopher. "I will defend my sister. Know that." He showed his sword, putting it in the attack position.

Christopher looked smugly at him and the weapon he had and replied tersely, "Sir, you are aware that with your sword held like that, you could never defend anyone. It's rather stupid on your part to think so, let alone to try it."

Anthony gasped, and his little face twitched painfully. Unflappable Anthony, who never cried—her little brother who was too proud for his age, too proud for any age perhaps—dropped his head and his sword.

For a few moments Anna could neither say nor do anything, because three things had absolutely upset her, and she didn't know which one upset her the most. The first was that Christopher Davenport had just humiliated her brother, a ten-year-old child. The second was that Christopher Davenport was truly bad, after all. She had had some doubts on the subject—doubts she hadn't admitted even to herself until that moment—due to the way in which he had held her close in the library with a sort of desperate tenderness. The third was that Christopher Davenport had called a little thing so much smaller and weaker than him "sir." Sir!

Maybe it was the last consideration that instilled in her the madness necessary to react. She moved in front of Anthony, and Lucy did the same, creating a wall between him and Christopher.

"Well, what's wrong," Christopher asked, not understanding. "The hilt was incorrectly—"

Slap!

The noise of it was louder than the sound made by the dishes falling on the floor. Anna forgot she was afraid of him; she forgot the possible consequences. In a fit of rage that completely prevented her use of reason, she raised her right arm, and, with all the force of a sacrosanct indignation incited by this most recent event and supported by past offenses, she slapped him so hard that Christopher's head remained to the side for a few moments. The imprints of five fingers slowly began to show on his cheek, as if he were branded by fire.

Shocked, Lucy put her hand to her mouth, and from behind his sister, Anthony also looked up in astonishment.

Beside herself, Anna yelled, "Out! Get out now! Out of my house!"

Christopher straightened his head and looked her in the eyes without anger. No, it was rather a sort of amazed attention. And amazed pain perhaps, which had nothing to do with the slap he had just received. It lasted for only a moment. Then, without a word, he turned abruptly on his heels and went to the doorway. He was nearly outside when Anthony's little voice stopped him: "Sir?"

"Anthony, no . . ." Anna started, but then she stopped short. Her brother had the *right* to say something to the man who had made fun of him with undue malice. Furthermore, the damage was already done: it could not get any worse.

(Of course. It couldn't get any worse, Anna. Do you realize what you have done?)

I defended my little brother—that's what I did. My sweet, defenseless little brother. She stepped to the side, and Lucy did the same, leaving Anthony in full view. He faced Christopher, who was waiting on the doorstep, standing straight and motionless as an obelisk. In one hand he held the gloves that he had not yet put back on. They were perfectly white and perfectly elegant. Perfectly without rips, as everything about him.

Anthony's clear eyes stared into his.

Poor baby. He won't soon forget this humiliation, Anna thought. When it's such an inevitable pain, the expectation can be very long, and her fingers tensed up as if she were making fresh-squeezed fruit juice. *He will probably say a few pathetic and childish sentences that will mortify him even more.*

A couple of seconds went by—a couple of seconds that seemed like hours. But, finally, the very odd little boy spoke. And with a voice clear and without any trace of fear, he said, "I give you permission to marry my sister if you would like."

For a few moments complete silence filled the room.

It seemed that even the countryside fell silent—even the trees and the birds in the branches decided suddenly to be quiet.

Then Lucy burst out laughing. It was uncontrollable laughter, and she tried to suppress it without success. Anna's mouth was open, and she could not close it. She looked at her friend with glassy eyes, unable to articulate a word or a thought.

Christopher remained impassive, the mark of the slap becoming more and more obvious on his face. He ignored the two girls and turned toward Anthony. "Sir," he said, "if you come with me outdoors, I will show you how to hold a sword."

And before his sister could do anything at all, Anthony ran to Christopher's side, and the two left the room together.

11

Marriage simplifies our lives and complicates our day.
—Edmond Rostand

Christopher looked at the map in front of him and sighed.

During the night a field to the west of the river on the DeMercy estate had been destroyed by fire. First the barn went up in flames, and then the fire moved toward the grain ready for harvest. It wasn't the major blaze that Christopher had hoped for. He had gone by there on horseback that morning and noticed that the damage was limited. Better than nothing, at any rate, and stopping in front of the burned remains there filled him with satisfied admiration. The family of farmers that worked there—that had worked there—was looking at the same scene. The thin farmer with dirty, tousled hair was crying. His wife was next to him, and she was holding a little girl by the hand. The wife and girl looked around, emotionless, but he—the head of the family—could not manage to hold back his sobbing. With his head hung low, he wiped away tears with his arm. The little child, who was maybe five years old, leaned her head as she contemplated her father's face, where tears mixed with soot.

With an irrational jerk, Christopher grabbed an ashtray from his desk and threw it against the wall, shattering it. Then he lowered his head, put his hands to his forehead, and slowly rubbed his index fingers on his temples. My God, how many years was it that he had been pursuing his goal without ever taking a break? He certainly could not stop now, but he would have liked to—at least for five minutes.

There was knocking at the door.

"Come in."

Matthew appeared in the office. "You do know there is a little bell if you want to call someone."

"Hmm?"

"That thing you broke." He nodded in the direction of the pieces of glass. "If you ring the little bell, someone would have come anyhow."

"And this is why you came in here, to tell me not to break the knickknacks?" he blurted.

"No, to give you some important news, stupid cousin," Matthew replied. "Daniel DeMercy got engaged this morning."

Oh, bloody hell. Christopher's mouth twisted. *Curses!* He had behaved so foolishly. Naturally, he should have forgotten about Miss Edwards following that afternoon four days before. Now that he thought about it, his cheek still hurt, and he rubbed it absentmindedly.

After the slap, that little brown-haired chap had taken him hurriedly toward a vegetable garden in the rear ("Hurry up, sir, or else they'll catch up!"), where he met Mr. Champion, and the old man—but he wasn't that old, no more than fifty-five years old, though he seemed much older—had welcomed Christopher with a twisted smile on his kind face. Arriving out of breath, Anna was kept from yelling by her father's presence, and Christopher was able to teach Anthony a few basics of swordplay without annoying interruptions. This little man was quite intelligent, he thought now with a smile. What a pity he had such a foolish sister. Perhaps that was why he sought so desperately to marry her off . . .

The smile on his lips faded as he looked at Matthew. The prospect of Daniel's marriage to Miss Edwards was cause for concern, he admitted. Wanting to humiliate Miss Champion risked delaying his plan. Damn it, he would have to get Lucy to fall in love with him and instead . . .

"Daniel will marry Lucy Edwards, I imagine," he stated with a resigned sigh.

"Chris, let me set the scene, instead of your jumping to hasty conclusions. So, as I was saying," Matthew continued calmly, ignoring the look that, right in front of him, certainly promised he would be murdered only after slow torture, "I was saying that probably the fire that we set last night heated up their tempers, because our spy informed me that there was an awful fight between your fath—Between Leopold and Daniel this morning. As you know, Leopold has always advocated for Daniel's marriage with Miss Edwards."

Christopher held his head in his hands. "Shit."

"Wait, because the best is yet to come." He paused emphatically, not seeming to want to continue.

In honest surprise, Christopher wondered how it could be possible that he hadn't yet killed him after twenty years. From time to time he had wanted to, deep down. And looking at his self-satisfied face, Christopher thought that perhaps the moment had come.

"So?" he sighed. "Are you going to tell me, or I am going to have to rip your smile off as I rip out your tongue?"

Matthew smiled. "Daniel has decided to ignore his father's instructions, Chris!" he disclosed all in one breath. "And this morning he announced that he is engaged to another girl, a girl who, according to Leopold, is as ugly as—"

"A donkey's arse, I suppose," Christopher said, finishing his sentence. He was relieved, but not completely; he needed to know more. "How rich is this fiancée?"

"That's the best part: she's absolutely penniless. And you already have her in your power, because you bought her promissory notes a few days ago."

Christopher stopped breathing.

"He will marry Anna Champion," Matthew concluded. "But I bet that you already knew. That's why you were on her from the beginning. Isn't that so? You really had me going this time."

With a tense smile on his face, Christopher said nothing.

***

Engaged . . . I am engaged. Anna repeated it again and again, trying to convince herself of it. *Is this what is feels like when a dream comes true?*

She tried to make sense of her confusion that morning, searching to analyze the developments. "The event," a marriage proposal—from the man she had hoped for, which she thought an impossible dream—left her stunned. Yes, stunned, not happy or excited—that was coming now—but stunned, because how on God's earth was it really possible that Daniel loved her? How was it that he missed her so much in the previous days that he was driven to knock on her door, throw himself at her feet, and ask her to marry him?

"Miss Champion? Will you marry me?" Daniel bowed his beautiful head of light-brown hair down and kissed her hand softly. His dark-green eyes—wide open, bright, and genuine—seemed even more lovely in the morning light.

Anna wasn't able to enjoy the moment intensely because the emotion that she felt was at once deep and comprehensible compared to the emotion of the previous days, which were so violent and absurd that they had drained her of all rationality.

She cleared her voice. "Mr. DeMercy—"

"Daniel, please. Call me Daniel, Anna."

Ah, the tenderness with which he pronounced her name was so different from that male voice that had spit on her in rage.

"Daniel," she began, embarrassed, "you know that my family has no . . . well, I have no . . . I have no dowry whatsoever, Daniel."

"No need to worry about that." For a moment a thought darkened his face. "Anna," he responded in a mortified tone, "I must confess something that you will find out soon enough. I'm not sorry, but unfortunately I cannot help it. And I offer you my apologies in advance." He rubbed his forehead uneasily. "My father did not agree with our marriage—if you will accept my proposal. And he will probably try to make me pay for it. But I have a good income from my mother, which I intend to use to support you and your loved ones. No dowry is needed at all on your part."

The depth of this gesture reflected the depth of his heart and his feelings for her. "I cannot allow you to clash with your father because of me!" she protested in dismay.

Daniel shrugged his shoulders in indifference. "It wouldn't be the first time in any case. And besides . . ." he said, lowering his head shyly, "life would not be worth living if one could not fight against bad masters—and bad fathers."

Anna looked at him and felt that she loved him. How could she not? He was all that was honest, fair, and good. He was a man who had always followed his own conscience, even in cases of personal loss—in love and in war. *And in the case of Rotherham,* Anna thought with a smile—although, as she reminded herself, without her mean little maneuvers of diversion, Rosemary would still be on the loose and not happily engaged. But this didn't break the general rule, did it?

"Anna, I have known I loved you for many months. I've been a coward to have not come forward before, and I hope you can forgive me. Am I a fool to think my feelings may be reciprocated? The truth is that . . ." He stopped, embarrassed, and his smile became that of a little boy, upset but adorable. "The truth is that since the first time we danced together—even before you trampled on my foot for the tenth time—I fell in love with you."

Was this not, Anna asked herself, perhaps the most romantic declaration of love in the world? "I have unbeatable weapons," she said, laughing, trying to hide her emotion.

Daniel said nothing and waited.

Ah, of course. The answer. She was supposed to answer, wasn't she?

"Do you love me, Anna? Will you marry me?" Daniel asked.

Is this love, then? This calm, this peace, this confidence that everything will happen for the best?

It was clear that she loved this man; he had always been her favorite, and for three months she had dreamed only of him, even if in the last two weeks she hadn't truthfully thought much about him, since she was too busy cursing Mr. Davenport. The striking difference between the two men took her breath away: Daniel DeMercy seemed like a giant compared to the miserable, contemptible, violent Christopher Davenport. Daniel was sweet, ironic, and able to feel childish joy; his enthusiasm was sincere, his heart was transparent. He was so delightfully different from the other gentleman, who even in Anthony's presence a few days before seemed unable to free himself from his strange severity. On that occasion he had taken his jacket off in the afternoon sun, stretched out his arm, and grabbed Anthony's wooden sword as if it were a damned serious matter and not a game. Anthony tried to imitate him, with the same look of seriousness on his childish face.

The scene had paralyzed Anna.

Never again, she had thought. *That must never happen again.*

She realized that Christopher served as a strong male figure, but what her family needed was a gentle, generous, and honest figure like the person in front of her. The world was full of bad masters, as Daniel had said; she would gladly keep them far away from the Champion children until they were no longer in a position to be in danger.

"Will you marry me, Anna?"

Anna heard the voices of Anthony and Dennis in the hallway, and she understood that she had no more time. Fortunately, she was sure of her choice.

"Daniel . . ."

It was impossible not to love him. *I will marry him,* she decided.

"Yes, Daniel," she replied. "I will marry you."

***

Unmoved, Christopher had listened to Matthew before asking him to leave his room. His cousin had given him a doubtful look, hesitating for a few moments, but finally he walked away. He knew him well enough to know when it was best to leave him alone.

Christopher sat on the edge of his desk with a glass of whisky in his hand. *It has finally come full circle, hasn't it?* he thought, expecting to feel satisfied. The developments relayed by Matthew were perfect: Anna was the ideal wife for Daniel, since she was just poor enough to not threaten his plan. And the cherry on the top of the cake was that Leopold was beside himself with this engagement. *Had I been tasked with choosing a wife for this clown, not even I could have done better,* he said to himself. *It's perfect, simply perfect.* He took a big gulp from his glass. *This is how Anna thinks she will strike it rich,* he realized, smiling with sarcasm. Daniel was not that rich in actuality. She would find out when he took everything away from the DeMercy family. *I really must offer my congratulations to her,* he decided.

He stood up and strode quickly out the door.

***

"Anna, you should know that meeting the father of one's own fiancée is a dreadful test even for the most loving heart."

Daniel had come back to her house that afternoon to tell her about his confrontation with Leopold, but especially to ask formally for Anna's hand in marriage from Mr. Champion. Anna couldn't help but laugh at his worried look. "Don't be afraid, Daniel," she responded. "I'll talk to him first and then I'll call you. Besides, my father isn't so bad; he'll talk to you about tomatoes, onions—in short, anything dealing with his vegetable garden—and if you prove yourself to be knowledgeable about gardening, he'll grant you my hand."

"And that is supposed to calm me? I'm even more terrified," he replied, and he truly looked it. "But, Anna . . . could you give me a bit of help?"

"Well, that wouldn't be fair. But if you insist and you promise me that in the future I can use this against you, I'll try to suggest the right answers."

"Use it against me? You're quite adorable."

He smiled lovingly at her, and Anna looked down, blushing because of what she read in his look. He gently put his hand under her chin, and then tenderly his lips got closer to hers.

That moment so long awaited and so long dreamt of; that sweet, caring face; those green eyes, which looked so brightly at her. Daniel moved closer, and Anna closed her eyes, ready to savor every moment—and hoping it would lack nothing it needed to become her one true *first* kiss.

***

The front door of the Champions' house opened suddenly, and Anthony came out and ran up to him. "Mr. Davenport!" he greeted him. "Are you looking for my sister?"

"You can call me Christopher," he replied, dismounting his horse. "And yes, I am looking for your sister. Is she at home?"

Anthony shook his head. "No, she's out."

"Do you know where she went?"

"No. That elegant gentleman came by again."

"Did she go off with that gentleman?" he said abruptly.

"No, he went off on his own beforehand. Anna disappeared soon after, and I believe that she is hiding somewhere to either laugh or cry. You know, she sometimes does that, sir."

"I understand." He got back on his horse quickly. "Good, now I must say good-bye, Anthony."

"Will you be back, sir?"

"Christopher."

"Will you be back, Christopher?"

"You can count on it."

***

Anna entered the secret garden—Lucy's and hers—looking nostalgically at the abandoned traps that they had set many years ago to protect their private space. A rusty water bucket hung from the cherry tree, empty and without life. Nearby a wooden figure with a horrible drawing on it—at least, it used to be horrible; it had an orange mouth, yellow eyes, a red body—was now faded, only a pathetic shadow of the monster that was meant to frighten any imprudent visitors. On the ground there was a rope, which was tied to a bell hidden far away in the bushes. She laughed and tried to pull it; the bell would not ring.

Today anyone could invade our kingdom, Lucy, she thought regretfully. *Luckily the reputation of this house keeps away even the most brave.*

And yet it had not kept her and Lucy far from each other—not at all. When they were children, they would approach the haunted house very slowly, having become familiar with the devastated garden, with the broken windows, and with the wrecked shutters. They didn't go into the house—that had happened only a few times; instead they would remain outside, in the garden, in a little corner all their own, a wide, green clearing where they magically became fairies, princesses, and wicked witches.

She went to that corner now. It seemed much smaller than she remembered. She sat under the mulberry, which welcomed her with its friendly branches in the unbearable heat of the afternoon. How long had it been since she had been in this place? She didn't know. Certainly many months. And yet as a child she never let a week go by without going there. *Everything was so simple then.* She sat down on the grass, holding her bent knees in her arms, telling herself that life sometimes forces us to make adult choices. And she thought about the choice that she had made that very day.

***

What a pity Miss Champion isn't at home, thought Christopher, and no one seemed to know in what damned hellhole she might be found. Incredibly frustrated, he took the road and left, moving away quickly from the redbrick house.

Where did you go, damned girl? he wondered. *I only want to congratulate you.* It was true: he wished very much to offer her his best wishes. That would have been extremely polite, and he would have so enjoyed seeing her face, conceited by the prospect of a marriage that was so *significant.*

He smiled in cruel anticipation.

He continued galloping down the beaten path as if he had the devil after him, and he gave only a furtive glance at the haunted house, passing in front of it like a bolt of lightning. Lucy's word's echoed again and again in his mind: "That is the old haunted house of the village. All the children are terrified of it, and many say that they hear horrible screams coming from there."

He continued to spur the horse, moving quickly straight ahead. And Lucy's voice said again, with an artificial ring that was secretly amused, "Of course I am afraid, like everyone. I always keep my distance from it, you know."

He pulled on the reins forcefully, and the horse stopped in a flash.

I always keep my distance, you know.

He remained motionless in the middle of the road, in the sun.

Of course I am afraid, like everyone.

He turned the horse around and went back in the other direction as quick as the wind. He arrived at the rusty gate, stopped, and got down from his horse. He looked at the path that led to the crumbling house, surrounded by wildly growing bushes.

The witches' house.

Anna Champion, I know that you're in there.

***

Under the tree, Anna found the old bell. It was missing its clapper and didn't ring anymore. She had a shudder of anxiety, but that was normal. When she and Lucy were little girls, they had avoided going in that place when they were alone. Together they could overcome the world, but when they were alone, they were captivated by the same ridiculous superstitions that the farmers believed—even if they would have never admitted it, not even to each other.

Anna shook her head, laughing at herself. She wasn't a child anymore, and this afternoon she needed to be alone and to think. And to calm down.

Because Daniel's kiss was . . . perfect. It was the kiss that she had imagined millions of times, making her speechless. It was exactly as she had imagined it—his lips drew closer slowly, timidly; he delicately grazed her lips with his, then suddenly moved them away. Then, as if they could stay away no longer, his lips touched hers again, more boldly, more decidedly, and infinitely sweetly. Finally his tongue had met with her gentle and curious tongue, finding space within her slightly opened mouth.

The perfect kiss.

The sweetest kiss that could be imagined.

Is this what it feels like when a wish comes true?

Daniel had moved from her, and Anna had stared at him. "Daniel," she murmured. Right there in front of her, his eyes were so beautiful, so blissful, so loving. Lowering her face, she had taken his hand. She was quiet for a bit; then she raised her head. Daniel's heart broke when he saw her expression.

"Daniel," she had whispered as a tear rolled down her face, "forgive me if you can. I can't marry you, Daniel . . . I don't love you."

***

Christopher entered the garden, stepping over the sticks and paying no attention to the trash. A bucket swung on a rope from a tree as if hanged. He went in that direction.

***

An ant was walking slowly on one of Anna's legs, taking advantage of her seated position. Anna smiled at it thoughtfully. "It's time for you to go home, little one," she said. "And me as well."

She gently lifted a leaf close to it. At first the little ant did not want to get on; then it seemed happy with its new haven. Anna was about to place it safely, but the sound of brutish footsteps made her hand shake. The ant fell through no fault of its own. Anna listened without moving, with the dead leaf in her hand. Someone was trampling senselessly on the fallen branches and ruins of the garden. In a moment of insane terror, she thought that it might be a witch passing through there to steal her soul. She got up suddenly, holding her skirt tightly in her hands.

Lucy, someone has entered our garden.

She turned toward the noise and saw the intruder. For a moment her vision blurred; then in his dark, angry eyes—in his horribly contracted face, in his closed fists—she saw her own terrible fate.

"Anna Champion," muttered Christopher Davenport. "What a wonderful surprise."

Without asking or wondering, Anna ran away, searching for impossible salvation.

***

Christopher saw the atrocious awareness in her eyes, the spasm of her face, the mute scream of her mouth. He wanted to smile at her and tell her, *"Anna, don't be afraid. I want only to offer you my congratulations. I will not touch you, Anna,"* but when she fled he was upon her with one leap.

12

Memory is the only paradise out of which we cannot be expelled.

—Jean Paul Richter

They fell down on the grass side by side. Anna was able to get away from him by rolling sideways, and she attempted to get up off the ground, but it was in vain, since Christopher jumped on her and wrapped his arms around her.

"Unhand me, sir. Unhand me at once!"

They fought furiously in the tall grass and the dry, dead twigs. Anna struck him with her fists and scratched his face and neck, drawing blood. Her dress was a rumpled mess and had ridden up indecently on her body. She began to kick frantically, but his legs were wedged between hers, spreading them apart. Finally Christopher managed to grab her by the wrists and hold down her arms as he lay on top of her.

What am I doing? he asked himself. *What the hell am I doing?*

He was panting heavily.

"Please let me go!" she screamed. Her hair was disheveled, her face distraught, and her eyes wide open. The pink dress she was wearing was pulled up above her white knees. It was ripped and had dirt and grass stains on it. "I beg you, let me go, Mr. Davenport!" Her voice cracked and it suddenly became very childlike, regressing back to an age of nameless fears. Her face was locked in a horrible grimace. "Don't hurt me . . . please . . . Christopher . . ."

She could say no more and wept desperately.

"Oh, Anna, I'm sorry," he mumbled. He lowered his face into the hollow of her shoulder, and the scent—bread, apples, and what exactly?—nearly overwhelmed him. "I am so very sorry," he repeated, kissing her neck and causing her to give a frightened groan, "but I can't let you go." He closed his eyes tightly and swallowed hard several times. *These damned people took everything from me,* he thought, and he realized he was close to tears—how long had it been since he cried? Almost sixteen years—*They took everything from me, Anna.*

He felt her tightening up, and she whispered a hopeless "No" that was so soft he could barely hear it. What was unmistakable was the sound of her delicate weeping. Her tears made his hair damp, and his wildly beating, broken heart boomed inside him. Christopher breathed in deeply against her shoulder, with her warmth so close, and he wondered again, hardly believing it possible, *My God, what am I doing?*

The answer was so horrifying that he hadn't the courage to admit it, and yet he didn't stop. All of a sudden he let go of her wrists, put his hands between her legs, and squeezed brutally hard against her most private areas.

"No! Sir, no! Don't do that to me. Please, Christopher!"

She began to beat him hysterically, desperately, on his lowered head, on his back, pulling, hitting, but it was as if this man felt none of her blows as he attacked her body with his abusive, cruel hands.

"Davenport! Christopher, please! Please, please, no!"

She tried to stop him, but it was no use, and she heard the sound of tearing fabric. The last layer that protected her was removed, and there she lay, defenseless and uncovered beneath him.

"No!" she screamed, sounding like an animal screeching, her voice unrecognizable and her face transfigured in horror.

He positioned himself more squarely on top of her, crushing her with his weight, while she shouted madly and ripped out his hair, trying to pull his head and mouth away, which had begun to kiss her face and neck. Christopher pulled down his pants and he grabbed her pelvis violently, raising it up and pulling her groin toward his.

"Don't do that to me! Please!" Anna howled up to the dazzling blue sky. "Christopher! Please, don't do it . . . no!" she screamed desperately, trying to free herself from his fierce grip. Christopher spread her legs open by raising her knees in an unthinkable, obscene position, and her private parts—her most intimate and secret feminine flesh—was in full view. The sunlight illuminated every detail and showed every nuance of color.

"God, please! Please, please, no!"

He didn't hesitate for a single second—perhaps one second, only one second, when he asked himself again, *My God, what am I doing?*

The most brutal part of his body—that felt no mercy for the desperate cries or the atrocious screams—drew nearer to the opening of what it was searching for, touched it, and sensed its warmth, while Anna wriggled to break free from his hold, from that fate, begging for mercy, struggling like an animal to the slaughter, reduced to a savage, pathetic state.

"No! Please! Don't do that to me! You can't possibly. I don't believe, no . . . Oh, please . . . Please, no! No!"

He raised his right hand and struck her on the face, then again. Back and forth he hit her face, her soft features, with the palm of his hand. He slapped her ears, her temples, her cheeks. He slapped Anna, who was dazed by his strength, his deliberate and blinding strength, and she stopped fighting back in the barrage of slaps, no longer understanding anything, except for a moment, a single moment of clarity. For a single moment she understood that this was the end of her.

Christopher drew her toward him, bending his head down to her shoulder.

“They won’t take you away from me,” he mumbled, and, leaning against her, he suddenly thrust into her. He felt a sharp pain as he invaded her unprepared and tight opening, and he was inside of her.

***

Anna felt a sharp pain when Christopher entered her. She screamed again and again, not to gain pity from the man who was bearing down on her and tearing her up inside, since he was impossible to move to pity, but because the pain was incredible. For a moment she thought she would die and she welcomed it as a blessing, but death did not come, and the pain came back more cruelly with each thrust.

“Oh God, no! No! No . . .” she screamed, her voice cracking several times due to the stabbing pain and her wild cries, which kept her from breathing.

The man who was on her, hiding his face, was panting hotly into her shoulder. He was pushing deeply into her, and he ripped mercilessly into her virginal body. His scent mixed rage, sweat, mint, and alcohol, and it covered her, mingling with her. His slight afternoon stubble scratched her chin, and though it left no marks on her skin, she worried about the marks that were being made underneath—the bitter gashes on her soul.

“Have mercy . . . Have mercy! Enough! Please! It hurts me. It hurts badly!”

This man did not hear her. He did not answer her screams. He didn’t react to her scratches and punches, which grew ever more weak. He used and hurt her body as if it were a shell with no feelings, enjoying the damage he inflicted inside, as though cutting her with glass or a blade, cutting her into piece of pulsating flesh, then cutting her some more—always more. Anna called desperately for help, but no one came to save her. No one could have heard her on the barren road, and if a feeble scream had reached the ears of a solitary passerby, superstition would have driven him to run far away from this evil, voracious house.

"Have pity, Christopher, please! Please, enough!"

She cried and cried without taking a breath, without being able to stop. Pinned down under his body and lying on the green but burned grass, she felt her inner parts being torn apart by the man who had ruined her forever, and she felt him steal from her one of her most beautiful possessions, on both the inside and the outside. Her screams scared the birds from the garden, while the trees motionlessly watched her torment. Her memories of this place were now defiled forever.

When Christopher raised his face and went to kiss her, the look of horror on her face was immeasurable. With a scream she pushed him away as he fell off her. She tried to get away, rolling over off her back and putting her hands on the ground to get on her feet, but he pulled down on her shoulders, pressed her to the ground, and struck her face, making blood run down her cheeks. He climbed on her again and brought his hand forward between her thighs, raising her pelvis and drawing it near him. He penetrated her again, from behind like an animal.

"No! Christopher! Please, no!" She reacted desperately but with no more strength in her body or her soul. "How could you? How?"

"Shh," he whispered, speaking for the first time since the nightmare had begun. He was panting, and his voice was hoarse. Her pain seemed to mean nothing to him. "If you are good, it will be over. It will all be over quickly."

"Let me go . . . please . . . Chris . . . Christopher!" she sobbed, and continued to cry silently, no longer fighting back, no longer screaming, exhausted. She put her hands on the sides of her face, burning from the summer sun, then grabbed the grass between her fists, biting her lips to not think—to not think, dear God, to not think—but there he was, inside her body; there he was, dear God, there he was. He was inside her womb. Oh God, my God . . .

"It's almost done . . . be good . . ."

He began to move again inside her, slowly. And slowly he began again to take pleasure in it. Anna was still at the mercy of this man, and the liquid heat that filled her—her own blood—made his movements less painful. A flow of red was taking away the last of her extinguished strength, and her physical suffering as well. Anna would always have the gashes on her heart, however, and she wept out of powerlessness and humiliation while the breathless, sweaty man crouched over her continued to steal what was not his, pushing hard and heavy inside her, in and out, without stopping.

"Don't cry," murmured this thief, leaning his mouth on her neck. "Don't cry, my dear."

With these words he bled her soul like he was bleeding her body. Anna felt dirty and guilty, and, miserable and dismayed, she cried more. "Don't . . . don't say . . ." she sobbed, but he grabbed her face, turned it toward his own, and tried to kiss her. She resisted, and Christopher only kissed one corner of her mouth.

(Be good, Anna. Wait for him to finish. You see? You see how happy he is with you? You see how much he likes you?)

No! she wanted to scream. No! No! And then fight and fight and punch him and scratch him. But she couldn't . . . she couldn't anymore. She only wanted it to be over. As she lay prostrate on the ground, with every fiber of her being abused, even her thoughts had been violated in that she could pretend she was somewhere else. She marked the passing time by his thrusts against her back, which shook her in a shameful, repetitive motion. Her face touched the grass, forward and back, forward and back.

"Here, almost there . . . just a little more . . . good girl . . ."

The sound of him inside her own body was a rhythmic and obscene tidal movement. Tears streamed ceaselessly from her open eyes, like salty raindrops of shame. They dripped on the green blades of grass and dampened the ground visible underneath, hot and swarming with life.

"Oh, Anna, Anna," mumbled Christopher, lightly touching her neck and cheeks with his lips. With his left hand he began to rub her groin with a horrible gentleness.

It would never be over. "No! No . . ." she begged despairingly. "No, it's not fair . . . no . . ."

Why was he humiliating her this way? How much would she have to endure? Giving up, she cried as he thrust deeper and deeper into her. "Now you are mine," he whispered, "you are mine."

He caressed her face and hair, hugging her tenderly with an absurd, crazy tenderness, and covered her face and neck with little kisses. His fingers played between her legs, insistent and tormenting. Even vile.

"No . . ." groaned Anna. "Please, Christopher . . . enough . . ."

"Shh . . . it's over, it's over . . ." With his nose buried in her hair, he breathed in her scent, as if becoming intoxicated. "Don't be afraid . . . it's all right now . . ."

Oh God. God, the man was everywhere. Inside her, outside of her. He touched her, licked her, filled her. He lustfully enjoyed her, and each gesture of his was followed by another and then another and then another. Confused, Anna felt all of his breaths, all of his moans, all of his kisses. His sweat dripped down on her; his pleasure dripped down on her. He greedily nourished himself from her belly, and he drank from the spring of her juices, which were not red or painful, as there was no longer any blood. Drops from her slipped between his fingers; drops from her flowed at his touch like a brook of velvet and oil.

"Do you feel it, Anna . . . ?" he murmured, and his tongue savored her skin, leaving saliva where it was still wet with tears. "Do you feel how beautiful it is now?"

She leaned a cheek on the ground, in the fragrant grass that was saturated with tears, and she closed her eyes. The beating of her wild heart and her breathing left her dazed and dizzy. She couldn't manage to think clearly: maybe it was the smell of the tall grass that was clouding her mind. Or maybe it was the warmth coming from the ground.

"Oh, Anna . . . you are like paradise . . ." His whispering entered into her like his breath. Like his body. "My queen . . . my magnificent queen . . ."

He took her face in his hands and turned it toward his own, and Anna didn't react, confused by too many caresses, succumbing to too many stimulations. He kissed her eyelids, her cheeks, the corner of her half-opened mouth. He put his lips on hers, searching for her tongue.

"N-no . . ." she begged, bewildered.

"Shh . . ." He put his thumb on her lips, pushing it a little into her mouth. "Oh, Anna . . ." he moaned, and with his hand he pulled her pelvis toward him as much as possible. "My dear, I can't resist anymore . . ." He leaned his forehead on her shoulder, and for a few moments he stopped moving, taking long, deep breaths; then, shaking, he pushed in her again. "Anna, Anna . . ." he called softly. "Oh, Anna . . . come to me, my darling . . ."

What was this man saying, and what did he want from her? Anna didn't know, and she couldn't understand it, and, befuddled, she stopped wondering about it. She felt hot, drugged by the scents of the garden and her body, possessed and touched without decency, overcome by an odd languor.

"Yes, like that . . . Oh, it's good like that, my darling . . ."

What time was it, and how long had they been there?

Anna did not know. She had forgotten—just as she had forgotten herself in the confusion of her senses. She felt her womb warming up unbearably, as if something were trying to escape, to erupt, to find a way out. She moaned, and her mind went blank. She could no longer remember anything or anyone. Between her legs she felt an intense pressure, and she felt something coming, as she felt necessity and urgency. Christopher kissed her mouth as she breathed unevenly. Under his hand an unstoppable, palpitating warmth was growing, and this warmth finally exploded suddenly in little waves—so many little shocks that it made her startle uncontrollably.

"Good girl . . . Oh God, you were so good, my love."

He lightly kissed the nape of her neck and took his hand away from her private parts, which were sensitive and swollen. For a few moments Anna was somewhere else, in a place without memories, where only the deafening sound of her own heart existed, and she vaguely felt him move inside her more vigorously. At last, with a spasm he collapsed and finally pulled out of her.

13

The spectacle of a battlefield after combat is sufficient to inspire princes with the love of peace and the horror of war.
—Napoléon Bonaparte

For a few minutes they stayed on the ground, motionless. Anna was underneath him, and she was breathing quietly, without crying. Christopher was on top, trying to calm down his own excited heart. He knew that she could not move, sensing her heat; under him he could feel the innocent body that he had raped. He breathed deeply and sat up. With a certain awkwardness, he straightened out his pants and covered himself.

He looked at the girl breathing quietly next to him. She was stretched out, her skirt raised, and she was dirty, with blood on her dress and skin. Her body was cruelly exposed, and he saw her chest going up and down slowly. She had one cheek leaning on the ground, as if it weren't worth the trouble to raise her head. He grabbed the skirt by the hem and, slowly pulling it down, covered her injured body. She didn't react. Christopher remained silent, incapable of saying anything to her. The quietness was astounding after the atrocious screams from earlier; that horrible battle was like a distant dream in the fading light of day.

It seemed that Anna would never move, nor say anything at all; however, she suddenly spoke. In the silence of the garden, in an incredibly clear voice she said, "Now are you going to kill me?"

Christopher was so stunned that for several moments he couldn't even open his mouth. "Kill you? Of course not," he answered, running a hand through his hair. "I will marry you, naturally."

As if dead, she didn't move at all; then she began to laugh incoherently with a high, deranged laugh even more frightening than her screams from earlier. "Kill me, sir, because I will never marry you, and if you leave me alive, it will be you who dies, by my hand."

She put her palms on the ground and pulled herself up on her knees. Seemingly without effort she got on her feet, and she turned her back to him, but Christopher noticed her closed fists as she swallowed her pain in order to not show weakness.

He also stood up. "You will never manage to kill me, Anna," he explained to her calmly. "And you *will have to* marry me. You have no other choice."

She suddenly spun around and gave him a forceful slap that even he did not see coming. "Do not call me by my first name! I don't want to hear you say my name! Do not dare ever again!"

Christopher straightened his head and looked at this beaten, scratched face. A drop of blood had left a red line on her cheek, separating it in two, as if it were a broken plate.

He nodded his head and repeated, "You will have to marry me, Miss Champion. You don't have any alternatives."

Anna took several steps away from him until she reached a tree. She didn't lean against it, however, but stood up straight and looked him in the eyes. "I prefer to die," she replied with an emotionless look. Her statement was so clear—that alternative was infinitely better than marriage to him—that he felt the rage which he had just calmed begin again to swell up within him.

"Really?" he asked her coldly. "I believed you cared dearly for your family. Would you leave them on their own, then?"

Her eyes opened wide, and she seemed to return to her senses. Unrelenting, Christopher continued: "Perhaps you think your fiancé will take care of your loved ones. You aren't taking into consideration that once I have informed him of this . . . thing . . . he will challenge me to a duel if he is a man. And have no fear: I will cut him to pieces."

Alarmed, Anna looked at him. "My . . . fiancé?"

"If you have a fiancé," he said, correcting himself. Good God, all he needed was for her to figure out that he was spying on the DeMercy family. With this girl he made one mistake after another. "If you will tell me his name, I can—"

"I have no fiancé!" she shouted, upset. "You should tell nothing to no one! No one must know—"

"Everyone will know if you're going to be obstinate about this," he snapped at her. "I will tell your father myself. He didn't seem to be in good health when I saw him a few days ago, but certainly you know most about that."

"No! You won't do that! If you dare, I . . . I'll denounce you, and they'll hang you, you know it!"

"You're living in a fairy tale, miss. It would be my word against yours, and it would be very easy to find someone ready to swear that you're hardly a virtuous woman, be sure of that. You're no longer a virgin now. Anyone could come to the trial and affirm that he had had you. It would all be quite unpleasant for you, and also for your father, I believe."

"N-no one . . . No one would say—"

"You have no idea what people are willing to do for money." Christopher's voice became low and sweet. "Do you really want to get yourself bogged down in such a quagmire? Life is already so complicated as it is. I don't know if you've heard about the fire last night that burned the fields on the west side of the river, toward Underhill. Fires break out with such unfortunate frequency in the country, don't you find? I hope that never happens to your house, Miss Champion."

She put a hand on her belly, as if punched in the stomach. "How . . . how could you?" The tears that it had seemed could never come back to her dried-out eyes began again to fall down her cheeks, mixing with blood and dirt.

"Oh, now, don't begin to snivel again!" he snapped.

Once and for all this broke her down. The world was too ugly a place to look at, and she covered her eyes with a hand. "Why do you want me to marry you by force, sir? I will say nothing to anyone—no one will ever know—but I cannot marry you, I beg you. You have already . . ." She stopped, unable to continue. She swallowed, and her mouth convulsed. "Why do you hate me so much?"

(Why do you hate her so much, Christopher?)

There was a moment of silence. "I don't hate you," he finally responded. It's true, he was angry with her, even now. He had an uncontrollable rage in his chest that he could not quench, because this girl was so damned . . . so damned . . . Oh shit, he didn't even know why, either. He would, however, marry her at any cost. The decision was already made, insofar as the impulse to have her . . .

(To rape her, Christopher. You raped her.)

. . . had suddenly come to him, and it wasn't a bad idea, after all. For him to become her husband was a tedious prospect, admittedly, but he wasn't a romantic, and he had never considered marrying for love. Honestly, he had never even considered getting married. To tell the entire truth, he had not given any thought to what he would do with his life after his vendetta against Leopold was finished.

(His vendetta against Leopold . . . and against *Daniel.* Yes, because sometimes even the damned princes from fairy tales don't get what they want. Isn't that so, little brother?)

Practically numb, Anna looked at him. "So, you love me? First . . ." she said, closing her eyes, as if the memory of what had just happened prevented her from continuing. "First you said . . ." But she couldn't finish, and the sentence died like a whisper on her lips.

Christopher gazed at her silently. *Have I said to her that I love her?* he wondered. He rubbed his forehead, trying to remember. *Perhaps . . . yes, perhaps something of the sort, it is true.* What a bunch of nonsense, now that he thought about it, and he probably only said it to make her stop crying. Because usually he didn't whisper such sweet words while he was having sex. In fact, he didn't whisper anything at all.

"Don't make too much of words said in certain . . . moments, Miss Champion," he advised her curtly. "You don't realize it, but when a man . . ." He broke off the sentence because she was dreadfully pale, and he feared he would see her fall to the ground. He carried on in a different way. "I believe, miss, that you overestimate my treachery—which, I must say, I find flattering. At any rate, it's my duty to inform you that this is the first time that . . ." He hesitated, searching for the right word. "That a . . . mishap of this sort has happened to me. I intend to make amends whether you agree or not."

Anna looked at him as if he not only raped women every day but killed them, cut them up, seasoned them, and ate them. Having no response, she leaned against the tree behind her.

Christopher clenched his fists, and if there had been stones in his hands, he would have reduced them to dust.

"You're a silly girl," he said to her. "And you will marry me, because you cannot do otherwise. And besides . . ." He looked at her askew. "Besides, you could be pregnant. Haven't you thought of that? No, you're too stupid. But I don't intend to leave behind any bastards." He almost stuttered on the last word. He closed his eyes and reopened them; he opened and closed his fists. Neither helped.

Silently, she gave him a look of desperation mixed with contempt. This girl was supposed to stop making *him* feel guilty, Christopher decided. Perhaps there was a need to clear things up a bit. "I will marry you therefore, and quickly, because I intend to assume my responsibilities. Although you did deserve it, since you provoked me to do the unthinkable."

And it was true, damn it, bloody true. Because he could deal with his hatred for the DeMercy family, he could handle the heat, he could bear the alcohol, he could put up with everything. But by God, if she hadn't prodded him in so many ways he would have left her in peace, if . . .

Her face seemed to fall. "No . . . no . . ."

"Stop babbling once and for all!"

(Why, Christopher? Why are you still hurting her?)

Anna raised her head. This was not the reaction he was expecting, nor did he expect the direct and accusatory look.

"You don't believe in what you are saying, and I don't even know why you are saying it." Besides disgust there was also surprise in her voice. "But this much is clear to you—it couldn't possibly be anything else, not even for a man so lacking in a conscience such as yourself: I despise you. You cannot marry me, and you know it. I despise you and I will always despise you."

Always. He shrugged his shoulders. "Patience."

Very little was necessary to kill a look. Sometimes only a single word.

"Please, sir." She was begging him now and as pale as morning fog and just as hopeless. "I cannot marry you. The thought that you . . ." She lowered her head, overwhelmed. "The thought that you could . . . I could not . . . I would die from it, sir."

"Listen." Christopher ran his fingers through his hair, calling on as much charm as he could. "I have already taken what I wanted from you. I am marrying you because I have dishonored you, and for this reason I can wait for . . ." He searched for a word that might not frighten her. He couldn't think of one. "I will be patient with you,

Anna. I will let you have all the time that you need to get used to me." He softened his tone, seeing the horror in her eyes. "Don't be afraid. It won't . . ." He paused and put a hand in front of his eyes, closing them. His head was aching and the screaming that day would be with him forever. "It isn't my intention to harm you," he continued gently. "I—"

"But what are you saying?" she said incredulously, interrupting him. The incoherence of these words seemed to upset her such that it made her forget her pain. "You! Do you have the courage . . . ?"

Christopher bit his lower lip as the silence shattered the residual song of that day. Finally he said, "I give you my word."

"Oh. Your word." Anna nodded with a painful force. "And tell me, is it worth much, truthfully?"

"Anna . . ."

"Remember . . ." She ignored him and, smiling unbelievably, said, "Remember that once you told me you were a cheat."

"Anna . . . Miss Champion," he added, correcting himself. "I will not continue to discuss this with you. I will give you until tomorrow morning to become reasonable, after which I will speak to your father."

There was fear in her eyes and the primordial instinct to protect her own. "You can't possibly introduce yourself in my house with your face in that condition!" she screamed. "My father will understand immediately . . ." she added, stopping short and she swallowed several times. "Don't come tomorrow, I beg you!"

Christopher touched a cheek, and he found it painful and scratched, like a field in ruins. He was silent, his hand on his cheek, lost in thought. Finally he nodded. "I will come to your house on Thursday afternoon, then."

He noticed a drop of blood had remained on her skin, and he felt himself getting a bit choked up. *God, she is a child. Only a child.* He took out a handkerchief and came closer to her, offering it with unexpected sweetness. "I will be a good husband for you, Anna," he murmured.

She looked at his outstretched arm with the handkerchief as if it were a trick, and her mouth began to tremble. She leaned a hand on the tree, and her body doubled over uncontrollably. With her arm on her stomach, she vomited out her pain and her soul, shaken by unstoppable retching.

14

Remorse: beholding heaven and feeling hell.
—George A. Moore

Somehow Anna began to make her way back to her house. Christopher followed a few steps behind. She walked on, alone, looking straight in front of her. It was very late, and the sun already left a few red streaks across the sky. The road was the same, looking so familiar at dusk. It had certainly not changed; it was not as if it were long and endless, distorted like a hallucination in the fog. Anna saw the redbrick house in the distance. In several places the walls looked heartbroken and darkened, with deep wounds. But all it would take would be a bit of paint to make this place beautiful again. Or maybe not.

She walked faster. The road would have to end sooner or later. And even the noise of footsteps behind her would have to end—those footsteps that followed her did so victoriously and proudly. She would have liked to run, for her family was surely worried about her unusual delay. She would have liked to run, but she couldn't. She couldn't look like a runaway to the man walking boldly behind her without hesitation or doubt. No, and she raised her head higher.

She reached the entry road lined with lindens, and she walked along it, hiding behind the trees. The garden was deserted; she did not walk in front of the house. Someone was probably watching from the window, waiting for her return; she could not be seen in this condition. The children would be frightened, and her father . . .

Keeping herself out of sight, she went to the rear of the house to enter through the window of a closed-off room—covered with big white sheets and left to collect dust and woodworm—which guaranteed her a means of escape, mostly for strategic evasions in case of annoying visitors, such as the irksome Mr. Clarke some time before. She stopped in front of the window, avoiding looking at her own reflection in the pane, struck by this thought: *Did it really happen? But when? Two weeks ago? Or two years ago? Or even two hundred?*

She placed her hands on the window and opened it. She did not look at her bleeding fingers, her broken fingernails, her uncontrolled shaking. Slowly she tried to raise herself up to get inside, and it was as if countless shards of glass were cutting her from the inside. She was finally able to get into the room, and she walked to the door, bumping into a table as she did. The white sheet moved, uncovering a broken shelf underneath the old piece of furniture.

Anna put her ear up to the door, then opened it and went into the dark hallway of this unused part of the house.

"Anna!" Nora shouted from behind, her voice petrifying Anna. "Anna! Anna . . ." Nora's voice cracked, then became a whisper that seemed like the peeping of a baby chick that had fallen ill. "Dear heavens, Anna . . ."

She heard the old woman run up to her. She couldn't move, and Nora took her by the hand and made her turn toward her. The round and barely wrinkled face of the woman trembled, and her double chin shook without any dignity.

"Anna, oh my God," she said in a whisper. Then she took her other hand as well. "My child, what happened to you? Your dress . . ." She stopped. Her mouth was half-open, as if she were going to say something else, to add something else. But she said nothing. She couldn't say anything. She couldn't because the horror of asking was too great. She wished she could deny what she saw and deny that something ugly had happened. She wished she could deny, but her fat, ageless face suddenly became old, and she could say nothing.

Anna tried to say *"I'm fine, it's nothing,"* but all that came out of her was silence. And in the silence she threw herself into Nora's short arms, searching for healing for the wounds that were so much larger than this little woman.

"Anna, my God, Anna . . ." Big tears ran down Nora's face, big tears that ran through the creases and dry skin. "Anna, what have they done to you, my little baby? What . . . ?" Not able to find a word, she fell silent. Not even a single word to console her baby in tears.

And so they stood, crying in each other's arms. Nora began to whine with a low guttural sound, like a childish weeping, coming from a tired, crumbling body. Like a pain that would never go away.

(Anna, what are you doing to this elderly woman? Maybe you want to break her heart.)

With her head on Nora's chest, Anna felt a sudden panic. Her hair stood up on her head, and she couldn't catch her breath, as if she were watching a fire burn everything dear to her. She stood up straight and raised her head. She looked at her destroyed Nora, and with her hand she caressed her head, the pink of Anna's fingers showing underneath through the thin, fluffy white hair. "Don't cry," she murmured while stopping her own tears. "Everything will be fine. I . . . they will not know."

She took her hand and led her into the uninhabited room. Nora followed her like a doll knocked about in the wind, her quick, authoritative ways having vanished in the sudden awareness of the helplessness of love.

"Oh, Anna . . . no . . ." she sobbed, and began again with her unending whining from deep down.

"Nora, listen to me." She took her by the shoulders, gently shaking her. "I need you. You must be strong. You will tell everyone that I am sick—even Lucy. At least for a few days, until I look normal again."

Nora raised her hand and stroked her face. "Anna, Anna, who . . . who . . . ? I . . . I will kill him, I . . ."

"No, no," she said, shaking her head, with a smile peeking out among the scratches and the dust on her face. "Listen to me. Everything will be fine."

But Nora could not believe that. She could never again believe that. "Anna, no . . ."

"He wants to marry me," she said, her mouth twitching. "No one would know anything."

"No!" Nora winced in pain, and the full horror of her exclamation exploded. "No, Anna, you don't deserve it . . . You will not marry him! Instead, I will kill him, I—"

"No . . . Nora . . . I don't know . . . I don't know what I will do," she responded with an exhausted sigh. "Please, now I only need to sleep. I want to sleep, just sleep." She felt the tears coming back in her eyes and pushed them back down inside. She would have time for crying. "Everything will take care of itself," she assured her finally. "I promise."

Nora kept her head low, sobbing quietly. The stress and suffering of that day, which went on and on, suddenly became too much, with its pushing and beating, and Anna could no longer bear it. A vise was squeezing her. It would kill her if she didn't scream, if she didn't . . .

"I need you, you don't understand!" she exploded. "Please help me! You *must* help me!" Her voice stopped abruptly, and hot drops of anguish streamed down her face in the impossibility of deciding anything whatsoever, even the time of her pain. "Please! Nora!"

The old lady jumped. And in addition to the desolation in her eyes, which had softened over the years, Nora showed the regret of not being strong enough. Of not being cut from the right cloth. Of being old and defeated.

A moment passed; then, with a trembling hand, she stroked Anna's cheek. "All right," she said, and her cracking voice sounded incontestable. "I am here. With you."

"Thank you. Oh, thank you." Anna smiled at her between her tears and sobs. Weakness makes one stronger, and Nora seemed to grow, a giant in an apron.

"I'll take you to your room," she said determinedly. "I will tell your father and your siblings that you had a cold. I will prepare the water for a bath. I will make you some hot broth."

Quickly this giantess wiped her eyes and did all the things she promised—and all at the same time.

***

Christopher roused himself. How long had he been there? By now it was dark; the moon was out and almost full, risking his discovery. He needed to leave; the last light in the redbrick house went out a while ago. The girl had gone in several hours before, walking as straight as an arrow in her spoiled dress, which moved about her like a flight of butterflies, and perhaps now she was in her spotless, innocent bed.

A scream came to his mind, the specter of a far-off echo, a desperate and atrocious scream. It was only a memory, but for a dreadful moment Christopher thought he had actually heard it. He turned toward the haunted house, which smiled ravenously not far from him.

15

An engagement should come on a young girl as a surprise, pleasant or unpleasant as the case may be. It is hardly a matter that she could be allowed to arrange for herself.

—Oscar Wilde

The first night she fell asleep exhausted after the bath she took by herself without Nora's help. She lay in the bed and fell immediately into a deep and forgetful sleep.

During the night she woke up suddenly and felt a pulsating pain in her body, like a sleeping monster—like the monster she had created so many years before out of a wooden plank, with an orange mouth wide open in a shout. Bewildered, she wondered what that monster had done inside her, then remembered. She got out of bed and went to the window. The moon was white and nearly full as it reigned over the dark sky—the sky that had been a dazzling blue a few hours before.

She walked to her water basin and washed her face for a long while, erasing the memory of a kiss. The last kiss, the one she had not refused her executioner. A kiss that when eaten from her lips left her absurdly hungry. While the drops of water ran down her skin, she asked herself if she could ever forgive herself for this kiss. Physical pain would go away, but as for the other wounds, she was not sure.

She wiped her face and went back to bed, where she sprawled out with her eyes open, without sleeping and without crying.

Nora went out of her way for Anna in the days that followed. She pampered her, she soothed her, and she made her eat all the foods she liked. She kept away visitors, including her siblings and her father. The family members could only greet her briefly, while Anna hid her heavily made-up face—makeup was something she had never used before. Nora treated the scratches and bruises with stinky herbs that she claimed worked wonders.

The night before he was to come to their house, Anna found herself in front of her open diary. She had written down the various possible alternatives, and there were only four—four sentences encompassed her entire future.

She reread the first sentence: *Seek justice for the offense.*

Then the second: *Kill myself.*

Then the third: *Marry Christopher Davenport.*

And finally the last: *Kill Christopher Davenport.*

She crossed out one, then another. Only two possibilities remained.

She spent that night with her eyes wide open in the dark yet again. When Christopher appeared at her house the following day, the marks on her face had practically vanished, and the bleeding had nearly stopped. Faint traces of red on her white lingerie were the only remaining proof of what had happened.

***

Christopher arrived at the redbrick house wanting to get it over with—and quick. Perhaps once the marriage agreements were made he would be able to get a good night's sleep without resorting first to alcohol, which he did not handle well. It was definitely due to aftereffects that he felt so worn out. Before leaving, he looked at himself in the mirror. His eyes were deeply sunken in and his coloring was sallow, while the scratch marks were healing but still slightly visible.

(She will not marry you, Christopher. You know that, don't you?)

These last few days he had stayed mainly at home, to allow his wounds to heal. But there was someone else with even deeper wounds than his . . .

(Anna.)

. . . namely, his brother. He had gone to London to lick his wounds, according to what had been relayed to Christopher by a surprised Matthew. Surprised because the unexpected breaking of the engagement with Daniel came like a landslide down the side of a mountain. "Chris, you'll never believe what happened. The engagement was over from one day to the next," he had explained to him, disappointed and disbelieving. All things considered, his reaction was understandable: Christopher had omitted a specific detail from the story—a rather important detail, in fact. "That's the last thing we wanted. Isn't that so? And Leopold . . ." Matthew hesitated, not knowing whether or not to say it. Finally, after a sigh he spit it out: "Leopold is in seventh heaven, as you can imagine. Maybe that's why Daniel decided on Sunday afternoon to leave."

Sunday afternoon. Good. That meant that Anna didn't hesitate a moment to tell him. She must have sent him a letter that very day. *That can only mean,* Christopher told himself, *that she will marry me. For sure.* He repeated it to himself again. Then he took a breath and knocked on the door of the Champion house. And he waited. And he waited some more. And some more. He remembered the first time he had been there. The front door had been left ajar, because that day Anna was expecting a dear friend. Instead, now he was waiting, and everything seemed to ward him off. Christopher was used to it, and he knocked again without getting upset. After a few minutes he heard a noise behind the doorway and his heart skipped a beat. But it was the face of Anna's little sister that appeared when the door finally opened.

"Are you the king of the tomaspiders?" asked the child, looking at him with her nose in the air. Her chestnut-brown ringlets were lighter than the color of her older sister's hair, although there was a resemblance in the soft features of the cheeks and the smile.

"The tomaspiders?" he asked.

"A tomato-spider, sir!"

The little girl seemed truly appalled at his ignorance and in fact was quite unforgiving, Christopher recognized.

"Is it another fairy tale?" he asked.

She nodded with the vigor of her young age. "It doesn't end well for the king of the tomaspiders, sir."

"Grace." Anna's calm voice called the child, and Christopher's heart skipped at first, then began to beat in an irregular pattern.

She appeared slowly as she walked up to the door. Her face was half covered by her hair. Delicate tendrils obscured the nearly invisible bruises—invisible to everyone else, perhaps, but not to him. She was wearing a faded yellow frock that was particularly ugly, and yet Christopher seemed blinded, as if he were looking at the reflection of the sun in a stream.

Anna did not look at him. "Grace, what did I tell you? Go finish your lessons along with your brothers."

The little girl began to show a pouty frown. "All right," she grumbled, and she ran off without looking back once—or perhaps she did just the once.

Standing motionless in the threshold, Christopher cleared his voice. "Good afternoon, Miss Champion," he said calmly in a half whisper.

She didn't respond or look at him. Her eyes were fixed on the garden, and she seemed unaware of his presence.

He took the biggest breath possible, then exhaled for a moment. "I would like to speak to your father, miss."

The short cook that lived there—how old was she? A hundred?—leaned out through the drawing room door and looked at him as if he were a shit stain—more accurately, a very large shit stain and a very smelly one.

Anna stepped aside to let him come in. Her face seemed emotionless, devoid even of fear—so still and different from the face he had begun to recognize, her changing face of a thousand expressions.

(You stole them from her, Christopher.)

He followed her into the drawing room. Her steps were slow and made no noise. Neither did his. The cook stood at the door, as if she wanted to stop him from coming in. She had a wooden spoon, which looked surprisingly disturbing in her hand. Anna put her hand on her shoulder. "Nora," she said with a dull voice, "let me and the gentleman alone, and keep the children with you."

"Are you sure?"

She nodded her head. Nora gripped the spoon tighter, and she turned to go into the kitchen. But she first stared at Christopher, looking closely at his hands, seemingly expecting still to see the blood that had to have been there. Christopher opened and closed his fists, trying to calm himself down. *Everything is going very well. Perfectly.*

Anna went into the vacant drawing room, filled with afternoon sunlight. She went toward the window, keeping her back to him. Christopher stopped in the middle of the room and remained standing and looking at Anna's back. She had not yet even looked at him since he had arrived.

Let's get this over with. "Where is your father?" he asked abruptly. "I don't have all day."

With her fingers touching the corners of the windowpane, Anna didn't move. Her head was tilted to one side, and the curve of her neck, left visible due to her hairstyle, was white from paleness and from the sunlight. Distracted, she said nothing for several seconds.

"I must clarify a few details with you, sir," she finally said in a voice that did not belong to her—that voice which was not her own.

"And you keep your back to me?" Christopher asked, bitterness swelling inside him. He tried to keep it down. "I have completely underestimated my good fortune if you are afraid of me so much that you can't manage to look me in the eyes."

"The first thing," she began, ignoring him, "you must allow me to continue to take care of my loved ones when we are married."

When we are married.

Christopher breathed once, then twice, then three times, and then he breathed again and again. After five days of breathlessness, he welcomed the air like a benediction, and he enjoyed every breath.

"I will accept your decision in this regard," he responded after several seconds.

"The second thing," she said without moving at all or giving any sign that she heard him. "Under no circumstances will you mistreat my family. If I observe that the violent attitude with which you treated me is commonplace for you, I will leave you and denounce you, sir, without caring about the consequences."

"I already told you, miss," he replied dryly, "that it is not my habit to mistreat—"

"Oh, quiet!" She put her hand to her forehead and shook her head, as if she couldn't manage to listen to any more. He remained quiet, watching the profile of her body, her hair, and her damaged dress. "Third thing." She was tired, as if she had been walking for days. "My father cannot move from this house, so it is here that . . ." She seemed unsure and appeared unable to maintain any longer the composure she had shown up to that moment. "Here is where we must live. After we are married."

Maybe he hadn't understood. "You must be joking!" he exclaimed.

But no, not at all. She had no desire to joke with him. Astounded, Christopher looked around. The drawing room was pathetic, and the house was shrunken and falling apart.

"How do you expect a man like me to live like this, amongst fleas?" he exploded. "And look at me, for God's sake!" His hands felt itchy as he ran them through his hair. Bloody hell, he could not move there. His plan included nothing of the sort. Richness, yes; opulence, yes; ostentation, yes; but . . .

"A portion of the house is closed off," explained Anna without turning around. "If we reopen all the rooms, I am certain that will be enough for you, and besides, you will always have your house to give dances and parties. No one will oblige you to stay here."

Christopher pretended that he didn't hear the last sentence. *God, it is all so small, so dingy inside!* The old sofa was made of worn velvet, and the rugs were faded.

"I cannot accept any other arrangement, sir. If you will not consent, I cannot marry you. My father . . ." She stopped, knowing it would be absurd to explain the reason to him. "Sir, we should not marry against our will," she added with a more lively voice. "Thus I ask you to reconsider it and to give up on the idea."

"Don't be ridiculous," he responded with an icy tone. God damn it, he did not need this complication. His eyes darted from the old parlor table to the broken-down sofa to the beat-up pillows. Yes, even the pillows were a disaster. Maybe they were once pretty, but the years—and the childhood fights, with all the happy playfulness and wild tossing of the pillows—had ruined them. In fact, the first time he was here he had noticed them. Standing in the doorway together with Lucy, he had noticed Anna—yes, of course—and the children sitting on the floor near her, and her soft voice telling them a fairy tale.

And he now remembered that all around them were these same old pillows. "All right." He was shocked by his own words. "All right," he repeated, more convinced. "But you must allow me to renovate this place, and quickly. Furthermore, there needs to be adequate staff. I will take on all the expenses, obviously."

She nodded her head, but her shoulders drooped, as if he had beaten her. She leaned her head on the pane. "I ask you only, sir"—and she seemed in pain when pronouncing the words—"I ask you . . . I ask you only to limit the inconvenience and the noise for my father and my family."

God, turn around, Anna. Look at me. "I will do everything possible," he replied with great difficulty, for the words did not want to come out of his clenched jaws.

"One last thing," she said. Then she was silent, and she slid her finger across the glass pane, making it move around as if lost in the transparence. "If you attempt," she said, after a long pause, "if you attempt to come near me after we are married—"

"I already told you—"

"I will kill you, sir."

(Are you also an inconvenience and a noise, Christopher?)

To hell with it. "I will manage to keep myself far from your bed without trying too hard, miss."

She was silent for a few minutes, then said, "I will speak with my father before you do. The circumstances of our . . ." she said, pausing. "The circumstances of our engagement must not be known."

"As you wish." Christopher filled his lungs with a couple of huge breaths. "I will request a marriage license, and we will marry in two weeks' time at the latest. It will not be difficult to justify the hurry, given your father's health conditions. Now turn toward me."

Anna did not move.

"I expect cooperation from you, miss. Is that clear?"

Silence.

"Now turn toward me and answer me. Remember that you are the party to profit from this marriage; therefore, I demand that you stop with this attitude."

Anna said nothing. She moved her forehead off the glass and looked outside pensively, as if she were looking for a response in the trees, in the ruined park bench, and in the withering rosebushes.

I will not go up to her, Christopher told himself. *I will not take her by the arms and turn her around. I will not shake her to make her look me in the eyes.* He took a step, and at that moment Nora appeared from the kitchen door.

"Shall I make you a bit of tea, Anna?"

She turned toward the short cook, and he saw her pale profile. "No. The gentleman will have nothing."

Christopher felt a hot flush of anger rise up in his head. If this girl thought she could continue to behave like this, she was ready for the mental hospital. "Actually, I would like some tea, Nora," he blurted.

The cook came in the room, and she seemed to become suddenly younger and perhaps even taller.

"I do not take orders from you, *sir*," she replied, and if the words had been spit upon him, he would have been completely soaked.

His astonishment left him with his mouth wide open for several moments.

"Are you eating flies?" giggled the damned midget. She wrinkled her nose at him as if he reeked of a horrible odor.

Enough is enough, thought Christopher. "If you believe!" he exploded, shouting at her, "that you allow yourself to—"

"Mr. Davenport."

Anna's calm voice interrupted him. He turned toward her as she looked directly at him with clear eyes, and he wasn't able to look away. *I did not take that spark from you, Anna.* And his temper melted in him, and he felt like crying. *I knew it, my darling. I knew it.*

"Mr. Davenport," she repeated, her tight lips making a thin line, "remember what I told you."

Christopher put his hand up to his eyes, trying to calm his emotions. *Must I allow myself to be humiliated by a shriveled-up old cook?*

Never. Not even in a million years. He breathed deeply and for a long while, then reopened his eyes and glared obnoxiously at the crone, who seemed very tall, even if she wasn't even five foot.

He breathed. "Would you be so kind as to bring me some tea, Nora?"

He said these words politely—or something like it—and Christopher could not understand why they came out like a sharp squawk. However, he would not be able to do better, even if he wanted to. He eyed Anna. *Was that good enough? Is she a bit more peaceful now?*

(You want her to be peaceful, Christopher? Ha!)

Anna forced a smile for the old lady. "What did I tell you, Nora, dear? The gentleman will be nice with us." Already her eyes didn't look at him any longer. His fiancée was again pretending that he didn't exist, that he didn't . . .

Fiancée.

(Your fiancée, Christopher.)

"Christopher!"

He turned toward the side door, where Anthony appeared, running—as he always did, from the time he learned to run—up to him. "Hello, sir."

At least one person in the room is not looking at me like a rotten cabbage, Christopher thought. And as much as he was getting used to being treated like a vegetable, he genuinely felt relieved. "Hello, Anthony."

Anna grew pale and moved closer to her brother. "Anthony, why didn't you stay in there?"

She stayed as far as possible from Christopher, but he nevertheless believed he could smell the scent of apples and of a flower. But which one?

"I finished my lessons, Anna. Sir," he said to him down low, given their foot and a half difference in height. "Have you come for my sister?"

"Anthony . . ." said Anna, reprimanding him and putting her hand on his shoulders.

But what does she think I am, an ogre? Christopher was stunned—furiously but absurdly stunned. Good God, I will not eat her brother! For Christ's sake, after five days of tension, this girl is really pushing her luck a bit too much. "Yes, I came for your sister," he replied curtly. "To ask for her hand, in fact. I recall that you already gave me your consent."

Anthony nodded without surprise. "Are you marrying him, Anna?"

She tried to smile. "Yes, Anthony."

"Does Daddy know?"

"Not yet."

Anthony became pensive. "Can you manage all right in a vegetable garden, Christopher?"

The question completely lacked any kind of logic, and Christopher looked at him, doubting he had understood it. "Vegetable . . . garden, Anthony?"

"Yes. Tomatoes, onions, carrots. My father will want to know if you understand agriculture. Do you know anything about it? Planting season, harvest season, things like that?"

Christopher put his hand to his forehead and rubbed it. God, this family was making him lose his mind. "Honestly, no." He shrugged his shoulders. "I imagine that won't be a serious problem."

From the look on Anthony's face, it was obvious that it would be a very serious problem. "I think it will, sir."

"Really?" He thought for a few moments. "You could give me a hand, then."

But Anthony shook his head. "That would not be fair," he explained.

"Oh." He held back a mocking smile. "So you play fair, then? That's a good thing, really it is." He paused. "What if in exchange I taught you another couple of fencing moves?"

It is all so simple, he thought, *when desires are involved.* In fact, the little boy's face lit up.

"All right," he responded.

"No."

Dumbfounded, Anthony turned his eyes toward Anna, who had spoken flatly, and Christopher felt his muscles stiffen forcefully in order to contain his anger. *Now that is enough.* He took a step toward her, and he saw her pupils get bigger. He moved to her side with his back to Anthony and brushed his side up against hers. She grew pale, as if she were on the verge of fainting, but Christopher nevertheless leaned his mouth down to her ear. He very deliberately nearly touched her skin.

"Miss Champion, take note," he whispered harshly. "From now on I will be a part of this family."

Her face had a spasm—of panic, memories, and pain—but she did not move, and Christopher did not expect her to. She would defend her family members even if it cost her life, and in fact when she hissed in response, her voice did not shake. "You should pay close attention to what you say and do, Mr. Davenport."

"Don't worry," he answered sharply. "Now go talk to your father and then call me." He took a step back, turning toward Anthony, who looked at them confusedly. "We can begin if you like," he said. "What can you tell me about tomatoes?"

16

No, it is not the body which is ailing, but the soul.
—Alexandre Dumas, père

The smell of cocoa was everywhere when Anna came into the kitchen. Her father greeted her with a crooked smile. "Good morning, Anna dear."

She smiled at him and gave him a little peck on the cheek. They heard quick footsteps in the little hall between the kitchen and the drawing room, and shortly after Dennis and Grace came through the door.

"What a smell!" exclaimed Dennis. He saw the biscuits on the table and walked up and took two of them in his little hand.

"Dennis," Nora scolded him. "Eat one at a time."

"Did we become rich?" Grace asked her. "You have made sweets every day this week."

"Humph."

Anna looked at Nora, and she knew very well that it was because of her that the round little cook began very early in the morning to make dough: she was trying to stimulate Anna's appetite, since it had diminished under the weight of thoughts that affected her mind as well as her stomach.

She put on a forced smile for her and gave her a kiss on the cheek. "Nora, but what time did you get up?"

Not answering, Nora pointed instead at the biscuits. "Try one. They are good." Her logic—"I get up early, you eat biscuits"—was flawless, and Anna took a chocolate Florentine, sat down heavily at the birch dining table, and leaned on her elbow with her chin in her hand.

Anthony entered the kitchen, scratching his head. He was sullen as he sat down next to her.

"Morning," he said.

Dennis looked in a corner of the kitchen, and his mouth dropped open as he stopped chewing. He let out an enthusiastic "Oh!" spitting pieces of biscuit all over. "What are those?" He pointed toward several wrapped packages and baskets of food and fruit, which were piled up in a little mountain of different colors.

Anna hadn't noticed them, and her hand stopped in midair as she was about to put a biscuit in her mouth. "Who sent those things?" she asked suddenly. Blood rushed to her head before she even heard the answer, because she knew.

"Mr. Davenport, dear," replied Mr. Champion, rubbing a bristly cheek.

Her hand shook with anger, and her back stiffened.

"He is a fine young man," her father added.

How could he, that pig?

"I have used up all of our flour to make the biscuits," Nora informed her. "I didn't use any from those baskets."

(Ah, Nora knew how to read her thoughts!)

"Are these things for us?" Dennis asked.

The excitement in his eyes was tinged with disbelief. It had been years in the Champion house since they had seen so many colors all together.

"Yes, Dennis," answered Mr. Champion. "You and your . . . your siblings."

Forgetting about the sweets, Dennis ran toward the gifts.

"They're not all yours," protested Grace, racing next to him.

"Dennis, don't touch anything!" Anna shouted.

Frightened, Dennis and Grace stopped short, and even her father eyed Anna strangely. "Why not, Anna, dear?"

Trembling with helplessness, she could not answer—after all, what could she say? *Curses! Damn you to hell, bloody Christopher Davenport!*

"Anna, you can't hurt . . ." Mr. Champion stopped, short of breath.

Oh heavens, would this ever end? "Of course, Daddy," she agreed hastily. "You are right."

Dennis approached the presents, looking doubtfully at one of them. Then he stopped hesitating and began to open them, and Grace ran to his side with a shriek. Only Anthony continued to eat his breakfast in silence. He watched, frowning.

From a gold package Dennis pulled out a doll. He wasn't interested in it, and he left it teetering on the corner of the table.

"Dennis!" Grace screamed at him, outraged.

Her brother ignored her and let out a yell, because in the next box he found a brand-new toy: a colored tube maybe eight inches long. The child put his eye up to the end with a hole, rotated the other end, then gave an "Oh!" of wonderment, as if he were witnessing some kind of magic.

Grace straightened the doll's hair, carefully arranging her blond tresses. "I shall call you Margaret," she said to it. She turned toward Anna. "She's beautiful, Anna. Look!"

The doll's vividly painted pink cheeks and shiny hair gave it a vulgar look. Its dark-red velvet dress was rich, like a prostitute's, and her blue eyes looked at Anna as if she were mocking her. Anna put her biscuit down on the table and got up suddenly with the feeling she was suffocating.

Without knowing that this sound pierced his older sister's heart like a dagger, Dennis opened another package. However, his voice lacked enthusiasm when he said, "Oh, books."

Anthony quickly raised his head. *Oh, Anthony, no. Not you, too.* But he slowly stood up and walked up to the box. "Philosophy!" he exclaimed, astounded, and his voice expressed such joy that Anna's heart made a painful creak only she could hear. *That accursed man,* she thought with a sad smile, *really knows how to play his cards well, that's for sure.* Tears, which had become her constant companion, flooded her eyes. It was such a rare occurrence—rare until a few weeks earlier. But she was no longer that other person: she had given up, spending her nights consoling herself, huddling as tears ran down her cheeks. There she remained, on her damp pillow, and she felt that something deep inside her was melting as she sank into oblivion; that was the only way she managed to fall asleep. Even now she lowered her head toward her chest, trembling with lack of confidence, and she quickly made for the door.

"Anna, wait," Nora called out, holding an envelope out to her. "There is a note for you."

Not understanding, she took the white, sealed paper and looked at it blankly. Then she collected herself, noticing the cook's sadness, and left in a hurry to hide in the back room, where everything was covered with white sheets, and where she could be alone for a while. *"But that place won't be yours for long—isn't that right?" laughed a male voice inside her head. "I'll make off with it, like all the rest."*

Anna closed the door and leaned against it, letting herself slide down to the floor. She remained in that position, with her forehead against her knees, and the pain showed on her flushed face. Weak, stupid, pathetic.

She would marry that man.

That cruel and violent man, dangerous for her and for her family. And if he ever wanted to touch her again . . .

Oh God, help me.

No. She would not allow him to. She would rather kill him. She would find a way; she would . . .

She wept desperately without being able to stop. Christopher had promised her time. *Time!* A corner of her mouth went up in a mock smile. *How much time does he think it will take? A month, a day, an hour?* She remembered the baskets in the kitchen, those colorful fruits, the wrapped boxes filled with poison. *He can buy anything and everything. He will even buy the affection of my family.*

She raised her head and looked stupidly at the note that she held in her hands. She opened the seal on it carefully, as if a hex might come out of it, and read.

> *Miss Champion,*
> *I opened accounts in the village shops for you and your family. Purchase everything that you need, without worrying about the cost. In particular, I would like you to buy a new wardrobe.*
> *C. D.*

She stared at the note, upset. Now he wanted to buy her.

***

She's doing it on purpose. That's what Christopher thought, facing the closed front door of the Champion house. He knocked for the third time. Making him wait for a long time before she let him in was becoming an annoying habit, and it was definitely not a coincidence. Oh no, definitely not a coincidence. He finally heard someone coming up behind the door, and as the door opened, Anna's face appeared, without a smile. Christopher clenched his jaws.

She stared over his shoulders and into the distance. "We weren't expecting you this morning," she said flatly, without any niceties or greetings.

"You're not very polite to your fiancé, I see," he responded coldly. "At any rate, I will be here often to follow up on the work being done to your house, so get accustomed to it." He paused briefly. "I need to talk to you about that."

"I have guests. Go away."

"I will be quick about it, only five minutes. Let me come in."

"No."

Christopher made an incredible effort not to grab her by the neck. "Miss Champion, I have already told you that you must change your attitude." Irritated, he ran his hand through his hair. "It will not work like this, I warn you."

She did not even seem to hear him—after being invisible, now he was inaudible. Each time he was in front of his fiancée, his physical presence seemed to be dangerously losing impact.

"Why did you send those things this morning?" Anger was obvious in her loudly hissing voice. *Dear God, is that why she is so cross? Because of the presents?* "But what did you think you were doing?" she continued. "You wish to buy my family with a few—"

"Stop being silly. I don't wish to buy anyone," he said, lying. *How do I talk to someone who won't look me in the face?* "I merely wanted to offer some gifts to your brothers and sister. I thought I was doing something you would appreciate. Now let me come in." He pushed on the door with his hand, but Anna held it closed.

"You . . . must . . . not . . ." She was able to speak only in short spurts. Christopher noticed her mouth, tight and full of rage. "Never again. I will not allow it. We want nothing from you."

"Oh, really?" Damn it, he needed to remain calm, but by God could she provoke him! "Miss Champion, listen." *This girl must have some brains somewhere; they just need to be found, right?* "You must understand that it's necessary for you to accept my money. I cannot tolerate you continuing to live in these shabby conditions. Don't make me ashamed of my wife!"

"Ashamed? You? Of me?" Anna seemed so upset that she turned her eyes toward him. Her look—honest to goodness, the look she gave him!—was so filled with hate that she was not afraid. "You, sir, know nothing about shame!"

"Anna." He pinched the tip of his nose and closed his eyes. "I gave in to your demands, as absurd as they were." He furiously opened his eyes again. "And now you will accept mine, by God! Let me in!"

He pushed the door violently, shoving it suddenly with his hand, and Anna jumped back as if she had been burned. Christopher entered and took big strides as he made for the drawing room.

"Mr. Davenport!" The charming Miss Edwards was sitting on the sofa, and she stood with a gracefulness that she seemed to be born with. "It's a real pleasure to see you."

"Miss Edwards," Christopher said, greeting her. In truth, he was dumbfounded. He did not think anyone was with Anna. "The pleasure is all mine."

Anna joined them, pale but composed. "Mr. Davenport cannot stay long, Lucy."

"Mr. Davenport, Anna has just now told me the wonderful news. You have my warmest congratulations."

"Thank you, Miss Edwards." An idea popped into his head, and he added with a calculated spite, "I wish that you could help my fiancée with the preparations for the wedding. Your impeccable taste would be invaluable." *And maybe you could even manage to get some sense into her!* he thought to himself.

Anna looked at him as if he had slapped her, and even Lucy seemed confused. "We were just talking about that, Mr. Davenport. Nothing would make me happier, and Anna knows that. And if she wants," she said, stressing the last three words, "I will gladly help her."

A genuine smile lit up Anna's face. She and Lucy turned to face him as if they were a wall.

It seems that my request means very little to Miss Edwards, Christopher understood, bothered. *It will be difficult to get her on my side.* He was about to respond when they heard banging with incredible force on the front door, and they were all three caught off guard a little and jumped. Lucy went to the window and stretched out her neck to see who had made this racket.

"Were you expecting someone, Miss Champion?" Christopher asked.

Anna didn't look at him or respond.

"I believe it's that relative that lives with you, Mr. Davenport," said Lucy. "I have seen him only in church, but I would swear that it's him."

Matthew?! He really couldn't have . . . Christopher went to the window. "It is indeed my cousin," he admitted, and God only knew how he hated saying those words aloud. *Damn it.* It was obvious that Matthew would have to meet Anna sooner or later, but first Christopher wanted to give him a piece of his mind, a very long and detailed account listing all the bones—a few that his cousin was not even aware existed, he was sure—that he would break in case he happened to let slip out something he shouldn't.

Another loud thump startled them.

"Leaving him outside will be pointless, Miss Champion," he said, sighing and rubbing his forehead with his fingertips. "This could go on for hours. I will have to introduce him to you, if I may."

"Oh, how wonderful!" Lucy exclaimed. "It's been ages that I've wanted to meet him."

"Mr. Davenport," Anna said to him. "If you would like to go open the door for your . . . relative . . ."

Relative? I would say that he's rather a horrible pain in the neck. "Of course. Perhaps he has only stopped by to tell me something. We'll be here just a few minutes, in any case."

He hurriedly left the room and went to the front door. He threw it open and found the nuisance smiling in front of him.

"Matt, what the hell—?"

"Cousin!" he interrupted in a voice so loud that the girls could definitely hear him—they could have heard him halfway around the world. "Well, why this face? Who died? Ah, of course, that's your usual face."

"Matt, what are you doing here?"

"Are you going to ask me in or not?"

He had to. "Matthew," he said seriously, "I don't know what you have in mind, but be sure you watch your tongue."

"Oh, I wouldn't worry about my tongue if I were you, with hair like that. What did you comb your hair with this morning, a hysterical hedgehog?"

Christopher sighed. "It's been a while since I threatened you with physical violence, hasn't it?"

His cousin scratched his head as he thought about it. "About a half hour, it seems to me. Maybe forty-five minutes."

"Good, it's time for me to start again, then. You shouldn't have come here today, and you know it. Now behave well if you want to keep each of your arms in one piece—at least until tonight, when I will break both of them."

Matthew laughed. He did not seem worried. "I don't understand why you are so worried, Chris. You see? I've put on my serious face."

Resigned, Christopher gave up on arguing. He led him into the drawing room, and the first words out of Matthew's mouth when he stepped foot inside were "You must be Miss Champion, I suppose. I have been so curious to meet the young lady who has captured my cousin's heart."

The fact that he had not even introduced himself was the least worry at this point. But why hadn't Christopher wrung his neck when he had the opportunity? For example, this morning. This morning would have been perfect. Or even yesterday morning, or . . .

Anna forced a dull smile. "You are Mr. Davenport's cousin?"

"Absolutely, miss, at your service. We are related, but I assure you that stupidity was a trait he alone inherited, so . . ."

For a moment Anna seemed to forget her fiancé was there. As she looked at Matthew with her mouth gaping open, her color came back.

Christopher quickly thought over the possible options.

One: eliminate his cousin on the spot.

Two: introduce him to the young ladies, who are looking at him strangely, each in her own way.

"This is Matthew Davenport, a distant cousin of mine," he informed them coldly. "Miss Anna Champion and Miss Lucy Edwards."

Lucy smiled at Matthew warmly. "I was aware that you were living in Mr. Davenport's house, but it's an outrage that we haven't met before, don't you think?"

"I don't mingle much in society, in fact. I leave that to Chris. His character has predisposed him for it, since he is always so cheerful and cordial."

Lucy let a little laugh slip out before she covered her mouth with her hand.

Laugh now, Matt, thought Christopher. *We'll talk about this later.* He was about to run his fingers through his hair, but he barely stopped in time. He glanced at Anna. She was a bit more lively, or did it only seem so to him? He almost welcomed Matthew's presence.

Almost.

Now it was time to get him out of there before he could cause some irreparable damage.

"Your cousin is very nice, Mr. Davenport," said Lucy. "Why haven't you introduced us before?"

Christopher said nothing and approached Matthew. "Matt," he whispered, taking him by the arm and squeezing it rather strongly.

"The ladies want to be alone, and now that I think of it, I have something to say to you. It's *very* important." He pulled him by the arm, but Matthew wriggled free, and, paying no mind to the danger—and the ridiculousness—he ran to hide behind Lucy.

"Miss Edwards," he said as Christopher eyed him with a silence that promised him a painful future, "tell him that I am not bothering you, please."

Lucy sniggered and gave Christopher a critical look. "Shoo, Mr. Davenport, you are dreadful," she scolded him. "Your cousin is a positively delightful young man."

Positively delightful will earn him a good beating, he thought, but he wisely decided to remain quiet. Matthew, however, did not do likewise.

"Today my cousin informed me that he will very soon marry you, Miss Champion," he said. "I wanted to meet you immediately, but he did not wish to bring me with him, so I decided to come alone."

"Makes sense," Anna muttered.

"What makes sense? That I came alone, or that he didn't wish to bring me with him?" He didn't give her time to respond—but Anna looked so taken aback that she probably wouldn't have been able to say much—and he went on: "The fact is, ladies, that I didn't believe there could exist a girl willing to put up with him on the entire face of the earth. So I scurried here to figure out what could drive a young girl in full possession of her mental faculties to marry such a sourpuss."

Oh, shit. "Matthew!"

"Calm down, Chris. I am not worried I will offend Miss Champion. Anyone who decides to marry you must have a great sense of humor."

Lucy laughed and even Anna smiled, although stiffly. "Don't worry, Mr. . . . Davenport." She seemed to have problems, and she gave a few coughs. "In fact, it's a question that anyone would ask."

Christopher felt anger growing inside of him. His cousin's wit was so out of place here. Didn't he notice that Anna wasn't at all amused? He thought him smarter than that.

Instead Matthew seemed to notice neither her tension nor her unnatural paleness, and he asked her again, "Is it possible that he took advantage of you in a moment of weakness to get you to accept?"

Anna blinked her eyes, not knowing how to respond. Luckily, Lucy got her out of the awkward situation.

"Now that I think of it, Mr. Davenport," she interrupted, "Anna was sick until two days ago, and then she was engaged to your cousin. Do you think her fever may have debilitated her that much, in your opinion?"

"I'm not sure. It's possible. How high was it?"

"High enough, it seems, since she didn't get out of bed for several days."

"Oh, it was nothing," Anna mumbled, growing paler. *If she continues like this,* Christopher said to himself, *she will disappear right in front of my eyes. But don't these two realize the agony Anna is in? What a couple of insensitive fools!*

"Anna, what do you mean, nothing?" Lucy objected, amazed. "Nora threatened me with a knife when I tried to get around her to see you in your room."

Nora. Nora and her disturbing wooden spoon. Christopher, who remembered it well, understood fully Miss Edwards's state of mind.

"Really?" asked Matthew, as if lost in thought, and he slowly turned toward Anna. Despite the fact that he continued to smile, it seemed that his face suddenly changed, and Christopher felt the first signs of danger. Matthew was smarter than that, after all. "You were feeling so ill that you did not want to receive visitors, Miss Champion?"

"Oh, nothing serious, sir." She gave a light laugh. "Nothing serious. Really."

"Matthew, we must go now." Christopher walked up to him and grabbed him by the arm. His cousin did not protest, and this—contrary to what it seemed—was not a good sign.

"It was a real pleasure to make your acquaintance, Mr. Davenport," said Lucy. "I hope to see you again very soon. Next Friday, promise me you'll come to the ball at my house."

"Certainly, Miss Edwards. Now that I have had the honor of meeting you, nothing could stop me. And I would like to ask you one last thing before going." He took a step toward her and whispered something in her ear. Lucy laughed and shook her head, then murmured something in reply. Matthew smiled as he listened. His eyes, however, remained serious. "I understand," he said aloud. "It must be the proximity to my cousin, then. He tends to have that effect—"

"Matthew . . ."

"Let's go, then. Miss Champion, would you be so kind as to accompany us to the door?"

Christopher hurried to intervene. "That is not at all necessary."

"Please," Matthew begged her with a strained smile. "Just a few more seconds in your company before leaving me alone with him."

"Matt, what the devil . . . ?" He stopped talking, because Lucy was looking at him, baffled.

"Of course, Mr. Davenport, I will gladly accompany you," Anna answered. "It'll be just a moment, Lucy."

All three of them made for the door, and they reached it in silence. Christopher opened it swiftly. "Miss Champion," he said in taking his leave of her.

Matthew raised an eyebrow. "You call her 'Miss Champion,' Chris. Very romantic of you."

"Matthew, you are really going too far."

The cousin seemed to be convinced of it. "Good," he said finally. "Let's go, then. Miss, it was a pleasure."

They left. Anna went to close the door, but Matthew, spinning around, put his hand on it and held it open. "Ah, I just remembered something funny," he said as if by chance. "You said that you were sick, didn't you? So sick"—he closed his eyes halfway and stared at her attentively—"that you were not able to leave your room."

"Oh, but it was—"

"It was nothing, I know," he said, finishing her sentence gently. "Do you want to know an odd thing? Chris also had a problem that kept him at home for several days, nearly a week. Do you find that to be a peculiar coincidence?"

"That's enough, Matthew. Let's go."

"Hush, Christopher."

Maybe he should grab him by the neck and throw him off the front porch, thought Christopher. Or maybe he should stop him from speaking further with Anna. But he knew it would be pointless, because Matthew had understood.

Bloody hell.

Matthew turned back toward Anna, whose head was bowed. In a low voice he said to her, "You should know, miss, that it seems that my cousin was attacked by a rabid tomcat. He was covered in cuts and scratches that, by the way, greatly improved his ugly face." He let out a joyless little laugh. "He told me he took a bad tumble, and if you look closely you can see a few scars on him still. You don't want to raise your eyes and have a look? No . . . ? I understand. Never mind."

"Matthew . . ." Christopher didn't finish the sentence. What could he say, anyway?

"To tell the truth, he himself seemed like a rabid tomcat during those days," Matthew went on. "He was beside himself. Really, Miss Champion, you should have seen him."

Anna looked up, confused. She looked stunned, but in her eyes there was something else—a light, a light that seemed like . . . hope?

"Did you think that I didn't notice, Chris?" Matthew said, smiling bitterly. "And, coincidentally, this morning you tell me that you're getting married. Like that. Out of the blue. I don't want to hurt your feelings, dear cousin, but I must confess that I have the impression your fiancée would rather be dunked in a cauldron of boiling hot soup than become your wife."

Christopher stared at him without saying anything. Anna was also silent, leaning against the open door in order to hold herself up.

"God, Christopher." Matthew's voice was barely a whisper, but it was a harsh whisper. "What have you done . . . ?"

17

The best mirror is an old friend.
—George Herbert

"God, Christopher, what did you do?"

Matthew's face seemed to wither suddenly, as if the skin just hung on it. Nothing more remained of the cheery chap from a few minutes before, and with a heavy heart Anna turned toward her fiancé to see if his cousin's suffering touched him.

Obviously not.

Christopher was emotionless—or rather, he was smiling. "Matthew, try not to cry if you can manage. And since when are you blasphemous in front of ladies?"

There was not a single hint whatsoever of shame on his face, and Anna stared at him, unbelieving in spite of everything.

"I didn't believe you to be capable of that, Christopher." But in his low, distressed murmur, Matthew seemed to be speaking to himself. "Never. Not even in a hundred years. I really am as stupid as you say." A half smile came over his face and he looked down, as an upset girl might have. "I have always helped you, and you know it. But this is too much, really too much. Do you understand?" He blinked to drive back the tears, and Christopher gave him a look of impatient annoyance. "Don't you understand? No?" Matthew's voice became furious. "Do you really think your past gives you the right . . ." He suddenly stopped, as if invisible scissors had cut the words while in his throat. Shocked, Matthew turned toward Anna. He seemed to have forgotten about her presence until that very moment.

What past? thought Anna. What right?

For a long moment everyone was speechless. The two cousins seemed stunned, both he who had spoken and he who had listened.

"Chris, I—"

Without letting him finish, Christopher came at him, slamming him against the doorjamb. "What the hell do you think you're doing, Matthew?"

"Mr. Davenport! Christopher! Leave him alone at once!"

Anna ran between them and put her hand on her fiancé's arm, forgetting the horror that he had done to her.

Blind with rage, Christopher looked at her. "Anna, don't get yourself mixed up in this!" he growled. "Stay out of it!"

"Stay out of it, Miss Champion," Matthew echoed, although he was calmer. He was motionless in the hands of his cousin, who kept him raised off the ground by the collar of his jacket, like a half-empty sack of potatoes. "This is between the two of us."

"Mr. Davenport, I cannot—"

"Move away, Miss Champion," Matthew reaffirmed, grinning at her as if he were drinking tea rather than dangling in the fists of his colossal and violent cousin. "Let us settle it our way."

Is he crazy? Nice but crazy? Anna wondered about that, with her heart in her throat and her head about to burst from the blood pumping too fast, but she took a step back as he had asked her.

"So, Chris, what do you want to do?" asked Matthew. "Do you think you will feel better afterward?"

Christopher clenched his fists harder on the jacket. "Oh, to hell with it!" he blurted out, dropping him all of a sudden. He walked away with his back to him, looking toward the short, tree-lined pathway. "You shouldn't have come here today," he muttered wearily.

Anna began to breathe again. Perhaps Matthew knew what he was doing. And maybe Christopher cared for him. The thought came to her with the urgency and the hope of an unforeseen and yet long-awaited piece of news.

Matthew straightened out his jacket. "Miss Champion," he began. There was a darkness on his face and in his big brown eyes. "Miss Champion," he repeated, clearing his voice. "I would like . . . I would like to apologize for a little bit ago, in the drawing room. For the things I said. I beg you to forgive me."

Anna nodded, and a lock of her hair landed in her eyes. "There's nothing to forgive."

Matthew turned his head toward his cousin. "Chris . . . ?"

"Hurry up, Matthew. Let's get going."

He didn't even turn around to look at him.

Matthew's jaw tensed up. "For the love of God, Christopher!" His chest moved up and down with a deep breath one, two, three times. Finally, with a loud voice he said, "I apologize on behalf of my cousin, Miss Champion. Feel sorry for him."

"That's enough!" Christopher took a step toward him, and Anna moved closer, ready to choke him. If only he dared to . . .

Matthew wearily raised his hand. "Let's go finish this conversation elsewhere, Chris. Miss Champion, it was a pleasure to meet you."

"Call me Anna," she said on impulse, touched. This thin boy, who seemed almost like an adolescent, was taking her side—that of a perfect stranger—against someone who seemed to be more of a brother to him than a cousin.

Matthew smiled warmly at her, his eyes lighting up in a way that seemed almost unreal, and he immediately became again the boyish young man whom she had met in the drawing room a few minutes earlier. "I caused quite a stir, didn't I?" he bragged in an impossibly witty way. With a look of satisfaction, he began to smooth down his hair. "You may call me Matthew, obviously."

Anna let out a hysterical little laugh. "I am very happy to have met you, Matthew," she replied, realizing she truly was happy. For the first time in nearly a week she felt herself growing a bit relieved. "We will see each other again very soon, I hope."

Christopher turned toward them suddenly. "Matthew, I will not wait another second."

It seemed he was having problems containing his anger, with his narrow eyes darkening, turning almost black in the full daylight.

(Is it only anger? Or is there also pain inside him, Anna?)

But what was she thinking? The stress was making her nonsensical, or maybe it was her absurd need to be able to believe that, despite everything . . .

"Miss . . . Anna . . . yes, we'll see each other again soon," Matthew confirmed.

He kissed her on the hand, squeezing it gently with something akin to affection, before going down the five steps of the front porch. Christopher followed him angrily, without saying good-bye to her or even looking back.

Anna ran after him. "Christopher!"

He did not stop. She caught up to him by running and, touching him, grabbed on to his sleeve, standing in the shadow of his incredible height. Christopher turned toward her, massive and frightening, but she was fearless.

"Mr. Davenport," she said, "if you so much as touch him—"

"These affairs do not concern you, Miss Champion!"

As he shook his arm violently, she let go, and with unusually big strides he went off. All Anna could do was watch the two of them mount their horses and ride away quickly down the lane. Christopher

Davenport against Matthew Davenport, with nearly an eight-inch height difference between the two, she estimated anxiously. *My fiancé is quite a gentleman, if anyone still has any doubts.*

***

"Are you in love with her, Chris?"

They had arrived at Rockfield Park without exchanging a single word, given their horses to Joseph, and now were walking toward the entrance of the house.

Christopher stopped, looking at his cousin to make sure he hadn't gotten a bit of a sunstroke on his stupid head. "In love, of course!" he replied mockingly. "God, Matthew, you should really grow up."

"You're right. I don't know how a thought like that came to my mind." He gave Christopher the look that he knew all too well. Shit. The sermon was about to begin. "Bloody hell, let's get it over with, Christopher!" he screamed definitely louder than normal. "You owe me an explanation."

"I'm warning you, Matthew," he answered tensely, "stop being such a pain in the neck, because I have reached the end of my patience for today."

It was true. The ungodly heat of this damned July, and Leopold, who would not see him the last two days under the pretext of previous commitments, and the problems he was having finding workers to fix the Champion house—these were all things that overwhelmed him or made him explode.

(And think of the smile she gave to Matthew and Lucy. But not to you, Christopher.)

"Christopher." Matthew lowered his voice and had sad eyes, like those of a small child preparing to be slapped. "You raped her after I told you about her engagement, and in some way that makes me your accomplice. I must know why you did it."

Christopher opened his mouth to speak—"Shut your trap, Matt"—but what came out was this: "I don't know! I don't know, God damn it!" This shocked him, and even his voice surprised him. It sounded so desperate. "I don't even like this girl. Christ!" He kicked a cloud of dust up in the air. He took a deep breath, then another and another. With his hand over his eyes, he tried to slow down the mad rush of blood in his veins. He began to speak again, calmer. "It happened, and that's all there is to it, Matt. It happened. I believe . . ." He paused. "I believe that my hatred for Daniel forced my hand a bit."

"Forced your hand a bit?" Matthew looked at him shocked. "God, Christopher, you wanted to spite your brother: Is that what you're telling me?"

It didn't sound good at all, he admitted, but he didn't know what had come over him a week earlier. Why in the devil had he done what he had done? "Naturally," he replied, shrugging his shoulders, "this is how things ended up. And now I have to marry her. It's comical, don't you think?"

"Oh, absolutely! Comical, he says! Are you completely out of your mind?"

Christopher raised his hand to his forehead. God, what heat and what confusion. He needed to go inside and drink something cold and strong, or maybe only strong. "Listen, there's no need for you to make this sad face. I'm marrying her, aren't I? I'll have to put up with her for the rest of my life, and I would say that is more than punishment enough."

"Dear God, Christopher, what are you saying? Are you listening to me at all?" Matthew hit himself on the temple with a hand to make Christopher understand what he thought of his mental state. "You're not really able to reason, are you? This girl is terrified by you! She can't even manage to look you in the eyes!"

Oh really? I hadn't noticed. "Don't waste your time feeling sorry for her," he replied tiredly. "She is the worst witch I have ever met, and if there's a victim in this marriage, it certainly isn't her."

Matthew couldn't spit out an answer even if he had tried. He opened his mouth, then closed it again, and then again opened it and closed it. Nothing came out.

His eyes, however, were judging Christopher. Bloody hell, they were judging him.

"She was asking for it, for God's sake!" Christopher burst out. "You weren't there, Matthew, but I assure you that she provoked me beyond all limits! I don't know what came over me. I didn't plan it, but it happened, damn it, it happened. I can't do anything else about it now." He looked at his cousin while slowly rubbing the back of his neck with his hand. "I won't be a bad husband to her," he assured him in a hushed tone. "I will give her everything she wants. You must believe me, Matt."

"But Chris, what are you saying?" he asked him with no more anger, but now with suffering in his eyes. "You don't realize what your life will be like, if she loves—"

"DeMercy?" he said, sarcastically finishing his sentence. "Certainly, she would have been happy with him, of course."

"You know very well that Daniel is not like his father, Christopher!"

"Fine, take his side, then!" He suddenly raised his arm, pointing down the lane with an anger as stiff as his movements. "Reveal to him the plans for my vendetta. Let all these years of struggling go up in smoke. You'll do it all for Anna, right? While—"

"But how can you say such a thing?" Matthew interrupted frantically. "You know that I would never betray you! But what you have done is inexcusable, and you *must* know it! You must beg forgiveness from this girl!" He gestured to emphasize his words in order to convince him, with the desperation of someone who sees a friend drowning and reaches out his hand, only to see him sink into the sea. "Dear God, when did you become so hard like this?"

"I *am* like this. You're the one who never wanted to understand that," replied Christopher, suddenly becoming calm. His anger was extinguished by an overpowering bitterness that weighed heavily on him, so much so that he felt an incredible need to lie down. "But maybe now I will convince you of this, and you'll regret not leaving me in that park twenty years ago."

This remark hit Matthew so hard that he would have thought it possible to see the slap marks on his face. "You really are a pig, Christopher," he said in a low voice. "That's a low blow, and you know it." Of course he knew it and said it deliberately. And it worked: the look on Matthew's face had softened. "Chris, listen . . ." He gulped and looked at him uncomfortably. "I'm sorry to have said that at Miss Champion's house earlier."

Christopher looked at him with his eyes half-closed. It was over; the sermon was over—at least for today. "I don't want to speak of it anymore, Matthew," he answered after a full minute of silence, and then he went toward the house without saying anything else. The soft footsteps of his cousin followed, but he didn't try to catch up to him.

It's so easy to manipulate you, Matt, thought Christopher as he walked through the front entrance of Rockfield and passed through the luxurious rooms, which were far too large. *That's the problem with people like you who have tender hearts: it's pointless to use violence, because it's more than enough to talk to you about friendship, love, and other rubbish like that, and immediately you back down.* Matthew had always been such a good person, even when he was little. *And in twenty years you haven't changed at all,* he reflected with mocking contempt. *You're still the same, the same trusting fool from back then.* Time had not hardened Matthew—certainly not. But it had hardened Christopher, and his cousin was right about that. And it was a good thing, because

Christopher was no longer a weakling nor a bloody victim. He was no longer the little child who ran away from the Covent Garden brothel.

(Not from the Covent Garden brothel, Christopher. From the hands of Bernard Jones. Do you remember Bernard, Christopher? Bernard the ogre?)

He remembered it all, and with surprising clarity. The elegant carriage they climbed into after leaving the brothel. The expressionless coachman who had opened the doors for them. And Bernard, who couldn't wait anymore when the carriage stopped for something blocking the street. "Do you want to see something?" he had asked Christopher, and his eager question seemed to reverberate inside the carriage like a mad grasshopper.

From the little carriage window he couldn't see anything, although Christopher kept looking outside. "What?"

Bernard's left hand was touching his trousers. "I have it here. Come closer. I'll show it to you."

But Christopher couldn't move. Why did he feel this mysterious panic gnawing at him in the pit of his stomach? This all seems so odd, he had thought, and Bernard definitely seemed odd, didn't he? "I don't want to see it, your thing." He was pushing up against the carriage door. The air inside there smelled of sweat, and there was also a hint of another odor that was hardly noticeable, something sweet and sugary.

"Come now, don't be bad." The ogre moved his hand around on the fly of his trousers, and his voice came out in little spurts without breath. "I will give you sweets—a sack of sweets." He reached his hand out toward him—a slimy hand, with fingers as white as fat worms—and he grasped Christopher by his hair, pulling him down there low, toward his overflowing belly.

"Let go of me!"

Christopher wriggled free like a snake and bit his hand, filling his mouth with blood and sweat.

"Ah! Bastard!" Bernard held his wounded hand with his other one, and he was stunned, as if he were insulted, his pouty face about to cry. Ignoring his pain, Christopher had opened the carriage door, jumped into the street, and run as fast as he could without looking back. Maybe someone was following him; he didn't know for sure. He also didn't know where he was going or whom to ask for help. He only knew that he had to run away, and he ran so far that he felt his heart would explode—he ran at breathtaking speed. He spent the night in Green Park, and the next day he met Matthew—and Matthew asked his mother to take him back home with them.

His mother had said no.

***

Anna rolled from one side of the bed to the other. The light sheet had slipped off one corner, uncovering a foot. Irritated, she turned over again, then gave a snort and sat up, letting the sheet fall on the floor. She got out of bed and groped her way toward the window, moving the heavy curtain to the side. The moon was on the wane and it barely lit the tree-lined lane and the park bench. The swing was moving slowly in the light breeze, as if a nighttime sprite had decided to play right there that night, swaying in the pale, ethereal moonlight. As a child, Anna had thought that this sprite could have been Cecily, her little sister who survived barely one year. Anna's mother had remained silent for several months after Cecily's death, and Anna had felt lonely and sad in the house, which was suddenly lacking in joy. She had felt the need for a female friend, and she began to speak with Cecily as if she were a real presence. What laughter she had, what games she played, and what races she ran with her little sister in those empty rooms of the house! Then she had met Lucy when she was seven years old, and she still thought that it was Cecily who had brought them together on that rainy day so long ago in the field between their houses. Since then

Cecily had not come back again to visit Anna, but even now, almost twelve years later, she tried to spy the mischievous presence of her sister.

Thoughts flooded her mind, and for the first time they were thoughts that gave her a bit of courage for the future. *And to think that I didn't want to meet Matthew Davenport.* She knew, like everyone in the village, that he lived with Christopher, even though he was often away on business. The idea of meeting another Davenport seemed to her to be something so repugnant that she had hoped it would never happen. But Matthew had shown human characteristics, unlike his cousin. She smiled as she remembered the note he had delivered that afternoon:

> *Dear Anna,*
> *I noticed your concern this morning and I am writing to reassure you: I am still in once piece. Christopher has declined to challenge me, much to my disappointment; I have never lost a fight with him, and I assure you that in the past my face has seriously hurt his fist, leaving light scratches more than once that were even visible a few times to the naked eye (if one had only truly tried to examine them carefully).*
>
> *Dear Anna, these words cannot express how happy I was to meet you. I hope to see you again very soon, perhaps at the home of your adorable friend, next Friday.*
>
> *Cordially,*
> *Matthew Davenport*

Anna had dry eyes. She did not want to cry, not as she did every night, haunted by the horrible afternoon six days before. The memory of that hot breath on her neck and the ingratiating voice of that invader inside her was always with her, like a shadow. She shook her head to avoid thinking about it now. She had to act, and the starting point could be what she had discovered this morning, that cryptic phrase: "Your past doesn't give you the right to . . ."

. . . to do what you want, she thought, finishing the sentence.

What had happened to Christopher? What had made him so cruel and so convinced he could act beyond the boundaries of any morals? She decided she would find out. It was a pity that she couldn't ask Lucy for help. Together they were unbeatable at solving mysteries both large and small, such as the first they had solved, The Secret of the Stolen Shovel Left in the Sun, and the memorable one only three weeks before, The Disappearing Pudding—or, Who Left Rosemary with Nothing to Eat?

Lit by the small moon, which shed a pale, new light on her keepsakes, Anna straightened her back. *The first step to figuring this out is Matthew,* she said to herself. Perhaps now that he knew what his cousin was capable of, he would turn his back on him to become her ally. And perhaps with his help, the wedding would be off. *And if I discover something that can destroy you, my vile fiancé, I will not hesitate to use it.*

18

What's in a name? That which we call a rose by any other name would smell as sweet.

—William Shakespeare

"What is your horse's name?"

"He doesn't have a name, Grace," answered Christopher. In fact, what could possibly be more stupid than to give a horse a name? "You children can decide if you like," he added nicely.

He was in the kitchen of the Champion house for his mandatory visit to his fiancée. Anna did not like these visits at all, and Christopher was aware of that, but it was unavoidable to maintain the appearance of an idyllic engagement. And in any case he couldn't help but come, because he needed to monitor the renovation being done on the cottage. Mr. Champion definitely could not take care of it, and as far as the idea of leaving it to Anna—which he had reacted to with *"Ridiculous!"* when she proposed it to him two days before—he hadn't even really considered it. Women definitely knew nothing about such things.

"Shall we call him Noumenon?" Anthony suggested.

Noumenon? wondered Christopher, puzzled.

"No," Grace retorted with an imperious frown on her round little face. "Let's call him Basil!"

"And what about Farty?" Dennis said. "Is Farty no good?"

Anna, sitting and sewing something near the window, said softly, "I do not think Farty seems very nice for a name."

Christopher turned toward her, shocked. When they were in the same room, Anna spoke to him as little as possible—only about the progress of the work on the house and of practical things—and she used very few words, exhibiting a remarkable ability to be brief when she wanted to. When she was with the others, in fact, it seemed that she could never be quiet. On that day Anna hadn't even looked at him. If she chimed in, it was most definitely because of the horse and not because of him.

Her head was bent over a little light-pink-and-green frock as she sewed a torn pocket. Her hands were pale and quick as they moved gracefully, as if pushing the needle through the fabric required a delicate touch. The light that came through the kitchen window shined on her. The white dress she was wearing hugged her body. Christopher seemed to feel her warmth, as if she were right next to him—or under him—and not across the room. He was silent, barely breathing.

"So, Prolegomenon then?" Anthony said, trying again.

Christopher blinked and turned to the little boy. "Sounds good," he acknowledged, "but you do understand that calling him a name that I do not understand could get me into trouble. What if someone asked me what it means?"

"I could explain it." Anthony lifted the book he was reading and showed him the word on the cover—and if that was the title, Christopher didn't want to know what horrible things could be lurking inside. *What a family of loonies!*

"Perhaps you could explain it to me, of course," he replied, giving an uneasy glance at the tome. "Or," he added in a decisive tone, "we could call him Basil."

Grace clapped her hands, but it seemed the other two wanted nothing of the sort, and they began to argue and hit each other.

"Prolegomenon!"

"What about Fartybit? Because it's only a bit smelly, right?"

Christopher sighed, raising his hands. He was quick to calm their tempers. "Don't fret," he assured them. "Soon you will have three horses, to which you can give all the names you want." It was true: the work on the stables was progressing quickly, and the horses and the carriage for the Champion family to use would arrive in a few days' time.

This tactic seemed to work, because Anthony and Dennis stopped arguing after several exchanges of final last words and a couple of imaginative insults.

"It's decided. It will be called Basil," said Christopher as he watched the three children calm themselves. That morning, for the first time everything seemed to be going in the right direction: even Nora had limited herself to only a few humphs under her breath, and she had grabbed the knife only once—and not to use against him but rather to peel potatoes. "Do you want to take him for a ride?" he then suggested, leading them outdoors.

What a huge mistake.

His dreadful fiancée suddenly looked up. "It's not a toy, children," she said. "Leave Basil alone."

My God, it wasn't possible that she was against him even in this? "Come on, children," he called. She wanted to fight? He would give her one. "Come."

He left quickly so not to hear the annoying protests, and Grace and Dennis ran after him.

Anna joined them outside in the open space beside the house. "Dennis! Grace!" she called them back indignantly. "Basil is not here for your entertainment." She didn't even deign to give Christopher a look, and she walked up to the horse and stroked his muzzle with a tenderness he had not been given for many years.

Christopher could have strangled her. "Come on, Dennis," he snapped. "Come, I'll help you on."

Anna turned to him furiously, and Christopher felt an elated pang stab him in the gut. *You are looking at me, Anna. You are looking at me.*

"Don't contradict me, Mr. Davenport."

"It is you who should not contradict me, Miss Champion," he retorted sharply, coming close enough to her to be able to stand over her. "I did not think that even *this* would bother you."

Her eyes flashed, and Christopher wondered if by chance she were trying to burn off his eyebrows with the power of her mind.

"You are not to discuss my authority in front of the children," she hissed without backing down. She raised her head higher, and her cheeks flushed. Her lips seemed redder than ever.

"You know very well that I will do it," he muttered.

He walked so close to her that he was almost touching her. Anna did not move. He took another small step, and his jacket touched her dress and her soft breast.

Her cheeks suddenly lost all color.

Christopher smiled cruelly. "Stop making a fool of yourself and go away, Miss Champion."

They were so close to each other that all he needed to do was lower his head to kiss her lips, or lower it a bit more to touch her neck and chest, which rose and fell quickly under her light clothing. The sun was beating down, and the heat was affecting his mind. He hoped that Anna would give up soon, because he felt a bit dazed, and he was afraid he might say—or worse, do—things that were not advisable.

She continued to look at him for a few moments longer, but finally fear got the better of her. She moved away from him by taking a step back.

"I am fulfilling all of your requests, Mr. Davenport," she mumbled, looking down. "Don't make things so difficult for me."

"You haven't put on your ring, miss."

That clear stone, on a simple and elegant mounting, had been left in the box right after he had given it to her. Anna did not wear it. She hadn't even looked at it, not even when he had slipped it on her finger in front of her own family members.

"I will wear it in public, sir." She turned back toward the children. "Dennis, Grace, come into the house," she ordered them flatly before turning and walking toward the entrance.

Dismayed, Grace first looked at her sister, then to Christopher.

"You can have a ride if you want, Grace," he said.

Ah, desire! So irresistible at the age with no half measures, shining so brightly in Grace's eyes! And yet the little girl shrugged her shoulders and, with one last look of regret, ran after her older sister.

Christopher sighed. "Shall we take this ride, Dennis?"

"Yes!"

Christopher hoisted him up on the horse—no, onto *Basil*—surprised at how light and thin this child was. "Hold on tight," he urged him. "Are you afraid to be up there by yourself?"

"No." Dennis seemed tiny, but he clung to the horse's neck without any fear. At nearly seven years old, he showed remarkable courage. "Christopher, do you think he likes his new name?"

"Of course," he replied distractedly, looking toward the house a bit. Anna was no longer outside at any rate, and Christopher pulled Basil by the reins, making him walk slowly in some small semicircles in the confined, stony area in front of them.

"He would have liked Fartybit more," Dennis said.

"Really?" He looked at his pocket watch and realized to his great disappointment that he was late for his first appointment of the day—*incredibly* late. "Dennis, one more time around, and then that's enough," he informed him.

"All right," said the boy obediently.

It was quite unexpected for him to be obedient, to tell the truth, although he was probably too intimidated by Christopher to throw a tantrum. Dennis didn't say a word when, just a bit later, Christopher took him back into the house. Inside, Christopher said good-bye to Mr. Champion and the children and even Nora. But he did not see Anna, who was no doubt holed up in some corner, where Christopher knew she would stay so long as he was around.

Despite his delay, he lingered in the yard, casting one last look at the windows of the house. Perhaps there was a shadow behind one of the upper-floor windows, but he could not say for sure. That was it for the day: his tedious chore was over, and he would not have to see his unbearable fiancée again until the next day.

He climbed on Basil, who Christopher was sure liked his name, making fun of this spitefully affectionate little boy. Before leaving, he gave him a pat on the neck to thank him. "Would you really have preferred Fartybit?" he asked him. It was not odd that he addressed these few words to his proud, strong horse, who had followed him for the last three years with bashful affection. The horse, however, never answered. "Or maybe you would have liked Proleg-something."

He spurred Basil lightly, and he began to trot before moving faster and eventually into a gallop. He did not seem resentful for the name he was given, nor for not being able to choose it for himself.

(Besides, no one gets to choose his own name. Isn't that so, Christopher?)

***

"We will say that you are the son of my cousin, Mark Davenport, and his wife, Isabella, who died two years ago in the West Indies," Matthew's father, Frank, had said to him when he welcomed him into their home. Just three days earlier Christopher had escaped from Bernard, and he had wandered all over London with almost nothing to eat. Just three days earlier Mrs. Davenport had dragged Matthew away from the park, screaming that she would never let Christopher come into her house and that Matthew would never again see him.

Just three days earlier his name was Christopher Smith.

Things change in three days. Sometimes even in three minutes they change. And a last name can change even more quickly, because it's nothing more than a series of letters arranged one after another.

Davenport.

And so they decided, and so it was, but Christopher had told himself that he was then, and would always remain, Christopher *Smith*, son of Martha Smith. He firmly believed that, and he continued to say that for four years, until he decided that it wasn't true, that he had been lying to himself. He wasn't Christopher Smith, not anymore. He was Christopher Davenport, the respectable son of Mark and Isabelle. He was Christopher Davenport, and Martha Smith—this whore—meant nothing to him; even less than nothing. He remembered the feeling that this thought had given him, a strong dizziness that made him grasp the door handle of the carriage as he was getting out of it. Just a few minutes before everything had been normal: he was in the carriage together with his aunt and Matthew, and they were going to the barber's, as they did every two weeks, to have their hair cut. Christopher looked out at the people and the shops through the carriage window; he was sitting sloppily, with his right leg under his left thigh. Matthew was sitting opposite him, and he wanted to do the same. Christopher remembered that Mrs. Davenport had raised an eyebrow. "Matthew, sit down correctly."

Putting both feet on the floor, his cousin obeyed. The coach stopped on Fleet Street, and Mrs. Davenport got out, calling her son. "Come, Matt."

Matthew followed her, and Christopher was right behind him, crawling on the soft seat cushion. He had grabbed the door handle while putting his foot on the step, and he paused for a moment to look around. Several people were walking on the sides of the street, looking curiously into the shop windows and street vendor stalls. It was a quite busy area, where men wore overcoats and hats and carried walking sticks, and women wore bonnets and elaborate little caps. The buzzing of the street was cheerful and calming and quite harmless.

"Stop, arsehole!"

The hair on his arms stood up, and his stomach tightened, as if in a vise. He turned to his left, toward the unexpectedly cruel voices, childish and angry, as if he were reliving a scene from his forgotten life. Four children were chasing another child, who was running away furiously—he ran and he ran. He must have been eight or nine years old, and he was as gaunt as a skeleton, with a little freckly face and brown hair dark with dirt. Around his neck he had a white handkerchief—at least, it had once been white, because now it was a filthy, nondescript grayish-beige color.

"Murderer!" the children were yelling, and they were throwing something at him—maybe stones or garbage. "Murderer!"

At this moment, in his mind Christopher imagined he heard a voice echoing. *If we are sure we can beat them up, we stop.*

If we are sure . . .

But he hadn't stopped since Simon died, had he? And he hadn't been chased by anyone through the street for four years. Now he went to get his hair cut at the barber's. Not like those kids over there, who wore ruined clothes and chased after each other as if they were running for their lives; not like the boy who was being hunted down, who had just barely turned a corner in search of an escape route.

That way we can get them some other time.

Before he even had time to think about it, he had jumped out of the carriage, bumping against Matthew's shoulder. His cousin had fallen to the ground.

"Oh heavens!" Mrs. Davenport had shrieked.

Matthew had perhaps been hurt, but Christopher didn't bother to stop, running at a breakneck speed behind the gang of children.

"Christopher!" his cousin had screamed, worried. "Where . . . ?"

Christopher didn't hear the rest. Turning onto the side road—which was long and narrow, and deserted, alas—he saw the haggard boy with the freckles and the handkerchief. He was maybe a hundred yards away, and the four children in the gang had reached him and were surrounding him. Two children, who were roughly the same age as Christopher, had grabbed him. Another child, who was smaller, stood off to the side. The small one was maybe four years old, probably the brother of one of the older boys. The last child, who was the tallest—and who really was a young man—had to be eleven or twelve years old and seemed to be the leader of the gang. He was wearing a shirt that was too big. He was thin and bony, with a face that was sunken in and a bulbous nose that seemed disproportionately round compared to the rest of his lean frame. His slender body showed an unusual strength, and his cruel scowl scared the little boy, who was paralyzed with fear.

"Leave me alone!" he cried, green and white spittle running down his face.

"Leave him alone!" yelled Christopher, running toward them.

Four pairs of eyes immediately turned toward him. "What the 'ell?"

Christopher stopped about ten yards away from them, frozen by these stares, his boldness vanishing in an instant. Suddenly he realized he was alone against a gang of violent and angry children. *What the devil am I going to do here?* They would massacre him. What kind of crazy idea had come over him?

"What the 'ell do you want, arsehole?" the leader asked him, staring at him with two dark and enraged eyes.

Christopher suddenly felt the humiliating need to pee. "Leave him alone," he repeated, but quieter, with a voice that seemed embarrassingly like a mouse squeaking.

The leader looked fiercely at him. "Say it again, you bastard. I didn't hear it good from over here."

Gathering all of his courage and staring at the bulbous nose—because looking him in the eyes was out of the question—Christopher repeated, "Leave him alone! What do you want with him?"

"What the 'ell do you care?" The leader looked at Christopher's fine clothing. "Go back to your mummy."

With very clear eyes, the little four-year-old looked at Christopher, amazed. "He's the son of a murderer," he explained to him with a gentle little voice, and he raised his hands in the air as if to say, *That's the end of the discussion, right?*

What the hell do I care? thought Christopher. *So he's the son of a murderer.* "Leave him alone," he repeated for the fourth time, his voice almost inaudible.

The gang leader seemed torn between running toward Christopher and finishing the fight with the child he had his hands on. "Come over here and say that, shithead."

Bending his knees, Christopher picked up a stone from the ground and held it up with his shaking hand. "You're the shithead," he answered with the voice of a mouse, and with a mad fear he threw the stone. Out of fright he hadn't even aimed at all, but against all odds the stone struck the boy—not very hard, but it struck him.

"Ow!" The boy rubbed his hurt shoulder, looking more surprised than wounded, but he immediately forgot about the child they had cornered. "So, you want to die!"

"John, did he hurt you?" asked the little boy with clear eyes, giving Christopher a look of silent but outraged reproach.

No answer from John, and Christopher stepped back, his heart pounding fast and loud in his chest. As if following specific orders, the three children—immediately followed even by the littlest one—took a step forward, letting go of the murderer's son, who had stopped crying and was staring at the scene, wide-eyed and hopeful. He didn't seem able to help Christopher; he wasn't even able to wipe the greenish spittle off his face. He was stepping backward, and Christopher was sure he would be gone in a few seconds. There was only one thing left for Christopher to do: run.

"Stop, you jackrabbit!"

The children seemed dangerously close behind him, and the sound of their footsteps grew louder and louder.

"Now we are going to beat you to a pulp, arsehole!"

Christopher ran faster. *If I can get back to my aunt and Matthew, I'll be safe,* he said to himself. No one could run as fast as him, and no one could catch him. *I can do this.*

"Stop, you son of a whore!"

With not even fifty yards to go to the street, he stopped, as if insane. Just in front of him was the end of the alley, and salvation.

No, he thought, and he turned toward the gang.

He stood still while the children ran up to him. A stone thrown by a little blond boy hit him in the stomach, giving him the most shocking joy of his entire life. *It doesn't hurt!* he understood in a flash. A river of elation boiled over him, flooding every part of his body. *I can beat them!*

Another stone hit him in the left eye, causing both pain and blood, but absurdly it didn't matter to him, because this pain did not *hurt* him. It would be more than fifteen years before he would be able to understand it, but this was it—this was life, this was pain, and that's why it didn't hurt him. He stood still, watching the brats come closer, ten yards away from him, then five, then three, and then John stopped, opened his arms. "Now we are going to tear you apart, arsehole," he said, strangely calm.

Without a sound Christopher hurled himself at him. The smallest child stood off to the side, but the other two immediately threw themselves into the fray. Christopher ended up on the ground, where he was kicked furiously. He felt punches and his hair being pulled, but it was as if he were a long ways away, outside of himself. He bit, scratched, and hit like a trapped, mad animal. They tried to hold him down, but he got away, frantic and violent. A punch square in his face made him see bright spots, but by dodging he was able to avoid another punch, and he felt his *own* fist strike someone else's soft flesh. He was slapped once, twice, three times in the face, and he immediately began to bite and kick, striking in every direction with no clear target—just striking, blindly striking. He heard a couple of sharp cries, but he wasn't sure from whom. Christopher, on the other hand, didn't shout, even though he was being hit again and again. He was also hitting them, and at a certain point he had scratched the face of a child who was on top of him, and under his fingernails he had flesh and skin. That child touched his cheek and noticed his hand was red and slimy with blood. He quickly scrambled to his feet.

"Phil, what the 'ell are you doing?" roared John, trying to hold Christopher by the arms while Christopher kicked the other child in the leg.

Phil lowered his head in shame and took a step back. He saw the three children on the ground as they writhed about furiously, then turned toward the entrance to the street. His lips quivered, and his hand again touched the bloody cheek. "I can't do this, John!" he said, his voice cracking. "It hurts too much!"

He took another step back, and then, abandoning all dignity, began to run away.

He was running from him.

Christopher felt himself shake with a joy so great that his eyes filled with tears. *Simon, my captain,* he thought as a punch in the stomach made him lose his breath all at once. *I beat him! I beat one of them!*

"Phil, where the 'ell—?!" John thundered as Christopher gave him a right hook on the mouth.

"Phil!" the littlest boy, who was looking at the brawl as if dumbstruck, called out desperately. Then he began to cry and ran off behind the other fugitive.

"Chris! Christopher!"

Christopher was on the ground, ripping a tuft of blond hair from a berserk child. He turned to hear the voice of his cousin, who he saw at the entrance to the street. He was being held back by Mrs. Davenport, who was yelling, beside herself, "He's a delinquent, Matthew. Do not go over there! I knew that we shouldn't take him into our home!"

A punch landed, and Christopher's head thudded against the ground. On top of him were John and the other boy in the gang, the frail but fierce blond boy. Thrashing about, Christopher had managed to give him such a bite that he almost severed a finger. The blond boy screamed in pain, holding his bleeding hand. "I'll kill you, you bastard!" he yelled, and he wasn't far from keeping his promise. They were truly massacring him, but Christopher felt like he was wrapped in a large pillow. *Where is the pain?* he wondered. *Where is the fear?*

The blond boy grabbed him by the arms to hold him still, but Christopher—biting and kicking to defend himself from John, who was still beating him—was able to shake him off. John threw himself on top of him, and they began to fight, rolling about in the street and striking each other with closed fists. The blond boy got up to reenter the fight, but the son of the murderer—yes, it was he who reappeared from who knew where, probably after first having run away—jumped on his shoulders from behind and put an arm around his neck. The blond boy thrashed about frantically, managing to throw the other boy on the ground.

With a good tug, Matthew broke free of his mother's grip, and he began to run toward them. "Chris! Christopher!"

"Come on, John!" screamed the blond. "People are coming!" Beaten and without stopping to wait for his companion, he ran off.

"Coward!" John shouted from the ground, squeezing Christopher with his arms as he took several punches to the head. He managed to break free and move to the side by rolling away and getting on his feet in a hurry. He was in pretty bad shape: on one side of his face he was dripping with blood, and his mouth was also bleeding.

Christopher was back on his feet and facing him. "Now step forward," he said to him. The son of the murderer ran to his side.

John had seemed hesitant, and he glanced over at Matthew and Mrs. Davenport, who were running up. "I'll catch you when you're alone, murderer!" he shouted, and, turning his back to them, he fled the scene.

Fled.

Shaking from the nerves, upset, and pale, Christopher stood there with clenched fists. He couldn't feel the pain from his wounds or the warm blood running down his face. *I am sure of it, captain,* he said to himself in a senseless daze. *I beat them.*

Matthew ran up to him, out of breath. "Chris . . . ?"

Christopher turned toward him, and Matthew took a step back, raising his arms in front of him. "Chris, it's me."

For a few moments he didn't understand who this child was—or where he was—or what he should do next. He then thankfully came back to his senses. "Matt," he said in a soft whisper.

And he collapsed to the ground.

"Mummy!" Matthew shouted, terrified, kneeling at his side. "Chris . . . ?"

"Don't touch him!" screamed Mrs. Davenport.

"I'm fine, Matt," he said, letting out just a whisper. But it was true: he was fine. Better than he had ever been.

The son of the murderer hunched over him. "Hey, thanks. You were tough," he said to him with respect. "I am Robert Barrett. What's your name?"

"Christopher . . . Smith," he replied. Then he closed his eyes and everything went black.

19

I am not in favor of long engagements. They give people the opportunity of finding out each other's character before marriage, which I think is never advisable.
—Oscar Wilde

"Oh, Anna. Now what excuse could you possibly give me for choosing this horrible corset?" Lucy had gone with her to the milliner, and laid out on the large table there were countless dresses, lingerie, and other items not easily identifiable in a specific category. "You don't fancy that little pink thing," she said, pointing to an accessory that was left off to the side in a corner and could have been anything from a powder puff to a brooch to a baby sparrow that fell from a tree and ended up by mistake on this table. "In fact, it's not clear what it's for, is it? Well, it is awfully cute nevertheless, and I believe I will take it for me. However, Anna, for you to choose this lingerie that is so ordinary . . ."

The milliner looked at the two young women, dazed, as if she couldn't quite make sense of the scene in front of her. There were these two girls, weren't there? One was blond and a vision to behold, cheerful and full of excitement and good taste. Perhaps she was the bride-to-be.

No, in fact. That was the other girl, who was dull and sullen next to her, and who, with a grimace, had rejected all of the most beautiful dresses of the entire collection and all of the most interesting items of lingerie, only to opt for cotton and practicality. And yes, Mr. Davenport—who had been so charming when he entered her shop a week earlier that she almost fainted with emotion—had left an account open just for Miss Champion.

Love is definitely an incomprehensible thing, thought Marie as she let out a sigh.

"Pardon me?" asked Lucy.

"No, nothing," she replied. "I will leave you two alone for a bit so that you can decide in quiet. I'll be back shortly."

She left through a door that exited to the rear of the shop. On the street there were carriages passing by every so often, and there were a few people walking on foot, peering inside, but all was quiet in the sun-filled shop. For the moment there was only Lucy and Anna there, much to Anna's relief. The sweet scent of women's perfume hung in the air, mixed with the vague smell of dust and glue.

"You can't tell me that you don't feel the least bit guilty for poor Marie," Lucy whispered. "Without a doubt she will drown her sorrows in the bottle of sherry she keeps hidden in back. Why are you doing this?"

Anna smiled. "I have nothing against her. But do all of these lacy things seem normal to you? Go ahead"—she picked up a pastel pink and white dress left on the table—"look here. No one could figure this out."

"Come now, Anna. You wouldn't put it on every day, of course. Besides, you'll have a personal maid, won't you? She will help you get dressed and . . . Oh, look at this!"

She pulled a soft blue dress out of the pile. It was so poufy that it seemed as if it might float up at any given moment, rising crazily like bread.

"Lucy, put that thing away." She smiled. "I don't need a personal maid, you know. I like to be independent."

"But you cannot be the wife of Mr. Davenport without a personal maid, Anna! Your husband will not agree."

Whatever he wants, of course, thought Anna. Mrs. Davenport? She shuddered at the very thought. There were only ten days to go before the wedding, and she was busy taking care of the work on the house, reopening the rooms, and moving furniture and memories. Her days were filled with running, choosing, and turning. Evening often came without her noticing. The moment she dreaded the most each day was the visit of her fiancé. The children, however, waited anxiously for him, and not only because of the gifts he brought them, she admitted painfully. No, despite his rigid personality and the fact that he practically never smiled, they liked him. To see her family welcome him with something even close to affection caused her pain, and she knew that it was foolish. After all, Christopher was only behaving as she had asked: politely and kindly.

"Do you like this muslin?" Lucy said, calling Anna back to the reality of flouncy laces—*And of material made of madness,* thought Anna as she considered the puzzling items on the table. *But who on God's green earth would have thought to combine these fabrics in this absurd way?*

"Come now, Anna, don't make that face. You'll need elegant clothing: you'll have a much more active social life now."

"I don't see why." She shook her head. "I am sure that Mr. Davenport will get along well enough by himself." It was true: her fiancé continued to participate in nearly every social event, but he never insisted that she go. "Anyway, I'll be there tomorrow night, won't I? I'm so anxious to see Mr. Pembrooke again." *And Matthew Davenport.* She could not pass on the party at Lucy's house for anything in the world. She absolutely needed to find out something that could result in calling off the wedding without risk of retaliation. It was obvious that she could not marry him. Even now, at the thought of him—his

"Good morning, Miss Champion," the only words he had muttered to her that morning—her heart tightened into a knot, along with her stomach. The first week of their engagement had alleviated her fears a little, but they would not go away completely: How could they? This man was so fierce, and, what was perhaps even more distressing, so *tall.* What happened in the grass—those very hard slaps, the immense pain that followed, the humiliation he made her suffer, slow and shocking—defined his character. He had wanted her, so he took her, and although he asserted that this had never happened to him before, Anna was not able to believe him. She had a maddening fear of him. He had taken her then, against every law. What would he do, she wondered obsessively, when he was her husband, with the rights of a husband?

No, she could not marry him. She knew almost nothing about him, except the scarce biographical commentaries that circulated among those in the village, and those didn't clear up any of her doubts whatsoever. Who was he *really*, and what was his past? She did not ask him; she did not want to ask him. She denied him even words and looks.

Lucy began to rummage in a container on the table, full of colorful bits and pieces that gave off colorful, shiny reflections each time they were moved, and she pulled out something that upon closer inspection could actually be a ribbon. *Since when are ribbons supposed to shine like that?* Anna wondered. Without saying a word, she stood there, watching the shiny velvet hanging from her friend's hands like a venomous snake. *So this is what is expected of Mrs. Davenport,* she told herself. *We used to be the queens of the world, do you remember, Lucy?* she thought regretfully. *And now look at me: I am buying clothing with this man's money.*

20

It is not so much our friends' help that helps us as the confident knowledge that they will help us.

—Epicurus

"And so you are guaranteeing me significant earnings, Davenport?"

With a slight shake of his head, Christopher pushed a lock of hair out of his eyes to better see eye to eye with his father. "Certainly, sir," he replied. *The first few times, at least.* "At any rate, you know me, and you know that I myself will invest in this deal."

In the noisy room of the Edwardses' house, people were walking about like ants racing, scrambling to have a dance, a glass, or a sweet from the overflowing buffet table.

"After the fire from a couple of weeks back, I thought trying a new type of investment could benefit me," Leopold mused. "Really a damned shame, that burned field. It must have been that farmer . . ."

"The farmer, you say?"

"Well, yes, starving wretches like that do nothing but revolt."

"Do you think he did it on purpose, then?"

"I don't know, and I don't care. Maybe he simply forgot a fire he had lit. These people don't have a lot of brains, you know. They can only do simple things without understanding why." He snorted, irritated. "In any case, I would have had him arrested if he hadn't run off. Damn it."

Indeed, that was quite a bit of bad luck. By bribing judges, Leopold would have made sure this farmer was put in jail and wouldn't see the light of day again. It was probably Matthew who helped him get away safely, along with his family. His stupid cousin was exactly the kind of person to take things like this to heart. Yes, he had most certainly helped them leave the village and the county—and quickly; perhaps even so quickly that they hadn't the time to say good-bye to their friends and family. The face of the little girl who didn't cry while facing the burning field flashed in Christopher's mind, and he ran his hand over his forehead as if to erase the nagging thought.

"I will find him, you know," Leopold assured him. "He will not have gone far, this son of a bitch. And for that matter . . . All right, Davenport. You've convinced me."

It's done. I've done it. A wave of fierce joy washed over him with the violence of a river overflowing with stones and memories, memories tossed about by the current like broken branches.

His father went on: "After all, the asking price isn't high, and besides"—he gave Christopher a knowing look—"I want to trust you because I like you, Davenport. It seems that you're the only one who enjoys life in this land of the dead. And about last night . . ."

"Last night, sir?"

"Yes." He lowered his voice, smiling at him with all the pleasure of a pig in front of an acorn—and Christopher had the feeling he was the bloody acorn. "You have been extremely prudish after you were with that whore . . . Yes, the redheaded one with the big breasts."

Christopher thought about the girl with the sweet face from the Bridgetown brothel. *She must have been sixteen years old,* he thought. *Seventeen at the most.* "Beatrice," he replied.

"You remember her name!" Leopold exclaimed admiringly. "You are a true romantic. I must confess that from mine, I only remember her beautiful arse." With a satisfied expression on his face, he put his hands on his hips. "It isn't like the London brothels, but it is rather well stocked, wouldn't you say?"

Christopher agreed with a nod of his head. The girl who had gone into the room with DeMercy—pale and thin with long blond hair—was even younger than the one he was with.

"And what did you think, Davenport?" continued Leopold. "Did you enjoy . . . ?"

For Christ's sake. "Of course, sir." He had not even had this girl. He had asked her to say nothing to the others in exchange for a big tip. Beatrice had looked at him without emotion, with her big, clear eyes. They had stayed in the room chatting, and Christopher had asked for some information about the brothel. Once Christopher had finished this vendetta with his father, Madam Amaryllis would have the dubious pleasure of seeing Christopher again, to be taught the lesson she deserved—that was for sure. After about twenty minutes, beyond the minimum time, Christopher left the room, and he had waited for his father outdoors, taking in deep breaths of air until his head cleared under the light of the street lamps.

"Well," said Leopold. "You young people need a guide for the pleasures of life, don't you think?" A shadow passed over his face, and he looked at Daniel, who was quite a distance from them. "When will you go back with me? Oh, pardon me," he added quickly with his typical bloody smile, "you're going to be married, and these things will no longer interest you, I guess. That girl over there, correct?"

He pointed toward Anna, and Christopher turned to look at her. She was talking to Matthew, and she laughed with a look of happiness, moving her hands as if drawing in the air. She was dressed simply in white and beige. The dress was new, and Christopher had paid for it. This thought made him feel stupidly proud, and a pleasant sensation warmed his lower abdomen.

"That's Anna Champion, correct?"

Said aloud by his father, that name seemed almost like blasphemy, and it made Christopher clench his fists. He tried to open them back up. *You know very well who she is,* he thought angrily. *She was engaged to Daniel, don't you remember? And then she jilted him precipitously, telling who knows what story. I raped her, Daddy, and if you knew this, you would like me even more.* "That's correct," he responded, and he looked over at her again. Matthew was shaking his head, and Anna seemed to suddenly lose her coloring, as if their conversation had turned more serious—damned serious. *Matthew, pay careful attention to what you're saying,* he thought uneasily.

***

Anna had intended to get further with her research during the evening, but she had already been talking to Matthew for three and a half minutes without making any progress. Anyone would have been nervous by then, but she was trying to not show how tense she was. Christopher was off in a corner of the room with Leopold DeMercy, and he was watching her like he was a prison guard. Anna knew he was watching her without even turning her head toward him, as if by some strange animal survival instinct. *Drat.* Like always, her heart began to beat madly, although Christopher was more than thirty feet from her—good heavens! *I must hurry before that horrible man joins us.*

"Matthew, I know so little about you," she said, changing the subject abruptly and interrupting him in the middle of a sentence. "Why don't you tell me more?"

Matthew was not fooled, and he smiled. "What would you like to know about my cousin, Anna?"

She blushed and looked down.

"Don't worry," Matthew added politely. "I understand your situation. I'll tell you what I can."

"You must take me for a coward, I know. And I am, don't you see?" She wasn't able to hold back the shaking in her voice, and she hated herself at that moment. My goodness, she was about to cry in front of a stranger: her pride was completely gone. *You have taken so many things from me, Christopher Davenport.* "I truly am a coward, because . . ." she said, bracing herself. "Matthew, I need to ask you something. Your cousin told me . . ." It was difficult for her to think back to what Christopher had said on the grass—because she had too many cruel thoughts overwhelming her, and . . .

She shook her head, trying to get rid of them. "He told me that if I decide not to marry him, or to denounce him, he could take revenge on my family. Is . . . is that possible, do you think?"

Matthew looked down, which was already answer enough. "Yes," he replied without hesitating.

She heard her heart make a dull thud inside her, like the sound of a stone falling. Even that was meaningless. "But then if you know what he is capable of, how can you remain so close to him, Matthew?"

His cheeks turned a shade that is known, in technical terms, as "shame red." "No, you don't understand . . . Anna . . ."

"If I decide to denounce him," she interrupted him, "would you testify against him?"

The shame red changed suddenly to get-me-out-of-here red. "No," he whispered, or maybe he was only moving his lips. He looked up, not sparing himself the sight of her sad eyes. In some way he felt responsible. "Please don't look at me like that. Would you denounce your brother? Would you denounce Lucy Edwards?" Anna didn't respond, and he continued, hesitating. "Don't think that I don't understand your pain, Anna. But I am certain that my cousin . . . isn't . . ." He did not finish the sentence, as if he wasn't able to or couldn't say more. "I understand your concerns," he said. "But I can assure you that he never . . . never. Never, Anna, before. And he will never do it again. I know that my word means nothing to you, and I cannot blame you. But you must believe me, even if you hardly know me. Even if I am the cousin of that"—he grimaced—"gentleman. You must believe me. I would not lie to you about this."

He was convinced he was telling her the truth, and Anna understood that. But he was not there in the grass, he couldn't . . . "How can you be sure?" she asked him softly, thinking back to those moments seared in her heart and in her eyes, which were already getting ready for tears. *Not now, my friends.* "It was an impulsive act, and he can't control himself, as you are well aware—"

"Anna . . ." Matthew interrupted her again, putting his hand up to his forehead, as if he were rearranging his thoughts.

He jumped on me, Matthew! He surprised me in that garden and he jumped on me in a random game of animal instincts! And you come to me and say, "He will never do it again"? But Matthew was so sure—so absurdly sure. Why? "Matthew, you seem to be hesitating. There is something that you're not telling me, I know it."

He was silent and resolute, and his face gave her no hope. He would not betray his cousin; that much Anna understood with agonizing clarity. *I will have to marry him. I will have to marry Christopher.* She held her breath for a long time, until it hurt her. *I must not cry. I must not.* "You have known him for a long time," she whispered, panting tiredly like a baby bird that had fallen out of its nest. "Please tell me what to expect when he becomes my husband."

There was nothing but silence as Matthew took a few breaths and the furrow on his brow became more pronounced. "I have known him forever, that much is true," he finally replied. "And I have seen him in all of the most ridiculous situations. Once I even saw him laugh, if you can believe it. But this is the first time that I've seen him . . . like this." He made a slight nod of his head to his left, where Christopher was still speaking with Leopold. "I don't know how to answer you, Anna. Not even I know." He rubbed his temples with his fingers, as if trying to put together words to make a sentence that was difficult to say. "Listen," he began, "I know that what I'm about to tell you will sound dreadful, but I must say it anyway, even if I'll seem worse than what you already think of me. Anna . . . perhaps with time . . . perhaps you could find good things about him, about Christopher. He's not all bad, believe me. If you could spend some time with him . . ."

Over my dead body. "I could do that," she lied, curling her lips, "but I need to know more, Matthew. You—"

"My, what serious faces," interrupted a voice dear to her—Lucy's—over her shoulder. She was so close it was alarming.

Anna stopped breathing. *It's the first time that I'm not happy to see her,* she realized with a kind of surprised fatigue. Recently, all of these things happening for the first time seemed to her like painful suffering in her soul. She looked at Matthew. *For the time being I will have to settle for this.* She mustered a smile on her face and turned toward her friend. She quickly looked down awkwardly: Lucy was with Daniel.

***

Leopold smiled like a cat sitting on a sofa. "A wife is a necessity. Isn't that so, Davenport? Not always a nuisance, but really quite always a necessity."

Out of the corner of his eye, Christopher saw that Daniel had just been introduced to Matthew and that he gave Anna a cold smile. She responded to it by blushing and giving him a sad, embarrassed look, with her head tilted to one side. Christopher started to clench and unclench his fists, controlling his breath and commanding his heart to slow down its pace, for God's sake.

"Do you agree? Davenport?"

"Absolutely."

"It was really quite smart of you to find a wife so much beneath you. She will always be grateful to you. Poor girls are the most submissive. Isn't that so?"

Definitely, and Anna Champion in particular. He turned his gaze away from her, only to find Leopold staring at him with what seemed to be derision. *He thinks I'm in love with her, as if I were a schoolboy,* he noted, annoyed. *And I'm the one who is to gain his confidence?* "You are right," he recognized. "A docile wife is just what I need. In any case, simply because I am to be married it doesn't make a man stop being a man. Am I right? I will admit that I miss sweet Beatrice already."

"Now you're talking, Davenport," Leopold said, lively and now relieved, with no lingering sign of derision, Christopher noticed. "For a moment I feared that you, too, had started writing poems at sunset, as my son does."

Christopher laughed earnestly without having to force himself. Hearing his half brother be denigrated was enjoyable, damn it. "Really, sir?"

"Oh, yes." Leopold seemed distracted, and then a half smile lit up his face. "Well, Davenport, what do you think about this evening? I adore coming to the Edwardses'. The best liqueurs, the best wine, and the food is first-rate. And besides . . ." He paused with a gleam in his eye as if he had a sweet tooth and he just saw a cake. "Besides, Mrs. Edwards is a very nice woman, don't you think?"

One by one Christopher's hairs stood on end, and his state of shock prevented him from answering. He hoped he wasn't gasping, but if he had fallen into a lake of icy water he would have had an easier time of breathing, that was certain.

"I see that you think like me," laughed DeMercy, amused. "It seems that you and I have a lot of things in common, young man."

A lot of things, you filthy piece of shit. Christopher did not want to ask whether or not his father had had this woman before or after him. *It happened only one time,* he thought, trying to calm the nausea he felt. *One time, and that's all.* He hadn't wanted to see her again after, and even he didn't know why. And Louise hadn't taken his refusal very well, either, and every once in a while she would cast a little insult at him . . . even in public. But for God's sake, for her to tell his father! He hoped at least that she had spared him the details, though from Leopold's sly grin he suspected she hadn't. It's not that there was really that much to know, anyway. He had gone to her estate, as they had arranged, and she was waiting for him in the garden. The lights were on inside the house and the sound of a piano—probably Lucy and her melodious fingers on the keys—echoed out across the night. When Louise had approached him, Christopher had taken her quickly on the pavilion table, lifting her skirt almost without looking at her. He had very desperately wanted to erase the memory of the evening prior, a memory that burned inside him like hellfire—the memory of a stolen kiss from an impudent girl. He hadn't managed very well to rid himself of the memory, he now realized with bleak irony, since in less than a month's time he was going to marry that same impudent girl.

He turned toward her. She had a few locks of hair dangling in front of her rosy and white cheeks, and she was smiling, but her eyes were shy, and something had obviously upset her, since she had become unnaturally stiff. She was speaking with Daniel, and he was looking at her face—no, not her face.

Her lips.

"Pardon me, DeMercy," he said, "I really must ask my fiancée to dance. It's one of those nuisances necessary to keep the family peace. Don't you agree?"

"I suppose so."

Christopher glanced over at Lady Eleanor, Leopold's wife. Sitting in a corner with two other ladies, looking down, and not participating in the conversation, she was instead lost in her own thoughts. *Leopold has certainly not danced with his wife for many years,* Christopher thought. Maybe he had never danced with her.

"Well, then, take me to see your lovely fiancée, Davenport." The hungry glow in Leopold's eyes grew stronger. "I have yet to offer her my congratulations, after all."

***

"My most sincere congratulations on your engagement, Miss Champion."

Only Anna understood the bitter irony of Daniel's words. He looked at her in a seemingly resentful manner with such a strange look in his limpid eyes that was so unlike him. He made her blush intensely when he stared persistently and deliberately at her lips.

She looked down, confused. "Thank you, Mr. DeMercy."

"Anna, do you realize," said Lucy, "in just over a week you can be my *chaperone*?"

"When that happens," Matthew interjected with a cheeky smile, "I do hope you'll leave me alone with your friend, Anna."

Anna had her reasons to be upset with Matthew, and good ones at that. And yet looking at him she discovered much to her surprise that she could not stay angry with him for long, especially with him looking back at her with such incredibly big eyes.

"Make no mistake, I will be very strict," she replied with a sincere smile in spite of herself. "Especially with you. You are a dreadful libertine."

Matthew laughed back smugly as he arrogantly puffed out his chest. "Oh, Anna, you are following our deal perfectly." He turned toward Daniel and Lucy. "You must know that nothing can ensure the success of a young man in society better than a reputation of being a dangerous seducer, and I begged my soon-to-be cousin to spread this rumor."

"So, young women like libertines. Is that it?" asked Daniel. His tone was acceptable, but Anna understood the sarcasm beneath the remark and his desire to hurt her in his wounded look.

Oh, Daniel, I didn't turn you down because of Christopher. She was in agony for having lost his esteem, but not the pride that was eating away at her heart. The worst was seeing his innocence contaminated by all this nastiness, which was so unlike him. *I'm sorry, Daniel, I didn't want this. But love—I didn't know what it was, and I still don't know. Maybe I'll never know.* She looked into his green eyes, darkened with resentment. *But for me, it's not you, Daniel. It's not you.*

"Of course, libertines, Mr. DeMercy," Matthew confirmed. "If they are incredibly charming, like myself, then it's a walk in the park. And, Anna . . ." He gave her a sweet look that seemed to still beg for forgiveness. "Would you like to be the first girl with whom I dance? You will be envied tremendously by all the young ladies present."

"With pleasure," she said. "But I warn you: it will be your first dance of the evening and probably your last. You may not know that I am a very poor dancer. Even the strongest and sturdiest of boots are no match for my cloth slippers once I get to kicking them."

"I can confirm that," laughed Lucy. "But you must also be aware that every one of Anna's kicks is a sign of destiny and should be taken with the right amount of respect and gratitude. Perhaps you don't know the story of Sir Colin and Rosemary Rotherham."

"I'm all ears. Kicks of destiny are, in fact, my favorite subject." Something to his left caught his attention, and he stopped smiling. He said coldly, "Oh, here comes my cousin."

Something inside Anna collapsed, and in its place confusion, fear, and pain rose up. *My God, why can't he let me be?*

Matthew glanced at her and then let out a little sigh. "Ladies and gentlemen," he muttered, "if we begin to talk about the weather and we avoid any interesting topics, perhaps he'll go away."

"I don't think that would work, Mr. Davenport," Daniel said flatly. "You cousin loves to talk about the weather."

Lucy looked at him quickly, both a bit surprised and a bit cautious. Lucy wouldn't forget about the art of good manners, even in bad company. She turned toward Leopold and Christopher with a beaming smile, and the two men smiled back. Matthew was introduced to Mr. DeMercy, and Anna recognized in Matthew this same unchanging look, the unmoving smile. But more so than anyone else, Christopher had that smile. Perhaps he also had another smile—the mocking one that he gave to her unsparingly. Here he was, less than two steps away and every bit as threatening and dangerous, even in a room full of people. It also seemed like he was strutting even more stuffily than usual, if that were possible. *Maybe the wedding will fall through, after all,* she said to herself, sickened. *If he continues to puff himself up like that, he will certainly explode sooner or later.*

"Miss Champion," Leopold said to her, "my most sincere congratulations on your engagement. Mr. Davenport is a rare man." Leopold was enjoying himself. He was doing his very best to make Daniel pay for his little rebellion.

Daniel, however, seemed to not even hear him. He was completely cold and perfectly still; perhaps his mind had left his body for a moment while it went for a stroll.

"Thank you, Mr. DeMercy," replied Anna. *Rare indeed—Christopher is certainly that,* she said to herself. *Maybe unique, but even that is too much to take.*

"You're quite welcome. It's always a pleasure to talk to intelligent girls such as you."

"You're very kind."

"I also wanted to compliment you on the carriage you arrived in this evening. It's new, isn't it, Davenport?"

Why is he saying this? Anna stood there in disbelief. Perhaps she had misunderstood him; certainly he hadn't—

"Really quite splendid, Davenport," Leopold continued. "And very fine horses. There has been much talk about the amount of money you spend on gifts to your fiancée."

Anna felt the blood run from her face. *But what . . . ?* Lucy opened her mouth as if dumbfounded. Matthew had the look on his face of someone who had swallowed a cockroach and felt it crawling inside their throat. Only Daniel seemed unfazed, like an empty husk from which a cruel hand had stolen every emotion.

"Oh, it's nothing, sir," Christopher responded, so satisfied that he seemed even taller, if that were possible.

The music on the dance floor stopped, and the silence that blanketed them seemed deafening.

"One would be hard put to find another generous young man such as he, Miss Champion." As always, Leopold's voice got lower but yet more powerful. As always, all those around him hung on his every word because of his inexplicable charisma, which defied logic or morality. "He's spending a fortune to renovate your house, isn't he? Very few men would do that. Let me say that you have been truly fortunate in the choice of your husband."

Anna hadn't any idea how to respond, and tears of rage filled her eyes. Despite the fact that Leopold was right in front of her and despite the fact that he was actually talking with her, she still could not believe it. She could not believe that he was saying such things, nor that he was going out of his way to mortify her in front of everyone.

And in front of her fiancé.

A fiancé who, supposedly, should defend her.

A fiancé who knew all too well that his debt to her could never be repaid.

A fiancé who smiled at Leopold and replied, "That's exactly what I always say to her as well."

That's exactly what I always say to her . . .

That's exactly . . .

Why were the tears in her eyes getting bigger? Why did they want to roll down her face, despite everything? She knew she couldn't expect anything else. She knew it, damn it. She knew it, and yet she had expected otherwise. She had expected justice at last.

Lucy took a deep breath, and her chest suddenly seemed to swell. Anna knew that she was about to break out in an indignant protest. *Please, Lucy,* she said to herself, closing her eyes. *Don't make my humiliation worse.*

It wasn't Lucy who began to speak.

"You're completely mistaken, Father."

Anna opened her eyes.

"You're completely mistaken, Father," Daniel repeated. "And you are also mistaken, Davenport. It is you who are fortunate, sir."

"Daniel." Anna couldn't help but say his name, and she then fell silent, overwhelmed by the feelings that flooded her chest and drove out the bitterness. She wasn't sure, but perhaps she shed a tear. What she did know was that she felt happy and that she was about to burst. His innocence was not gone; her Daniel had returned.

He smiled gently at her. "Anna, now I truly need that sign of destiny," he said to her, and it seemed they were the only people in the crowded room. "Would you dance with me?"

"With pleasure," she replied with all the emotion that filled her heart and her voice. Daniel took her by the hand and led her to the dance floor without even bothering to look back at the others.

21

The art of living is more like wrestling than dancing.
—Marcus Aurelius

"It seems you won't be dancing with your fiancée, after all."

Leopold always found the amusing side of things. Amusing for him, of course, typically meant someone else was not at all amused. With his eyes full of mockery, he looked at Christopher.

(Laugh with him, Christopher. Win his affection.)

But Christopher didn't even answer him, and not because he couldn't decide what to say or because he suddenly couldn't tolerate him. In fact, he almost didn't hear him. His eyes were fixed on Anna, whose gloved hand was held tightly in Daniel's, and who was crossing the room, passing between people without seeing them.

A young blond man came up to Lucy to reclaim the dance she had promised him. "Certainly, Mr. Roskin," she replied, and she seemed quite relieved at the prospect of parting with them.

Matthew whispered something in Lucy's ear, and she smiled as she walked away. Christopher didn't even notice that as he watched his fiancée enter the dance floor. Anna held her head high, her eyes shining brightly and her cheeks the color of red apples—and she had that same scent, as Christopher knew all too well.

"If you'll excuse me, gentlemen," said Leopold with a smile curved in just a hint of ridicule, "I'm also going to see a lady about a dance she owes me. It seems one of us should be able to manage that, don't you think, Davenport?"

Christopher looked back at him. "Of course," he replied flatly. "See you later, DeMercy."

Leopold walked away. As soon as they were alone, Matthew patted him on the shoulder. "Good work, Chris."

Perfect. Now for his sermon—just what Christopher needed! "Don't be absurd, Matt," he replied, irritated. I couldn't have possibly behaved any differently, and you know it."

Anna was in the middle of the dance floor, facing Daniel. She was not wearing the amber pendant that Christopher had given her a few days before—the one he had chosen personally for her, since he thought it matched the color of her eyes—and her slight cleavage immodestly showed her milky skin.

"Oh, really?" Matthew responded. "To me it seemed you were enjoying seeing Leopold humiliate your fiancée."

The music began. Daniel moved toward Anna, but there seemed to be a certain awkwardness between them, since they could not manage to look each other in the eyes.

"Don't say such rubbish. No one wanted to humiliate her," said Christopher. "In saying that, Leopold wanted to hurt his son, and as far as I'm concerned you know very well that I couldn't criticize him for that."

"Certainly, of course not." Matthew sighed. "Chris, attempting to punish her because she considers you a worthless heap will not improve her opinion of you. You do realize that, don't you?"

Daniel was saying something to Anna, and she was answering with seriousness. Whether because of her emotions or her embarrassment or her constant absentmindedness, which made her bump into chairs and people, Anna stumbled. Daniel caught her before she fell.

(What else would you expect from a bloody fairy-tale prince?)

He held her body in his arms. He was touching her dress, the one that Christopher had purchased. The ring on her finger, the one that Christopher had also purchased, gleamed.

"You're talking rubbish, Matthew," he responded mechanically. "It isn't . . ." All of a sudden he closed his mouth, because what was taking place on the dance floor prevented him from finishing his sentence. Anna had gotten back up after the awkward incident and was readjusting her dress with ostentatious carelessness. She had to recognize that Daniel was trying to remain serious. He truly did try. He turned his head to not look at her. He did not want to laugh, so he bit his lips harder and harder, but to no avail. The corners of his mouth rose up relentlessly. She noticed but, in a dignified way, pretended to cough again and again. And she pressed her hand to her mouth to stifle what was bursting from beneath, trying to escape.

Daniel looked at her. Unfortunately, she looked at him.

And that was the end.

Laughter—free, uncontrollable, illogical in this stuffy room—seized them as if in a trap. It captured and imprisoned them, blinding them with the tears that filled their eyes, deafening them from the shocked remarks of the other dancers, and shook their bodies.

Bombs of joy that left their shrapnel in a man who, just a few yards away, watched them with blood boiling madly in his veins.

(There's no room for you, Christopher.)

With his mind fogged over by his beating heart, Christopher suddenly made for the dance floor. Matthew grabbed his arm and held him back. "Christopher, don't . . ."

Oh sanity, refuge of the strong, where the hell are you when you're needed? Christopher shrugged his arm. "Don't get mixed up in this, Matthew!"

"Do you want to punch Daniel in the middle of the room? That's a brilliant idea, Chris!" He nodded his head enthusiastically and let go of his arm. "Listen to what we'll do: while you are beating him to a pulp, I will go home and pack our luggage. Because after the brawl things will be over for us here, you know this."

Christopher put his hand over his eyes. *Shit! Shit, shit, shit!* He felt his heart beating furiously, and he had to calm down. He had to, damn it. He knew that Anna loved Daniel, right? And it made absolutely no difference to him. And so then, for God's sake, why was he taking this so badly? *Because this is embarrassing me in front of everyone, that's why.* He breathed more calmly. *That's the only reason.*

"Chris, listen," Matthew said, "the only way to improve your situation is to make sure that Anna falls in love with you sooner or later."

"Christ, you sound like a little girl! I don't want her to love me, by God!" *For crying out loud, could this goddamned night get any worse?* "I want her to fear me, and I will succeed all right. Bloody hell, she will be my wife in not even ten days!"

"*If* she marries you, Christopher."

What was his stupid cousin babbling about? "Don't talk nonsense," he replied dryly. "She has no other alternative."

"I would not be so sure if I were you. She has many doubts about this marriage. And, Christopher, perhaps I shouldn't even say this, but since it's you, I must. 'Doubts' is not exactly the word I would use to define her mental state regarding you. 'Total refusal' or 'absolute opposition' or 'determined will to flee' would capture the concept better."

Christopher stared at him tensely. Could he possibly be right? He turned toward Anna, his fiancée. Because she was *his* fiancée, by God! Daniel was whispering something to her, and she was shaking her head sheepishly. She flashed him a smile like a pearl between the pink and red of her mouth. While dancing, her hands touched Daniel's, and their bodies came closer and then moved away, only to move closer once again.

"Listen to me, Chris," Matthew continued, following his gaze, "begin to woo her. Admit that you behaved disgracefully, fall at her feet, and beg her forgiveness. It's the only thing you can do."

Never in a million years. "Or . . ." he replied.

"Or what?"

Or I will find a way to make her more reasonable. This witch hates me? Perfect. She doesn't want me in her bed? Just as well. She isn't even beautiful, and . . .

("You are like paradise," you said to her, Christopher.)

. . . and there were women willing to please him everywhere. Lately his commitments had obligated him to an annoying chastity, but he would get over that soon enough. Tonight or maybe tomorrow. Or the day after, at the latest. For God's sake, it didn't matter. The important thing was that he did not want Anna. He didn't want her; he would never ask to make love to her after the wedding. Unless she wanted him, of course, in which case he would be clearly obliged to satisfy her.

("Unless she wanted him." Ha!)

But, my God, he would no longer allow her to expose him to ridicule. *I'll find a way, you witch.*

"What's going through that head of yours, Christopher?" Matthew's voice sounded very exhausted, as if this continual battle drained his strength. "Isn't what you did to her enough? I'm warning you, I will not allow you to . . ."

"Stop it. I'm not going to do anything." He stared at him innocently, then even gave him a smile. "In fact, I will try to treat her better from now on." *At least, until just after the wedding. I don't want to scare her.*

Matthew seemed more worried than before. It was probably the smile that gave away his intentions. *Yes, I have obviously overdone it,* Christopher thought. Paying no attention to Matthew's whiny voice, he looked over at his fiancée's shining face, lit up with happiness. *Don't fool yourself, Daniel.* Deep inside him, his rage swelled up and then dissipated as he remembered. *You will never see her as beautiful as I have seen her.* The sight of her in the grass came to him. He recalled her very hot cheeks, which glowed even brighter than they did now. Even though they were wet from crying, they burned his mouth when he kissed her. He had licked the sweet flavor mixed with salty tears from her skin, and finally he had kissed her damp, parted lips. She had responded to his kiss and had enjoyed him, her face burning with abandon and pleasure.

Only I have seen her as beautiful as that.

***

"I was unreasonable, Anna," said Daniel hesitantly. The composure he had maintained, even when she had rejected him, was gone. He no longer wanted to hide his pain. Perhaps he was ready to let it go. "You . . . you were being honest with me, but it wasn't easy to accept. I mean, I . . . I, Anna . . ." His voice trailed off. After all, he had said what he needed to.

"Daniel . . ."

"Pardon me. I am not blaming you. But surely," he said laughing, a bit strained, "I am embarrassing you."

It's the least I deserve. "Nothing could embarrass me after my near fall a few moments ago," she said, letting out a smile. She wondered what color her face was turning; it was hard to know if it was more purple or crimson. "And thanks again for the heroic rescue."

Alongside her, Lucy was dancing with a gentleman who Anna barely knew—Roskin, Redskin, something like that—and she wasn't enjoying herself, judging by the dull expression on her face.

"Well, that's what friends are for, right?" Daniel asked.

Anna looked back at him. "And to prevent clumsy girls from falling down on the floor?" she asked with a hint of a giggle returning to her lips. She hoped she would not begin to giggle again. Good heavens, how embarrassing that was earlier. One of those things you would never want to happen to you, and then, when it does happen, it becomes one of the best memories of your life.

Even Daniel chuckled. "To laugh about falling down, if anything."

This changed the smile on her face. Anna was touched now, and she shyly lowered her gaze to hide her emotions. She came to think that affection did not show itself easily, as anger did. Maybe it had something to do with the fear of making yourself vulnerable. "So, we're friends then, Daniel?"

"If you would do me the honor." His voice had the same emotion.

"I will honor you by falling down many more times, then." She laughed and looked up. "If you will do the same."

"Of course," he replied with a playfulness that was hardly audible. "Besides, that will be the only way to remain in your arms."

(That's a pain that stings, isn't it, Anna?)

She looked down again, feeling guilty. *Love is so strange, Daniel. It's strange when you have it and even stranger when you do not.*

He was silent for a while. He looked pensively across the room. "As your friend," he began, seeming oddly serious, "may I point out that your fiancé has a strange way of showing you his affections, Anna? Pardon me, I didn't mean to hurt you," he added quickly. "I swear that I will never ask you why you have decided to marry such a person." He paused. "Why did you decide to marry such a person, Anna?"

"Daniel!" Anna laughed loudly and looked away from him. She didn't respond. She could not think of a possible answer, but sooner or later she would have to find a credible phrase, because everyone continued to ask her the same question. Why are you marrying him? What about him made you fall in love with him? Lucy wasn't too insistent, but even she, although truly happy about the wedding, asked for some information every once in a while. Anna said nothing. She probably offended Lucy with this behavior, but good heavens, what could she say?

She could feel her fiancé's eyes on her, like an incredible weight—a terrifying stone around her neck. For the love of God, why did he have to stare so intensely at her? Perhaps her friendship with Daniel bothered him. No, that was a ridiculous thought. Christopher didn't care about her at all. Wasn't that so? He was marrying her only because of the *incident*.

(Or maybe he loves you, Anna.)

No. No man in love would have . . . no. Anyway, Christopher knew nothing about her engagement with Daniel, which lasted for an entire six hours during a hot morning almost two weeks before. She shook her head to not dwell on what happened in the afternoon later that day, but as always to not dwell on it was impossible.

Oh how she had paid for her refusal to Daniel.

She caught a glimpse of her fiancé, and her legs became weak. There was no saving her now, she thought desperately; within nine days' time she would be his wife, and his eyes still looked as hungry as they did that afternoon.

22

Ask no questions, and you'll be told no lies.
—Charles Dickens

A red and white corner of the card—the ace of diamonds—stuck out from under the cuff of the little boy's sleeve. He and Christopher were seated in the drawing room with a deck of cards in front of them, laid out on a nice little parlor table. The morning light filtered delicately in, giving a soft glow to the redone room.

"Like this, Christopher?" asked Anthony, concentrating. He raised his arms, showing his sleeve.

"Don't be silly, Anthony," he responded sharply. "You would be challenged immediately to a duel. The best way . . ."

Anthony looked behind him and shook his head slightly. Christopher became quiet immediately without turning around, but from the light footsteps that he heard and because of his sixth sense, which had warned him even before Anthony had signaled to him, he knew that Anna was there. He was surprised: she never voluntarily came into a room where he was if it wasn't necessary. It was strange.

Anna walked up to them. This was strange indeed.

Christopher was sitting on a new, quite impressive sofa that was soft, cozy, and blue. He was reluctant to get up to leave, but he had to, unfortunately; if he stayed there, it would be difficult for him to keep his calm, which he needed to do at all costs. After the dance the previous Friday, he had vowed not to frighten this girl *before* the wedding; he would have an entire lifetime *afterward* to do that. He hadn't even invited her to dance, to avoid any temptation to shake her by the shoulders until her hair became all mussed. Keep calm: that was the order of the day. It was such a simple thing, and yet God only knew why Christopher was rather certain that he could not manage it if he were in her presence. The rage of that night still burned in him like lava in his bowels—fiery, thick, and red.

"Miss Champion," he greeted her coldly.

Without responding with her own greeting, Anna looked at the cards on the table. "Anthony, what are you doing with those?" she said pointing, amazed.

"Nothing, Anna." *Not exactly a successful bluff,* thought Christopher. That lie is as obvious on Anthony's face as a chocolate mustache.

"Anthony!" Wide-eyed in disbelief, she wasn't able to utter a word for a few moments. "Is that a card that you have hidden up your sleeve?"

"No."

"Deny, always deny, Anthony," Christopher had told him a few days before.

"Even when there's no possibility whatsoever of being believed, Christopher?" the boy had asked.

"*Especially* then. You have nothing to lose, right?"

Outraged, Anna turned toward Christopher with a look on her face that promised nothing good to come from it. She was stunned and angry—in a word, she was unpleasant, as always. "Mr. Davenport, you're *not* teaching my brother how to cheat!"

"Did you want something, Miss Champion?"

"Mr. Davenport! Do not—"

"For pity's sake, Anna, since when do you feel the need to croak at me so?" he snapped at her before realizing it. *Keep calm? That was child's play.* "Couldn't you keep quiet, like usual?"

She seemed to make an incredible effort to keep from screaming, or maybe from scratching his eyes out. She breathed deeply with her eyes closed, and only after a few moments did she reopen them. The look on her face, which was unusually determined, indicated that it was not cards that she wished to discuss. "Sir, I came here because I need to have a word with you," she said. "Alone."

Why did she want to speak with him alone only three days from the wedding? Christopher suspected that it was not for the pleasure of his company.

"Anthony, can you leave me alone with Mr. Davenport, please?"

Saying nothing, her brother nodded, and as he stood up from the sofa the card slipped out of his sleeve, falling gracefully onto the floor. No one said a word, and Anthony made for the door rather quickly and ran outside without hesitation.

Anna did not sit down, so Christopher stood. She took a few steps and tried to look at him. She seemed unable to, and so she turned her back to him, going to the window.

"I will not talk with you, miss, if you do not face me immediately."

She slowly obeyed, but she continued to avoid looking at him. "Mr. Davenport, I wanted to inform you . . ." she said, pausing. Anna was having trouble speaking, and she looked at a point above his head.

Christopher felt as if he couldn't breathe. "So, what the devil do you want?"

She leaned against the wall and began to wring her hands forcefully. My God, she felt like she was trying to roll them into balls. "You should know . . ." she stammered at last. "Sir, I wanted to inform you . . ."

Something outside had fallen—maybe a ladder or a brick—and the noise filled the room as well as Christopher's mind.

Has she changed her mind? he wondered.

Would she marry DeMercy? What had she said to him? What?

"What?" his voice thundered. "What do you have to say to me, miss?"

Anna gasped, frightened. "Sir, I am not pregnant," she revealed quickly. She dropped her hands down to her sides and regained a semblance of composure. But her face, red as fire, stood out against her white cotton frock in a color contrast as strong as it was striking.

Christopher did not speak for several minutes. He was not certain how he felt. Although perhaps it was too early to say with absolute certainty, it seemed that he would not be a father—not right away, at least. *Father . . . to become a father.* Dear God, it was true: sooner or later it would happen. Sooner or later Anna would ask to become a mother; that was inevitable. This girl who couldn't even look him in the eyes while standing in front of him would be the mother of his children. Sooner or later.

"I thank you for this information," he finally replied. *Look at me. God, look at me, Anna.* "I imagine, however, that I would have noticed it on my own, given a couple of months," he added with gratuitous sarcasm. Of course, that did not help make her want to look up at him.

"I told you for a reason, obviously."

A reason? Something tightened in his stomach. Without knowing why, he already knew. *Keep calm. Keep . . .* "Do enlighten me, then," he blurted out. "I don't have time to waste."

Anna glanced at the playing cards on the table, without mentioning them. "Sir, you had said . . ." Her mouth twisted, and she strained to speak. "You had said that our marriage was necessary because I could be pregnant."

For a moment Christopher did not realize what she was saying. He did not *want* to realize. And yet it was all so clear: it had been from the beginning. This realization came to him like a bucket dropped into a well. *She never stopped hoping.* Inside him the bucket continued to drop deeper and deeper. *She still hopes she won't have to marry me.*

"Now you can withdraw your offer, sir."

Christopher stood motionless, his fists clenching. *Forget Daniel, Anna.* He tried to overlook the dark feelings that began to creep inside him. "What you have said to me changes nothing," he responded curtly. *Could this girl ever be quiet? No, certainly not.*

"Sir, be aware that you will never have any children by me."

The feelings in him grew, and Christopher could no longer control them. They rushed to his brain, preventing him from thinking clearly.

"You'll be free to find a wife . . . keep away!" she screamed, raising her hands in defense; two steps and Christopher was upon her.

He didn't listen to her and grabbed her by the wrists, slamming her back against the wall and pushing against her with her hands pinned back. He stayed as far back as possible from her, at least as far as the length of his outstretched arms, but he felt very clearly the fury that was rushing through his body. Fury—and not only that. Bloody hell!

Although terrified, Anna did not scream. She could not—the house was full of people, and they would have heard it, which would make their engagement seem quite special indeed, wouldn't it? *Isn't that so, you goddamned irritating wicked witch?*

"Let me go immediately!" she hissed, trying to free her wrists. "Someone will come in!"

Her body was giving off a sweet warmth that was soft and cozy. Christopher looked down and squeezed her wrists harder. He was not getting any closer to her; he could not get any closer. But dear God, how much he wanted to push her against the wall, against himself.

"Christopher, let me go!" she said, trying to sound commanding. "I only wanted to give you the possibility . . ."

He looked up and Anna stopped in midsentence, while her eyes grew wider in terror.

(We aren't playing anymore, are we, my dear?)

"Must I make you pregnant in order to marry you?" His voice sounded perfectly calm. "Is this what you're telling me?"

Distraught, Anna shook her head and tried to speak, but nothing came out, not even a sound; just a fearful grimace appeared on her mouth—her mouth as red as a cherry, parted slightly like an apricot opens in half.

Oh damn it. As if shot, Christopher released her wrists and stepped back immediately. A sudden realization came to him, a realization that, although completely new, was indisputable: *I will not be able to keep my promise. I will not be able to.* He yelled this to himself, and he knew it was irrefutable. Bloody hell! He wanted this woman, and there was no getting around that. *I cannot wait long, Anna.* He felt a regret and an urge, an urge that disgraced him, but that was there without a doubt. *I'm sorry, sweetheart.*

He walked away quickly, going to the other side of the room. She rubbed her painful wrists, frightened, as if she were reading his thoughts.

And if she were able to do that, I would say farewell to marrying her. Goddamn it, sometimes his own stupidity surprised even him. He tensely cleared his throat and ran his hand along his sleeve as to shake off an invisible speck of dust. "Be careful when you say certain things, Miss Champion," he said nonchalantly. "It sounds like an invitation."

"N-no . . ."

"Oh come now, don't make that face." He laughed mockingly. "You don't have much of a sense of humor, I see."

"Amuse yourself with whatever women you find who appreciate your charms, if there are any, sir," she replied, disgusted. Now her face was as pale as her dress. "But not with me. I will not allow you to touch me ever again in any way. Is this clear?" She began to rub her wrists without realizing it. "Or I . . . or I will tell . . . I will tell Matthew."

She sounded quite pathetic, and Christopher burst out laughing—not that it was particularly amusing to him.

"Really, this is a horrible threat," he replied. "Doesn't it seem excessively cruel to you?"

He felt the need to hurt and frighten her, without understanding why. He was quite satisfied with the results. Her eyes filled with tears.

"You gave me your w-word, sir."

It was barely a whisper, and it came painfully out of her throat, swollen with fear, and through her lips trembling like butterfly wings. Her words were nothing more than a prayer, begging, surrendering. And that was what Christopher wanted, wasn't it? Still, he felt a frustration, one that seemed terribly like pain. He put his hand to his forehead, bowing his head slightly. "I will keep my word," he said softly, "as long as you do the same, Miss Champion." He knew he had said the right thing because Anna turned white again. "In three days' time we will be married," he continued without inflection, "and I do not want to hear any more talk about this. Is this clear to *you*? Don't push me to do anything that you might not like."

She closed her eyes. She couldn't bear the sight of him, and that was all she could see, after all. To Christopher she seemed nauseated—and perhaps slightly dazed—when she mumbled, "Sir, you *truly* are the worst person that—"

"Oh, don't start with that again, all right? I already told you that I find your voice irritating to no end."

Without another word, he headed for the door.

"Christopher."

He stopped at the door, his back to her. "What is it now?"

"You're not deceiving me, are you, Christopher?"

He put his left hand against the doorjamb and lowered his head. "Don't worry, Miss Champion," he responded sharply. "I will keep my word, as I promised."

He raised his head and left without looking back.

23

A wonderful fact to reflect upon, that every human creature is constituted to be that profound secret and mystery to every other.

—Charles Dickens

Anna took Margaret gently from the settee where she had been placed and brought her to the secretary desk, setting her down next to her diary. The candlelight illuminated the doll's shiny face, giving it an unusual mobility of expression, as if it shared in Anna's state of mind.

Anna dipped her pen in the ink and wrote, *"Tomorrow I'm getting married."*

"The day has come, Maggie."

The doll looked back at her calmly with its clear eyes, and it remained resolutely silent and motionless. Anna didn't expect anything else for that matter. She touched the doll's face with the stylus, brushing a blond ringlet to the side. She felt much less lonely in the dark of night with the doll as her confidant. And yet she had hated her the day she saw her for the first time. Damn it, she had thought when Grace had forgotten the doll and left it in a corner as she went back to her beloved drawings and colors. Anna had taken it and gone quickly into the kitchen. She had put the toy—an unworthy semblance of the human shape and ridiculously helpless—on the rubbish bins and decided to bury her among the old peelings and spoiled food. Anna had held the doll upside down; Margaret's little hat had fallen in the waste, standing out like a red spot in this stinking filth, and her blind eyes looked at the garbage. The blond curls were stretched down, disheveled and shiny. A doll. It was just a doll with flushed cheeks and vulgar clothing that someone had made to sell the doll more easily.

"Who did this to you, Margaret?" Anna had asked her.

She felt a sudden but familiar pain rise in her throat. She had picked up the hat and shaken it to knock the waste off it, and she had put it gently back on her head.

You are a victim, my little Maggie.

She had taken her to her room, and ever since she had become her confidant during the sleepless nights.

"Today is the last night that we spend here," Anna now murmured. "Tomorrow we are moving into a new room."

Her new room was waiting for her on the other side of the house, the reopened side. The whole house had been updated, except her father's room downstairs—so as not to disturb him—and her own. Anna had wanted her room to stay just like it was until the moment she would have to leave it, on the following day. Now, however, her room would suffer the same fate of the other rooms: it would be furnished in a delicate and cheerful style and shine like a ring sticking out of the sand.

She looked at the worn, inexpensive furniture among which she had grown up. The dark, imposing chest that had frightened her so much as a child was now closed and empty. Although now scared, Anna felt her heart sink. The old sofa was worn and broken-down, and the mattress was soft. And—up until just a few weeks before—the four-poster bed had allowed Anna to close the light bed curtains and dream she was sleeping on a cloud, pretending to be the little girl everyone said she no longer was.

She wrote, *"Every piece of furniture is a part of me that I leave tonight."*

"You'll like the new room—you'll see, Maggie. It's more suitable for you than me."

The room had been decorated in delicate pastel shades. Lucy had chosen them, and Anna had not objected to the sweet decorations on the walls, nor to the big, fluffy bed, nor the elegant and ostentatious settee. She would have preferred something simple, more like what was in her room as a little girl, but she kept that to herself. Christopher would have been indignant about furnishings that were too poor, and if everything needed to shine to make him happy, that's the way it would have to be. And besides, she thought bitterly, what type of decor could soothe the terror brought on by the door to the adjoining room, which was her future husband's?

She did not know what she had hoped for in her own marriage, but it was not this, and Christopher was certainly not the man whom she had imagined marrying. It made her feel bad that the children liked him so. How was that possible? They should have been frightened by him, like they were by the bogeyman hidden in the old armoire at the end of the hallway. *No, that armoire is no longer there,* she remembered suddenly. *It was given away, together with its dreadful occupant, and now it is scaring other children in another house.*

And the bogeyman who would be her husband would live with her and her family, starting the day after. Anna looked at her wrists where the purple bruises still showed on her pale skin. She flipped through the pages of her diary and found the options mentioned before.

"Kill Christopher Davenport," she read.

***

Across the county, in his room lit poorly by a lamp still burning, Christopher could not sleep. He got up from his bed and went to the papers spread on the table, full of calculations and arrows. It would still take him a month, perhaps two, to carry out his plan.

Tomorrow he was getting married.

Once his vendetta was over—when torturing Daniel would become pointless—what would he do with this silly girl whom he had taken as his wife? He expected bitter regrets, he knew that, but reconsidering it now was useless: he had dishonored her, and the wedding was unavoidable. Anna as well had no choice: she would say her vows the next day. She would not refuse to marry him; she would not change her mind at the last moment. Christopher repeated again and again all the reasons why such a possibility was inconceivable, illogical, and senseless.

What a pity he was dealing with a girl who was inconceivable, illogical, and senseless.

A phrase echoed in his mind, a phrase that no one would have thought to say in the situation in which, absurdly, it was said.

Go to hell, Mr. Davenport.

24

Marriage is like life in this—that it is a field of battle, and not a bed of roses.

—Robert Louis Stevenson

Never before had a couple with such dark circles under their eyes come to church to be wed as on the following day. That overcast morning—it looked like it might rain—a small crowd gathered to attend the wedding of Christopher Davenport and Anna Champion.

"Dearly beloved," boomed Reverend Graham's voice in the nave of the church, "we are gathered in the sight of God, and in the face of this company, to join together this man and this woman in holy matrimony . . ."

Anna looked straight ahead at the elderly reverend without allowing her eyes to look to her right, where her fiancé stood proud and silent in his dark, solemn suit. With great difficulty her father had walked her down the aisle, and she herself had felt her legs nearly give way while Grace—in her new pink dress full of lace, which gave her the look of a cloud at sunset—walked in front of her, dropping rose petals with the precision and grace of an artist. Anna had not looked up at the man who was waiting for her at the altar; she wasn't able to, and it wouldn't have been wise, for she would have run away immediately. She had thought she would not be able to finish walking the last three feet that separated her from Christopher, but since she had done it in the past—in a desperate moment—she would not allow herself to be weak, and so she stood up straight and tall, walking proudly.

The reverend continued to speak in the obligatory pompous manner: "No one should enter into marriage unadvisedly or lightly, or to satisfy only carnal appetites . . ."

Lucy's presence near her failed to cheer her up, but it still gave her a smile: her friend had spent a good hour arranging and rearranging her hair and making her up a bit. She had wanted to put on a bit of blush—fortunately very lightly—to hide the dark circles from the sleepless night before. Anna had not said no, because being pampered by Lucy had a calming effect on her nerves. Her friend talked to her of gossip and trivia to help her get over her anxiety, and although behind her absent smile Anna didn't hear a single word, she felt some relief. At least one person in the house wasn't mentioning Christopher Davenport to her.

"Marriage is intended for their mutual joy and for the help and comfort given one another, in good times and in bad . . ."

(Run away, Anna.)

She could not run. She could not, because if she had turned around, she would have seen her whole family in front of her. She would have seen her father, who made her worry because of the happiness he showed on seeing her marrying such a reliable and level-headed man as Christopher Davenport. She would see Anthony, elegant in his new suit, who was motionless and frowning as he upheld the burden of being her eldest brother. She would see Dennis, who wriggled around restlessly in the pew, bothering those around him and trying to get Grace to join him in his mutiny. Dennis had little chance of succeeding; the little girl was undoubtedly staring wide-eyed at her big sister who was getting married while she imagined different worlds and new fairy tales. Nora had definitely already cried in her handkerchief. She disapproved of the marriage, but Anna had been able to bring her around to the idea a bit, thanks to the kind appearance of the man at her side.

"However, if any person can show just cause why these two people may not be joined together in marriage, let him speak now or forever hold his peace."

She felt Christopher at her side, calm and determined. That man never seemed to have a doubt or a hesitation.

And Anna didn't know what to do.

With horror, she realized that the moment had come. The reverend was about to question them. *Oh God, I do not know! I do not know what to do!*

"Do you take this woman to be your lawfully wedded wife . . ."

Lawfully wedded wife. Anna heard the words as if far-off, like words repeated in a muddled echo.

". . . to live together in God's ordinance in the holy state of matrimony? Will you love her, comfort her, honor her, and keep her, in sickness and in health . . ."

Love her, honor her . . .

". . . and, forsaking all others, keep yourself only unto her, until death do you part?"

Anna's heart didn't even have the time to stop beating.

"I do," said Christopher.

***

It was almost over, he thought. A tiny little word from the hen next to him and it was over. One little word.

"Will you take this man to be your lawfully wedded husband, to live together in God's ordinance in the holy state of matrimony?" Next to him, Anna was so silent that she probably wasn't even breathing. "Will you obey him and serve him, love him, honor him, and keep him in sickness and in health and, forsaking all others, keep yourself only to him until death do you part?"

Christopher kept his gaze straight ahead. He did not look at the girl on his left. He was not anxious, and he certainly didn't have any fear at all.

A second went by with no response.

The absolute silence seemed to collapse the walls of the church. Christopher felt them close in on him like the lid of a coffin. He did not move, did not even blink. But in that place he had no air. Someone would have to throw open the door and soon; otherwise, they would all suffocate.

Two seconds of silence.

Then three.

Christopher kept his eyes on the worn and saggy face of the reverend, who gave a baffled smile—a smile that seemed to tear at his dry, unwell skin. Someone coughed awkwardly, and off to one side there was a nasty chuckle. There was a swarming crowd of people behind him—a hundred, a thousand, a million people—and he felt them moving, breathing, huddling against each other like worms in a box.

Four seconds, and not a sound came from his fiancée's mouth.

Christopher definitely needed to loosen the knot of his cravat: it was too tight and starched, and it was choking him. But he did not raise his arm or put his hand up to his throat; he stayed perfectly still, suffocating in silence.

"I do."

The answer echoed in the large, brightly lit church. The voice of his fiancée—*my wife*—was fresh and sweet as it trickled over him like the happy skipping of a stream in spring.

The reverend smiled, relieved. "Who gives this woman in marriage to this man?"

James Champion stepped forward, and Christopher looked at him. His father-in-law was leaving his daughter in his hands.

Finally.

He took her by the right hand and realized that it was shaking uncontrollably. He loosened his grip, his touch gentle. *Oh my dear. Her hand was icy cold.* Christopher looked upon her; she was pale and tired, with a simple hairstyle and a modest dress lacking almost completely in lace. She wore no jewelry, as if it were any other day, but this was the day she became a wife. His wife.

Repeating after the reverend, Christopher began to say his vows with a strange urgency, as if the girl next to him—who still hadn't looked at him since she entered the church—might turn and run away, or vanish in a flash of light and a puff of smoke.

"I, Christopher, take you, Anna, as my lawfully wedded wife." She lowered her head, avoiding his eyes, even while she was marrying him. "To have and to hold, for better or for worse, for richer or poorer, in good health and sickness, to love and to keep dearly, until death do we part, according to the holy laws of God." He barely squeezed her hand, and her shoulders jolted. "And thereto I pledge my faith to you."

He released her hand and waited.

***

How many times will you ask me to say yes? Isn't it enough that I am here, with everything else that I have done? She had to give her consent over and over, just as she had done a minute ago, when her mind had gone completely blank. The terror of saying yes was equal to that of saying no; she didn't know what to say, and in the void the words that had just been said by her fiancé were still lingering: *I do.*

Hoping that her shaking was over, she reached out and took the hand of the man at her side. "I, Anna, take you, Christopher, as my lawfully wedded husband." Her voice was not her own, but it seemed like it, and yes, it did come from her mouth, but it was not her voice. "To have and to hold, in good times and in bad, for richer or poorer, in good health and sickness, to love and keep dearly and to obey." *Is this man smiling? Probably. He has already asked for my obedience, and he has been satisfied with that, as always.* "Un-until death do us part, according to the holy laws of God." She closed her eyes. "And thereto I pledge my faith to you."

She let go of his hand and opened her eyes.

The reverend gave Christopher the ring, and the wedding band shined a little bit in his palm.

A tiny little circle of gold.

Christopher took her hand, but she was unable to open her half-closed fist, so he grabbed the tip of her ring finger and gently managed to extend it. Then, touching the skin slowly, he slipped the wedding band on it. His fingers were steady as he said, "With this ring I thee wed. With my body I honor you."

Her hand dropped heavily down to her side. The ring was burning her, attached to an invisible weight that pulled her down. And yet the ring was so small and harmless.

The reverend took them by their right hands and joined them. "That which God has united let no man put asunder."

It was almost over—or had it not yet begun? Dazed, Anna heard the sentence "I now pronounce you man and wife."

Confusion clouded her mind and took over her legs, her muscles, and her heart. She was now Mrs. Davenport. She was no longer who she was yesterday, nor this morning, and not even the person she was a minute ago.

"You may now kiss the bride."

No! No! She took a big gulp of air but couldn't raise her head. She felt Christopher's fingers under her chin.

No!

He lifted her face with an almost shy, unusual gentleness. Anna looked at him for the first time in the entire ceremony—and her legs went weak and her heart leaped into her chest and then sank to her bowels with a drop that gave her belly a cramp.

No!

Her husband leaned toward her. Fear took away her sense of reason, and Anna turned to the side, avoiding him—and allowing him only to kiss a corner of her mouth. He stopped an inch from her lips and then, with his gentle but relentless hand, he straightened her face. He put his lips to hers, covering them for a moment, and their marriage was then sealed with a kiss.

25

Find no joy in promises, and no fear in threats.
—Proverb

All right, her husband was dreadful. All right, he wasn't at all what she would have chosen voluntarily. But . . . but if it stopped raining after a terrible storm, you would appreciate it, wouldn't you? And besides, to be honest Anna felt almost calm—a little reluctantly, because it didn't seem fair, but calm. Damn it, it wasn't a crime. Why should she ever need to whine? Her concerns were lessening for the first time after a month of fear. A week had gone by since the wedding, and Christopher hadn't attempted to come near at all—although when she went to bed, she locked the door between their rooms and wedged a chair against it—and treated her in a cold, unfriendly manner. He behaved within the expectations of formal courtesy, however, for the benefit of whoever was there with them—and there was always someone present—which, at any rate, did not prevent his presence from seeming pervasive, even from a distance. Even at a distance she seemed to be able to smell his scent of freshly cut grass and cinnamon. And also, more recently, of cacao, because he was mad for Nora's biscuits. The cook hid them from him, but somehow Christopher always managed to bribe someone. Anna was sure that he was corrupting her brothers, returning the favor with toys, little trips, and money.

She sighed. What a wonderful teacher he was, her husband. She saw little of him, because she avoided him, but also because he was away from the house most of the time, returning only for the main meals. One day he was in London, and they didn't see each other at all.

On a couple of occasions she had heard him come back late at night. *Maybe he has a lover,* she now thought. *Who knows who it is. I hope it's not still Mrs. Edwards.* She turned her head to take a quick look out of the kitchen window. The hot sun of the latter half of August warmed the countryside. After finishing their lessons with their new tutors, Dennis and Anthony went to the stables with Philip, the valet who also took care of the horses, and Lewis, the one-eyed coachman. Her father was resting—*He almost never leaves his room anymore,* she thought with a pang in her heart—while Victoria, the old maid hired at Christopher's request, was in bed with a cold and being cared for by Nora with her concoctions. Even little Grace was with her, since she took her role of physician's assistant very seriously.

Anna was in the kitchen washing the dishes from lunch while humming a farmer's song out of tune. She hummed because she never happened to be alone for a few hours during the day, and being able to concentrate on her own thoughts almost seemed like a party. *Who could Lucy have for a fiancé?* she wondered, thinking it over. She washed a dish and set it on its side to dry. *Daniel?* Lucy was not interested in him, and it was probably better that way, seeing that the young man still seemed to harbor affection for Anna. *Affection, not love maybe.* Perhaps it was never love, she thought. *In fact that kiss that he had given her . . .* She set another plate to dry. *If not Daniel, Matthew?* She had little to do with him anymore, but the more she knew him, the more she liked him. Lucy felt the same way. *It seems it often goes that way . . .*

"Anna, what the hell are you doing?" her husband's voice asked from behind her. His voice was abrupt, as it always was when they were alone. Alone. Something that hadn't happened for about a week, and that would never need to happen now, obviously, or ever again.

Anna froze with her hands in the dishwater and immediately stopped humming. For a moment panic prevented her from thinking; her blood rushed so quickly that she was stunned and had to lean against the edge of the cabinet to hold herself up. *What is he doing here at this time of day?* She grabbed a towel to her side and slowly wiped her hands.

Calm. Pretend to be calm. Don't be afraid.

She turned toward him.

(Don't upset him, Anna. Everything will be fine. Someone will come soon.)

"I'm washing dishes, sir," she replied.

She was caught in the act, and even if she had wanted to—and she did want to, damn it—she couldn't say anything else.

He did not like these words at all. Standing in the kitchen doorway, he looked at her as if he were mad. "That's not your duty, and you are well aware of it," he responded, annoyed. "What's gotten into you?"

Irritation soon replaced her fear, as no one was able to release an entire range of negative emotions in her like her husband. Anna puffed out her cheeks and then pushed the air out of her mouth before she could stop herself. *My God, how pedantic he is!* "It's only for today," she explained, trying to hide the annoyance in her voice. "Victoria is not well, and—"

"The staff in this house is totally inadequate," he said, interrupting. "You have employed people who are all sick, incapable, and definitely unfit to manage a household. If you do not want to let her go, you will still need to hire another domestic—one able to perform her duties."

"And where would we put them, sir?" She called him "sir," and she knew she should not. Christopher had told her to call him by his first name after the wedding while the carriage was bringing them back home. (And those ten minutes in his company, in that very confined space, had taken all the air and the color from her. Fortunately, that was all he had said, and afterward he became silent.) In public she did call him by his first name. (Had this ever happened, she now wondered? Perhaps not. She hadn't even talked to him, in fact.) In private, however, the situation was different. Wasn't that so . . . *sir*? "We have filled up almost every spare room just with the staff required for the carriage, and—"

"Don't talk such nonsense; there's still space. You have carte blanche—you do know that—and if you can't be bothered to find more help, I will. This isn't the first time I've done it, and I do not want to see you doing things you should not be—dusting, sweeping, polishing the silverware." Irritated, he walked into the room and stood a few feet away from her. "This all has to stop, Anna. My wife *must not* perform domestic chores. You do realize what this would look like if I arrived here with some guest?"

Anna forced herself not to take a step back—partly because she wanted to show she was brave, and partly because the kitchen cabinet would not allow her to go anywhere. "Oh, what a scandalous sight I agree, sir," she said, unable to contain her sarcasm. *To hell with him and his empty pretentiousness.* "And with that sensitive disposition that you have, I just don't know how you would manage to survive the shame."

Christopher frowned, and for a moment Anna feared she had gone too far. However, she realized that his face *seemed* angry, and he *seemed* annoyed . . . but . . . but was he really? She couldn't help but wonder. She had seen Christopher enraged several times, but now he seemed to be acting. But why?

"You need to hire another maid, Anna," he said. "And a cook to replace Nora."

Perhaps she had misunderstood him. "What did you say?" she asked, dumbfounded.

"Nora will remain as your companion, obviously," he clarified quickly, "but she can't possibly cook and then sit down at table with us."

Anna closed her mouth and considered it. Nora was elderly, and indeed it was time for her to rest, and maybe her husband would be satisfied with this one concession, forgetting about his other senseless demands. "I will try to talk to her, sir."

"Good. But you need a personal maid and a nanny."

"Absolutely not! There are already too many of us in this house." She hoped he understood from the look on her face that the one too many was, more specifically, him. "You keep your valet, but I have no need for a personal maid. As for my siblings, I look after them myself, as you know."

"Must you always be so unreasonable, Anna?" said Christopher, running a hand through his hair. "We could—"

"I have agreed to everything, sir!" she blurted. "You asked me to let you manage the accounting of the house. You asked me to accompany you on your evenings out in society—"

"Which you have never done, however, inventing a thousand excuses every time."

"You've asked me to be accommodating and many more absurd things. You must leave a bit of room to breathe now!" she exploded, exasperated. She turned away from him and grabbed the dish she had left to dry. "Now will you please let me finish, because I have other things to do today. Don't you?" she asked him bitterly. "Soon I have to go out on a visit—don't you remember? The social calls that you force me to make in the neighborhood, sir."

She grabbed the towel and wiped the plate, trying to ignore the itching feeling on her neck; her husband was staring at her, and she felt it, making her as tense as a violin string.

Good heavens, but why doesn't he go away?

She pretended to not care and raised her arm to place the dry plate on a shelf, getting on her tiptoes. She heard her husband approach, and the plate nearly slipped from her hand.

"Let me help you," he murmured. *What was that in his voice? Tenderness? My God.* His tone had no hint of the arrogance from a moment before, and she was paralyzed with her arm raised as she stopped breathing. *No, please, no!*

Behind her, Christopher raised his hand to take the plate, barely touching her fingers, and then put the plate away slowly.

Anna quickly lowered her arm. Why was her heart making so much noise as it shook with fright like an earthquake?

"Thank you," she mumbled without turning around.

Her husband did not respond but stood behind her, far too close. Anna went to step to the side, but he put his hand on her right hip.

Her worst fear. She turned suddenly. "Sir, do not touch me!"

But what the devil was in his eyes? Was it misery that burned there? Why? She fell silent, feeling her face begin to flush. She moved again to step away, but his hands held on to her firmly. He was not wearing gloves, and she felt the warmth from his light touch on her skin, even through her light clothing.

Someone will come, someone. Soon. God help me. Anna put her palms on his forearms, pushing on them to move them. "Sir, let me go! Don't . . . !" Her voice trailed off. Where was his arrogance? Why was his mouth bent like that? She couldn't manage to look away. She felt lost, and she didn't know why: was this the monster who terrified her? She stood still while she felt a surprising emotion deep inside her.

"Anna," he murmured, pushing her against the cabinet, leaning on her body. She still did not move. She felt him close—he was on her, dear God!—and still she did not move. She was frozen, even in her mind, her thoughts scattered everywhere. Christopher raised his hand and placed it on her cheek; it was warm and dry. And again her belly relaxed, as if she were crying.

"S-sir . . ." she stuttered.

"Anna," he repeated softly, tilting his head toward her face, "won't you give a kiss to your husband?"

Their mouths were very close. Her heart . . . Where had her heart gone? That damned thing was in her throat, thumping so loud inside it hurt her. "Let me go, sir," she muttered. And still she stared at him, at his eyes, and still wondered, *Is this the monster who has swallowed me whole?*

"Please, Anna."

Please.

She was so stunned she couldn't move. He stroked her cheek with his thumb. His lips were within a finger's length of hers. His breath was already inside her.

Why am I not pushing this man away? She blinked once, then twice, then again and again. And then again, until she remembered. The grass. The library. Even the kiss he had given her on their wedding day.

(He never listened to what pleased *you*, did he, Anna?)

She turned her face to the side, darkened with grief and hatred. "Let me go," she ordered coldly. She was no longer afraid. She knew that he would not force her: for once it was written in his eyes, sincere and implicit in his request to kiss him.

Christopher let out a soft moan and dropped his forehead to touch her cheek. His breathing still touched her skin, and his warmth continued to blend with hers. He stood there for a few moments while cheerful noises of nature at play came in through the open window. Then he put his hands down, raised his head, stood up straight, and took a step back.

That was it, his metamorphosis.

Here again was her husband, changed back into the same man as before, with the same hard, cruel expression on his face, arrogant and distant.

Anna walked quickly toward the door, stiff and without looking at him again.

"Anna."

She stopped in the doorway and turned toward him. He showed no sign of emotion.

"I will not wait forever," he informed her matter-of-factly. "This must be clear to you."

Here was the monster. Anna stepped back and then ran from the kitchen with her heart pounding in her chest violently, making her almost blind with fear.

***

Shaking, his hand penned his signature on the document: *"James Champion."*

"Good," said Christopher, "now you have nothing left to worry about."

His father-in-law nodded without answering, exhausted from fatigue. In the room of the Champion house that Christopher used as an office, the afternoon heat was stifling.

"Gentlemen, are we done here?"

"Of course, Mr. Davenport," responded one of the two lawyers called for the matter, a gentleman who was short and round, with bulging eyes like a bullfrog's.

"Good. I'll see you out, then. Mr. Champion, I'll call Nora. She will help you back to your room."

"Thank you, son."

When time has finished its work, thought Christopher, *all that's left for men to do is watch things fade.* Despite his continual medical visits, his father-in-law's condition was getting worse day by day. Sometimes he didn't even remember his own birthdate. *Ah, time . . . what a son of a bitch.*

"Gentlemen, if you'll follow me," he said to the two lawyers. Guiding them, he walked toward the front door, and when he opened the door to have them exit, there stood his wife. To be honest, it was a slight problem—"problem," otherwise known as an "unforeseen event." *Damn it, I didn't need this.* He tried to hide his bad luck. "Back so soon?" he asked her coldly.

Anna looked at the two men with him rather surprised. "Yes," she replied. She seemed to be waiting to be introduced.

Prepare yourself for quite a long wait, then. Christopher quickly saw out his two guests, then, without another word, walked toward his study, meeting Nora and Mr. Champion in the hallway.

Another slight problem.

"Dad," he heard Anna exclaim, "why are you on your feet?"

"Ask your husband," said Nora bitterly, as eager as always to call negative attention to Christopher. "He has tired him out."

"Who, Christopher?" said Anna, surprised. "Christopher!" she called out.

He quickened his pace and returned to his office, closing the door behind him. He was only temporarily saved, because a moment later Anna opened the door forcefully. "Why did you need my father, sir?" she accused him from the doorway.

Christopher walked to the bottle of whisky he kept on a small table near the window, turning his back to her.

"Sir, who were those people you brought here? Usually you take care of your business affairs at Rockfield."

He slowly opened the bottle of liquor.

"Mr. Davenport, I demand an answer."

Christopher carefully poured a finger of whisky in a glass, then picked it up and walked to the desk. He didn't sit behind it, however, but merely leaned on it, facing his wife.

"I am not leaving until you answer me, sir."

He took a sip from the glass. Anna still wore a hat on her head and she was carrying a parasol. She brandished it in a rather disturbing way indeed. He sighed, for soon she would begin screaming like a madwoman. "Your father is not well," he finally responded.

She was silent, and pain flashed on her face like the shadow of an enemy's hand. Then she murmured, "What do those people have to do with that?"

"Those people are lawyers," he explained. Would it be better to take the long route to explain it or say it quickly? It would be better to not say it at all, but . . . "Your father has appointed me as guardian of your brothers and sister and of all his possessions."

That doesn't sound so bad after all, does it? Perhaps I am worried for nothing. Anna might take it fine. Pretty well, at least. In actuality she took it very badly: she seemed to lose both her color and her voice. She just stood there gasping for air like a fish in a meadow.

Bloody hell. Christopher raised his hands up to halt the impending explosion. "And it's the best solution, Anna," he said calmly. "Your father cannot continue—"

"You?!" she screamed, beside herself, taking a step toward him and pointing her finger at him in a rather melodramatic way. "You?! Their guardian? You are mad! You! You will never be—"

"I already am. As of today," he replied dryly, abandoning his gentle tone. "You have no say in the matter."

"I have no say? I am their sister, and I know what is good for them! And it certainly is not you!"

Ah, no? "Ah, no? That's odd, because I have a sheet of paper that certifies precisely the contrary."

The irritation was mounting inside of him. He attempted to calm down. He could try to argue logically with her, rather than humiliate her and make her cry. He thought about it. *Logic and Anna Champion: no, impossible.* He decided to try, anyway.

"Come now, Anna, this changes nothing for you and your loved ones," he began. "I am the best person to handle the affairs of your family. And as far your siblings are concerned, you can continue to see to their education—perhaps with less leniency, but—"

"Are you advising me on how to educate the children?" If he had given her advice on how to cut them into pieces and cook them, she may have taken it better, he was certain of that. "Did I hear correctly? You!" The anger seemed to make her taller. "I wouldn't trust you with the education of an earthworm!"

Christopher slammed his glass on the table, and liquor spilled everywhere. He jumped to his feet, filled with rage and more—something else, similar to a fever, that was getting damned tiring.

Anna gasped, and fear flashed in her eyes, but the outrage was too much, and she went on, beside herself: "You are a violent person with no morals! I am their older sister, and I will not allow them to remain under your guardianship!"

He took a deep breath before speaking, putting a hand on his forehead. After a couple of seconds he regained his self-control and replied, "You are their sister, that's quite true, but first of all, you are a woman, and it is assumed that you should behave as such. Keep in mind what your position entails—embroidering and chatting with friends—but leave the serious things to men. You know very well that you could not provide—"

She wasn't listening, her cheeks streaked red with anger. "I will stop you!" she interrupted him. "You do not . . . I will move immediately to . . . I will speak with my father right away!"

"Oh, good," he replied, nodding with exaggerated enthusiasm. "Why don't we go there right now, then? I can't wait to hear what you have to say to him. Maybe you could scream it at him, hmm, Anna? Or explain to him *why* you don't want me to be the guardian of your siblings. Or would you prefer that I explain it to him myself?"

She raised the parasol, pointing it at him like a rifle. She still had rage in her eyes, but the hope was already gone. *Ah, what a silly little girl, his wife.* "You! You did this all behind my back; you did it on purpose!" she accused him. "How did you manage to convince my father? How did you convince him to say nothing to me?"

I have my ways, Anna. Christopher didn't respond.

"Why did you do it?" she asked him again. "Do you believe you can control me better this way?"

I don't "believe." I "know" it, dear Anna. "Oh, so that's what you are afraid of, then?" He took a sip of whisky and slowly swallowed it. "You think that I did it to . . . *control* . . . you?"

Anna's face twitched. "You are a disgusting, vile creature. You have no shame!"

This girl knew exactly how to bring out the worst in him, thought Christopher. And considering that even the best in him was not particularly good, the situation was serious. "Anna, control yourself. They will hear you," he said, maintaining his calm, but only by making an effort, because he already felt the strong need to yell. "Or come in the room and close the door." He took a few steps toward her, then stopped. It would hardly be wise to go any closer, for sure. "You say you are in a position to protect those children, and yet you lack the courage to dare stay in a room alone with your husband."

"Husband!" She lowered her voice, and her eyes flashed with hatred. "You know that I would have loved to kill you instead of marry you, but I can always take care of that!"

(It's nothing, Christopher. Your heart is breaking a bit, but it's nothing.)

"You'll stop now, Anna, or as true as that is, by God . . ." He clenched his fists and stopped himself, making an immense effort to not rush up to her. And shake her. Forcefully. "You must become more sensible than you are now if you do not want to suffer the consequences of your attitude. You have asked me for time to get used to me, and I am giving it to you—you must recognize that. I can put up with your lack of discipline with the patience of a saint, but I'm warning you, it will not last forever. You must not forget that you are my wife, and you will begin to act like it sooner or later. You have duties toward me, and you know it."

How red with fire her cheeks became when she got angry! And her furious eyes finally looked up at him. "Me? Toward you? Oh no, Christopher, *you* have a moral duty to disappear off the face of the earth—and quickly!"

(It's nothing. Nothing. Breathe.)

He began to feel himself getting dangerously hot. His heart beat faster, and his blood ran madly through his veins. What was worse was that he began to see everything in shades of red, and then he clearly understood the danger. He understood that he was about to lose control. He understood that he was going to hurt her. "For your own good, Anna," he said slowly in a very low voice, drawing out every syllable, "go away now. And quickly."

There was pain and panic in her face, tears in her eyes. Anna bit her lip. She certainly could not mistake his fury, so she backed away until she disappeared from sight. The footsteps of her frightened escape echoed down the hallway.

Christopher went to the office door and slammed it with such violence that the walls seemed to shake. He stood with one hand over his eyes, listening to the absurd sound of his heart beating.

That did not go so badly, he said to himself after several minutes as reason dissolved the darkness of his mind and of his senses. *She only threatened to kill me a couple of times, after all.*

26

There are strings in the human heart that had better not be vibrated.

—Charles Dickens

"Very well, Davenport," Leopold said to him, his smile like a stake through his heart, "we can go see that land if you would like."

"Gladly, DeMercy. I'm buying it from you at a good price." *And I'll get it all back—be sure of that.*

Leopold walked around the desk and tapped him on the shoulder. "I enjoy doing business with you," he said before breaking into a laugh. "And other things, of course. But perhaps you can't say the same, young man; yesterday you lost a lot of money. Without batting an eyelid, I must admit. You are a horrible player, Davenport."

He gave a resigned grimace. "It's true, sir. Maybe you could teach me some—"

The door swung open without warning and Daniel rushed into his father's office. He stopped suddenly, dumbfounded, noticing Christopher. "Mr. Davenport," he greeted him coldly. "Pardon me for the interruption, but I didn't know you were here. Father," he said, his darkened face growing ever darker, "I need to speak to you."

Even princes enter battles sometimes, Christopher thought with glee. For the first time maybe, he was really about to have fun at Riverstone Manor.

"Not now, Daniel," answered Leopold, annoyed. "I am busy, as you can see. And you're old enough to know that one knocks before entering a room—and especially in this room."

"Father . . ." *Oh, there, there,* thought Christopher, *what do we have here? Was Daniel so angry that steam was coming out of him like a boiling kettle? Were his fists clenched so tight that he was wrinkling the papers he held in his hands?*

"I cannot wait, Father."

God only knows how much Christopher would have loved to be present for this argument between father and son. Oh, he would have paid any price to see that. But damn it, it was impossible to stay in the room; it would have clearly been rude.

"I can wait in the drawing room, DeMercy," Christopher said.

It was Daniel who shook his head in response. *What a good little brother!* "No, Mr. Davenport, stay. I would have come to speak to you in any case."

A bit less good. "Oh?" he said with a vague uneasiness. A ridiculous uneasiness, he immediately reminded himself, because he definitely was not a dandy like Daniel, who might have suspicions about him.

"Yes, I wanted to know . . ." Daniel read something from a piece of paper he held in his hand. "You just purchased the fields from the Shadows family, isn't that so?"

I would say that is none of your business. Such a direct question was an indiscretion that he did not expect from this big baby. Daniel always used words in such a pointless and roundabout way. "Your father will certainly be able to clarify all the details of the contract we have signed," he responded flatly.

"I don't even think so," snapped Leopold, rather irritated, as if slightly sickened by Daniel. "Davenport, ignore him: he will definitely split your soul in two with some complaint or another. You can tell from the expression on his face. You see? When he has these grimaces, it means that he's about to begin whining like a little woman. Daniel, get out of my sight . . ." Christopher was beside himself with glee at these words—what a wonderfully resentful tone the senior DeMercy was using with his son!

Daniel did not move, seemingly unhurt by these words. "You cannot sell that land and you know it, Father," he exclaimed angrily. "This agreement that you signed with the late Martin Shadows guarantees his widow the legal rights to use it while she is alive." He walked up to Christopher, handing him the contract. "I imagine that my father has not told you all the details of this . . . *affair*."

Christopher ignored the outstretched arm of his half brother. "You are mistaken, Mr. DeMercy. I am fully aware of that."

Surprise and anger rested on Daniel's paralyzed face. For a few moments he could not speak, too crushed with bewilderment. "You mean that you already knew that there are usufruct rights to this land?" he finally asked, unable to believe it. "The widow and her children—"

It was better to clarify the situation. "I mean to say that the contract you're waving about like a flag has a flaw," said Christopher. "The clause is invalid. I will make use of that land immediately as I see fit. I am sorry for the widow, obviously," he smiled carelessly, "but I can do nothing about it. She will have to go."

It is no small feat to shake your eyes, wrinkle your brow, and curl up your lips and your nose all at the same time, but Daniel succeeded very well. He even managed perfectly to shut himself up in an outraged silence.

Leopold laughed. Christopher had to admit that his father understood the art of laughing. He knew when to use it as a deadly weapon, when to use it to cajole, when to use it to seduce. He was able to adapt every nuance. In this instance, derision, disgust, and delusion were threaded in Leopold's laugh, as well as genuine amusement. Yes, that was what made him so good at it. He truly had so much fun in humiliation. *The subtle line that separates the professional from the artist,* thought Christopher, *is all right here.*

"What did I tell you, Davenport?" Leopold's tone was the perfect continuation of his laugh. "My son has a tender heart. Daniel, I already allow you to live in this house. Don't ask me to put up with your presence in my office."

These words struck Daniel to his core. The response that he gave, Christopher suspected, was directed at him and not at his father.

"I do not stay in this house for you, and you know it," he replied curtly. "And I will not allow you to commit this injustice, Father. Martin Shadows was a good friend of mine—he was even your good friend, my goodness! How could you behave like this? And you, Mr. Davenport . . ." He turned toward him. "It's not possible that you're not touched by the situation of this widow and of—"

"Why don't you support them yourself, Daniel?" interrupted Leopold. "With your money, of course. Also, at this rate it won't last you long, seeing as how you give to every poor person who asks you for it. Will you come begging from me, then?"

"I don't want your money, and you know it. I want a father able to behave in a decent way for once—just one goddamned time."

"That's disrespectful of you, son." There was no anger in Leopold's voice. In truth, his son's words seemed to have practically pleased him now. "Now get out, or I'll take my belt and make you squeak like a mouse, just like when you were a child. And you'll scream even more than you did then, since you get softer every day that goes by."

Daniel paid no attention to him and gave Christopher a look that promised a fight. He didn't bat an eyelid. *Careful, little prince,* he warned him silently. *You do not want to challenge me. You'll wrinkle your clothing.*

"I don't hope for much from my father," Daniel said, "but I demand an explanation from you, Mr. Davenport."

And your face, Daniel. You'll wrinkle your face as well. "Oh really . . . you 'demand' . . . ?" He had problems containing his anger, and he was silent for a few moments before continuing. "I shouldn't have to answer you, Mr. DeMercy," he finally said, "but I will out of the respect that I have for your father. Business is business, and when you have your own responsibilities, if you ever do, you will understand what that means." Who knows what kind of insect Daniel saw when he looked at his half brother—a very ugly and very black one, judging by the nausea on his face. Christopher would have liked to ignore it, or at least find it amusing, but he realized that a real danger existed in letting himself be taken by anger. "Now I'm leaving, DeMercy," he said quickly to his father. "I'll leave you alone to finish this conversation. We can put it off until tomorrow."

"No, stay," Leopold invited him. "And you, Daniel, do as you please. Help that woman, support her children, throw away your money. Maybe to thank you she will let you have her, and God only knows how much you need that. Now get out before I kick you out."

Christopher smiled tightly. "Don't be so strict with your son, sir," he urged him condescendingly. Then, knowing he should not do it—forcing himself not to—he turned toward Daniel and addressed him directly. *To hell with it,* he thought. *This shined-up clown really needs two words of advice.* "I am certain that you'll soon get a dirty conscience when your turn comes to make decisions, Mr. DeMercy," he said.

The little brother narrowed his eyes and did not back down. "Mr. Davenport," he replied dryly, "I'd rather dive headfirst into the ground from a hundred feet up than become like you. And I'm sure," he said, lifting his chin, "that your wife is not aware of how you conduct business."

Christopher felt a disturbing feeling boil up to his neck and his head. "This isn't business for women, don't you think?" he asked him.

His voice sounded particularly nervous. "A gentleman like you should know what is appropriate and what is not to women's ears."

"I would have sworn that sooner or later you would mention that girl's name, Daniel," Leopold sneered. "You're so predictable. And you, Davenport, excuse him: my son is attacking you because your wife broke his heart." A moment of silence descended while Leopold observed Christopher carefully. "You don't seem surprised, young man," he concluded. "You already knew, I guess, that my son was engaged to your wife for a brief—fleeting, you might say—period."

Christopher gave a curt nod. "As I told you, sir, I never sign a contract without knowing all the details." He smiled mockingly at Daniel with the strongest desire to hurt him. To have Daniel in front of him in person when he already saw him every day in the eyes of his wife was really too much. "I am very sorry for your sickened heart, Mr. DeMercy."

Daniel shook his head, and the grimace of his lips—of disgust—returned to his face. "I am also sorry, but for your wife, Mr. Davenport." He did not seem embarrassed; he had witnessed the exchange between Leopold and Christopher without showing any emotion. "Anna deserved better."

Christopher felt the blood pounding against his temples. He knew he had gone too far, but turning back now was impossible. "And the best, I imagine, would be you."

"Anyone," replied his half brother, his voice escaping his throat choppily, "anyone would be better than you. How long have you been married? Ten days?" he burst out, no longer able to restrain himself. "And already you have been unfaithful to her, for God's sake! Do you believe that she does not know what places you frequent?" He gave his father a disgusted look. "You are humiliating her brutally, Mr. Davenport. Don't you have even a little respect for her?"

He shouldn't smash his brother's face. He shouldn't. Not here, and especially not in front of his father, who watched with a delighted smile. "DeMercy, I am warning you," he said seriously, finding it difficult to open his clenched jaws, "do not mention my wife anymore, or I will make you regret it."

Common sense seemed to elude Daniel in that moment. "I don't know how you managed to convince her to marry you, but you fooled her, that's for sure," he said, raising his voice in accusation. "If she knew what kind of man you are, she would run a thousand miles away from you. Maybe she has already understood—she is frightened whenever you're near, and it's clear you don't make her happy, Davenport!"

(It's clear, Christopher. Or maybe you thought that she was happy with you?)

"Don't be absurd," Christopher replied, clenching his fists. To make matters worse, he was sure that he would be using his fists very soon. "She is my wife and she will not leave me. She will certainly never be with you, if that's what you're hoping for." He laughed, but he was not enjoying himself. This was definitely the furthest thing from enjoyment that he could imagine. "How long was your engagement? A day?"

Even Leopold burst out laughing, and this time it seemed authentic. He had every reason to laugh, after all. "Oh, even less than that, Davenport," Leopold pointed out. "Just barely six hours, or am I mistaken, Daniel? An engagement that lasted only from morning until night. You really know how to charm the women, my son."

It lasted a whole day, Leopold, Christopher said to himself. *And my wife finds him far more charming than me, I assure you.*

"Be careful, Daniel," his father said to him. "Mr. Davenport will rip you into little bits if you continue to provoke him. You've never been good at defending yourself."

Daniel did not seem to hear him. Instead he stared at Christopher, his green eyes burning with contempt. "Anna is too pure to love a man like you. Somehow you've tricked her. I already suspected it, but now I'm sure of it, Davenport!"

"I've already told you once," Christopher growled, "don't mention my wife!"

"Daniel!"

A frightened voice coming from the doorway suddenly made them all turn. Lady Eleanor was in the hall, and she looked at them, shocked. Her dress hung on her like loose skin. "Daniel, what's going on?" she asked in a faint voice. She was pale, and her hair was down, as if neglected. "There was yelling . . ."

Daniel suddenly seemed to deflate. "Mother, I—"

"What the devil do you think you're doing in here?" Leopold said. "Go to your rooms!"

"But the y-yelling . . ."

"That was your son, who squeals like a female in heat. Why don't you loan him your dress, Eleanor? It'll definitely look better on him than on you. Now get out of my sight. Right now!"

"Father, have some respect for your wife," Daniel said, suddenly calm. "It's all right, Mother," he assured her softly. "It was just a friendly misunderstanding between me and this gentleman."

Lady Eleanor did not seem reassured, and her half-closed eyelids next to the bags under her eyes accentuated her ill appearance. "Will you come with me, then, Daniel?" she begged him. "Please."

What a disheveled woman, thought Christopher, coldly looking her up and down. *She wanted to marry Leopold, and now she is nothing more than a floor mop. And it suits her, better than this famous dress does.*

"All right, Mother," Daniel replied, glancing at Christopher. "We'll have to discuss this again, Davenport."

"Count on it."

Daniel turned to go to Lady Eleanor in the doorway. "Come." He took her arm delicately and walked away with her.

Leopold shook his head. "What a fine sight, eh, Davenport? I don't understand who that son of mine takes after. Were it not for the fact that my wife has always been as ugly as a horse, I would say that he is from another man. But I found it difficult to have sex with her in order to create my firstborn, and I had to, bloody hell! I wonder who could do that voluntarily."

"It's not a bother," Christopher said, playing down the situation. "Please excuse me for overreacting. It's just that I am used to defending my things."

"It shows that you are a man with balls," he said, and he patted him on the back. Then his father smiled at him like the son he had always wanted—which, after all, was funny—and at another time Christopher would have appreciated the irony. But preventing that was a nagging voice in his head.

Anna is unhappy with you, Davenport.

But she's mine, Daniel. She's mine, and there's nothing you can do about it.

But she wasn't Christopher's—and he knew it.

27

Oh no! Why cry out against passions? Are they not the one beautiful thing on Earth, the source of heroism and enthusiasm, of poetry, music, the arts—in other words, of everything?
—Gustave Flaubert

"Here comes that elegant gentleman, Anna."

She looked up from her pastry dough that she was kneading vigorously. "What elegant gentleman, Anthony?" She wiped the floury dough from her hands onto her apron and snorted. A visit this afternoon was unwelcomed; she was making bread and she needed to finish before her husband got home and began to grumble. She went to the window and saw Daniel. "Go and let him in, won't you, Anthony? Bring him in here."

"Send Dennis," her brother answered. "Or leave him outside. That's what you always do with Christopher."

"That's not true," she lied. Anthony did not seem convinced, and Anna gave up. "Dennis would you go . . . ?"

Engaged in a fierce pillow fight, the child declared a truce and ran to the door.

Sitting at the kitchen table, Grace looked up from the drawing she was making. "Can I draw his portrait, Anna?"

"Of course." Daniel had definitely never seen a portrait like the ones her sister made. "It will make him happy."

Soon the quick steps of her brother were followed by Daniel's slower steps echoing in the hallways.

Anna met him at the doorway. "Daniel, what a pleasure to see you," she said.

Daniel kissed her on the hand gently. She was charmed as she looked at him. It was obvious that heaven shined brighter for some than others. That day her ex-fiancé was very handsome: his outfit made his brown hair, lightened further by the sun, stand out; his symmetrical face was a bit tanned; and his physique seemed more muscular to her than it had the last time she'd seen him. Only his eyes seemed dull, subdued, and the smile on his face was forced.

"Anna," he greeted her politely. "Am I bothering you?"

"It's no bother, you know this."

From the opposite corner of the room, where chairs were arranged to create two different fortresses, Dennis yelled, "That's not fair, though! Anna! Anthony . . ."

"Shh, children," she scolded, "we have a guest. Anthony, don't annoy your brother. Who taught you to behave that impolite way?" But she knew all too well, unfortunately. "Play fair, or I'll make you stop right away."

Anthony shrugged his shoulders and threw a pillow at Dennis while he wasn't looking.

"Excuse me, Daniel, if I'm doing a dreadful job of welcoming you," said Anna with a resigned sigh as she gave up on scolding her brother again. "But I'm sure you don't mind, do you?"

"Not at all, Anna. Please continue what you were doing."

She put the kettle on for tea. "Anthony, when the water is ready, it's up to you to fill the cups. Nora is out, and Victoria is reading to Daddy."

She turned back to the table and began to knead again. "Daniel, make yourself at home," she said. "Take a chair and sit next to me."

"I'll stand next to you if you don't mind." The troubled look had somewhat disappeared from his face, and he looked at her in a way that made her regret not welcoming him more formally.

"Is there a particular reason why you're here, Daniel?"

"Why, yes." He became very serious and moved closer to her to speak in a low voice. "Could you possibly send your siblings into another room?"

Why, what for? "I'll try," she quickly answered. "Dennis, Grace, Anthony, why don't you go find Victoria and Daddy?"

"I'm drawing the gentleman's portrait!" exclaimed Grace indignantly.

"You can finish later. Victoria might need help reading that big book all by herself. Do you want to help her, Anthony?"

Her brother looked at her and then at Daniel. *He won't move from that spot, Anna thought sadly. He will defend Christopher's territory. Ah, little brother, if only . . .*

"All right," Anthony answered. Anna always forgot how difficult it was to predict that child's actions. "Let's go. Come on, Dennis."

"No, I'm staying here." His little voice sounded spiteful from behind the stack of chairs. "I want a biscuit."

Anthony turned toward Anna and shrugged his shoulders.

"It won't be easy," Anna sighed. "Come on. Two biscuits each if you leave right now."

After some hesitation, the ranks of the opposition fell; the first to surrender was Dennis, and Grace followed suit. Each holding two biscuits in their hands, they left without further protests.

"A biscuit does wonders, Daniel," said Anna, smiling. "Won't you have one?"

"Gladly," he replied. He never left her side, even after the children had gone. He turned his back to the table and leaned against it, facing her. "Did you make them yourself?"

"Oh, no. The biscuits in this house can be made only by Nora. Once I tried to make them instead of her, and I found two frogs in my bed. It was a general mutiny, you . . ." Anna looked up from the dough and blushed. She even forgot to finish the sentence as she noticed the way he looked at her. *Gracious, is it possible that he has not yet forgotten about her?* "You said that you must speak to me, Daniel."

His expression reflected grave concern, but not concern about her—rather, for her. "Indeed." He took a deep breath. "Anna, I would not wish to be indiscreet . . ." He scratched his head with a sigh. "But what am I saying? Of course this will seem indiscreet. The fact is that . . . Anna, I must absolutely make you aware of an issue regarding your husband."

Her heart jumped, and her hands trembled in the dough. *Christopher? What has Christopher done? And why is Daniel looking at me so seriously?*

(An incident in the grass, Anna? Another incident in the grass? Why did you allow this to happen?)

No! I know, I'm sure of it! I'm sure of it! Oh God . . . God, please . . . "Tell me, Daniel. Did he do something . . . something that wasn't . . . that wasn't right?"

Oh, Christopher, Christopher. She still did not understand her husband and had no way to know what to expect from him. At times he seemed almost human—for instance, when he was talking with Matthew or Anthony . . .

(And for a moment there was something gleaming in his eyes, wasn't there?)

. . . but then he became distant and unfathomable. Was there darkness and only darkness inside him? Or was there something buried alive, peeking out from underneath? There were a thousand questions but not a single answer. She was sure of only one thing, and that was the hatred she felt for him. It was a hatred that she nourished, nurtured, and grew; it was a hatred that she never wanted to extinguish or forget.

"Do you know anything about the business affairs your husband handles?"

"Business affairs?" She let out a big sigh of relief after her memories and fears had stopped her from breathing. "It's a business matter that you want to talk to me about, Daniel?"

The tense look on his face told her that it was nothing to be happy about. "Anna, it is possible that your husband will not be happy to see me here when he comes back home today. A little while ago we had a—how would I put it?—a disagreement . . . at my father's house."

"You had a discussion about business, you say?" She formed a loaf and began to make another one. She loved making bread; it was so relaxing. Christopher wanted to take away even that pleasure from her. He wanted to take away everything from her. "Nothing insurmountable, I hope. At any rate, he will not be back for a couple of hours, so if you'd care to discuss—"

"Anna," he muttered, embarrassed. "It was not a simple discussion. It was more of an argument, I would say. Due to business . . . and to you."

Anna forgot about the bread. "To me? How? . . . Why? You shouldn't have told him . . ."

Horizontal lines showed on Daniel's forehead, furrowed deeply in astonishment "There was no need to tell him anything, Anna. Your husband already knew about our . . ." He paused, searching for the right word, the right epitaph. "What shall we call it? . . . Our morning of madness."

"What are you saying?" Christopher knew about her and Daniel? But when, and how? "I had no idea! He never mentioned a word to me. Do you think that he found out from your father, Daniel?"

"I don't believe so. Today seemed to be the first time that the topic came up for them."

"Really? That is odd. I told him nothing, and I don't know . . . Oh, the water is boiling. What must you think of me! Excuse me. I'm really a shameful hostess."

"Shameful is not the word that I would have used," Daniel replied. The smile that he gave her was all that was necessary to clarify his opinion of her.

She felt her face getting warm and said quickly, "In any case, if Christopher didn't ask me anything about . . . about that morning . . ." She paused, because the subject unfortunately did not help her face regain her natural coloring. "That means that the issue for him has no importance," she concluded after a few moments. *Otherwise, he would have told me so for sure with two thousand useless and arrogant words and that dark look of his.* She watched Daniel pouring the tea in the cups and blamed him silently. It was unfair, she knew, but she couldn't help it. *It's also your fault, Daniel,* she thought. *If I hadn't gone that day to brood in that garden . . .* She sighed and tried to banish the memory, though it still haunted her after a month. There were a few hours here and there, though, when she managed not to think about it. She went back to working the bread to manage her tension, pressing on it, smashing it, deforming it forcefully.

Daniel walked back to her with the tea. "No, I don't think of it as you do, Anna," he replied politely. "In fact, I believe that your husband is quite jealous."

"Who, Christopher?" Anna looked up suddenly. "You must be joking."

The breath that Daniel drew in was so deep and heavy that he seemed to take all of the air from the room. And still it wasn't enough for him, and he kept the air in his lungs for a few moments.

"Anna, pardon my impertinence, but I must ask you this," he said hesitantly. "It doesn't seem to me that you are happy. Am I mistaken?"

"Daniel—"

"Anna, your husband exhibits behaviors that worry me," he said, interrupting her. "I must be frank with you, even if this could jeopardize our friendship, but it is my duty, and . . ." He didn't finish the sentence. "Take the business deal that he just finished with my father," he continued. "He will throw a widow out of her home, along with her two children, and he has no financial reason to do it, since he isn't driven by desperation."

"That's not possible!" Anna exclaimed. She put down the dough and wiped her hands quickly on her apron, her anger combining with absurd amazement. The same absurd, never-ending amazement, damn it! Good God, when would she admit that Christopher's soul was completely black? "My husband will do this—are you sure? Does Matthew know? We must involve Matthew. He will certainly—"

"Anna, you talk to Matthew Davenport to get your husband to listen to you?"

Damn it, she had spoken without thinking. She looked away, picking up the bread again.

But Daniel continued to stare at her and read her. "Anna," he murmured, "it seems to me that . . . it seems to me that your husband does not treat you . . . does not treat you . . . correctly. He reminds me of my father sometimes."

"Not correctly?"

In public Christopher wasn't affectionate, of course, but etiquette did not allow him greater public displays even if he wanted to give them—and in any case, he didn't mistreat her in obvious ways. She wondered cluelessly whether Daniel was referring to Mrs. Edwards.

Was he outraged because Christopher was cheating on her? She didn't have the courage to ask the question and remained silent.

"Sometimes it seems to me that you are scared of him," Daniel stated. "Am I mistaken?"

Anna was stunned. "Frightened by him . . . ?" *Oh, you might say it like that if you wanted to use a euphemism. But dear God, how did you manage to figure it out? Not even Lucy knows!*

Daniel noticed her reaction and his face darkened. He waited for an answer that never came; then he rubbed his forehead with his fingers, as if making a difficult decision. "I have never told you anything about my childhood," he finally said. "Maybe I should have."

"Daniel—"

"I recall my mother. When I was little, Anna," he said, speaking quickly, as if he was afraid he might change his mind. "She was a sweet and kind woman, and above all, naive. She cried often, but around me she was a different person, with genuine smiles that made me understand how it could have been if she wasn't married to my father." He took a sip of tea, just barely wetting his lips. "He has always treated her badly. Always. On one occasion I saw her fight back, and my father beat her terribly. So terribly that the memory will haunt me all the days of my life, Anna. I was a child."

He kept staring into space, as if crushed by the memory. "It was a sunny afternoon and I happened to go into her room by mistake. I wanted to see her, but my father was there with her. What he was saying . . ." He swallowed, and his throat moved up and down quickly. "He was holding a belt, and to this day I still hear the noise it made when he whipped her. I was there, Anna, I was there . . ." Ah, the shame—fifteen years were not enough to erase it, and he wondered briefly if a hundred would be. Deep down, he knew, though. Daniel could live forever and it still would not be enough. "I tried to defend her at the beginning. I yelled at my father, and he . . . he looked at me, and he was so tall and so big. He turned the belt on me and hit me on the belly, where it is softer . . . and I . . ." He paused and was silent for a moment, unable to continue. But the secret that weighed on his soul had to come out. "I . . . Do you know what I did, my mother's son? I ran away, Anna. I left her in his hands, and I ran away."

In front of her was this same child who ran away, sweet, cheerful, and intelligent. A child who had refused a terrible physical pain and as a result received a bigger pain—a painful burden—still without forgiveness.

"Daniel . . ." She took him by the hand, and with astonishment she felt the warmth of her tears running down her face—but they were not for her, not this time. How long had it been since she cried for someone else? "Daniel, you were just a baby!"

He put his other hand up to his eyes, closing them. "You don't understand, Anna. You don't understand." He shook his head. "My mother stayed in bed for two weeks because of the beating she received, and when she recovered . . . she was never the same as before. Something in her died that afternoon." He was silent for a few seconds, squeezing Anna's hand until it hurt her. "My father had never been so cruel before, and never again did he repeat anything so serious. Do you understand? If only I hadn't run away . . ." He was silent for a few minutes, and Anna too fell quiet. All she could do was hold his hand and listen.

After clearing his throat, Daniel continued: "After that day, my mother shut herself up in an unreachable place inside herself, all alone. Every time I came home from boarding school I found her more distant. Anna, that was my mother—that woman who eighteen years ago stayed with me an entire morning playing with old sheets, building caves all over the house—my mother died each day, and it was all my fault. Now . . . now her soul wanders almost blindly. She walks by rooms without seeing the people who are right there with her. She spends her days without humming any songs, without looking at any flowers, without reading any books . . ." He swallowed down several big gulps of air, as if drowning the past.

(But the past is a bastard that always comes back, Daniel.)

"I do what I can, but I am not always there to defend her from my father, who still . . ." Overwhelmed, he bit his lip. "Anyway," he said in a weak voice, taking his hand off his eyes and letting it fall to his side, "now it is too late. I had my chance and I threw it away, and I can do nothing more than regret my choice."

(Choice? But what choice did you have, pet?)

"Daniel, you're mistaken!" she said to him with the urgency of someone who could possibly make a difference. "You couldn't save your mother—but how could you? Only she could save herself. Only she *can* save herself; it's not too late! Why doesn't she leave him? Why does she stay with a man like that?"

He raised his head. His eyes, with their attentive gleam, looked into hers. "Why don't you leave your husband?"

Anna winced and said nothing. She pulled out a handkerchief and wiped her cheeks and her eyes.

"My mother's reasons are that . . . she is damaged," responded Daniel. "She has no more soul. She hasn't the strength to get up out of a chair, let alone leave my father. And what's worse . . ." He closed his eyes, because the words were difficult for him to say. "What's worse is that she loves him, Anna." His voice trembled. He had to pause to regain his composure. "I believe that despite everything," he said in a whisper. "Despite the way that he treats her, despite the cruelty he shows her, despite his guilt for crimes against justice, if not against the law . . . I believe that despite all that, my mother still loves him. And she will not stop hoping that she can change him back someday." He smiled sadly. "It's dreadful, Anna, loving someone who doesn't deserve it."

Her tears prevented her from clearly seeing Daniel's eyes, but she was able to detect another secret hidden behind the green of his irises, a secret perhaps worse than the first. "You also love your father, don't you?" she whispered to him.

"And you, Anna?" he retorted. "Do you love your husband?"

***

Christopher had left Leopold rather quickly. He had decided to cancel the last two appointments of the day because he needed to see his wife.

That stupid woman.

She might disappear any minute, according to what his half brother had said.

He got to the redbrick house, but he stopped to look at the building from a distance, as he had done the first time. He dismounted his horse and slowly led Basil by the bridle.

He arrived at the end of the lane—and he saw it.

DeMercy's horse, tied up in front of the stables.

Blood rushed to his head, nearly making him blind. For a moment he stood perfectly still without even breathing; then he left Basil in the lane and headed at once to the rear of the house, where there was a window his wife had passed through once—once when she needed to enter without being seen. He got in easily and quickly, and quietly went toward the voices in the kitchen. He met no one, as if the house had fallen asleep together with its colors and noises.

He appeared in the doorway. Daniel and Anna were nearby. She was wearing an apron and was in tears; her hands covered in flour, she was holding his hand. Daniel seemed upset and looked at her as if he wanted to read inside her.

"What a touching romantic scene," he said, entering the room with quick, long strides.

Anna and Daniel turned at the same time, letting go of each other's hands. Anna looked panicked. Daniel looked surprised and angry.

"Davenport," said his brother. He walked around the table, moving toward him. "So we meet again."

Christopher smiled and hit him.

The punch came so quickly that Daniel found himself on the ground before realizing that he had even fallen. The satisfaction that this blow gave to Christopher was indescribable, and it only increased when he saw the trickle of blood that came from his half brother's lip—a drop that fell and stained the white handkerchief he wore around his neck.

"Christopher!" Anna cried out. She ran toward him, opening her arms up in front of Daniel. "Christopher, what are you doing?"

"Don't get in the middle of this, Anna!" he yelled, shoving her to the side. She fell heavily on the ground, with a little cry of fear and pain. This pain was not physical—at least not only that.

Daniel got back up after the moment of dizziness brought on by the unexpected punch. On his feet now, he looked down and saw her on the floor. His face wore the expression of someone seeing all of his worst fears take place.

"You bully!" he screamed.

"I warned you, DeMercy, and if you try it again . . ."

Daniel pounced on him like a battering ram, striking Christopher's stomach with his head. The blow threw him onto the table, causing him to hit his back. Some white loaves fell to the ground, raising clouds of flour.

Distraught, Anna stood up and pleaded, "Please stop it! They will hear you! You, Daniel! At least you!"

She held out her arms toward the two, but it was impossible for her to intervene: they were much larger than she and too busy attacking each other to listen. Christopher grabbed his half brother's head with his right hand, pulled him by the hair, and gave him a punch in the face with his left fist before raising his foot and kicking him in the belly, tossing him backward. Daniel was moving uncontrollably, and

Christopher dove for him but missed and hit the floor. Daniel jumped on him, striking him with a punch in the nose that sounded like wood splitting in two. Christopher felt the blood pouring from his face onto his mouth and neck. He was dazed, and his half brother was able to get over him, holding him to the ground and sitting on top of him, unleashing blows like hailstones on his face wildly, one after another.

"Daniel, please!"

Trembling, Anna approached the two, holding her hands out. Daniel stood still and motioned for her to stop, stretching out his arms to the sides. "Anna, don't get close! Stay away!"

(Watch out, Daniel. In a battle, you never take your eyes off the adversary.)

Christopher shoved him to the side, trying to lift him off him. He failed, but Daniel moved enough that it allowed Christopher to lift one knee, which he used to give him a horrible blow to his lower abdomen. He used all of the strength he could in that position, and with incredible satisfaction he saw his brother change color, exhale suddenly, and fall to the side with his eyes closed in pain.

"Please, please stop!" Anna begged.

Christopher leapt onto his brother, sitting on his stomach and pinning his arms under his own legs. He grabbed his hair with his left hand and raised his right fist, ready to hit him with all the strength he had. He hoped that Daniel had looked in the mirror before leaving, because his distinguishing features would very soon be rearranged.

Anna ran to him. "Christopher, please!" Demented, she grabbed at his raised fist. She did not understand how dangerous that was.

"Anna, get off!" he growled, pulling his fist from her hand.

"Anna, go away!" yelled Daniel, trying to break free. "Anna, please!"

Could she listen to them? Had she ever? No, and she dropped to her knees beside them. She stretched out her arms, and Christopher almost fell down in amazement when she closed her arms around him and hugged him. Yes, she hugged him, absurdly—under these circumstances it was mad to do it, and the last thing that one could expect. To Christopher this seemed so logical, so comfortable, and so soft.

Anna leaned her head against his chest at the level of his heart, which beat with quick, deafening noises. "Please, Chris," she said. "Enough. Please."

These three, all on the ground, were a very strange sight: Daniel lying lengthwise; Christopher on top of him with his fist in the air; and Anna, who was hugging him with her head down.

"Please, Christopher."

He closed his eyes. The warm embrace of his wife entered inside him with bitter emotion: he knew that it was only a ploy to distract him from Daniel, but he wasn't able to think clearly. He knew he was a fool, and he knew that she was cynically using her power to get him away from the man she loved—but he could not push away her tender body. He couldn't even manage to ignore it. His arms fell to his sides and he remained motionless while Anna wept on his jacket, and the emotion came over him against his own will.

(You're ridiculous—you know that, don't you? A ridiculous puppet in the hands of this woman.)

He opened his eyes and grabbed her wrists, freeing himself from her embrace. He stood up immediately, pushing her away, and Anna placed a palm on the floor to keep from falling down again. After a moment she got up as well, supporting herself with her hands, and Daniel sat up, his pale face destroyed.

"Christopher?" called Anthony, peeking his head out through the door. "Anna?"

All three of them turned toward the doorway; Daniel hurried to his feet.

"Anthony, leave, and keep your brother and sister away," said Christopher calmly with the impassivity of a man hiding a secret—the secret of blood stirred to emotion by a hug. He readjusted his jacket and noticed the taste of blood in his mouth. His face must have been a disaster if it looked anything like his half brother's did.

Disobeying, Anthony came into the kitchen. "I'll pick up the bread," he said, turning to his sister. "I'll straighten up a bit, Anna. Daddy will be here soon."

There were loaves on the ground. The kitchen looked like a tornado had hit. Christopher's and Daniel's faces seemed that they needed to be more than "straightened up." Anna put a hand over her eyes, which were still wet. "Anthony . . ." she began, but then stopped, perhaps because she did not know what to say to that little boy, who seemed to be the most mature person in the room.

Christopher looked at Daniel. "Never show your face in this house again, DeMercy." His voice was calm but firm—a voice to be taken bloody seriously. "Next time you will not get away with so little."

"I liked you better when you spoke like a book of printed rhetoric, Davenport." His voice was low, because *he* remembered Anthony was there. He didn't want him to hear, but little children always hear everything no matter what. "Nevertheless, I realize that you are very different from what you want others to believe."

"Please, Daniel," pleaded Anna, keeping her eyes on her husband, as if controlling him with her gaze. "Go now."

Daniel shook his head. "I cannot leave you here with him, Anna." It was an observation, not a hypothesis. "He's dangerous, and . . ."

You still haven't understood how dangerous. Christopher made again to approach him, but Anna reached her arms out in front, stopping him. "Daniel, stop it," she ordered him without looking at him, instead staring at her husband with steady eyes. "And you, Christopher, calm down. I will not allow you to be violent in this house."

Daniel moved to the side to get around her, but she would not let him. She came closer to her husband—and with the same bittersweet amazement from a moment before, Christopher was again hugged by his wife. She was like a shield between him and Daniel.

A hug doesn't cost you anything, Anna? he thought with the same tiresome irony, while an annoying hoarseness forced him to clear his throat. The pain, which was very different from that of his bloody nose, burst like a boil deep within him. He broke free from her hands, but without strength. He stepped back.

"Please, Daniel, leave," said Anna. "Don't be afraid for me. My husband will not do anything to me."

"Anna, I—"

"Go, Daniel. Soon my father will come, and he must not see you with your face like that. Go through the dining room. You know the way."

"Anna—"

"Out! Before my family gets here—please!"

But Daniel did not want to go. Something flickered in his face, a terrible fear of making the wrong choice. "Anna, I can't! Don't you understand? I can't leave you with—"

"This is my home, Daniel, and I'm ordering you to leave. Out now!"

It seemed to him that she had asked him to kill her instead. "Dear God, Anna . . ." Shocked so much that he was blasphemous in front of a woman, he stared at Christopher, and his green eyes stood out in sharp contrast to the red of the blood on his face. "If you hurt her, Davenport!" he said with a voice that came from God only knows what part of him—some cavernous, secret, and maybe ancient part. "If you so much as touch her with your finger, I will kill you, I swear it."

"Leave, DeMercy," said Christopher, but wearily, as if the anger from moments before had left only a trace. "Leave, unless you want me to kill you myself here, in front of my wife."

Anthony dropped the broom he had in his hand, causing all three of them to turn suddenly. They had forgotten about him, as they were lost in their own speeches, the kind made by adults who thought the child invisible.

The little boy ran up to them, his face serious and determined. Anthony knew what to do, as all eleven-year-olds do. "Come, sir," he said curtly, and took Daniel by the hand. "I will show you to the door."

He pulled him slightly, but gently. Daniel looked at him blankly and glanced toward Anna.

"Go, Daniel, please," she begged him. "If you stay, it will be worse."

In his eyes an old pain mixed with a new one. Defeated, he let himself be dragged away as if pulled along in the tide. At the doorway he turned one last time to look at her.

"Go, Daniel," Anna said to him in a calm tone. "Don't be afraid for me. It's not . . ." She stopped talking suddenly. "Don't be afraid," she repeated softly. "Don't worry, Daniel."

(Does it hurt, Christopher? He came at you from every direction.)

Daniel slowly disappeared around the corner, and shortly after they heard the front door shut.

Anna and Christopher remained quiet in the kitchen. Anthony came back a moment later. He began to straighten up the mess, ignoring the two adults as still as statues in the middle of the room. Children are used to quarrelling, after all.

Shocked and puzzled, Anna looked at Christopher, and he took a moment to study her as well. He considered her looks, her red lips, her smooth, white neck, and the apron she was wearing, which was covered in flour. A white smudge was on her cheekbone, which stood out against the pink of her cheek—which he hadn't noticed when he came into the kitchen. Maybe she had just done it, wiping the tears away with her floured hands. *The power this woman has over me must end,* he thought with a sort of dispassionate despair. *And there's only one way.* He left the room and headed for his office.

***

For several minutes, fear kept Anna from moving. *My husband was beside himself,* she thought. *Beside himself.*

And again she was surprised by the fact that she could be surprised. She suddenly became aware of this hidden desire to not want to believe in Christopher's violent nature despite the evidence that continued to pile up in front of her eyes. But what else did she need to know to be convinced that he was capable of killing someone?

Anthony watched with attentive eyes. *Good heavens, he's so young,* thought Anna. She smiled at him to hide how frightened she was. "Did you see, Anthony? You and Dennis aren't the only ones who fight. Were you scared?" *Because I was—very scared.* She rubbed the hip she had fallen on when she fell. Christopher had shoved her without even a hint of regret.

(But you embraced him, Anna, didn't you? And he stopped.)

She didn't know what had gotten into her. In a state of sanity, she would have certainly never thought that a hug—a hug from her—could dissuade her husband from doing anything.

"No, I wasn't scared," Anthony responded. He was undoubtedly surprised by the question. With a knife, he was scraping dough off the floor. He didn't look up toward her. "You need to fight for your own things. Christopher always says that."

Your own things. A shiver ran down her spine, which still hurt her from the fall a little earlier. "Oh?" she asked him worriedly. "But, Anthony, you know that you don't have to listen to everything that—"

"I know, I know. You already told me that," he interrupted her, puffing. *And his tone . . . so abrupt, so impatient . . . It sounds eerily similar to that of someone else. Someone tall and mean.*

(What have you done to your family, Anna?)

Her insides tightened, pierced by fierce regret.

(Why did you allow him to come into this house?)

She felt the need to leave the room and be alone, to cry inconsolably. "Anthony, can you finish here?" she asked him quickly. "Oh, you're almost done, I see." She smiled. "I'll be right back and we will prepare supper."

She went running to her room. The pain, like always, demanded the tribute of tears and torment.

28

But an infinity of passion can be contained in a minute, like a crowd in a small space.
—Gustave Flaubert

Christopher was in his wife's room. He looked at a doll resting on a little table in front of him as the trees visible through the window slowly began to cast longer shadows in the late-afternoon sun. He had wiped the blood off him, but he seemed to have some kind of animal on his face—a swollen, red creature that bit him where he should have had a nose.

He grabbed the smiling doll from the little table. *Anna is just a little girl.* The very blond locks and the garish colors of this toy seemed very different from the fresh simplicity of his wife. He would have been less surprised if he had found, say, a hoe or a pistol in that room rather than such a fancy object.

A slight noise made him turn toward the door.

(She's here, Christopher.)

Something jumped in his chest as the door handle turned, and a moment later his wife opened the door. She stopped dead.

"What are you doing in my room?" she asked, frozen in the doorway. "Put down that doll and leave."

I really don't think so, witch. "Come in and close the door," he ordered her softly. "And don't even attempt to debate it, unless you want me to pull you in here by the hair."

Anna bit her lip and entered into one endless moment in which memory and fear cast shadows over her face. She closed the door behind her. "What do you want?" Her voice was firm, but Christopher was sure it wouldn't be for long. "It's nearly time for supper."

He put the doll down on the table and walked to the window, with its open curtain, putting a greater distance between them. Then he turned toward his wife and sat with his back to the windowpane, crossing his arms on his stomach. Anna stayed where she was—they were at two opposite ends of the room, with the bed in the middle.

No one spoke. Seconds passed slowly.

Christopher studied her carefully, and she tried to study him too but could not manage it for long. She lowered her head and gave up, defeated and frightened. "Sir . . ." she began, then suddenly paused. She wrung her hands tensely. "Sir, perhaps you should have the doctor look at your wounds. If you would like compresses for your nose . . ."

Christopher continued to stare at her, and her voice trailed off. She began again: "Daniel," she said, looking up at him, straining her eyes. "Daniel had only stopped by to inform me of . . . a business affair . . . that you finished, sir. It seems that there were a few problems, and . . ." She stopped in midsentence. "I would like you to reconsider," she then continued, ignoring his cold eyes. "That land is . . ." Frustrated, she paused. "Why are you so fiercely against him?" she suddenly asked. "I don't believe you did it for the money—it doesn't seem to me that you are wanting; you throw money away with both hands. And certainly you didn't do it for me. Maybe you are so violent that you seize every opportunity to attack someone."

He said nothing, slowly crossing his legs in front of him. He continued to contemplate his wife, who still had the apron on—which, he wagered, still smelled of flour and warm bread.

(She still has the smudge on her face, Christopher.)

He pulled away from the window, suddenly sitting up straight. Anna had a flash of fear in her eyes, but she didn't move—she even stiffened her hands, which she held tight one inside the other just below her chest.

Christopher went to the little table and sat on the edge of it. He hadn't come any closer to her. "Anna," he said, stretching his legs out in front of him, "perhaps you remember the conversation we had a few days ago."

"Conversation, sir?" she asked quietly. Then she seemed to understand. "About the guardianship . . ."

"Exactly."

She tensed up like a bow. "Why are you bringing it up now?"

He smiled, relaxed and serene, but inside he was putting out flames. "Because, my dear wife," he said quietly, "I have decided that you will pay for your lack of discipline with your family members from now on."

Silence. A silence filled with a dismay that took the form of a perfect O on her mouth. Still, something was missing: she was not afraid. Anna didn't believe him, Christopher understood. "You can't be serious," she said when she regained the ability to articulate a thought. "You just want to scare me."

No, I am deadly serious, Anna. "Oh, you'll see." Christopher shrugged nonchalantly. "To begin with, I will sell this house. Perhaps you don't know it, Anna, but I hold the mortgage in my possession. And the payments lately"—he smiled—"have not been regular, unfortunately. We are moving to Rockfield, as we should have at the beginning."

"But what are you saying? Have you been drinking?"

"Quiet. I'm not here to argue with you. I only came to tell you that I will not put up with other rebellions on your part." *Because you are mine.* "You belong to me, Anna. And it's time you understood that."

She winced as if he had thrown a foul-smelling liquid on her. She glanced at the table, although there was nothing of importance on it—some papers, a book, that nauseating little doll. "I am not one of your things, sir," she replied, her face twitching.

Of course you are. "Of course you are. And now listen to me carefully, because I will not repeat myself." He paused to emphasize his words. "I will buy a small house for your father and Nora," he said, raising his hand to stop her from protesting. "I have already found it, Anna, and it's not far from Rockfield. I will not prevent you from going to see them, don't worry. But I do not want invalids underfoot."

"Christopher, you aren't saying . . ." The sentence slipped out without her realizing it. She put her hand over her mouth.

He stared at her in silence, and after a few minutes he began to speak. "I don't even want your siblings in the house."

Shocked, her mouth wide open, she couldn't say a word. All that came out was mute disbelief.

"They can live with your father or go to boarding school—that is up to you to decide. What do you prefer?" He waited for an answer, which didn't come. He hadn't honestly expected one. "Well, I'll decide, then," he concluded. "That's all, Anna." He stood up quickly. "Tomorrow I will let you know the details of the move."

She found her voice. "Why are you telling me this absurd nonsense, sir? You love my family and you would never hurt them."

You love my family.

That was the first time he heard her say something positive about him, Christopher realized. And ironically it wasn't true. "Oh, how wrong you are, Anna," he muttered. His voice sounded bitter even to his own ears. Because he did not love anyone, and the idea of love—positive, necessary, even right—caused him a sort of inexplicable discomfort. Oh, he felt sympathy for a couple of people in the world, that was true—sympathy that would never prevent him from pursuing his goals. (And that's life, Anna. Either you win or you lose.) And he would win that night in between his wife's thighs. Because if she did not give in, he would carry out his threats just as promised. He didn't want to, but he would do it. He would continue to wear her down in a thousand ways until she broke under his fingers like a flower stem.

"I don't believe you."

You don't know how to read my eyes, then. "Think what you will," he answered. "In fact, you'll only have to wait until tomorrow to find out how serious I am." He eyes fell on the doll with the purple dress. "It's time that you grow up, Anna. But I see that you still play with dolls." He reached for the porcelain face smiling at him from across the table.

"Don't touch it," she ordered him, and he heard in her voice that she was alarmed.

(You have already won, Christopher.)

He picked up this childish object, and with his finger he brushed a blond curl off her colorful, shiny face. His wife did not move, did not come closer to take the doll from his hands, but her face had a strained grimace. Her eyes watched, wide open. *It's a doll, Anna. Only a bloody doll, and I am your husband, by God!*

"Put it down right away, sir!"

She wanted it to sound like an order, but it seemed to him like a plea. Christopher smiled and almost felt her pain. *Oh dear.* "Anna, you don't know much about me," he began gently. "Let me explain something to you. How do you think that I got to where I am now? I started from the bottom, you know. I could have never done it if I had any scruples or any second thoughts."

He looked at the doll in his hands, as if reflecting, and he gently touched its face. Then he raised his arm and threw it against the wall. The doll's smile exploded into countless fragments. The impact seemed to fill the whole room.

"No!" Anna put her hands up to her face.

The perfect features of the doll no longer existed; they were shattered into disjointed, irregular pieces. She had only one blind, very blue eye left, while the other had been swallowed by a black hole right in the center of her face.

"No . . ." whispered Anna. "Oh, why?"

And in her eyes, in one quick instant, she changed. One quick instant—the blink of an eye—and the alleged falsehood became true. She finally believed him.

"Please, Christopher." Her voice grew faint, subdued. "Please don't blame my family. They haven't done anything. I'm sorry for what happened. It won't happen again. Please, don't . . ." The sentence faded into a whimper. Tears streamed down her face, mixing with flour. "You see, I'm begging you . . . Are you happy now? I have done everything you wanted, sir . . ." She lowered her head, with her hand over her eyes.

"Everything that I wanted? I wouldn't say that." Victory swelled up inside of him; an immoral victory, a shameful one—even he could recognize that. He knew that his disgrace was truly in not feeling any shame. "You defy me all the time, and you know it. Today you made me look ridiculous with your friend. No, don't say a word, Anna. Since you aren't capable of satisfying me in the few things I ask, I feel free to do the same."

"I will change, Christopher. I will change. I will avoid everything that bothers you. I . . . I swear to you, I—"

"Be quiet. I don't know what to make of your words. You've said this before, and you haven't kept your word."

"Christopher!" She was motionless and distraught. "You can't be serious, you can't be! Anthony adores you! You even took him to London with you last week! You would not do that. I know you wouldn't do that . . ."

Christopher went to the door and opened it, ignoring her. He started to leave, but she approached him, reached out, and took his hand. She touched him—she really and truly touched him. "Christopher! Christopher, please!"

He broke free from her grasp abruptly but paused and leaned against the doorjamb.

(You see how destroyed she is, Christopher? You can ask her for anything that you want now. Ask her, Christopher. Ask her to fulfill your every desire.)

"All right," he murmured, as if suddenly convinced. "All right, Anna, I will give you another chance."

Hope blossomed on her face like a rose. It lit her up sweetly, and she seemed even more gentle, even more beautiful. Even more his.

"But you will change your attitude," he continued. "You will need to show me your goodwill."

"I will," she replied, broken and reborn at the same time. "Do not doubt. You won't have to complain about me. I will employ all the staff that you ask me to. I will no longer do anything in the house. I won't—"

Oh, Anna. What do you think I care about all of that? "You will be obedient and respectful."

That hit her, and it hit her hard. Her eyes sparked with a residual flash of rebellion, but the flames were extinguished when she sighed in resignation. *Now I'll tell you what I really want, sweet wife of mine,* he thought, and he felt a pain mixed with a tender feeling he couldn't ignore in the pit of his stomach. *The light in your eyes will go out and fear will take them over.*

"I will be, I swear to you, Christopher, I—"

"And tonight you will not lock the door to your room."

Anna stopped talking, stopped moving, stopped breathing. Frozen by the thought, she seemed to turn into a marble column—or rather, a piece of chalk ready to crumble to pieces at the slightest touch.

Christopher turned and left without waiting for her answer.

***

The room seemed to smile at her with its soft pastel colors, so strange at that moment, when everything should have been red, black, gray, purple. She looked at Margaret, all in pieces, and a voice inside her told her the story of a broken woman.

. . . she walks by rooms without seeing the people who are right there near her. She spends her days without humming any songs, without looking at any flowers . . .

Was that the fate that awaited her? There was a door between her room and that of her husband.

(But he isn't your husband, is he? Not yet. He will become your husband in a few hours.)

There was a door, and it would not be closed that night.

Margaret was a purple spot on the floor, and her curls shined oddly among the porcelain fragments. A part of her face was still intact, while the rest was gone, leaving a dreadful hole where there had been a winking blue eye and a proud smile. Anna walked up to her and knelt at her side.

"Excuse me, Maggie," she mumbled. "You had to suffer this time, but soon he will come after me." She put her hand on her stomach, and she rocked back and forth. "What can I do? What?"

Matthew? Could Matthew help her? She thought back to Christopher's eyes, to the decisiveness with which he smashed Margaret because he knew it would hurt Anna. No, Matthew couldn't stop him. Maybe—just maybe—he could hide the Champion family. Or help them escape. But her father . . . her father . . .

(Do you remember the grass, Anna? Do you remember him inside you?)

Yes, she remembered. And she remembered the terrible pain she felt, and she remembered thinking she wanted to die that day. She touched the side of the little porcelain face that was still intact. "You were right, Maggie," she said, a tear falling on the broken pieces. "Sooner or later we all give in."

***

Christopher went back to his room after supper, leaving Anna and Nora together with the children in the dining room.

During the meal he had said very little. Grace and Dennis had pestered him with questions about his destroyed face, and in fact it would have been strange if they had not. Anthony had said nothing, and neither did Mr. Champion. Nora had looked at him suspiciously and didn't seem very convinced by his answers—"I bumped into a shutter, Grace, and no, I didn't fight against the king of the mashed-potatoers."

"That's a good thing," the little girl had replied. "When it's a being made out of mashed potatoes, you never know what to expect. It can take on any shape, but the color is always yellow. Isn't that right, Anna?"

Christopher had looked at his wife, who tried to appear calm.

"Unless you encounter a gravy-shaper," she had responded, her hand shaking. When Christopher passed her the green beans, the tremors in her hands caused one to fall off the tray. He would have liked to put his hand over hers to stop the uncontrolled movement.

He had barely eaten, and he had remained quiet without joining in any of the conversations, even when Dennis had asked him, "Will your nose stay crooked, Christopher?"

He shrugged his shoulders without answering.

"Hopefully," Grace said. "You're more handsome this way."

The little girl had a rather peculiar idea of what was beautiful, and Christopher had not considered that to be a compliment. He glanced at his wife, whose mouth had flashed a bitter grimace, and he couldn't bear one more minute of being the only one to notice it. He got up quickly, excusing himself by saying his nose hurt, and went to his room, where he threw himself on the bed.

He was still there after almost two hours. Two hours of brooding with an arm over his eyes.

My God, what am I to do?

The place was different than it was a month before, and the situation was different, but the question was the same, and the violence would be the same, and if the first time it hadn't made him a monster—he had behaved like a monster without being one, or so he thought—now what other explanation could there be?

(You liked it, Christopher. You liked raping her.)

The image of his wife and Daniel hand in hand made him strengthen his resolve on the matter, which had begun to falter. How much longer before Anna became the lover of his half brother? He would stop that. She was his wife, by God, and she would share only his bed.

Very soon she will come back to her room.

Christopher sat down, rested his elbows on his knees, and put his head in his hands. Wasn't he like his father? Wasn't he really about to manipulate a young girl's heart in a premeditated way without any excuse that might allow him even to consider the possibility of having a conscience?

She's the one who forces me to do these things. Her, it's all her. Desperation pounded against his temples and in his chest.

(And what's that underneath, Christopher? Isn't that excitement? You can't wait—tell the truth.)

Shit. Shit, shit. He got up and looked in the mirror: he had a swollen nose, a wound under one eye, bruises all over, and dark circles around his eyes. Anna already hated him, and now . . .

I will not hurt her. And this hatred for Daniel will go away, and this anger against her will disappear.

He heard someone—his wife—entering the room next door, and his heart began to beat madly. *I could restrict myself only to talking to her tonight,* he thought as he opened and closed his fists to calm down.

I am not a monster, by God. I am not my father.

He waited about ten minutes, then walked up to the forbidden door, which had teased him with her sweet and terrible song for ten nights. *I won't go in,* he said to himself. *I will tell her through the door that if she doesn't want me, I will stay out.*

But his hand went right up to the door handle and lowered it gently, as if it were made of glass. For a dreadful moment he thought he felt resistance, as if it was locked, but then he pushed forward with his fingers and the door opened easily.

29

How quick come the reasons for approving what we like!
—Jane Austen

Anna was standing near the window when Christopher came into her room. She had turned her back to the door and was looking out. She was wearing a nightgown that reached almost to the floor—very practical but hardly feminine. Her very long hair was not imprisoned in the bun she always kept it in but pulled back in a soft ponytail that went down her back. As Christopher looked at her hair, his mouth became dry, and he knew that he had just lied to himself. He would take her—and that night.

Anna turned toward him in the room lit by a candle and the moonlight coming in through the open curtains. "You're not laughing, sir?" she asked. She held herself tightly in a solitary embrace, her left hand wrapped around her right arm. "Do you want me to give you a round of applause?"

Christopher did not expect such a direct attack. He took a deep breath and raised his hands to calm her. "Anna . . ." he murmured. *I really need to make love to you.* "I don't want to hurt you."

She smiled, but there was nothing cheerful to be found in the crooked crease of her lips. "You don't want to hurt me, I understand. You have an odd sense of humor—has anyone ever pointed that out to you?"

"It won't be painful, Anna. If you are afraid—"

"I'm not afraid. You simply disgust me."

(What about that, Christopher? How much does that hurt?)

"Didn't you say that you would be more careful?" he asked her, feeling a pain in his chest. "Those aren't exactly the words I was expecting to hear."

"Oh, but my words are of no interest to you—not really, sir. I understand now. All of those things that you challenged me with this afternoon—all of these trifles—were only a farce. Isn't that so?" Christopher said nothing, and she went on: "I don't understand why you would want to resort to that trick. You could have taken me anytime without my consent, as you are accustomed."

"That is not the way that I want you. I have already told you that." He took a step toward her, but the contempt on her face made him stop. "If you give me a chance, I will make it pleasant—"

She looked as though he had struck her with an open hand. "You make me ill, sir. Do what you must, but don't demand anything else from me."

Christopher sighed. *God, it is not easy.* "Listen," he said. He ran a hand through his hair, lowering his head. "There's no need for you to look at me as though I am about to cut you into a thousand pieces. It's normal for . . . You're my wife, and you know it. And you want children, I'm sure."

"Not from you."

(Not from you, Christopher.)

"For you, I'm the only one here, and it's time that you accept that. That's why I am here tonight."

"No. You're vile, and *that's* why you're here tonight."

"I am your husband, Anna. I have the right to ask you for it."

"The right . . . ? You?" She shook her head slowly in disbelief, denying even the possibility of having heard those words. "Good heavens," she mumbled, "and you even have the courage to look me in the eyes while you say that."

"Anna, listen . . ."

"And this was your reason for hitting Daniel?"

Saying that name was not exactly the smartest move. "I don't think I need a particular reason to split open that buffoon's face," he responded. "His face is there for that reason, probably."

"Oh, you certainly 'split open' his face," she agreed, giving a knowing look at Christopher's destroyed face. A bit of liveliness sparked in her eyes when she spoke. Although she considered his pain, she couldn't help but feel a bit of joy. "It's a good thing that you're so happy about it, because after that edifying brawl from this afternoon, *your* face bears a striking resemblance to cat vomit. And I'm too polite to point out to you that if it had been a fair fight, Daniel would have probably beaten you."

No, Anna. He lost. And so will you. "I advise you to be careful with what you say. Don't defend your . . . *Daniel* . . . in front of me, because the next time I'll do more than slap him around a bit."

Fear flashed in her eyes. "Leave him alone," she ordered quickly. "You will leave him alone, Christopher, or I—"

"Or you'll what?"

"Sir, don't be angry with him," she said hurriedly. "Our brief engagement never had anything to do with you—at least, not until today. I do not know how much you know about it, but be aware that there is nothing between Daniel and myself, except for a close friendship."

A close friendship—of course, thought Christopher. And that close friend would now be your husband if it weren't for me and for what I did to you. And certainly you would not be looking at me with those eyes, would you? Those damned eyes full of hate.

He was silent, and his wife went on: "Who told you about it, by the way? His father?" She waited for an answer, but none came. "Our engagement barely lasted a half day, you know. Not even you can be so foolish as to think much of it."

Christopher watched her with narrowed eyes for a long while. Anna knew how to lie when she wanted to, but her paleness and her pain betrayed her. "If you keep him far away from my things," he replied with deliberate nastiness, "he will have nothing to fear."

This nastiness hit her right where he wanted it to: in her stomach. "Does it amuse you a lot when you refer to me as 'your thing'?" She spit these words out in helpless rage. "But the day will come when you won't laugh anymore."

Then, to hurt her even more, he laughed.

"Are you threatening to kill me again, Anna? Because you have been saying that for quite a while, and I continue to be in perfect health."

"You're not that healthy, sir. You're wrong. You are sick, rotten inside, and repulsive." Her eyes flared with disgust. "And you don't have even a little bit of dignity. Don't you feel embarrassed to take a woman who finds you as attractive as the scab on a leper?"

Her tone seemed genuinely and painfully surprised, and Christopher felt his anger surge up into his brain and take away his access to reason. *God, this girl always knows when to say the wrong thing.* "There, Anna, those are exactly the words that you should not say, and *especially* not tonight." He tried not to raise his voice, but it came out distorted, anyway. *To hell with this. It is time to get it over with.* "And now let's be done with this unpleasant conversation and move on to more amusing things, wouldn't you say? For once I think I will enjoy your . . . company."

He quickly took two big steps toward her, stopping in front of her.

"How could you?" Anna asked him without emotion. "How could you get pleasure from a woman who doesn't want you?"

"Oh, in many ways," he answered with a cruel smile. "And I will teach you all of them."

Anna tilted her head to the side and looked away. He was indifferent and distant; it was as if he was not in front of her. "I ask only that you do it in a hurry."

Anna, look at me.

He grabbed her arm abruptly and was on her, crushing her against the wall, hurting her deliberately. Her soft body pressed against his most sensitive parts. And she still did not look at him. She still looked like a soulless statue. He put his hand on her cheek and turned her face toward him. And what he saw shocked him.

(But what are you doing, Christopher?)

A man sentenced to hang, standing on the gallows while the hood is put over his head, would have the same expression in his eyes as Anna had then—wide open and ready to glimpse the last moment of light. His wife had hidden behind her words of defiance an uncontrollable, primal emotion—the one that makes the baby cry in the cradle, because, even before knowing what life is, it already fears death.

"Oh, Anna, dear," he murmured. "But you are frightened."

In his throat there was a pain, and it was new, relentless, and sharp. It was the pain of fear that he had forgotten years ago. *I only have this chance,* he thought in the moment of panic that stopped his breathing, *and if I am mistaken, I will kill her inside and I will die as well.* Why was he doing this to his wife? Why drag her into this revenge like a lamb to the slaughter? He looked at his wife, her eyes wide open, tendrils of her hair around her face, her pale complexion diaphanous in the moonlight. *But you will not die in my arms tonight.*

***

Christopher pulled away from her and put his hands on the wall next to his head, looming over her without touching her.

"Anna, don't be afraid of me." He leaned his temple to the side, lightly touching hers.

And she thought, *That pain, that awful pain, very soon.*

She had promised herself not to cry—but the promises of a broken soul are not worth much, are they? *Very soon I will be finished. Margaret is already waiting for me in her box. Very soon my smile will be destroyed, like hers, and I will also have that hole in my face. My eye will fall out then, too.*

"Anna, listen." Her husband took his forearms off the wall and moved closer to her. He put his forehead up to her hair. "I don't want to hurt you. Don't cry."

But Anna wasn't able to stop, because she suddenly understood the shocking truth: it was she who was the wicked one, not him. It was she who was supposed to save her family, and she couldn't. As much as she wanted to, she couldn't, not in a thousand years.

God, forgive me. Anthony, Dennis, Grace, and all of you who entrusted your lives to me without any doubts, forgive me. I am about to betray you, my beloved. I am about to commit the crime that will condemn me forever.

"I can't do it, Christopher!" she erupted, sobbing in despair. "Please, I beg you! Don't ask me to do that!"

A memory—a voice buried by guilt—said inside her, *"It was my fault. Do you understand? If only I had not run away that day, I could have saved her."*

"Forgive me please, and don't blame my family!"

Her shoulders shook without dignity, and her tears soaked the light cotton nightgown. She put her arms around her husband, burying her face in his chest, and felt him startle slightly. "Christopher, don't you understand? I would if I could, but I can't! Oh God, forgive me . . . I can't do it . . . I can't do it!"

Her terror had taken away her reason, and she held on tightly to him, as if seeking protection—clinging on to anything to keep from falling forever. Her desperate crying kept her from saying more. There was no air in her lungs, and she took long, painful intervals from one breath to the next. Her head was pressing on her husband's chest in an absurd request for consolation.

Christopher stood still for a few moments, and then he pulled his arms from the wall and hugged her around the shoulders. With one hand he stroked her hair, giving her little kisses on the top of her head. "Shh," he murmured. "It's all right." He rocked her slowly, swaying gently. "It's all right, don't worry," he repeated. "Don't cry."

He continued to rock her and kiss her hair until her crying subsided—which took an eternity. And when her tears finally finished, Anna continued to sob big gulps of air in his arms, in a strange embrace between victim and torturer. She could not think about the consequences of her refusal; she wanted to forget about everything in this unfair and comforting warmth, which she was sure would haunt her the next day. She didn't look up; she was not ready to read the death sentence in his eyes.

(What have you done, Anna?)

Christopher put his hand on her cheek and raised her face; their eyes met.

"Anna," he murmured, lowering his head and placing his warm lips on her cheek, chilled by the tears. "Listen to me. I will settle for a few kisses tonight—what do you think? Just a few caresses. I won't ask for more—I will not hurt you, no . . . I will not make love to you." He put his hand on her back and hugged her gently while he waited for her answer. "Can you manage?"

Could she? Could she accept to be touched by such a heinous man, willing to threaten her family—a family that loved him and welcomed him every night like a son? Could she please a man who routinely crushed the weak and innocent, as Daniel had revealed? Could she satisfy a man who on a July afternoon had thrown her in the grass, violating her dreams, raping her memories? With his mouth on her cheek and his burning heat against her, she wondered, *Can I do it?*

And what was the alternative? Strike again with the dagger of betrayal against her loved ones?

I have a second chance. I can make a different choice. How many times does that happen in life? "Will that be enough for you?" she asked him in a whisper.

"Yes." He spoke against her cheek, warming her face, and the sound he made was little more than a breath. "You shouldn't be afraid, you see? I will not go . . . I will not go inside you."

"You're not lying to me?"

"No." Her husband breathed passionately on her skin. "I swear to God, Anna. Let me hug you and kiss you only for a few minutes . . . just a few minutes . . . You can't imagine how much I need it."

He turned his head to the side, searching for her lips. Anna kept her eyes open while his mouth touched hers. She felt his heat and then his tongue, which was slow, gentle, and possessive all at once. She felt a cramp in her stomach and closed her eyes. A cramp of terror, or of a tearful remembrance, and something else she could not define.

Christopher kissed her slowly, without aggression. He held her, and then, moving his mouth to her skin, he asked, "Anna, am I that repulsive to you?"

She didn't answer but reopened her eyes at his strange and sorrowful tone. *What is the matter with my husband? Why does he behave in this absurd, inconsistent way?*

"Why . . . why are you doing this to me?" she asked him in a whisper.

"It's your fault, all your . . ." he answered desperately, his cheek against hers. "You've bewitched me, and I can't . . ." His lips brushed against her lightly, giving her little shivers. "You don't know . . . how much I've wanted . . . how much, my God . . ."

He kissed her again, and a feeling of dizziness made her hold on to him, her fingers grabbing on to his robe to hold herself up. *Oh, this man is so cruel,* she reminded herself. Even his kisses were cruel, because that cramp in her stomach kept growing. It rose into her chest and even higher, straight to her brain. Her husband came back to her lips, reclaiming them, biting them, touching them with his tongue, all around their edges. His hand on the nape of her neck pulled her toward him, driving his tongue completely into her mouth. His impetuousness jolted her; fear comingled with that indefinable emotion, but which one? What in her belly was creating that gnawing warmth? Was it panic or hatred? Whatever it was, it made her say to him, "Christopher . . . don't . . ."

"Five minutes . . . Please, oh please . . . just another five minutes more . . ."

He pushed her against the wall, and Anna felt something hard pressing against her flesh down low, ready to devour her. She opened her eyes suddenly, putting her hands up between her chest and her husband's. "Christopher!" she gasped. "Christopher, no, don't—"

"I swore . . . you know . . . Oh, Anna," he said hoarsely. "Give me . . . a minute, just one . . ."

His breath smelled of chocolate biscuits and cinnamon; she could almost taste it on him as he gave her little bites on her lips, licking them softly, kissing them lightly. "Your scent . . ." he mumbled, "your scent makes me go mad . . . But what is it?" With his hands he touched her body, her breasts, her hips. He put his mouth on her neck, and she bowed her head, shivering. *There's something wrong with me, my God.*

"Oh, Anna," he murmured, and he ran one of his hands between her legs, pushing on the fabric of the nightgown.

No, this couldn't be right. "No . . . Christopher!"

"A caress . . ." he said, with difficulty. "It's . . . a caress . . ."

That? That's what he means by "caresses"? Oh God, God . . . So this is how he intends to confirm my submission. By giving me pleasure, forcing me to answer. She felt hot, breathless, her heart beating madly. She was afraid, and he was so much bigger than her and so much more savage. And yet . . . and yet there were truly those times—those damned times when she had to stop and look at him absentmindedly against her will—in which he seemed almost sweet, and when, for a fragment of a moment, his eyes changed. In those moments his serious face became lighter, his eyes became childlike, defenseless, even sorrowful. But there couldn't be any good in him—she must have been mistaken about that. A feeling completely unsupported by logic could not defeat the thousand bits of proof of his evil soul. Christopher loomed. He stood over her with his massive force, his heat, with the sweet, fresh smell of his skin. And yet, as absurd as it was, his forced caresses turned out to be delicate and not unwelcomed, despite her panic that it was wrong.

(Don't you remember anymore who this man is, Anna?)

God help me. She felt her most intimate body part release liquid heat while his hand rubbed on her nightgown. *No, no, the fabric will get stained,* she thought incoherently. *I cannot get dirty, I can't . . .* And yet, besides the anxiety, there was a sensual pleasure she couldn't ignore. Her mind and her body were two entities, each fighting for different, irreconcilable objectives.

"Oh, darling, my darling . . ." he murmured to her, kissing her behind the ear, licking her softly and slowly lifting her nightshirt with his finger, searching for her.

No, I'm wet down there . . . You mustn't, don't . . . "No, no, Christopher!" She tried to stop his hand, but his was stronger, and he reached out to her. He touched her where she was the hottest, where it was the most indecent.

Shame made her lower her head, but her body didn't seem to feel any remorse. It wanted more; it wanted to betray her, because her husband had chosen the most cruel and sweet way to prove how much she belonged to him, how inextricably linked she was to him. Anna did not give in; she could not give in. She closed her legs tightly.

"Let me caress you please," he begged her. "Don't hide yourself, my darling."

He approached her mouth, raising her humiliated face, and he began to lift off her nightgown. *Does he want to undress me?* Anna wondered, upset. "No!" Frightened, she stepped back, putting her hands on his, opening her eyes.

Christopher lowered his forehead to touch hers. "I just wanted . . . to touch you," he said, having problems getting the words out. "Don't tell me no, Anna, don't . . . Just a few caresses . . . five minutes. One minute . . . one, please, just one . . ." He kissed her again and let go of the nightgown, which fell back down to her feet. "Come," he said, taking her by the hand and pulling her toward the bed.

(In the bed, Anna. He wants you in the bed. And you know what he will do to you once he's there, don't you?)

Anna did not move; she would not lie down for him like prey so that his jaws could devour her. He resented the panic that filled her and made her blind. "What . . . ? Don't . . ."

He got close to her mouth again. "I just want to hold you, Anna, just hold you," he whispered. He kissed her neck, breathing on her. "Just a few moments near you . . ."

He bent his knees a bit and raised her in his arms effortlessly. Anna was against his chest, trapped against him.

(Say no. Ask him to leave. Now.)

Fear pounded in her body and her head. His heat wrapped around her. She heard the beating of his heart and breathed in his scent. She closed her eyes and did not say no.

He set her down in the middle of the bed and removed his shirt. And when he lay down next to her, his chest was bare. "How beautiful you are, Anna," he whispered, rubbing her belly with his hand. "How beautiful you are, my dear."

The warmth of his skin startled her and put tears in her voice. "Christopher, please, I—"

"No, don't be afraid." He kissed her mouth while slowly stroking her hair. "I just want to hold you . . . just for a moment . . ."

Anna remained on her back, but he . . . he began again to take off her nightgown, and . . . Oh God, no, did he really want to see her nude? "No, Christopher . . ." She covered her eyes with her hands, not knowing what to do. Could she refuse? In addition to panic—and perhaps also hatred, she wondered—she had a ridiculous, unexpected thought: *And what if he doesn't find me to be beautiful?* "Don't undress me, don't—"

"Shh . . . wait . . ." Her husband leaned to the side and blew out the candle. The treacherous moonlight came in through the window, though. There was still enough light to allow them to make out the outlines of their bodies. "Is that better?" he asked her with a tenderness that rattled her bowels. He put his mouth to her ear while he resumed caressing her between her timid thighs. "Don't be ashamed, Anna . . . You're very beautiful . . ."

Am I beautiful? she wondered, confused.

"You really don't know it, do you, my dear?"

He kissed her face and neck. His tongue licked her skin. He moved to get on top of her by slipping in between her legs. Suddenly, his body was on top of her, and feeling it there filled Anna with a terrible memory that she could not push away. She winced and raised her hands in defense, but he put them on her chest to keep them down.

"Anna, I swore," he reminded her, his voice gentle but firm. "I won't go any further—you have to believe me. I only want to make you feel good, just this . . ." He kissed her face, scratching her lightly with his stubble. "Let me feel your skin . . . just for a minute, for a moment . . ."

He continued to caress her softly and sweetly, and Anna breathed heavily, trying to move to the rhythm of his caresses. His body was on top of hers, but it didn't weigh heavily on her. Unexpectedly light and unexpectedly protective, he began again to move his hand on her.

Slowly he lifted her nightgown, revealing her secret part, and then lifted it higher to show her navel and her belly.

"Open your legs a bit. Let me pamper you," he ordered her. She obeyed. "There we go, like that. Good . . ." His fingers made their way into the small space under the nightgown. He touched her, making little circles, moving rhythmically and delicately. He kissed her on the mouth while his panting breathing caressed her skin. "Oh, Anna . . . your taste . . ." He lifted her nightgown, uncovering her breasts. Then he took it off.

She was naked beneath him, covered only by his body. She was both afraid and ashamed, not just one or the other. Oh why didn't she remember who this man was? Why did she have this longing feeling in her stomach, her chest, and her head whenever he touched her skin?

"Don't look at me," she whispered, blushing, too guilty to open her eyes. "Please don't—"

"I can't see . . . I can't see anything . . ." He took her hand and kissed her palm sweetly. "Anna, am I so disgusting to you?" he asked in a whisper. "Won't you stroke my face?"

Breathing hard, Anna opened her eyes. In the half light, his wounds made him seem almost sweet and defenseless. He had asked her for a caress: Was it an order? Or was it a plea? He was looking at her helplessly. She gathered her courage and touched him for the first time. With a strange emotion, she felt the roughness of his cheek, his nose swollen by the punch, and his wolf's eyes, which distinguished him and gave off sparks even in the dark.

"And a kiss . . . Won't you give me a kiss, Anna?"

Shyly, she kissed him on the face, on the mouth, and on the corners of his eyes. She hadn't the courage to lick his skin, but she wanted to try the taste, to find out if was mint and cinnamon like his kisses. She couldn't; she had already gone too far, and she had to stifle the absurd impulse that urged her to caress him, to touch him, and to give him pleasure—the pleasure he was giving her. Anna vaguely imagined the regret and shame that would follow, and yet she couldn't manage to stop, and she held tight. She touched his body, which usually frightened her so, and his shoulders, his hips, his chest.

"Oh, Anna . . . Anna, my love . . ." Her husband's voice had a new, vulnerable sound, and he turned to kiss her, to play with her tongue, and to challenge her in a sweet and violent battle. He put his hand on her breast, and Anna felt his warmth and the shame and the injustice. But he kissed her, and she—why did she feel so comfortable underneath his body? Why did she feel that tense pleasure, as if waiting for something? Why was her husband's mouth on her breast?

She covered herself with her hands but did not protest. She didn't protest, not even when he licked her fingers while his caresses melted her, while he took one of her hands and placed it on his cheek. She didn't protest, not even with her husband's mouth kissing her nipple. He began to suck it gently, tickling it softly, as if he had the right.

(Do you see him, Anna? Do you see him taking everything from you?)

Bewildered, she let his lips set fire to her skin and let him touch her again and again—*How can I face him tomorrow?* They were only kisses and caresses—that's what he had said to her—and she had to accept that, didn't she? She had to—she couldn't do anything else . . .

"Oh, Chris, my God . . ." she said when he delicately pinched her sensitive skin. She bit her lips. The pleasure, the shame . . . No, no, she had to end all of this. *I have to ask him to stop now, she swore.* "Chris . . . please . . ."

"Anna, how much . . . how much I have dreamed of you," he murmured, continuing to kiss her, going lower still, toward her navel, and he licked her skin, teasing her with relentless tenderness, provoking her heat and her groans. *Oh, Maggie,* she thought as the wet caresses of her husband echoed immodestly. *Maggie, forgive me.*

Christopher bent her knees, raising them up. As if giving up, she indulged him. It was obedience, nothing but obedience. She let him spread her legs more and put his lips on her thigh. Although she was concerned when she felt something—a finger—slide inside, it was greeted with sweetness from a hot river.

"Chris?" she said, breathless.

"It's all right, all right, my love . . ." Christopher licked her slowly from the inside of her thigh and then moved lower. To where? Where he was touching her, breaking down all of her resistance? She had completely lost sense of time and limits. Five minutes had become fifty, she was aware, but she couldn't protest, not anymore. The tension in her body, her hot breathing, her sighs—everything in her responded naturally, in perfect rhythm with his kisses and his touch. She moaned, her eyes closed. She didn't want to open them—the caresses were so sweet; the kisses were so sweet. She didn't want to know why his head was down there. She didn't want to know where his lips . . .

She opened her eyes, shocked. "No!" She reached out her hand, grabbed him by the hair, and pulled hard, but he did not budge. His tongue made its way into her wet, scandalous furrow, and he licked it slowly. He licked it there, where all of her secrets were . . .

"No, not that, Chris, please!"

He licked her nectar, her obscene, hot nectar. He licked her where she was about to explode, to *make her* explode, make her explode . . . in his mouth.

"Christopher, no!" She pulled on him again, begged breathlessly, shook, and finally he came back to her navel, stopping the indecency. Her belly was inflated, as were her breasts. Everything in her was tense, asking, begging. "No, no! . . ." But what kind of woman was she? What on earth? "It's immoral, don't . . ."

Christopher laughed softly. "Oh, Anna," he said, resting his forehead on her abdomen. "There's nothing more moral."

"Don't laugh," she pleaded. "Don't . . ." *Don't laugh at me. Don't judge me, Chris.* And she felt fear, but it was different now, wasn't it? She was no longer afraid of pleasing him. She was afraid of *not* pleasing him. Right now she wanted him on her mouth; right now she wanted him to kiss her with tenderness and passion; right now she wanted—yes, *she* wanted him—while he maybe thought of her as a bad woman. She didn't have the courage to pull him toward her own mouth, nor to call out to him, nor to beg him, and she remained in agony, feeling a little bit dirty and a little bit beautiful, while his finger—a part of him—was inside her body, welcomed by her body.

"I'm not laughing at you, silly." Christopher went back to her breast and kissed it with possessiveness in every gesture, with sweet aggressiveness in every gesture. "It's my right," he had said to her. And Anna, conquered, stuck her fingers in his hair, watching him bend over her. She watched him possess everything of hers. Her legs spread wide, naked under his body, she was allowing him to do anything—she knew that. He had beaten her. And yet . . . and yet what showed on his face was not the satisfied derision of victory. No, it was as if he were lost, lost in her, and happy—an unmediated happiness; a natural, instinctive happiness. And when his mouth came back to hers, Anna greeted him with the same happiness, and with her fingers in his hair she held him close to her, kissing him with an unbridled passion, and, for the first time, voluntarily.

"How much you have tortured me, Anna, how much . . ." he whispered. "Did you really not understand, my love?"

He increased the rhythm of his stroking, as if to punish her, and Anna was lost, clinging to his body. The warmth that he had taken from her in the grass was coming back—it was inevitable; that warmth that she hadn't been able to think of without pain and shame. And the shame: would that also come back, she wondered with a last glimmer of clarity? She felt her husband insert another finger in her, and she could no longer wonder if it was bad or wrong, if *she* was wrong. Her husband would sooner or later ask to become her husband, to enter inside her, as his hand now had done. Maybe even the night after. But she couldn't worry about that now; not now that he was so sweet; not now that chills were shaking her body; not now that she wanted so, so much to keep him close to her.

"It doesn't hurt, does it, my love?"

Anna shook her head. Her eyes closed, and breathing hard, she pushed her own groin against his hand, forgetting about honor, forgetting about morals. Christopher took out the cruel part of his body, and she felt it press hard against her raised thigh. She stiffened and came to her senses. "No, Christopher! You swore!"

"I just want . . . just to touch you . . ." He turned with his mouth on hers. "I'll stay out, Anna, dear."

"Chris, don't—"

"Shh . . ."

He kissed her, and his devious member rubbed against her legs, but his fingers continued to plunge into her—first out, then in—in a smooth but disturbing movement. Again out, then in, then . . .

"Chris?"

He barely penetrated her—half an inch maybe.

"That's my hand, my love."

But weren't his hands touching her nipples, caressing them gently?

"Christopher . . . ?"

"Don't . . . don't worry . . . I swore . . ."

And then what was he sliding inside her . . . an inch . . . ?

"Oh . . . Chris . . . what . . . ?"

He buried his head in her shoulder, clutching her, and then he raised his head, searched for her mouth, and kissed her with a groan. He pushed forward slowly, keeping her knees raised. He gave her time to adjust to the invasion, moving slowly, trembling with the effort to control himself. Anna responded to his kiss, held on to him, and welcomed him. It wasn't a finger that finally filled up her secret part—she knew what it was and how deep it could go.

"Oh, Anna . . . you're my wife now . . . you're my wife . . ."

He filled her—her husband, who had fooled her and entered inside her.

30

The soul, fortunately, has an interpreter—often an unconscious but still a faithful interpreter—in the eye.
—Charlotte Brontë

She woke at first light in the morning, feeling a warm weight at her side. In the first moments of consciousness, she thought it was Nightshade. It often happened that the cat secretly slipped into her bed when she slept at Lucy's. But she was at her house now, and they had no cats.

She remembered, opening her eyes wide in the room: her husband had made love to her last night. It was his arm that was around her now even while he was asleep, and his breathing was difficult because of his injured nose. His sleeping body was nude, right behind her own.

He had fooled her like always, and the fact that she had found his kisses to be pleasant, as well as those caresses—and, finally, him inside her—made her close her eyes. She was naked under the sheet, and the morning light told her that it was time to get up, but his arm was pinning her down, although light and comforting. The fear of waking him up was too much even to get dressed: it would mean seeing him again, and he would certainly laugh at her, finally tamed.

(But you liked it—being tamed—didn't you? Tamed by he who was willing to do harm to your loved ones.)

Would he have really done it? Would he have really separated her from her family? she wondered, barely breathing so as not to wake him. Christopher, who taught fencing to Anthony. Who gave imaginative answers to Grace's questions—but softly, almost muttering, as if ashamed. Who didn't scold Dennis when he found him snooping in his room.

He seemed to believe it. His eyes seemed sure of it. Almost unhappy, indeed, in the belief that yes, he would do anything just to bend her to his will. Just to win.

And yet he could have any woman he wanted. He had had many, probably. But he also wanted her; however, whether that was out of desire or spite was something she didn't know.

And she . . . she would please him from now on, both in and out of bed? She would no longer put her family in jeopardy? She had already betrayed them once—almost betrayed them, almost sacrificed them on the altar of fear. Because if he had left after her refusal . . . The thought continued to torment her. A few tears formed in her eyes and then fell, and she would have wiped them away but she was afraid to wake him. In the light it was easier to make out the shape and profile of everything. She slowly moved her hand to her eyes, and she felt her husband's arm move on her. She froze.

***

Christopher awoke. He was lying on his side, and in front of him there were waves of brown, his wife's hair loose on the pillow. For several moments he did nothing, not even breathe; then he smiled and moved his arm on the soft skin of the girl in front of him.

He heard her sniffling. *Is she crying?* It seemed chilly with only the light sheet on the bed. Had he done something wrong? Had he hurt her? No. No, he was sure: his wife might love Daniel, or at least hate him, but she had enjoyed that night in his arms.

"Anna, are you awake?" he asked her with a thick voice.

She didn't respond for several seconds. "You have sworn falsely, sir," she finally said.

He smiled. He expected these words exactly. "Oh." Anna could not see him, and that was a good thing. She wouldn't have liked his grin. "Of course." Lying flat on his back, he pulled his arm off her and brought it to his eyes.

"Is it something you do often?"

Christopher thought about it. "No, not often," he replied. He removed his arm from his eyes and turned his head toward the nape of his wife's neck. "Usually after the first time it doesn't work anymore."

Anna didn't seem particularly amused. "I see," she said dryly.

"Anna, I didn't want to fool you," he murmured to calm the anger he felt in her. "I wanted you not to be afraid."

He put his hand on her hip, but she moved, annoyed. She sat up, putting her feet on the floor, and looked for her nightgown. She found it, picked it up, and raised her arms to slip it on. He looked quickly at her back, covered by loose hair, as she stretched to get on the nightgown. Her body was slowly hidden by clothing; fabric covered her shoulders and shoulder blades. He observed her wide, comfortable hips, and noticed a large bruise on her left buttock—he had given that to her the day before when he had knocked her down violently. The purplish color of the bruise contrasted sharply with her white skin. Her nightgown finally hid even that spot.

Unable to prevent it—without even trying, actually—he sat up in bed, put his arms around her waist, and bent down to kiss her on the cheek.

Anna bowed her head to the side with a restless shudder. "Christopher, go back to your room," she ordered him. She tried to remove his arms from her sides, but his grasp was very strong, and he got even closer to her. "Christopher! It's late. Let me go."

She's still afraid of me. God, will she ever get over that? "Don't be afraid, Anna," he whispered. "You should know that I will not hurt you." He gave her some kisses on the recess of her shoulder and gently licked her skin.

As shy as a bride—she was a bride, in fact—she stiffened. But Christopher noticed that her breath had begun to quicken and she seemed to shrink in his arms. He recognized this to be her childish reaction, but it was still their first wedding night, and . . .

"Sir," she said with her head down. "Sir, I would like . . . I need to know . . ."

Christopher raised his head from the curve of her neck and looked at her profile. "What?" he asked nicely. "Tell me."

Silence for a bit. "Do you love me, Christopher?"

The question rang in his head for a few moments, striking him for its sheer stupidity.

God, women.

No, Anna, I don't love you. You are only part of my revenge.

(But in the meantime you'll take all the pleasure you can. Isn't that so, Christopher?)

That thought bothered him. Come now, he didn't rape her at all. They were married, after all, and he . . . Oh, to hell with it. Irritated, he dropped his arm from her side and moved back a little. His wife took the opportunity to get up suddenly, and she walked away from the bed without looking at him.

"Would it make you feel better if I told you that I love you?" he wanted to know. He could lie if need be.

"It would help me understand your behavior," she answered without turning around.

(Then she would have all the answers she needs, Christopher. She wouldn't bother you with her complaints anymore.)

True. Maybe she wouldn't forget about Daniel, but, satisfied with his vanity, he could put her heart at peace. What did it matter if he told one more lie if it served a purpose?

I love you, Anna, he tried to say in his mind.

"I don't love you, Anna," he said. The words came out wrong. Perhaps he thought it too cynical to fool her about that as well. "But love isn't necessary for a good marriage," he added gently. "I like you and that's something, isn't it?"

"The same way you like Mrs. Edwards?"

"Mrs. . . . ?" He frowned. He had completely forgotten about that woman. *You would be amazed if you knew how different it is to make love with you. Different . . . yes . . . and more beautiful,* he had to admit. It was beautiful because his pleasure combined with hers, and he was attentive to her every moan, every thrill, every answer. He watched her with her back to him, proud and embarrassed. "Are you jealous, Anna? Do you want me to be faithful?"

"No, sir. Feel free to have as many women as you want."

These words were cold, and in fact he felt the cold under the sheets. Maybe it was time to get dressed and start the day. "I will not say the same to you, if that's what you expect."

Anna turned to look at him, and she blushed when her eyes met his; her pupils grew large and the memories from the night before prevented her from appearing indifferent. She quickly looked down. To Christopher she seemed more beautiful than ever, and he fought the urge to go to her immediately. He could surely talk with his wife for five minutes without jumping on her, by God!

"No, I didn't expect that," she answered. She played with her hands a bit, then sighed and changed the subject. "Sir, that widow that you will evict from her property—"

"Don't worry about that," he interrupted abruptly. "You'll see. It will be your Daniel who deals with it." *And maybe Daniel will fuck that widow; God only knows how much he needs it.* He gave a naughty smile that his wife couldn't understand and went on: "Since you care so much for the well-being of that gentleman, you of all people would not want to take away from him the pleasure of feeling so right and so superior to ordinary mortals."

"But what are you saying, Christopher? I cannot believe that your conscience—"

"Anna, do not get involved in things that you cannot understand," he said, and stopped talking. His tone was final and the same one used with a person whose opinion has no value at all. His wife drew back, mortified. She turned away and walked toward the armoire. He began to speak again, more gently: "Listen. Don't take an interest in my business, and in exchange you will be free to manage the house as you see fit."

She opened a door on the armoire, and her voice came out tinged with bitter irony when she said, "I was right, then. You find fault with my actions just so you can oppress me."

"Not really," he replied in his own sincere way. "But I'm willing to get down to some compromise." *Maddening, this woman is maddening,* he thought when he saw her shake her head. *Is she ever happy?* "I could do without, you know," he explained condescendingly, "but I want to meet you halfway, and you should thank me for once."

"Your kind heart moves me, sir."

"Good." It wasn't that he didn't hear her sarcasm, it was just that he preferred to ignore it. And in truth he wanted to move on to other things. "Come here now."

Anna gave up the search for a dress and closed the armoire. She moved toward the door that led down the hallway.

Oh, no. Don't run away from me. Christopher threw the blanket to the side in a hurry, got up, and headed toward her.

"Christopher, cover up!" Anna exclaimed, covering her eyes with her hand. Her face was so on fire she could have cooked breakfast on it that morning. "I have to go downstairs, sir," she mumbled. "I'm late."

She seemed to want to leave the room like that, in her nightgown. Christopher joined her at the door as she opened it. He was behind her, and he pushed against the door, closing it again.

"Christopher, what?"

"Anna, you're not still afraid of me, are you?" he asked in a whisper. He held her and began to lift off her thin, white nightgown. "I won't hurt you ever like this," he murmured. A detail occurred to him, and he added: "Never again, Anna." He kissed her cheek. "Do you believe me?"

***

How can I believe you? thought Anna without answering as he embraced her and tenderly kissed her neck. *You don't even ask me whether or not I want to make love with you.*

And her husband's hands were already touching her, sweet and overbearing, moving her body in an unfair and inevitable way. Hands that lied to her body; hands that declared love. Lying hands—liars just like Christopher, who told her the truth in only one instance. When he didn't tell her the lie that she wanted to hear.

(But what would that change for you, Anna? Perhaps you would not continue to hate him.)

Christopher spread her legs with those hands. *He doesn't really want to . . . in the morning!* "Don't . . . Chris, I have to go! This is not the time, don't . . ."

"It's our honeymoon," he whispered, caressing her. "Anyway, I will be quick, dear. Don't worry."

But he lied, like always.

***

When Christopher got downstairs, he found three pairs of children's eyes looking at him reproachfully.

"You're late, Christopher," Anthony pointed out, taking the last biscuit in front of him from the plate in the middle of the table. "The biscuits are all gone."

"I see." He looked at his wife. Surely it was her behind this boycott of his breakfast. Anna didn't raise her head from the tea she was sipping, too embarrassed to look at him.

"No biscuits, Nora?" he asked the cook, who was sitting at the table with Anna and the children.

"Humph."

"Mr. Champion isn't joining us today?"

"He already finished," said Anthony. "He went back to his room."

"Christopher," Grace declared, getting up from the table. "If I become a doctor when I grow up, I'll put your nose back in order."

"Oh." Christopher touched it. That damned half brother had hit him good, he admitted to himself. Who knew if he was in a bad way like him this morning. He hoped so. Indeed, he hoped worse for him. Unfortunately, it did not seem very likely. "Didn't you say that it looked good on me?" he asked, taking a teacup and filling it with tea. If even Grace thought it was ugly, there was definitely a need to worry.

"How stupid you are, Grace," Dennis said. "Don't you know that only men become doctors?"

"That's not true," protested the little girl. "Chris, tell him so."

Chris put the cup on the table and stood. His chair was also gone. Where had they hidden it? He looked around but didn't see it, and he answered with a sigh. "I don't know if there are women doctors, Grace. Anna, what do you say?"

His wife pretended not to hear him, blushing furiously. Christopher tried to imagine what their future life together would be like if she always stayed this shy with him. *No more discussions, no more bitter sentences, no more corrosive or disgusted looks,* he enumerated to himself. *Well, I could survive. It would be heaven, to be honest.* He wanted to give it a try. "Anyway, you will not have to do any work, Grace," he said.

"To support you, your husband will do all the thinking when you're married. So if I were you, I really wouldn't bother with the study of medicine and all the other things. Leave studying to your brothers. For you there's no need."

Anna looked up suddenly. "Christopher, what are you saying!" she exploded, glaring at him. "Grace, do not listen to this . . . this . . ."

She seemed unable to find the right word to define her husband's unwelcome advice properly. Christopher turned quickly to hide a smile.

31

There are books of which the backs and covers are by far the best parts.

—Charles Dickens

When her husband finally left the house—that day it seemed he never wanted to leave—Anna could have a careful look at the letter Nora had given her when she had gone downstairs. She had hidden it in a hurry because she quickly recognized who it was from: on the envelope was written *"Miss Roxanne Fogmind,"* and it had an unknown seal.

She now turned it over and smiled. "Who delivered it, Nora?"

"The farmer, along with that fruit in the corner," replied the little cook, who had not wanted to give up that role and was rather indignant when they proposed the idea to her. Perhaps she was convinced that a new cook would poison them or, even worse, make them lose weight.

Miss Roxanne required Anna's full attention, but where could she hide away to read that letter? The answer suddenly popped into her head: her husband's office. Not to get even, obviously. No. Oh, all right, maybe a little. However, it was also true that the children would not look for her there, and besides, it had been a while since she had looked through his drawers. Not that she ever found anything interesting, but . . .

She ran there quickly and unlocked the door with a hairpin in less than a minute. She was nervous as she did it: her husband's presence was so strong in that room that she was always scared of seeing him appear from behind the door.

She entered and closed the door behind her. She sat down by the window, where the view allowed her to see the road, and opened the letter from Miss Fogmind.

> *Dear Anna,*
>
> *I apologize for taking the liberty to write to you, but as you can imagine the anxiety after what happened yesterday—because of me—has given me no peace. Anna, I know that this will offend you, but I have decided to go to London to investigate your husband. I will not ask you again how he was able to get you to marry him, but I cannot manage to convince myself that your feelings for him came on as suddenly as you say—or that, to quote his words, it "blossomed overnight like a wildflower."*
>
> *I would like to hear from you, if you could possibly reply to this letter; I will wait impatiently to receive your response before leaving. I'm quite worried after yesterday afternoon. Anna, I hope that you know my friendship is unwavering and always present for you, and I pray you feel free to confide every one of your problems to me without hesitation. I could help get you out of any (any!) difficult situation. Anna, believe me, no scandal is worse than a life spent with a violent man.*

I would have come to your house this morning if the fear of causing a problem hadn't prevented me. Just say the word and I will rush to you; to crack your husband's face again would give me immeasurable satisfaction.

Warmest wishes,
D. DeM.

Anna smiled and walked to her husband's writing desk, and with her heart pounding loudly, she began right there to draft a response to Miss Roxanne.

Dear Daniel,
Or Fogmind, as you're now calling yourself—I wish you a good trip if you're leaving for London. A foggy mind will definitely be helpful there, don't you think?

Your concern for me, although very kind, is not warranted. Nothing has happened to me since yesterday afternoon—

(Nothing, Anna?)

She paused as her cheeks got warm—and her body, perhaps. Then she shook her head and began again to write.

Nothing has happened to me since yesterday afternoon that could possibly worry you. I know that you will not keep me in the dark regarding the things that you will find out, because we are friends, and for that very same reason do not be offended if I do not offer further explanations to this request of mine.

I wanted to reassure you, however: Christopher does not beat me. It never happened during our engagement, nor since we have been married. In any case, I will remember your thoughtful offer to help in case I may need it. I ask one thing of you: do not speak of your concerns with Lucy. I fear that she won't give me a moment's rest and that she may attempt to scratch out my husband's eyes to make a charming little knickknack out of them—a paperweight perhaps.

She finished the letter; time was running short.

With many thanks, dear Daniel.
Your friend,
Anna

PS You will be surprised to know that the closing remarks of your letter are the same ones used by my husband when referring to you. I imagine that this will displease you, and already I'm smiling at the look on your face right now (come on, stop it, Daniel, or you will get premature wrinkles furrowing up your brow). Maybe I shouldn't have mentioned such a coincidence, but I know that you will be able to appreciate the irony. Certainly, given your mutual sympathy, I believe it would be best if you and Christopher stay away from each other in the near future, even on any social occasions at which you both happen to be. A word of advice: my husband's nose has swollen so big that if one is in the same room with him it will be impossible not to be near him, insofar as he frightens others away.

Anna hurried to clean up the desk, removing all traces of her being there. Before leaving, she opened all the desk drawers, without neglecting the locked one, which was empty again this time.

She felt frustrated.

Where was her husband hiding his documents? Because they were there, she was sure of it. For example, the papers about guardianship. But where were they? She had already looked in all the books on the shelves. There weren't many, to tell the truth. Maybe Christopher was afraid of ruining his mind by reading too much. In fact, he was unaware of practically every aspect of human knowledge. Why soil such an immaculate ignorance with careless reading?

She continued her search. She checked all false bottoms—she discovered three of them—and found nothing. She looked behind all of the paintings and in the wastepaper bin. Nothing. Exasperated, she went back to the books—and she finally noticed something that had escaped her.

The fireplace.

The fireplace mantel had been redecorated according to her husband's instructions with heavy marble and stucco, and when she and Lucy had seen the gilded jumble of flowers and vines, they had thought that Christopher's taste was so gaudy it was almost illegal. *But maybe he wanted it this way for a reason,* she thought, and a smile appeared on her face.

***

Mr. Owen was left, and then he could go home. *Mr. Owen . . . Mr. Owen . . . Ah, yes, that stocky man with a bald spot who asked him for the small loan.* It wasn't so important, come to think of it. Practically nothing, thought Christopher. *That's enough for today,* he decided. *I'll notify him that the appointment has been postponed until tomorrow.* If he hurried, he could finish in time to get home for the afternoon fairy tale that Anna told the children. Not that he approved of such sentimental nonsense, mind you; he only wanted to find out what part in the story his wife would give him that day, and in what imaginative way she would kill him in the end.

He rose from his chair after closing his desk and stretched out his arms as wide as possible. He caught a glimpse of a book on a nearby shelf. It was an old edition with a brown cover, ruined in several places. He reached out, took it, and flipped through a few pages. He knew every detail, every scratch, every crease of the yellowed paper. He read:

> *. . . the castle and lordship of Otranto 'should pass from the present family whenever the real owner should be grown too large to inhabit it.'*

He closed the book with a thud. He put it back in its place and then returned to his seat behind the desk.

(You can't take a break, Christopher. Not even for half an hour.)

That book had reminded him of that once again, just like it had reminded him one cold afternoon twelve years before when he had gone into Frank Davenport's office to read it. Afterward he pinched it from Matthew. In truth, in the beginning he really just wanted to hide it. And he was convinced that sooner or later he would give it back to him—but first Matthew would have to beg him for days. Maybe months. To be completely honest, the idea that at thirteen years old Christopher had spent an afternoon reading a book (and his cousin's, no less!) sounded more like an impossibility than an actual fact. It occurred, however, following four random and simultaneous events.

The first was an afternoon of rain mixed with sleet. The second was that Matthew was in bed with a cold, and the third was that he had not yet noticed the theft after two days. Finally, the fourth was that a terrible danger loomed over Christopher. *Irritating an obese nanny with a shrill voice is definitely hard on the eardrums,* he was thinking as he ran for the dining room. *Maybe that's why they pick such fat ones.* He had stopped for a moment to grab the book from where he had hidden it—behind the sofa—before seeking out solitude and safety in his uncle's office, where Sonia would not look for him.

Hiding had proven to be a rather wise idea, because when the nanny discovered the mess in the playroom, she began to scream. Not that Christopher had any part in that disaster, mind you: it's only normal to damage furniture when one is trying to move a little wagon with steam. He had read about this machine, and he tried to reproduce the way it worked. It hadn't gone too badly. Moreover, it wasn't that the rug had been really burned. Not all of it, at least; if she had just cut a foot off the end, it would have been as good as new, but he doubted Sonia would have thought so. She was always making such a fuss over things. If he had tried to propose this solution to her—or if she found him in any case—she would have puffed out her big pink cheeks, run her hand through her frizzy, dark-blond hair, and then, putting her hands on her hips, barked a rebuke at him. Well, certainly more than one. Finally, she would have exploded in one of her favorite battle cries: "Now I'm telling Mrs. Davenport, Christopher!" Not that it would have made a difference. Even Sonia understood that if it didn't concern Matthew, the aunt merely shrugged her shoulders and immediately forgot about the whole thing.

I hope she doesn't tell Uncle, however, Christopher had wished with a slight sense of guilt. But honestly, what else could he have done that afternoon if not some scientific experiment? Matthew was in bed, and his aunt wouldn't allow him to get up. And the annoying tapping of the rain on the windowpane wouldn't stop and kept him from going out.

He was distracted from his thoughts because he had heard Sonia coming down the hallway. "Christopher!"

He evaluated her tone. There was irritation, certainly. Breathlessness (she was probably walking fast). Maybe a slight appetite. But was there a negligible trace of kindness, which might allow him to go out or hope for forgiveness?

"Christopher! Christopher Davenport, come out at once! Where are you, you rascal?"

No, definitely not. He remained silent, hoping that Sonia didn't come into his uncle's office. She passed by, and Christopher felt understandably relieved.

After an hour he came out from his hiding place underneath the dark wooden desk, and he walked up to the short table in the right corner. On it there was a bottle with an amber liquid in it that looked very tasty indeed. Christopher poured some into a glass and tried it. It burned his throat, and the smoky flavor almost made him vomit. *My uncle isn't right about everything, then,* he thought as he went to sit in the armchair with the book in his hands. He hoped that, despite having drunk that stuff, he would still be able to find out something about the letters he had given his uncle more than a year before. His mother's letters. Because it had not been easy for him to hand them over to him. For six years he had kept them hidden, and for six years he had reread them without even showing them to Matthew. For six years trying to figure out a few clues: a street, "East Street"; the school of a certain Mrs. White; and who L. was, of course. Six years without making any damned progress. And in the end he had given them to his uncle, because if there was someone who could help him get to the bottom of it, it was Frank Davenport. His mother's notebook—the strange diary that spoke of better, faraway worlds—was the only thing he didn't give him. Mostly because he thought that it would not be useful to him, but also because he wanted to keep it to himself. Only to himself.

Wrapped in an old gray blanket that he had found on the back of the armchair, he felt warm despite the cold. In reality it was freezing in his uncle's office: Mary hadn't lit the fire since Frank was out and would not be back until the next day. However, Christopher didn't leave, even though Sonia had stopped looking for him. He felt cozy with the slight odor of pipe in the air—*Maybe I should try to smoke it,* he had thought, but with the memory of his failed experiment with the whisky, he decided to give up on the idea.

He began to read.

> *Manfred, Prince of Otranto, had one son and one daughter: the latter, a most beautiful virgin, aged eighteen, was called Matilda . . .*

Typical book for Matthew, he said to himself. *It's all about the fierce battle between boredom and monotony.* In truth, this book wasn't Matthew's, and that was why Christopher hoped for something a little bit more exciting. But there was nothing exciting about Bridgetown in Kent, and even less so in the house of Mrs. Sharp, Matthew's maternal grandmother. It was there that his bad little cousin had discovered this *Castle of Otranto* when he had been there for a visit earlier that month. Christopher had not gone with him and his aunt—he had stayed with his uncle, who was unable to leave London—and he wasn't disappointed about it at all, since Mrs. Sharp had a strange way of curling up her nose when she saw him, and she punished him constantly. Not always unfairly, to be sure, but that didn't change the fact, did it? He had missed Matthew a little during those two weeks, he had to admit, but not seeing his aunt was nice, as was having his uncle all to himself for once. Going with him on the frozen Thames was a very exciting experience indeed. It was a pity his stupid cousin couldn't come, Christopher thought with regret, but they would have the chance to go back again sooner or later, maybe even the next year.

> *. . . Manfred had contracted a marriage for his son with the Marquis of Vincenza's daughter, Isabella . . .*

Maybe he could hurl the book against the wall and get another. He looked around; there were only periodicals and old registry logs.

> *. . . what a sight for a father's eyes!—he beheld his child dashed to pieces and almost buried under an enormous helmet . . .*

Oh, it's getting better, he thought with satisfaction, and he dived more quickly into the reading. He stopped only once, when he thought it was too dark. He left to bring back a candle, then immersed himself among the ghosts and giants of the book again.

> *. . . Theodore threatened destruction to all who attempted to remove him from it. He printed a thousand kisses on her clay-cold hands and uttered every expression that despairing love could dictate . . .*

Time flew by, and it was already nearly suppertime. The cold had made his fingers numb, and he felt stiff under the blanket.

> *. . . But Theodore's grief was too fresh to admit the thought of another love, and it was not until after frequent discourses with Isabella of his dear Matilda that he was persuaded he could know no happiness but in the society of one with whom he could forever indulge the melancholy that had taken possession of his soul.*

That was it; it was over. It wasn't bad, was it? And yet someone didn't like it; in fact, under the words "The End" some mysterious person had written meticulously:

On the sixteenth day of May in the year of our Lord 1798

We hereby find that:

The ending of this book is dreadful

We hereby note that:

Isabella's destiny is the worst that could be wished for

This document is drafted and signed by the owner of the book and by her best friend, who in full possession of their mental faculties (and also a full stomach) do swear, assure, and declare that:

They will never be second to none, by Jove!

A mysterious person, yes. This handwriting seemed strange to him. It looked familiar, it was true, but he didn't recognize it. Maybe because we only see the things we expect to see. Maybe because rain was still hitting the window and he was still under the blanket and he was still in the office that smelled like pipe tobacco, and everything bad—death and pain—seemed so out of place here. And yet . . . and yet these words were cheerful, and Christopher felt uneasy. And yet he was afraid to read the signatures under the oath.

No, that wasn't it exactly. He wasn't afraid to read the *first* signature. Because even though it was written in a more uncertain way, and less slanted, and larger compared to the writing that Christopher knew, the pen was unmistakable. Reassuring.

The owner of the book

Barbara Sharp

But underneath . . . underneath there was a second signature. Unknown yet familiar. So damned familiar.

Her aforementioned friend, and notary of distinction

"Notary of distinction," Christopher read. Then he read again, and he stared and stared at that phrase as if lost. Again and again. He gazed at it for minutes at a time until he became blind to it and he couldn't take his eyes off it. He wouldn't allow his eyes to read the signature underneath. Why?

". . . notary of distinction . . ."

"Her aforementioned friend . . ."

"Her aforementioned friend, and notary of distinction . . ."

Those *a*'s with the flourish, rounded, with playful curls. He didn't recognize them, did he? He recognized neither the bulging *d*'s, nor the delicate *n*'s, nor any of the flowery alphabet with which, in a notebook with a black cover, she had created a far-off world years after. A better world.

"Her aforementioned friend, and notary of distinction . . ."

He let his eyes look down.

"*Martha Askey,"* he had read.

32

Murder is always a mistake. One should never do anything that one cannot talk about after dinner.
—Oscar Wilde

He glanced at his wife, who was sitting under the window, sewing. It was absurd that he felt embarrassed just to talk to her. After all, she was his wife—*really* his wife. Already for several days now, and there was no point in him thinking about it at this time of the afternoon, he thought with a smile on his face. "Anna, could I speak to you a moment?"

She did not look up at him. "Aren't you going out today?" she asked, as if distracted. But she wasn't. She was shy, this silly girl, and she was trying not to show it.

"No. Can you come into my office? I have something to show you."

His wife seemed alarmed. "Now? What?"

Oh for God's sake. "Anna, it's nothing dangerous. Come."

She sighed. She put her sewing down and followed him to the room. "Tell me, then," she said, entering the room after him.

"You recall that Anthony and I went to London some time ago." He picked up a letter that was sitting on top of his desk and handed it to her. "I received the response that I was waiting for this morning." He hoped that Anna would not react badly to the news that he was about to give her. *But no, why would she? She will be happy, if anything. Absolutely.* "From the Westminster School. Anthony will go there next Monday."

Anna stood there. "What?"

"Anthony will go to boarding school," he stated. "He wants to."

She frowned. "What are you saying?"

Things were going rather well. "It's a good thing for—"

Her eyes opened wide. She understood. "No! How could you?" There was anger in her eyes, and pain as well. *Is she mortified?* "No! You said—"

Christopher raised his hands to stop this incoherent babbling. "Anna, listen—"

"Don't!" Her lips were trembling. "How? . . . Why?"

"Anna, listen—"

"What . . . what did I do wrong?" she asked him in a broken voice, clutching her belly in her arms. "What more do you want from me still? Why do you persist—?"

"Oh for the love of God, Anna!" Why did this woman not let him speak? "You have done nothing wrong. The boarding school is a good—"

"Why are you doing this to me? Why are you taking him away from me?"

"Anthony *wants*—"

"No! Don't take my brother away from me! Don't do it! Don't . . ."

It was impossible to reason with this woman. He was a fool to even consider it. He went toward the door and opened it quickly. "Anthony!" his voice boomed from the doorway. "Anthony, come here now!"

His voice echoed through the entire house, and Anna gasped. "Christopher, my father! . . ."

"Christopher?" Anthony called out as he came running.

"Oh, Anthony, you're here." For a man as tall as him to hail a little boy who was almost two feet shorter than him as a savior—that was saying a lot. "Please repeat to your sister what you told me about your desire to go to boarding school." It was a bit cowardly certainly, but the moment definitely required emergency measures.

Unperturbed, Anthony turned to look at his sister with a face as serious as that of a diplomat on a mission. "I would like to go to boarding school, Anna. Christopher said—"

"You . . . you want to go?" she said. Her voice was calm, but she was as pale as a sheet and didn't seem very believing of her younger brother. "You didn't . . . You hadn't ever mentioned . . . Anthony, why didn't you tell me? Why did you tell him and not me?"

Anthony shrugged his shoulders without answering.

"I have news for you, Anthony," Christopher said to him. He picked up the letter that his wife had let fall to the ground and handed it to the boy. "Start to think about the things that you would like to take with you, because there's only one week until your departure. You have been accepted at the Royal College of St. Peter."

Anthony's cheeks flushed, and his mouth dropped open. He didn't know how to show his joy in any other way, nor had Christopher expected him to, anyway. The boy had his own way of showing enthusiasm. He began to read the letter that his brother-in-law had given him, still looking very serious. *But . . . but . . . Eh? No, Anthony, that won't do, thought Christopher. Your eyes are starting to tear up, my boy.*

Anna still had the pale, startled look from earlier. *Why does she always have to make everything difficult?* "I will accompany him myself for admission next Monday," he announced. "You could come with us, obviously. Your brother will come back here every weekend if his studies will allow it."

Anna seemed drained. She put a hand on her forehead and rubbed it as if to collect her thoughts. "But . . . so soon?"

"School is about to begin, and Anthony cannot afford delays. He will have to follow the pace of his fellow pupils."

"And Daddy?" His wife's voice sounded faint.

"You will tell Mr. Champion. But he will be happy, I imagine."

"But why didn't you say anything to me, Christopher?"

Because you would have made a big fuss. "It slipped my mind," he replied.

"It slipped . . . Oh, I suppose it did," she commented dryly. She turned toward her brother. "Anthony, could you leave Christopher and me alone, please."

Damn it, she wants to argue. And the outburst will be incredibly noisy.

"Anna, there's no point to . . ." he said, but he stopped after he saw her expression. "Anthony," he said then. "If you want, you can finish reading that letter in your room. It belongs to you, after all."

Anthony nodded. "I will miss you a lot, Anna," he said. "And the others as well."

He seemed uncertain; then he motioned with his hand for her to stoop toward him. Anna humored him with some effort, as if held down by an invisible weight. Anthony whispered something in her ear, and then he went out of the office and ran to his room with the letter tight in his hands.

Anna stood up straight. Dismay darkened her eyes and face. "What are you trying to do, Christopher? Why do you behave in this way?"

"I don't understand you."

"Is this your way of depriving me of affection? Buying them with—"

For a moment he was tempted to call Anthony back. "Anna," he interrupted her, "you can't really think . . . Oh dear God! If it's because I haven't spoken to you about it, it was only because you would have complained."

"Don't lie to me." She looked at him carefully, and he felt uncomfortable. Why, then? He wasn't lying. "You didn't say anything, because you wanted it to be you who made my brother happy. Isn't that so?"

"What?" He was dumbfounded. "What are you saying?"

"You love this child. Am I right?"

Not that question. Not again! "Love? Is it always love that fills your little head, Anna? Not everyone sees the world in pastel colors, you know. Listen, he likes the school, he asked me to go, and I think it will be good for him. That's it."

"Answer my question."

Christopher let out a little puff of air from his parted lips. "You know very well that I find your family very likable," he finally admitted.

"Likable?" She laughed bitterly, shaking her head. "You haven't answered, Christopher. Let me be crystal clear. If I rebel against you—if, for example, I say to your friend Leopold DeMercy and your business associates what I think of them, or if Thursday night at the Mortimers' I don't wear the dress that you have chosen for me—well, if I don't do all the things that you ask"—she barely blushed—"you would take it out on me with my family members, wouldn't you? So you said."

"Anna, is it necessary to talk about this still?" There was an element of despair in his voice and in his flesh, too. "You already know that for me it is essential to have a disciplined wife, but you must recognize that I leave you a lot of freedom, and I don't seem to be the monster that—"

"Answer. Would you do any harm to my family? Yes or no?"

Christopher was silent for a few moments, tightening his jaws. "Yes," he finally admitted wearily. "You know it."

Anna looked at him with contrite attention. "And yet you seemed really happy for Anthony a little while ago."

"Damn it, it's clear that I wouldn't like it!" he exploded. "But why must you always discuss everything?" And why must he always lose his temper? "Listen," he continued more calmly, "now we're getting along fine, aren't we? There's no need to . . ." He paused. "Anna, listen to me," he continued gently. He approached her and touched her upset face, then lowered his head to kiss her lips. "Don't be so grumpy always. Aren't you happy for your brother?"

But she remained rigid and sorrowful, a living accusation of the deceit of Christopher Davenport. "My brother adores you, and you buy him by mimicking a nonexistent affection. How can I be happy for that?" She closed her eyes, and tears filled them and ran down her face.

(That hadn't happened for a while, had it, Christopher? And maybe you had hoped that it wouldn't happen anymore.)

"Anna, don't . . ." he started, so tired of seeing her cry, so tired of being made to feel the villain.

"You know what he told me just now?"

"No." He gave out an exasperated sigh. "Tell me."

"He said that now he can leave this house without any worries, because you are here to defend us."

One last tear rolled down her cheek. Christopher was silent, and his wife turned her head and left the room.

***

"Matthew, are you engaged to Lucy?" Grace asked as they sat at the table. Anna, Lucy, and Matthew were talking animatedly, while Christopher remained quiet. Mr. Champion had eaten supper with Nora in advance, because fatigue had prevented him from tolerating the noise and the late hour.

Lucy laughed. "Grace!" she exclaimed. "It's normally Anthony who asks these kinds of questions."

Hearing his name, the child shrugged his shoulders and gave an intimidated glance. Anna smiled to herself. *Even my conscientious brother has his weakness.* She looked at him affectionately. *He's nearly eleven years old. He has become a little man.*

Matthew didn't seem embarrassed and smiled at the little girl. "Hadn't we agreed that you would become my fiancée once you're grown up?" he asked. "Are you trying to rid yourself of me?"

"It's not that I don't like you," Grace assured him, using her fork to chase down a pea that was rolling on her plate. "It's that I'm not sure I want to get married. Christopher says that I have to, because I can't become a doctor."

Lucy choked on a mouthful of food. "Mr. Davenport," she said to him when she was able to catch her breath, "did you really say such a thing to Grace?"

"Yes, he said it," Dennis confirmed. "I was there."

Christopher casually shrugged his shoulders. "I just told the truth, and that's better than filling their heads with unrealistic ideas, like the rest of you do."

Lucy's face showed she was ready for a fight, and Anna grimaced. *It's useless, Lucy,* she tried to communicate with her silently. *My husband is a lost cause.*

Unfortunately, her friend didn't understand her reasonable message. "If everyone thought like you, Mr. Davenport, the world would always remain the same."

"I don't see why it should change."

"You don't see why . . ." Her astonishment stopped her from finishing.

"Women are intellectually unfit for scientific pursuits, Miss Edwards," explained Christopher. "Lying to Grace will not change this reality."

Lucy's face responded to this remark without words. Grace, however, did not seem to be very angry. "I don't care what you say, Chris," she insisted, and Anna felt her chest jump with pride. "When I grow up, I'll dress like a man and I'll be a doctor, anyway."

Christopher raised an eyebrow, surprised. He replied dryly, "I do not think so, Grace, but we'll discuss it again in the next fifteen years."

Anna put her hand to her forehead calmly. "Don't listen to my husband, Lucy," she advised her, and he glared at her. "He's intellectually unfit for . . . intellectual pursuits."

Even Lucy seemed convinced. "Well, then, let's talk to someone who is. Anthony, your sister told me that you're going away. You're going to London? To boarding school? Isn't that fantastic?"

"Yeah," he replied without looking her in the eyes, blushing slightly.

Anna wanted to smile but couldn't. *Oh, Anthony,* she thought, trying to chase away this selfish grief. *What will I do without you?*

Matthew scratched his head thoughtfully. "I wonder how it is that you want to go to boarding school, Anthony. I understand being forced to go, but *asking* to go . . ."

"Come on, Matthew, it's completely understandable," Lucy said. "The best experiences in life happen there, or at least that is what Daniel has told me—Daniel DeMercy. He says that only in school yards one enters into real battles and discovers real courage."

Anna froze upon hearing that name, but Anthony looked up, concerned. "He said that?"

"Exactly." Lucy smiled, unaware of Christopher's disapproving look—the one that Anna had noticed and was agonizing over. "Daniel attended Westminster himself. He should tell you some of his adventures. He could suggest the best place to hide your snacks and tricks for cheating without getting caught. I could ask him to come with me here one afternoon if you'd like."

Anthony glanced at Christopher, then shook his head. "I will probably have too much to do," he answered, but he sounded disappointed. "Thanks all the same, Miss Edwards."

She looked at him, puzzled. "I understand," she said, but she did not seem to understand. She turned toward Christopher, who had been watching the exchange between the two of them. "You will miss Anthony very much, Mr. Davenport, won't you?"

"I don't know," he replied. The indifference in his voice cut deeper than the knife he had in his hand. "I imagine everyone will miss him."

No, not you, Christopher. Anna swallowed the pain that hadn't left her throat since that afternoon.

"Never mind him, Lucy," Matthew advised her. "He has been in a foul mood ever since his nose got twisted."

"I see," said Lucy, smiling, looking at its new shape. She had thought of how she could get him back for his comments, and she seemed like a bear trying to get at honey. "But your profile is more interesting now, Mr. Davenport—and don't worry, we won't reveal the unspeakable secret behind it."

***

"Unspeakable secret?" Christopher asked. There was a fairly unspeakable truth, in fact, and that was why he was more than fairly certain that Anna hadn't said a word to anyone. And yet Lucy was grinning at him alarmingly. He gave his wife a questioning look, but she avoided looking back at him.

"Anna was not very clear," said Lucy, "but it seems that your accident involved a chamber pot, a parlor table, and a dark room. Is that right?"

For a moment he didn't move. "Chamber pot?" he repeated. Oh dear God. What the hell had his wife said?

"Come now, Mr. Davenport, that can happen to anyone, to stumble in the dark," Lucy said, consoling him, but the effect was ruined because she let out a giggle, then tried desperately to mask it with a cough. "Perhaps the consequences are not always quite so devastating, but . . ."

Worse than he expected. *I'm really going to spank you tonight, my little wife.* He turned to her to tell her this with his eyes, but Anna kept her head down and didn't look back at him.

(She's still cross with you, Christopher.)

There again was that annoying feeling in his chest that refused to go away. Maybe it was a bit of food that wouldn't go down, or maybe a mouthful of disillusionment. *She is never happy with me, never.* It wasn't logical for this to surprise him, and yet he was surprised. *She really is a hateful, unbearable . . .*

"Come now, Chris, don't worry," suggested Matthew. "If you'd prefer to tell everyone that you broke your nose defending some orphan from being assaulted, or some little old lady from being robbed, we won't deny it."

"Quiet, Matt."

"It looks like your cousin doesn't know how to handle losing, Matthew," Lucy commented.

"Really? Well, sooner or later he will have to admit that there are insurmountable obstacles even for him. But do tell, Chris; Anna left out one detail. Was the chamber pot full or empty?"

Does proper etiquette allow for strangling a harassing guest? Christopher tried to remember. Maybe so. "Very amusing, Matthew," he said. "But Miss Edwards, let me give you some advice: don't get too attached to him," he said, pointing at Matthew with the knife he held in his hand, "because later, unfortunately, I'll have to wring his neck."

He glanced at his wife, who finally looked up. He saw her smile timidly—with her chipped tooth showing between her red lips.

"Did you see, Matthew?" Lucy sounded genuinely surprised. Her voice was without a trace of sarcasm this time. "A real smile."

"Yes . . . I saw."

Even his cousin's tone seemed to show amazement, and Christopher turned toward them, struck by the accusation implied in their words. "Come now, that's not the first time that you've seen your friend smile, Miss Edwards," he snapped at her, annoyed.

Lucy tilted her head to the side and looked at him oddly. Oddly but kindly. Since she had gotten to know him better, she hadn't often looked at him that way. “Oh, but I wasn’t talking about your wife’s smile, Mr. Davenport,” she said softly.

33

Conventionality is not morality.
—Charlotte Brontë

Yet another social event, with yet more smiles and yet more noise. Anna stifled yet another sigh. It was a sort of retaliation for her, because she despised these balls and the compliments that inevitably came with them.

"Mrs. Davenport," said Miss Aberworthy, "what a marvelous dress."

Anna blushed uncomfortably. "Thank you. Yours is . . ." What could she say about this bright lilac dress, except that it was pretentious, pompous, and excessive? "It's very beautiful," she concluded.

"Mr. Davenport," said Mrs. Mortimer, "have you met my husband? He would like to speak with you."

Christopher looked around. "We'll certainly have a chance to before the night is over," he replied with one of his smiles that made no one bat an eye.

Even you can't bear this chatter, thought Anna. And it wasn't the first time. Her husband appeared suave, but she had begun to get to know him enough to notice in him the same boredom. *You don't admit it, but you can't stand it.*

"Mrs. Davenport, you simply must come and dine with us on Saturday," Miss Aberworthy said to her politely. "Have you received our invitation?"

Yes, but I don't want to come. Anthony is about to leave and . . . "Oh, really . . ." She tried quickly to find an excuse, but her husband gave her a commanding look. But of course he was thinking of his damned business affairs. And she could do nothing but obey.

(You're a puppet in his hands, Anna. Move like he wants. Hurry.)

"Of course, Annabelle," she responded sweetly. *Hurry, Christopher.*

She looked askew at her odd husband, his wolf eyes, his lips pursed so tightly, and his nose, which now had a small hump and curved slightly to the right. Until two months before she hadn't even known him; now they were married, and not only was he her husband but he was also her master. *Everything that has happened and continues to happen between us is wrong, sick.*

(But weren't his eyes sweet sometimes when he looked at her? And didn't his lips maybe have secret smiles? And his bent nose—yes, even that—didn't it make him nearly lovable?)

She eyed Mrs. Edwards, who was not far away, and studied her aged eyes, the small wrinkles covered with makeup, her beauty fading more day after day. *Mrs. Edwards, when Christopher was making love to you—if it's not still happening—did he murmur the same words that he murmurs to me? Did he embrace you with the same voracious sweetness? Did his eyes smile at you as if you were the most beautiful woman in the world?* She felt a strange pain in her chest while she thought this.

What the hell? she wondered, shocked. Where did those thoughts come from? *That man is a monster. My goodness, I must have . . .*

Lucy came up to her and pointed across the room from them. "Matthew and Daniel—over there—seem to be engaged in a serious conversation," she whispered. "I'm afraid your husband's behavior is contagious."

Anna smiled. Perhaps with a bit of difficulty, but she smiled. Anyway, between the two men there was an apparent cordiality, which cheered her up. She felt her husband looking at her, and she quickly looked away.

"Why don't they join us?" Lucy asked, annoyed. She raised her hand to attract their attention. "They haven't even said hello to us yet."

Anna lifted her arms in the air and feigned complete ignorance. In fact, she was probably showing off one of her best empty expressions. She was certain that Daniel would not come over, not as long as she and Christopher were nearby.

"Here they are," said Lucy. "They're coming."

A shiver ran down her stomach and her back. *They will probably only stop for a moment,* she thought, trying to calm down. *He can't avoid it: it would be an obvious show of bad manners toward Lucy.*

But as she looked at Daniel's face her uneasiness increased, because the young man approached with a swaggering smile and looked at Christopher with his head held unnaturally high. He kissed the ladies' hands and greeted everyone warmly—except one person, to whom he gave just a nod, which seemed more of an involuntary bobbing of his head. Christopher answered with the same enthusiasm. Anna hoped he wouldn't break his teeth from clenching his jaw so hard.

I must separate the two of them—and in a hurry. "Maybe we should go now," she said to him quickly, and her husband nodded coldly. "You wanted to meet Mr. Jackson, I recall."

"Yes." Christopher turned his head toward the ladies. "With your permission, my wife and I should—"

"Oh, wait a moment, Mr. Davenport," Lucy said. "Anna, you were going to run off before telling Daniel the news?" She turned toward him. "You should know that on Monday, Anthony is leaving for Westminster School."

Daniel smiled. "Anthony is going to boarding school? If I remember correctly the questions that boy poses, I believe that he will manage to embarrass more than one professor."

"That's very true," agreed Lucy. "But I think he's also scared. Oh, just a bit," she clarified, "but he's too proud to admit it, and I believe that it would help him to have some suggestions about life there. Would you go with me to see him one of these afternoons? It would be nice to hear you tell about the terrible and adventurous life that is hiding inside those cold classrooms."

Christopher stood motionless next to Anna, who held her breath.

"I don't know, Lucy," Daniel responded evasively. "That boy never cared for me."

Oh, but now he likes you, Daniel, Anna said to herself. *After all, you broke Christopher's nose. And my brother has a way of thinking that's all his own.*

"You are mistaken, Daniel," said Lucy, as if she were reading Anna's mind. Nothing got by that girl. *Almost* nothing. "A few days ago I had the distinct impression that he was rather intrigued by you."

"Really?" Daniel seemed pleasantly surprised. That was typical of him—to light up for a reason like that. "Do you think that may be possible, Anna?" he asked, ignoring her husband.

Completely contrary to etiquette, Christopher took a step toward Anna and put a hand on her hip. "DeMercy, don't feel obliged to neglect any of your *important* commitments for my brother-in-law," he answered. "He's a bright boy, and therefore he will be able to do without your . . . *help.*"

Daniel, don't give him any rope. Don't, Anna frantically thought.

"Oh, I'll find a couple of hours for Anthony, Davenport," he said, provoking him instead. "Any advice can always come in handy in life. For example, you cannot imagine the kind of free-for-all that can take place at snack time if someone's apple is stolen." He looked carefully at the crooked nose without showing the slightest sense of guilt. In truth, he seemed to be gloating. "I could teach a few punches to this boy, don't you think?"

Oh for the love . . . "Daniel," Anna interrupted quickly, "why don't you tell us about your stay in London? Have you seen—?"

Her husband squeezed her side tighter, drawing her closer to him. "Tell me, DeMercy. Did you happen to catch a cold in the city?" he asked him with perfect manners. "Your voice sounds a bit sharp tonight."

"Sharp?" said Mrs. Mortimer, and Anna felt the need to laugh hysterically. "I don't think so. I hope you're not getting ill, Mr. DeMercy, or I shall have to reassign all the seats at table tomorrow evening."

(Take advantage of the diversion right away.)

Anna stood on her tiptoes and got her lips closer to her husband's ear. That is, that's what she would have liked to do, but his ear was so very high up that it was practically unreachable. "Christopher, stop it," she whispered preemptively. "You're behaving like a child."

"That's not true at all," he said softly. And he gently lowered his face a little toward her. "Besides, he started it."

Anna lifted her lips a little. "That, Mr. Davenport, is the most mature sentence I've heard you say since I've known you."

She was happy and surprised to see him relaxing. He gave her a faint, barely noticeable smile, which softened her against her will. Christopher didn't spare any smiles on her at night, but those were a prelude to love. Even the sweet words he told her weren't worth anything in the disruption of his senses. During the day, however . . . During the day he remained distant, closed in his depths, in the inner battles that darkened his eyes. It was then that a smile became precious.

(But what has happened to you, Anna?)

What had Daniel told her a week before when talking about his mother?

It's dreadful, Anna, loving someone who doesn't deserve it.

Calling herself stupid, she moved, turning again toward the people around her. She noticed that Daniel was looking at her in an odd way, almost sadly, yet relieved; Daniel, who knew how to read her mind. She lowered her head, blushing.

Mrs. Mortimer waved her hand at someone. "If you'll excuse me," she said, "now I should get back to my husband."

"Mrs. Mortimer, I'll go with you," Miss Aberworthy said, joining her. "I have to ask Mrs. Robertson if she is satisfied with the new maid that I recommended. You know," she added with an embarrassment that Anna didn't believe for even a moment, "the behavior of the maid before her . . . Oh, excuse me." She paused with reluctance. "It's inappropriate to talk about this."

Who knows where Annabelle learned always to make the right face for the right occasion? Anna thought. *It couldn't be easy, given that there is no emotion involved. How does she not confuse them? For example, doesn't she ever happen to use the face for joy when she means to use the face for disgust, or to use the face for anger instead of the one for kindness?* Halfway between nausea and admiration, Anna thought that sooner or later she would really have to ask her.

Mrs. Mortimer's eyes sparked with delight. "Oh, certainly, Miss Aberworthy, you are absolutely right! It's better not to talk about certain things." She took her leave in a hurry; her mood had probably been lifted so much by the rumor mentioned that she wasn't worried any longer about how many people would be at her house for supper the next day. "Oh, Mr. Davenport," she said as she walked away, "remember that my husband would like to meet you."

"Certainly, Mrs. Mortimer. I'll join you in a moment."

The two ladies took their leave, and Anna heard Mrs. Mortimer say with what seemed like greed, "Immoral, you said, Annabelle . . . ?"

She couldn't hear Annabelle's response, and the five of them now found themselves in a very odd group. The ice was arctic, and Anna hoped that Matthew would break it a bit, but he did not seem to want to. He was watching Daniel and Christopher as if he was expecting them to handle it on their own. That was a completely inadvisable thing, thought Anna uneasily, given the previous—increasingly unsuccessful—attempts. The only one at ease was Lucy. Of course she had noticed the antipathy between these two—it was obvious—but at least she did not know that it wasn't a chamber pot at night that humiliated Christopher Davenport.

Daniel cleared his throat and looked right at Christopher, but—unexpectedly—without animosity. "I would really like to pay Anthony a visit tomorrow afternoon, Davenport," he said. After a moment, and very casually, he added, "If you don't mind." It hadn't been easy. No, not at all. The frog was still there in his throat, and he tried to swallow it. Anna respected him even more, if it were possible.

Christopher did not respond immediately. He had been taken by surprise—this man who always knew what do in battle was so often awkward in peacetime. He bowed his head, put his hand to his forehead, and rubbed it with his fingertips. "It will do him no good," he asserted. He paused and then looked up. "But you're free to do as you like, DeMercy."

Anna felt a strange feeling heating up her heart and her belly. *What is it that I see on my husband's face? Emotion?* She did not have the time to rejoice in it, because as fast as it appeared it vanished. The usual veil of arrogance and impenetrability had fallen back over his face.

His face turned to the left. Daniel followed his gaze, and the same dark veil also darkened his features: Leopold DeMercy was coming their way.

***

The family is all together, thought Christopher when Leopold joined them. He needed to talk to him too much to miss this chance.

His father said good evening to everyone. He was greeted by more or less friendly faces, and he took a long look at Christopher and Daniel, as if he were amazed to see them so close to each other.

"Daniel, are you not dancing this evening?" he asked his son. The tone was one of the two he reserved for Daniel: mockery. The other was annoyance. He looked up and down at Lucy, who was adorable in blue and white, with her blond hair that shined with all of the lights in the room. "You're not asking this beautiful young lady to dance?"

Daniel clenched his jaw, and his face seemed it was fighting mixed emotions. He was quiet for what seemed like a century as Lucy stared at him. Finally he broke this rude silence. "Lucy, would you do me the honor of the next dance?" His voice sounded like it was coming from inside of a medieval helmet, it was so distant and metallic.

"Thank you, Daniel," she responded, and she too sounded far away, but also sad. "I'm already committed."

"To dance with me in fact, DeMercy," said Matthew. "I haven't felt so excited since I was confirmed."

Daniel seemed hurt by Lucy's tone. He forgot about his father and tried again. "The one after that, then?"

"We'll see. I admit I'm a bit tired this evening."

"Daniel, you'll have to be faster in making your decisions," Leopold advised him. His deep and hoarse voice shook with a laugh he held back. "You're always too slow, my son."

How Daniel manages not to kill his father is something that defies all the rules of logic, thought Christopher. And yet it was clear that he hated him. And hatred, when it is not reciprocal, hurts as much as love. It was inevitable, because Leopold did not hate Daniel. He didn't love him, either. Nor, in fact, did he seem to have any feelings whatsoever for him.

"Ah, Davenport," added Leopold. "I need to talk with you about a matter later."

It is time, Daddy. He felt his heart beating madly, and he hoped he didn't show any emotion. He succeeded, not because he was cold-blooded, but because he had learned to pretend to be. "Now is also fine, sir."

"Oh no, not now." He turned toward Anna, who flinched slightly under his gaze. "Now I wish to have the honor of dancing with your charming wife. Will you do me this honor, Mrs. Davenport?"

(What do you think of that, Christopher?)

He stopped breathing—that's what he thought of it. At his side, Anna seemed to be floundering. Her aversion to Leopold was so apparent that Christopher feared he might see it written on her forehead. *Shit. Shit. Shit!* He turned to her, and his wife gasped. For a moment it seemed that they had gone back to the old days: the ancient fear covered her face, and her eyes sparkled with a hint of tears. She understood what her husband wanted her to do.

(You tamed her well, Christopher. Are you satisfied?)

"Of course, Mr. DeMercy," she responded, giving in.

Leopold nodded. "You don't mind, do you, son?"

Son. A few moments of silence slipped by. "Of course not, DeMercy," Christopher finally replied.

Leopold smiled. "Do you see how it's done, Daniel? It's not so difficult."

Anna was stiff and struggled to find her breath. Anna, with her damned hot temper, who could hurt him if she began to fly into a rage on the dance floor, had accepted a dance with Leopold! He put his mouth up to her ear. "Behave perfectly well," he hissed, "Otherwise . . ."

He left the sentence hanging. She lowered her face and didn't protest, but her lips curved into a distressed smile and she blinked for a moment or two.

The music was about to begin, and Matthew took Lucy's arm. Leopold did the same with Anna, whose face seemed suddenly without color.

Christopher and Daniel were alone. *It's not possible,* he thought. *This night can't get any worse.* He started to leave.

"Davenport, I have to talk to you," Daniel said in a tone that sounded resigned, stopping him.

"Is that necessary?" asked Christopher. His wife had reached the dance floor with Leopold, and she stood facing him. She kept her head bowed without looking at him.

"Yes, it is."

"DeMercy, I already told you not to interest yourself in my business affairs, if that's what this is about."

The music began, and Leopold's fingers touched his bride.

"No. Honestly, I wanted to . . . rectify . . . some of the things that I said to you in my father's office the other day." He took a breath, then continued: "It seems that your wife feels affection for you, as opposed to what I thought."

Christopher looked away from the dance floor. *My wife would leave me tomorrow if she didn't have a sick father and siblings under my guardianship.* "Obviously," he said. He looked at his half brother with a smile loaded with arrogance. *Maybe tonight something is going to go my way after all.* "But let me understand, DeMercy: are you offering me an apology?"

"I will not call it . . . Oh, very well." His little brother wasn't at all happy, and the embarrassment filling his eyes was quite a pleasant sight to Christopher. "But only for the things I said to you about your wife, Davenport. As for the rest, you are still a scoundrel, and you know it."

Christopher's smile broadened. "Well, I accept your humble apology, then," he replied mockingly. "And if you're quite finished now . . ." He again tried to leave, turning his eyes back to the dance floor.

"Wait," Daniel said, stopping him. "I have a request to ask of you. I hope that you have no objections to Anna and I remaining friends. We've known each other for a long time—years, one could say. And even if you and I have our differences . . ."

Forget it. "I can accept that. Between the two of you, there is a formal acquaintance but nothing else. And my wife," he said, giving him an arrogant look, "will respect my wishes, rest assured." He looked at her; she wasn't watching Leopold but was instead looking around her, avoiding his touch and his gaze.

Daniel slowly exhaled before answering. "Your jealousy is misplaced, Davenport," he replied, annoyed. "You insult your wife with this absurd behavior."

"That shouldn't matter to you. Live your own life and stop meddling in mine." *Listen to the words of someone who got married just to steal your fiancée away.*

"Oh, I'll gladly do that, but you just seem to pop up in my way, like grass in a field."

Leopold said something to Anna, laughing, and she seemed to get pale in anger.

"You know, DeMercy, your voice really is shrill—it's piercing my eardrums."

"It's for Anna that I'm forcing myself to talk to you, because I assure you that every word I say to you feels like an unforgivable waste of air."

"Have you finished? Your father is right when he says that you nag like a little woman."

"It's evident you hold my father in very high regard," Daniel replied sarcastically. "That must be why you seem like the very picture of joy now that he's dancing with your wife."

Should I punch him again? Maybe change his voice for good—and his sex life, Christopher wondered, staring angrily. Finally he turned on his heels and walked away suddenly, without responding.

***

It was the first time that she happened to dance with Leopold DeMercy, and she sincerely hoped it would be the last.

"You look lovely tonight, Mrs. Davenport."

Anna sighed. Did she really have to talk? "Thank you, sir."

"How do you like being a newlywed?"

That's a bit of a personal question, don't you think? And didn't this gentleman's smile seem slightly . . . suggestive? "Very well, sir."

"Anna—I can call you Anna, can't I?"

Absolutely not. The horrible look that Christopher had given her a short while ago made her remember that her name didn't belong to her any longer. "Of course, sir."

Leopold laughed. "Oh, let me say that you don't seem very excited by the prospect, Anna," he said, amused. "But by all means feel free to speak frankly with me. For a time it nearly seemed that you and I would be related—isn't that so?"

Anna was shocked: Why bring up this old story? And wasn't he holding her a bit too tightly, beyond what was allowed by etiquette? She didn't answer, moving away from him. She tried to focus on other thoughts. Lucy, for example. The way she looked unhappy a short while ago when Daniel had hesitated to invite her. *Is it possible that—?*

"I had underestimated you, Anna."

(Ignore him. Ignore him.)

Anna continued to follow her own train of thought. Lucy showed quite an excessive indifference when she was speaking about Daniel. But a few minutes before that dejected look—that for once she was not able to hide behind her social mask—there was really—

"I am almost sorry for being so opposed to the marriage between you and my son," continued Leopold. "Maybe you would have managed to get a bit of blood from this turnip."

These words called Anna back to reality abruptly. "Sir," she hissed indignantly, with anger preventing her from refraining, "your son has more blood in his body than you . . ." She stopped suddenly, biting her lip.

Leopold's low, gloating laughter seemed to wrap around her. "Oh no, don't stop, Anna. You were fantastic."

Have no fear, Leopold. The day will come when I can tell you everything I think of you. But would it really be today? Or was she becoming even more like her husband? "It was you who informed my husband of my engagement to your son, wasn't it?"

Leopold shook his head. "No," he replied with a twinkle of wonder in his eyes. "In fact, I thought that was a strategy of yours to make yourself look more interesting to him. It would have been clever—and moreover, it's evident that you have no shortage of brains."

No, it was you, Leopold. And now you're telling me a pack of lies. Because you still haven't gotten over Daniel's rebellion. Because you still haven't managed to stop it. "Are you trying to provoke me, sir?"

"Yes, Anna." *Well, you could call this man many things, but predictable is not one of them.* "You have a fiery temperament, and I would like to know if that's the reason why you attract men like bees to honey."

She opened her eyes wide, and her cheeks flushed. "Your manner of speech is inappropriate," she stammered, her voice barely coming out. "Stop at once, or I'll have to stop this dance."

"Oh no, you will not," grinned Leopold. "Your husband would not agree, would he? He's very keen on you being nice to me."

(He wants you to be nice to him, Anna.)

Although it was difficult, she managed to respond, partly out of indignation and partly out of fear that Leopold could be right. "My husband would not . . . my husband would not disapprove, sir."

Leopold laughed again, endearingly. "Oh, actually I do believe he would. You do not know him very well, Anna."

(You don't know him well *at all*, do you, Anna?)

"Why do you think that? Would you like to tell me something about him?"

"No, there's nothing that I would *like* to tell you."

"And what are you trying to insinuate by saying that?"

"Absolutely nothing," he responded, smiling innocently. "I like your husband very much."

Of course you like him, she thought, distressed, swallowing to get rid of the bitter sand that scratched her throat. *He will stop at nothing, like you. You are made for each other.*

"And I'm beginning to like you a lot as well, Anna."

She should have felt naked in front of his deliberately vulgar gaze, and instead she simply felt tired. She continued to dance as if moved by invisible strings, while her husband, not far away, watched her, like a master with his livestock.

(Good. That's it, Anna. Smile. Look polite.)

"Why are you so pensive, Anna?"

"Sir, don't hold me like that please," she replied without emotion, moving away from him when he got too close to her.

"Oh, I hadn't noticed. Forgive me," he responded. His eyes, however, continued to touch her indecently, and his smile remained ingratiating.

My husband is prostituting me, Anna realized finally. Because that was the truth, wasn't it? That's what her heart was telling her. *I've fallen into a cesspit, and the filth will never come off my body.* "You're disgusting, sir," she said to Leopold quietly, letting go of his hands, "and our dance ends here."

She walked away quickly, leaving him alone on the dance floor.

***

"You'll have to apologize to him."

Christopher commented for the first time on the incident in the carriage that brought them back home at the end of the evening.

Anna stared at him in disbelief. "What?"

"You heard me. You abandoned him in the middle of a dance, and even if he laughed about it with me, he was really quite displeased with you."

"And you're taking his side? His behavior was—"

"Quiet." His eyes were stern, the same eyes that lovingly called her his queen in the shadows of the bed. "You will apologize to him, and that's that. And be thankful that I'm asking only for that. I trusted you with this, Anna, and you disobeyed me. I'm warning you: I don't want this to become a habit."

"But Christopher . . ." She was having troubling speaking. But she had to explain it to him, and he had to understand. "That man insulted me. Doesn't that matter to you?"

"Don't be silly. What could he have said that was so serious?"

"It wasn't so much the words he used, but I assure you that the tone that—"

"Oh. Of course, the tone." He smirked. "Let me tell you one thing: I care nothing about his 'tone.' I need him, and you will offer him your apology at the first opportunity."

She felt so much pain from this, yet another disappointment. "Oh, Christopher," she murmured, more to herself than to him, "I didn't expect anything different from you, but why . . . why does it hurt the same?" This sad question came out of her mouth before she knew it, followed by another. "Am I worth so little to you?" she asked him, her voice cracking. "Am I worth so little that anyone can treat me with disrespect?"

Hurt, he seemed to feel her pain for a moment. Then he shook his head. "Don't be absurd. DeMercy was only joking."

"He most certainly was not—"

"Don't contradict me."

Her lips trembled. "How far will you go with your requests, Christopher?" she asked in a whisper. She had to know. She was afraid of his response, but she had to know. "Do you want me to go to bed with him maybe?"

Christopher's eyes became big, and Anna knew she had said the worst possible thing—the thing to never say under any circumstance. And when he suddenly raised his hand, she knew that he would hit her—he would really hit her. She put her arm up to her face in defense. She squinted her eyes and lowered her head between her clenched shoulders, and her heart trembled in her chest and perhaps even forgot to beat. And she waited. She waited for the inevitable strike.

It never happened, however. Sitting across from her, Christopher moved to her side, grabbed her violently by the hair, and made her raise her head. Anna opened her eyes, and she almost wet herself out of fear: her husband was beside himself.

"Never say a thing like that again," he informed her, his face distorted with contractions of rage, "if you want to stay in one piece."

Anna was petrified for a long while; then somehow her voice returned to her, as did her breathing. "So, Chris, if you care about me a tiny bit," she murmured with a little hope, "don't humiliate me in front of that man."

"I'll keep you far away from him from now on," he conceded in a whisper, softening his grip on her hair. "But when you see him again, you will have to apologize. I don't care how. The important thing is that you fix it. No," he said, holding up his hand to stop her objections, ignoring the pain given to her by the injustice of this treatment. "Say no more."

Anna swallowed hard, trying again to choke down that sand, or perhaps those thorns—she wasn't sure anymore. Then this dreadful man pulled her close and kissed her passionately and aggressively as tears of despair ran down her face.

34

Give me, O Lord, the sense of the ridiculous. Grant me the grace to understand a joke, so that I may know in life a bit of joy and I may be able to share that with others.
—Sir Thomas More

The letters from L. were in his flat in London. Christopher had brought only two with him to Coxton: the one concerning his birth, and the one that his mother was holding in her hands before she died. He kept them there, in his office in Rockfield, because he wanted to reread them before killing his father. *Or I could make him read them,* he thought, relishing this other possibility. This would help him pass the time. *Oh God, that would be a bit melodramatic,* he admitted to himself with a sarcastic regret, *but I'm not sure he would appreciate it: life would be so mundane if we didn't give it a touch of poetry. Isn't that so?*

In truth, to compel Leopold to read these letters would not be easy—Christopher was sure of it. He probably wouldn't give in, not even after being struck countless times, not even before dying. Not that it was necessary, however. Because the prospect of doing him in remained exhilarating, no matter how he imagined it. Oh, the word "murder" frightened him, and—unless he counted that man who committed suicide after he had ruined him and who sometimes haunted his dreams—he had always been sure to shy away from it. But "patricide"—that damned word *par excellence*; that concept that was by definition unforgivable—had a nice ring to it for Christopher. He knew it would be the best action of his life, and the most just. He had waited for it for years, and every day it seemed closer. Every day witnessing Leopold's smiles, which stuck to his skin; every day witnessing his sayings, which were consciously indifferent to other people's fate; every day witnessing the injustices that he scattered about like a trail of breadcrumbs behind him. Every day—and even more so, if possible, after the insult from the night before. Anna seemed so saddened, so inconsolable when he had told her that she must apologize to this worm. Even after having made love with him, even after having whispered his name . . . Oh damn it. Christopher rubbed his eyes, tired. He would go back home a little early that afternoon, he decided, and the fact that his half brother was visiting the Champion house, and that Anna still felt affection for him—for that idiot who seemed always like he had walked straight out of the tailor's—had nothing to do with it.

I don't know if she loves him, and I don't care, he said to himself as his horse reached the redbrick house. *The important thing is that she remains submissive. That's all I want from her.*

He calmly went down the lane of lindens. He left the horse with Lewis and went into the rear of the house. The limited presence of domestics, who seemed to come right out of the medieval "court of miracles," meant that no one would notice. He walked toward the kitchen, where surely they were gathered. In spite of himself, he also adored that informal room.

He came up silently, stopping outside in the hallway, and he heard the elegant voice of his brother say, "And so, Anthony, the trick is to hide not one but *two* pieces of food—whatever starts to rot the easiest—in your enemy's room. With each passing day a disturbing odor will grow around him, and the poor chap will try to find where it's coming from. When he finds the first of your graciously concealed—less graciously nauseating, I fear—items, he will think he is safe and stop looking. In his naiveté he will be convinced that the stench will fade away in a couple of hours. Unfortunately"—he sighed sorrowfully—"he will be sadly mistaken."

Lucy laughed musically. "Daniel, you are absolutely wicked."

"Lucy, you can afford to be merciful: no one has ever stolen the door to your dormitory. I assure you that after that everything is permissible."

"I want to go to boarding school with Anthony," Grace exclaimed, pouting. "Why can't I?"

"Because you're still too young," Anna explained sweetly.

Ah, that bloody habit of hers of not telling children the truth, thought Christopher, exasperated.

"That's not the reason," Dennis said, contradicting her. "Christopher told me that females cannot go there."

"Well, I'll go," she insisted. "I will disguise myself . . ."

In the hallway Christopher smiled, and then he entered the room. "But you'll have to cut your hair short, Grace," he said as everyone turned toward him.

"Chris!" cried Grace happily, and she got up from the table where she was drawing and ran up to him. She pulled him down with her hand and gave him a kiss on the cheek, and he felt oddly embarrassed in front of his brother. He stood back up quickly, went to the table, and stopped next to his wife.

"I don't care if I have to cut my hair," said Grace, who had not yet let go of his hand. "That's how much I want to be a soldier."

"A soldier now?" Christopher shook his head. He decided not to say anything and instead simply threw Anna a stern look. At least he wanted it to be stern. She smiled at him hesitantly. *Oh, my dear. I would not make you do it, really.*

"Yes," Grace confirmed. She seemed shy and pleading. "But you have to teach me to shoot, Christopher, like you did Anthony."

"Oh." He poured himself a cup of tea. *I will never teach you, Grace. It's not something meant for females.* "I can't. You're still too young. And by the way, Anthony . . ." He looked at the little chap sitting next to Daniel. "Do you want to shoot a bit more before it gets dark? Monday you are leaving, and we won't have another chance." Christopher noted that Anna nodded to herself as if she had expected those exact words. The idea of throwing Daniel out of the house, in fact, had something to do with his suggestion. Not everything, but definitely something to do with it.

"I'd like that, Christopher," Anthony replied. He looked at Daniel, and he seemed torn. "But I would also like to know what happened to your door, Mr. DeMercy."

The half brother put his hand on his chin, as if reflecting carefully. "We can combine the two—isn't that so, Davenport?" he asked. "I could keep you and your brother company while you practice shooting."

Damned half brother. He was doing it on purpose for sure. "I don't know, DeMercy," he said flatly. "I don't believe it's advisable for you to come near me when I have a pistol in my hands."

Daniel laughed loudly, amused, and stood facing him without the slightest uneasiness. "Do you shoot that badly?"

"On the contrary," he retorted with a veiled threat in his eyes. Not even very veiled, in fact. "I am quite proficient."

"What a coincidence," replied Daniel with the same look. "I am as well. Indeed, probably more proficient than you are. Therefore, I'm not afraid."

Lucy looked from one to the other with a cheeky smile. "So, Daniel, is this a challenge?"

"Obviously. Are you accepting it, Davenport? The winner is the one of us who hits the most targets."

Christopher pursed his lips with uncontrollable arrogance. "It's apparent that you like to lose, DeMercy."

"I'll take that as a yes."

Grace clapped her hands enthusiastically. "How wonderful!" she exclaimed, showing the dimple on her left cheek. She forgot about the impossible drawings that she was doing and ran outside. After a moment Anthony and Dennis followed her.

"Are you sure?" Anna asked them with a bit of anxiety in her voice. His wife seemed to be the only person in the room to find Christopher frightening. Perhaps it wasn't a good sign. "It's already late and—"

Daniel laughed and was perfectly calm. "Don't worry, Anna, your husband will not shoot me."

"I wouldn't be so sure."

"Did you say something, Davenport?"

"No, nothing." He looked at his brother, resigning himself to having to tolerate his obnoxious presence. *At least I will have the satisfaction of beating you, Daniel.* "Come on, then," he urged.

They walked down the hallway, and without talking they reached the room where the weapons were kept.

"One moment, Davenport," said the unbearable dandy with a suspicious twinkle in his green eyes. "A challenge isn't a challenge if we don't bet on something. Don't you agree? Unless . . ." He stopped and gave him a wry look. Christopher had to admit that Daniel also knew how to do wry looks rather well, if he tried. "Unless it's not being defeated that you fear, obviously."

Christopher opened a cabinet and pulled out two matching, polished pistols. "What would you like to bet?"

"That land we talked about a while ago," Daniel said without hesitation. Christopher looked up from the weapons and stared at him silently. His brother went on, undaunted: "If I win, you'll give it to me. If I lose . . . Well, what do you want, Davenport, if you win?"

To shoot you. "That you get out of my sight," he snapped. "DeMercy, you're an incredible pain in the neck."

"Yeah," he admitted, and he seemed very pleased.

35

Nothing would ever be discovered if we considered ourselves satisfied with what has already been discovered.
—Seneca

"Tomorrow morning my oldest brother leaves," wrote Anna on that sunny morning while the children were doing lessons with their teachers, and the house carried on without her. *"I knew that this moment would come, but still I wonder how I will manage."*

She paused to wipe her eyes, and a tear fell on the paper, staining it.

"And I cannot even stay at home to recover, because tomorrow evening," she wrote after having wiped off the mess, *"there will be a stupid dinner at Rockfield Park."* She looked at the dark-blue dress on a mannequin next to her and sighed softly. *"Christopher asked me to spend the night there after the evening is over. 'It will probably be late, Anna,' he said yesterday morning, and—I swear!—he seemed hesitant to me. Perhaps even shy. 'We could stay at Rockfield and come back Tuesday by lunchtime. Do you think that your family can get along without us for a few hours?' 'I'm sure they can,' I responded without the slightest hesitation. 'It seems like a good idea to me.'*

"My husband seemed pleased by this immediate response of mine; I believe he was expecting some objection. He came near me while I was embroidering by the window, and he leaned over me. 'We can consider it our honeymoon trip, then,' he whispered to me. 'Matthew is out of town.'

"I blushed and felt a bit guilty, given his excitement, and because the romantic implication of the situation had completely slipped by me. I accepted it only for one reason, in fact: to get into his office at night. Because I want—I must—find something to free me from his power. Because I want—I must—calm my heart when he is near me. Because the suffering that he gives me with his inexplicable behavior is troubling to me; I often find myself crying alone.

"Sometimes I sit by the window and willingly indulge in all those thoughts that make me sad. Such as when I think of having to apologize to Leopold tomorrow night. Such as when I observe the deception that my husband uses to win the affection of my family, and I remember the blackness in his heart that let him abuse me a month and a half ago. Such as when he comes home late at night and I do not even know where he has been—and his eyes are tired and despondent, as if he has been to hell and back.

"It also happened that night, and I could not stop myself. 'Christopher, it's three in the morning,' I said to him in an upset voice when he gave me a kiss to wake me. He didn't know that I wasn't sleeping yet. 'Haven't you already had a woman tonight?' He smiled in the dim light of one lit candle. 'That shouldn't matter, Anna,' he said with a whisper of irony. 'Didn't you say that you don't care if I'm faithful to you or not?'

"I felt so humiliated that he was laughing at me! I turned my back to him, and I covered myself up with the sheet. 'I don't care, in fact,' I replied with an annoyed tone, holding back the foolish tears that filled my eyes. 'I would just like you to let me sleep.' 'Soon,' he murmured, putting his hand on my shoulder and making me turn toward him. 'Would you mind terribly?'

"Still offended, I looked at him, but something in his appearance stopped the sarcastic comment that I was about to make from coming out of my mouth. 'Is something bothering you, Christopher?' I asked him, and I raised my hand to push his hair away from his eyes. 'Tell me what's wrong, Chris.' 'Shh,' he whispered. 'Come here.' His mouth kissed mine, and his hands touched me—and once again my questions were left unanswered."

There was a knock on the door to her room, and Anna stopped writing and looked up from her diary. "Come in," she said. "Ah, it's you, Christopher."

***

God, now she will complain. No, she won't "complain"; she will explode. She will murder me. She will tear my skin off, Christopher sighed. *It's better to say it quickly.* "Anna," he called out, "you'll have to see to the final preparations for dinner at my house. And you can't not do it today, since tomorrow we will be London to go with Anthony."

"But—"

"I don't want to hear any arguments." He raised his hand to stop her protests. "Today I will be outside of Coxton for some unavoidable commitments, and so you will have to do it. It will be your duty, among other things."

His wife made a face. "All right," she said.

"All right"? No grumbling or nasty threats—had he heard right? Christopher tried to remember if by chance he hadn't drunk whisky instead of tea that morning.

"But remind me about one thing," she added. "When preparing for a party, is one also supposed to set fire to the house?"

"I'd have to check," he said, thinking it over. He was relieved. Anna wasn't angry, not even a little. He approached her and said softly, "I wouldn't have put you in this situation if I could have avoided it, I assure you."

"Don't worry," she said with a shrug. "You know that from you I always expect the worst, so you can't disappoint me."

He grinned as he sat on the edge of the desk. "Is that what you write in your diary?" he asked, casting a blind eye on his wife's illegible scrawl. "Insults against me in your strange code?"

"Make no mistake, I never write about you. I wouldn't be able to find enough horrible words to describe you."

"Oh, really?" He cheekily put his mouth up to her ear, and in a voice so soft it was barely audible he whispered, "That will mean that I will ask you to repeat that sentence to me tonight, Anna. When I will be between your legs."

"Christopher!" His wife pushed his head back up and gave him a light slap—quite hard in actuality—but with a certain delicacy when compared to those to which he had become accustomed. "You're obscene," she accused him while blushing, and she looked down to her diary. "And what are you still doing here? I thought you said you had *unavoidable* commitments."

Christopher rubbed his cheek. "Yeah," he admitted reluctantly. He stood up, went to the door, and looked back one last time.

***

"Treasure Pyramid."

A cryptic title and a cryptic document. In the silence of her husband's office in Rockfield, Anna had almost jumped with excitement when she discovered a little red box under the fireplace mantel, hidden in the same way that Christopher had hidden things in the Champions' house. To be honest, she was supposed to be seeing to the preparations for the party, not investigating, but she was sure that Thea—the haughty housekeeper of the home—would fare very well on her own.

In the red box were documents. Only two, unfortunately, but they were interesting. One was "Treasure Pyramid." She quickly saw the figures and names listed; they were all strangers except for two: Leopold DeMercy and Christopher Davenport. It seemed like a kind of business; whoever participated paid a more or less conspicuous sum, and they drew a rather high short-term gain. Leopold's name appeared three times, with the stakes gradually increasing each time. *Is this why Christopher doesn't want to have a conflict with him?* Anna wondered. She didn't know, but she knew that in this Egyptian treasure there was something that didn't make sense. She rubbed her eyes, checking again the columns for accounts payable and accounts receivable. It was odd, since it truly seemed that the money that came into the accounts was never used to purchase or produce *anything*, but simply reinvested in the same pyramid. Practically every new revenue was used to pay the interest of the preceding investments, and since the figures in the accounts receivable were increasing (whether because the number of investors increased, or the amount paid in by a single investor increased), it was an open cycle. It really was a pyramid, Anna understood. Whoever was at the top gave *one* and took *two* from the second and third participating in the business deal; the second and third in turn took *four* from the fifth, sixth, and seventh—and so on indefinitely. *Or rather, not indefinitely,* she thought, disturbed. *There will come a day when the amounts to be paid will be too high, and new investors will not be found. Then whoever is at the bottom of the pyramid will have no gains and only losses.* She put her hand on her forehead and closed her eyes. The concern made her chest tighten up. *Certainly there must be an explanation,* she told herself reasonably. *I probably don't know the market like Christopher does.*

(Why does your husband hide these documents, then, Anna?)

The creator of this pyramid wasn't him but a certain Robert Barrett; Christopher's name appeared only as an investor. However . . .

I will think about this later, she decided. It was getting late, and she couldn't dwell any longer. She went on to the second document, which reported credits and gambling debts. Her husband's debtors were all unknown names; his creditors were people from all over the county. *It seems that bad luck is following Christopher here in Coxton.* The largest debt that her husband had accrued was with Leopold DeMercy. *That's strange, she thought,* frowning. Christopher seemed to be an ace at cards when he was giving lessons to Anthony. And wasn't he the one who claimed "to win always," even unfairly? It was strange indeed, but now she had to hurry to leave the room, since she had taken a look at everything that was in the box.

Almost everything, she thought, correcting herself. A moment before she replaced the files, in a corner she noticed two folded old sheets of paper that had fallen out as she hurried to close a file up. They were two letters, two pages yellowed by time—how old were they?—written in an unknown, slanted handwriting that was not her husband's. She looked at the first sheet; it was wrinkled and faded with dark spots in certain parts that made it almost illegible. It seemed that this must have been recovered from some inaccessible place. It had no date, and all that was written on it was the following:

> *I would forego all the years I have lived until now, all this time, which has dragged like a dead leg, just to relive a moment, just a moment, Martha.*
>
> *You were leaving from a decrepit building, and some of your lazy companions walked alongside you. The winter evening was cold, and you wore a gray coat and a gray scarf on your head.*
>
> *And a burst of color on your face.*
>
> *Your white smile and red lips, burning cheeks in the mist that rose from your breath; your blue eyes among the hair that fell out of your headscarf.*

That was the first time I saw you, Martha, and if in that moment someone had told me to ask what life is, I would have pointed to you and said, "It's that girl over there."

L.

***

When Christopher joined his wife in the bedroom that evening, he found her sitting at her vanity table. From behind he could see her long hair, which she brushed slowly, cascading down her back, and the reflection of her face in the mirror. As always he was quiet for a moment before he spoke.

"Is everything ready for tomorrow evening, Anna?" he asked.

During supper they had only spoken about Anthony's trip, which made sense. The little chap had said nothing, however, while Grace had cried. Dennis would probably cry the next day.

"Certainly, sir," his wife replied, moving the brush slowly through her shiny locks.

"Certainly, sir," my foot. They had told him that she had arrived at Rockfield and immediately disappeared. She had probably hidden somewhere in the house in order to read, leaving the staff to themselves. *Anna, I know everything you do,* he would have liked to say to her. *You're a fool not to understand that.* He took a deep breath and asked her again, "Didn't you do anything else today?"

"Well, I helped Anthony close up his trunks," she said nonchalantly. "And . . . Ah, yes, I went by the church to drop off some old clothes."

Oh, that's all, really, thought Christopher wearily. *And what did you and Daniel say to each other outside of the church?* He leaned against the wall without saying anything, put his hand up to his eyes, and slowly rubbed them.

Anna turned to look at him. "Christopher, is everything all right?"

Continuing to look at her, he didn't answer. Anna felt uneasy and put her hand on the nape of her neck before turning back to look into the mirror.

Christopher stood still, breathing slowly, trying to quench the anger inside him. *Oh, Anna, I always win with you. Isn't that so?*

He really should have shot his brother two days before, damn it. But instead he hadn't. Instead, Daniel had raised his pistol and taken aim at a bottle placed on a stump quite a ways from the house. He had pulled the trigger and hit the target. Christopher then took his pistol and brought it into position. Without hesitation he had raised his arm, and almost without aiming he fired, hitting his target.

Another shot by Daniel, and another bottle was hit.

Another shot by Christopher, and another bottle was hit.

A shot and a bottle.

A shot and a bottle.

Another shot.

Another.

And then Daniel aimed the gun and fired at the last target. And he had missed. Yes, he had missed. And horribly—by at least a foot!

Wild rejoicing exploded inside Christopher. Victory was such a common feeling for him, and yet every time it felt like the first victory. "Can't you handle the pressure, DeMercy?" he had teased, getting into firing position. "It seems that you have lost."

"It's not over yet, Davenport," Daniel had replied. He was calm and careful, without any regrets whatsoever. "You could also miss."

"No."

With the children reverently quiet, he pointed his gun and took aim with a firm hand.

And for a moment he could not shoot.

A silly thought entered his mind—that losing the challenge would be a perfect way for him to get rid of the Shadows' land. Losing the challenge could be a good thing, after all.

He had looked at the bottle in front of him and pulled the trigger. The children shouted, and the last target had been shattered.

***

Anna woke up and slowly moved from her husband's shoulder and turned over on her back. Christopher didn't stir and continued to sleep, breathing easily, as if his nightmares hadn't caught up to him yet that night.

Anna knew it must be very late. It was time to sleep, or the next day she would be a wreck for the trip with Anthony. But she had dreamt something—something that made sense of all the information she had. And that was odd, because her meeting with Daniel earlier that afternoon hadn't clarified anything at all.

"There's no Martha that I know of," he had said to her when she had asked him if he had ever come across that name. "Certainly not among your husband's relatives in London, with whom, however, he has no connection. Not even with Frank Davenport apparently, despite having been welcomed into his house as a child. However, if you are worried, I must admit that I found nothing unusual in his life . . . apart from the sheer dumb luck that he has in business affairs and gambling. In any case, no one has ever complained. And no one had anything bad to say about him—or good for that matter." There was hesitation in Daniel's eyes; then he had decided to explain. "Or anything *at all*, to be honest. Let's just say that mentioning his name got more than one door slammed in my face."

This information was none too reassuring, and what was more it wasn't very helpful. It was damned useless! She had risked incurring the wrath of her husband for *nothing*. If he had found out about the meeting she had requested with Daniel . . . *Fortunately, Christopher is in the dark about it. Good heavens, he would have made a scene about that!*

But that dream—it had slipped away from her a moment before she could grab it. What had she dreamt? She senselessly repeated the details that she knew.

"Do you really think your past gives you the right . . . ?"

"He has never done anything like this before, and he never will again . . ."

And then there was the pyramid and the gambling debts . . . and Martha and L.

With her eyes wide open, she stared into the dark for a long while, before tiredness made her drift into sleep.

36

Death may be atonement for our mistakes, but it will never correct them.

—Napoléon Bonaparte

My God, it is bitterly cold outside. Christopher woke up shivering in the darkness and put his hand over his eyes to cover the images of the dream still flashing in his mind. Monmouth Street, beggars who were lighting fires that were then probably extinguished three minutes later, the damp street, the cold, and the air that stung when he breathed in, like shards of glass . . .

He lay back slowly, trying not to disturb his wife's peaceful sleep. He wanted to fall back asleep, but the images of that unreal "court of miracles" would not go away. *What did George say when he saw Matthew?* he wondered with a smile. *"Just have a look at this little lord." That's what he said.*

He stopped fighting his memories, and he let them sweep over him. He found himself again under that portico on March 2, 1814, covered by a pile of old newspapers and somewhere between waking and sleeping. He again saw himself get up from his bed, called by George, and he relived the astonishment of seeing his cousin in that street, the last place he would have expected to see him. Three beggars were surrounding Matthew, and Christopher—in his memory, which now merged with a dream—got up and ran toward them.

London, March 2, 1814

"Leave him alone, George!"

With his face lighting up with a smile, Matthew turned toward Christopher. The look of fear disappeared from his face, replaced by such a strong expression of happiness that Christopher was afraid he would see him explode. Stupid cousin!

"He's your friend?" George asked, disappointed. He had wanted to beat up this little boy.

Christopher nodded his head and pulled Matthew aside against a wall fifteen or twenty feet away. "What the bloody hell are you doing here?" he said gently. "This is no place for you."

His cousin shrugged his shoulders. "Come back home, Chris," was all he said in response.

"You came here alone on foot? Do you know what could have happened to you in the streets at this time of night dressed like that? You're truly out of your mind."

"It's only nine in the evening." The calmness that Matthew answered with was extremely irritating. "It's still practically daylight out."

It was darker than dark could be outside, and they exhaled wispy puffs of vapor, which glowed under the lamplight.

"Right, practically daylight! Holy . . ." Christopher said before pausing to shiver. He wore a threadbare coat and rags, which he had exchanged for his new clothes earlier that afternoon to scrape together some money. "Who the hell told you where I was? Bob?"

Matthew said nothing, looking away.

"He's a goddamned traitor, then."

"What are you saying, Chris?" Matthew looked at him with the sympathy reserved for a sick friend. "He cares for you a lot—that's why he told me."

"Go away, Matt," he snapped. "I'll walk with you for a while, until we get to a safer area."

The thin boy in front of him seemed to be a baby still—at nearly fifteen years of age, he looked twelve—and he sounded even more childish when he retorted, "Only if you come back home with me."

"Matt, I told you on the note—"

"Oh, the note! Of course!" He pulled it out of his pocket with great enthusiasm. "Sorry, excuse my voice for a moment, because it should be a baritone, I suppose, to read such a work of art."

Christopher was cold, tired, and seriously considering killing his cousin, who eight years before had saved his life.

Ignoring the danger, Matthew continued: "I hope you have a few handkerchiefs on you, because I had to use three, your words were so moving." He coughed a couple of times and began to recite the words written on a piece of paper: "'Hi, Matt. I ran away. Do not look for me. Having you around was tolerable one day out of three. Bye. Chris.'" He paused, lowering the hand that held the note, and the look on his face changed. He became serious. "What can I say, Christopher? I had hoped that you would have made a bit more of an effort when bidding me farewell."

He looked away, embarrassed. "I didn't want to hurt you, Matt. It's just that I had to leave in a hurry, because . . . you don't know . . ."

"I know."

"How?"

"I know that my parents knew your mother."

Anger surged through him hotly. "Your father?" he said slowly. "Your father sent you? And maybe he's waiting for you around the corner."

"No. He wanted to come with me . . . Wait, let me finish. When I ran to him to tell him you had run away—"

"I had written—"

"If you didn't want me to look for you, you should have explained your reasons to me better, Christopher. Let me go on. When I told him that you had run off, he was upset—"

"Upset, my arse!"

"Wait, damn it! He was upset but not shocked. He told me the story of your mother and . . . and I understood why you had gone. I figured you would have not wanted to see him again, and so I pretended to wait for him. While he was getting his coat and hat, I ran off without him."

"So he doesn't know where you are?"

"No. I would have never told him where to find you. I came secretly. I've been looking around the city for two hours."

"Oh, you poor thing." He looked at the warm coat Matthew was wearing. "It breaks my heart."

"You want to compete for who's worse off, Chris? All right." He took off his coat in an angry huff.

"Matt, what the—?"

"Hey you, sir!" Matthew yelled, holding his coat out to George. "Take it. I don't need it."

Stunned, Christopher grabbed his arm. "Matthew, are you mad or something? What the hell are you doing?"

"I'll let myself die to convince you to come home," his cousin said flatly. *Maybe I should stop calling him "cousin,"* thought Christopher, since he would never call Frank Davenport his "uncle" ever again.

Matthew began to shake. The cold was dreadful, but Matthew was certainly pretending a bit, because he had only taken his coat off three seconds earlier.

"Stay away, George," Christopher ordered the older boy, who had come near.

"But—"

"Stay away." Christopher wasn't even thirteen and a half, but he was already nearly six feet tall, and he was rather well built for an adolescent. He was also a friend of the Barrett brothers. George let it go and walked away, muttering.

"If he doesn't want it, I'll throw it away," Matthew said. He actually threw it on the ground a few feet from them, into the wet street.

"Don't be daft. You'll come down with pneumonia." He went to pick it up and came back up to his cousin. "Come on, put it on."

"No. Not until you come home."

"Matthew, I can't! If your father told you, then how can you not understand? I don't . . ." His voice trembled, and that surprised him. He wasn't tormented by this at all; in fact, he was happy because he had finally discovered the name of the dog who had abandoned his mother. He had been wanting to find out for years, and this tingling in his voice had to be from the cold, most certainly. "Your father deceived me the entire time," he explained in an emotionless voice. "It's also his fault that my mother is dead. Put your coat back on—come on."

"No."

But didn't he care? Could he be so selfish that he couldn't put himself in Christopher's shoes for once? "If you don't put on the coat right now, I'll run off, and you'll never see me again, Matt," he warned him. "I'm counting to three. One . . ."

Shivering, Matthew looked at him, but he didn't move. And increasing the pathetic effect, his lips began to become a dangerous purplish color.

"Two . . ."

No movement, except for the vapor from his mouth and the chattering of his teeth.

"You'll never catch me, Matt. But if you put it on, I'll stay here to talk to you."

"Do you even know how to count to three, Chris? How long will it take you?"

"Go to hell, then!" He threw the coat on the ground right in front of the stunned beggars. "I don't care if you die. I'm leaving now, Matt!"

"Do what you like."

Christopher turned and began to run. There were no footsteps behind him. He didn't stop. Not right away. He ran a hundred and fifty feet before giving in and looking back. His cousin was still there where he had left him, calmly freezing.

Shit. And yet he should have expected that. Matthew had emotional blackmail in his blood: wasn't he the one who refused to eat for three days in 1806 to force his parents to let an orphan in their house—a bastard son of a whore?

"You're a swine, Matthew!" he yelled, turning and running back. "Put your coat back on!" he roared, grabbing him by the shirt.

"No."

He raised his right fist. "Get your coat back on, or I will break all of your teeth!" He stopped in midair with his closed fist, but his cousin didn't even blink. His big eyes were able to extinguish any anger. "Oh, bloody hell!" he exclaimed in frustration, letting go of him. "All right, then. If it's going to be like that, I'm taking mine off, too!"

With a jerky movement he took off his coat and threw it on the ground near the other one. His clothes, which were lighter than his cousin's, and his body were soon racked by chills.

"You're losing a lot of time." Matthew's statement showed exactly how much this gesture had hurt him—that is, not at all. "I feel that my chances of living are declining rapidly. Why don't you come back home with me and stop acting like an idiot?"

How can he not understand? Maybe Frank watered down the version of the story he told Matthew. "Matt, listen. He always knew who my mother was."

Matthew nodded. "Yes, inside he never had any doubt, even if he told me he wasn't certain until a year ago for some reason that he didn't explain to me." He breathed in the cold air and exhaled a warm, white puff. "And how did you discover it, Chris? I never thought that my mother might have had friends. Real friends, I mean."

"I believe it. No one ever mentioned Martha Askey, and even . . ." Without so much as a gravestone, not even her name remained. "They tried every possible way to get rid of her memory, but she hasn't been erased, not completely." Despite the cold there was pride in his voice. "I found her name by accident, and I confronted your father this afternoon." He swallowed, remembering how his heart fell when he read the truth in Frank's eyes. "It was really quite funny; you should have been there. He turned as white as a sheet, and he stuttered that it was a coincidence and that he didn't know . . . didn't know any . . ." He bit his lip hard. Martha Askey—denied even when she was long gone and dead. "Then he stopped lying, so now I know."

"He told me that he didn't want you to know, because the idea of revenge would have ruined your life. Don't look at me like that. I'm only telling you what he said to me—"

"He didn't tell me, because he was ashamed—that's the only reason!" Anger—anger was all he felt. "You don't know the whole truth, Matt. He and your mother—"

"They refused to bring you up as their son, I know."

Christopher swallowed his saliva, and it hurt. Maybe he was catching a cold. "My mother could have started her life over . . . No one would have known, not even her parents. All she would have had to do was not be seen the last few months of the pregnancy. But when she asked your parents, they said . . . they said . . ." He stopped talking to fight the emotion that was preventing him from speaking clearly.

When he was sure his voice wouldn't crack, he spoke again. "I'm talking rubbish, Matt. Never mind. I shouldn't have been born, and that's the truth."

His cousin shook his head, and now the guilt was on his face. "They wouldn't take you because of me, Chris." His mouth twitched in a strange grimace. Christopher hoped that it was because of the cold and not because he was about to start crying. "As a newborn I almost died, you know. My mother says that all the time—that it was a miracle that I survived the first year. My father told me that she was beside herself. She almost died out of despair. And when she said no to your mother, my father didn't have the courage to object."

"Your mother . . . What else could I expect from your mother? But your father . . ." His voice was shaking. "Your father had to know what would become of a twenty-year-old girl on her own with a little baby. He knew that her parents would turn her away. He sent her to her death, Matt."

"He looked for her later. That's what he swore to me, but he couldn't find her. If she had shown up—"

"Oh, so it's her fault, then. Is that what you're trying to tell me?"

Unhappy, Matthew looked down. "I'm sorry."

But there was no need to be. The rage inside Christopher against him was already gone. "It doesn't matter," he murmured. Matthew was frail—the cold hurt him even when he was warmly dressed. Oh damn. He rubbed his hands together and stomped his feet on the ground. "How about we put our coats back on?" he asked.

"You put on yours. I'm waiting for you to come home with me first."

I can't. "But I can't, for Christ's sake, don't you understand? He should have told me! He should have told me!" He put his hand up to his eyes, and he didn't even feel cold, since he was so hot from the hatred inside him. "Your mother didn't want me in her house, and that's fine! Your father didn't insist, and that's fine as well, damn it! But he should have told me! Bloody hell, he should have told me! And he never did—don't you understand? Never, Matt, never!"

"Chris, I know, but—"

"No, no, how could you understand? You?" Now he sounded desperate—and he was. He was damned desperate. "Your father has always known who my mother was, and he has always known who my *father* was!" He took a big breath, and then another, and then another. "And now . . . now *I* know, too. I know and—"

"You want your revenge, don't you? You want to go to Coxton and kill him."

"I have to get my revenge," he answered, and a strange calm suddenly fell over him. "I know that you can't understand, because for you she was . . . she was only a whore—isn't that so? But for me . . . for me she wasn't." He put his hand to his face, covering his eyes with his fingers. "She gave up everything to have me. Can you imagine what happened? I don't know how she ended up in that brothel. I can only imagine it was like drowning a little bit at a time, and all because I was there with her, like a fucking stone tied around her neck."

He lowered his head, and Matthew waited in silence for him to start talking again, holding his numb hands under his armpits to warm them up in the chilly night air.

"There are so many who are guilty for what happened to her," Christopher said in a tired voice, "but only one really matters: Leopold DeMercy." The man who had seduced his mother. The man who had destroyed her like a burning leaf. The man who was Christopher's father. "And he will pay. I'm leaving tomorrow."

"No, you aren't."

Christopher didn't even get angry at this. He didn't understand why his cousin was against it, but he knew he could convince him sooner or later: it was clear that DeMercy had to die.

"You would do the same thing in my place," he said quietly. "If someone killed me, you would avenge me. I know it."

"That's true." Matthew's admission was without any emphasis or doubt. "But I certainly could not do it with a cheap pocketknife—is that really what you're thinking of using? Tell me something, honestly: If you get revenge and then get hanged for it, would that make you happy?"

"Matthew—"

"Do you think your mother wanted that for you?"

"My mother . . ." Christopher lowered his head and smiled. He couldn't go on.

"You want to die for your revenge—is that what you want? You'll never get away with it, I know it. They'll get you. It's suicide. You don't even have a plan to kill your father."

"I do have one, actually," he said. "I was thinking about getting myself hired and—"

"You'll just introduce yourself to him dressed like this, like a tramp?"

"What does that matter?" he replied, shrugging his shoulders. "He won't be looking at my clothes."

"And so this is your grand idea of revenge, then? A patched-together plan that will never work."

"To hell with it!" he exploded, exasperated. "You know what I would really like; do you want to have a good laugh? I would like to make my father relive my mother's ordeal: throw him in the dust, and make him suffer more and more disgrace, and take away everything from him that makes him so proud! I would like to buy the estate where he lives and set fire to it! I would like to take everything he owns and leave him without a penny to his name. I want to ruin him. I want him to be so desperate that he has no alternative but to kill himself!" He paused, shivering with cold and anger. "But I know that's impossible," he continued a little later, calming himself down, and his eyes lost their sinister glow. "I will have to be happy with killing him," he concluded in a breathless whisper.

Matthew stood thinking it over for a few minutes, tapping his feet on the ground. "You're absolutely right, Chris," he finally said. "DeMercy wanted to become a lord, didn't he? That's why he abandoned your mother after he promised to marry her. A chance for a better marriage came up, and he couldn't let it slip by." He gave him a sorry look. "And you want to humiliate her more by making yourself look disgusting and filthy to him."

Christopher shrugged his shoulders, looking at their lifeless coats left on the ground, getting soaked. "It's freezing cold, Matt. Why—?"

"Listen. First you said that it's impossible for you to be able to leave him penniless with his face in the dust. But if we put ourselves to the task—"

"What stupidity," Christopher interrupted testily. "It's even absurd to—"

"No, it's not absurd. We just have to find a way." He lowered his head and put a hand on his forehead. "Maybe . . . maybe if he invests his money in the wrong way . . . if he buys shares, paying far more than their value, as in the South Sea Bubble . . ." He cupped his hands together and blew into them to warm them up. "You understand, right?"

"Hmm?"

"No, you don't understand." He let out a sigh. "Chris, studying a bit more really wouldn't hurt you."

"Will you bother to explain it to me, or do you think you'll keep looking at me with that grin until both of us become ice statues?"

"All right, all right." Matthew smiled, and inexplicably the night became less dark. Only he had the ability to do such things. "The South Sea Company was a company based on nothing, on a 'bubble.' On the Stock Exchange it's easy to lose everything in a moment. Hell, even Newton, with his big brain, lost quite a lot during the last century."

"Maybe he had studied too much," Christopher said to his cousin's know-it-all look.

"Don't distract me; it's cold out," Matthew grumbled.

Know-it-all, absolutely. Maybe a punch—maybe not too hard—is what I need to give him, Christopher reasoned. *That would warm him up, wouldn't it?*

"It's possible, Chris." The perfectly pedantic voice of his cousin came out from his mouth in white clouds. "It's possible to trick your father and bring him to financial ruin."

Christopher sighed. "Would you like to create one of these . . . bubbles in that case?"

Matthew thought about it and frowned. "I don't know. They have their limitations now, but we will find a way. I will help you. If not on the Stock Exchange, you could still offer him some kind of reckless investment." He watched him carefully, as if trying to dissect him. It was a bit disturbing, to be honest. Christopher rubbed the back of his neck with his hand.

"Obviously," said Matthew, "you couldn't introduce yourself to him immediately after starting your business. You should start at the bottom with a little swindling and gradually aim higher." He tilted his head to the left and again looked like a surgeon who was trying to decide which part to cut up first. "And no one is forcing us to limit ourselves to financial scams. You have many talents, Chris, and some are not very—how shall I put it?—proper. But still useful, that's for sure. You always beat me at cards, and it's not just luck, is it?"

Christopher smiled. Even in the cold he was warmed by a certain amount of satisfaction. "You have no proof that I cheat when playing," he said cheekily. "It's more likely that you're just not good at it."

"Or maybe I was never able catch you red-handed, which means that you're damned good at it." Matthew shook his head from shoulder to shoulder to warm up, shivering wildly. "You also have many friends." He looked at the gloomy street and the men who had gone to sleep a ways from them. "As you said, this is no place for me. If I tried to run away from home, I would end up floating in the river after a day at most. Not you. You know people who make me afraid even from a mile away, people who can be very useful in certain situations. There are loads of more or less legal ways to make money, Chris, and there are load of people who deserve to be cheated—and this is the best part of the whole thing."

Christopher scratched his head, fascinated in spite of himself. "Even if it were possible, I would have to wait years," he answered with uncertainty. Then he took a deep breath. "No. One stab in his chest and I end it all tomorrow."

"That's really great revenge, Chris. Congratulations. Even if you succeed—and your plan seems a bit vague, actually—it will take DeMercy only a moment to die. No, people like him should suffer only after they've been thrown in the dust, like you said."

"If my plan is vague, what about yours? It's full of unknowns, and it's practically—"

"We can do it, Chris," Matthew interrupted. "And besides, listen: it's not written in stone. You can always try, and if it doesn't work you can go back to the original idea, can't you?"

Christopher felt his toes falling off from the cold, and his hands hurt badly. But he still took the time to ask, "And what if while I'm trying to get rich and find a way to ruin him, DeMercy ups and dies?"

"No, he won't die. People like him never do." The explanation had nothing scientific about it, but it convinced Christopher instantly. Certain things were true, and that was that. "And if the worst comes to the worst, we can keep informed of the condition of his health," Matthew continued. He paused, and Christopher understood that he was about to say something he would not like. "My father—"

"No!" One of the beggars not far away who had dozed off lifted his head up, looking at them angrily, then ducked back down to his bed. "No," he repeated with a lower voice. "Your father doesn't . . ."

"Don't be stupid, Chris." He was angry now and no longer cajoling him. "Do you think this is a game? If so, you might as well really go to Coxton tomorrow. But if you want to get serious, we need him."

(He will betray you again, Christopher.)

"He will betray me, Matthew."

His cousin shook his head. "No, he will not be able to betray you, because he won't know anything. He will fork out a bit of money for our—what should we call it?—*enterprise*. He owes that to you, doesn't he?"

Silence.

"Take a good look at the reality, Chris. To get to your father, you need—"

"He's not my father."

"What?"

"He's not my father." It was a sudden realization, and as cold as the street. "Don't call him that, because he's not that. He's just a fucking pig."

Matthew stared at him, and the same realization appeared in his eyes. "You're right," he agreed. "He's only a pig. But to get to him you need money, Chris. And a name."

Of course, the name. Christopher was silent, clenching his fists in the ice-cold air. Oh, Frank had been so firm when he had imposed that name "Davenport" on him! Wasn't it now clear why? Martha had asked him for that years before, and in response at that time a no had killed her. A belated sense of guilt—that was his bloody name. And he could not get rid of it! He couldn't, for God's sake! Because Leopold DeMercy would never connect Christopher *Davenport* with the obscure and forgotten Martha Askey from his past, since that name—that damned name, that hated name—was good for something, damn it!

"Come on, Chris, let's go home. You can't ever become an important person if you stay in this stinking street without studying—and a lot, Chris, I warn you now—and without money. Even you know that."

He knew it, but he couldn't go back. "I don't want to see him again, Matt." Because that was the whole issue, wasn't it? Seeing him again. Seeing the man who betrayed him. "For me your father died today."

(Uncle Frank, Christopher. The one who taught you how to swim.)

Matthew looked down. "I understand." His voice crackled, like ice crystals in the street. "But you will not have to speak to him again, Chris, nor with my mother." He raised his head and looked him in the eyes. "I swear. I will talk for you. You have to come back home, though." He gave a timid smile. "Maybe they won't be your aunt and uncle anymore, Christopher, but I will stay your cousin, won't I?"

So it seemed. But dear God, what an absurd plan. And how damned cold it was! Christopher didn't answer right away. There probably wasn't the slightest chance of getting this bubble thing that Matthew was talking about to work, but surely the annoying "cousin" would have let himself die if he hadn't gone back home with him—or at least he would have caught another cold, with every possible symptom this time. And besides . . . what had he said? "It's not written in stone . . ." Let's try it, then.

"All right, I'll go back," he murmured, and Matthew's mood lightened as if he didn't feel cold anymore, which was probably the case. "But only until I'm rich enough to go off on my own again." He picked up Matthew's coat from the ground; it was wet, but fortunately the inside seemed dry. He handed it to him abruptly, and his cousin still would not put it back on. "I'll go, but on two conditions," he said clearly. "The first is that you must not criticize my methods, not even when you don't like them. Maybe for you this absurd plan is a way to distract me from killing DeMercy, but you've ended up in a mess that not even you can imagine, and if you want to get yourself out of it, this is the right time."

Matthew smiled again. "You're not as bad as you think, Chris. You won't trample on the innocent, and as for the others . . . Someone has to clean up after you, right?"

Christopher bent over to pick up his coat, and sadly he noticed that it was quite wet. Sighing, he slipped his arm in a soaked, freezing sleeve. "The second condition," he continued, "concerns your father. I told you things about him tonight, things that you didn't want to hear. I won't do it again from now on. I know that you love him . . ." He pursed his lips. "But you," he added, giving him a heavy look, "you will never defend him to me again."

There was a pause. "All right," Matthew replied hesitantly. "But there's one thing I want to say to you, Chris. My father loves you . . . No, just this once, please, I swear, then I'll put back on my coat. My father loves you, and he has never forgiven himself for not taking you in when you were born. I believe . . . I believe that he stopped loving my mother for that very reason. Or maybe he never loved her and that's the reason why . . ." The sentence trailed off. "Christopher, he wronged you, I know. But in the end he was honest, wasn't he? He could have not told you about the failure to adopt you, and instead—"

"Instead nothing! He admitted it only when I asked him why my mother hated yours."

Matthew shook his head. "No. He could have come up with an excuse. They were classmates in Bridgetown, weren't they? He could have said that they had quarreled for some reason, and instead he confessed everything to you. You said he was dishonest with you, which is true, but he wasn't dishonest today. And you, Chris"—he looked into his eyes, trying to make himself understood—"you broke his heart today."

Christopher stared at him grimly. "Are you finished?"

"Yes."

"Then put back on that bloody coat."

37

Anything is better than lies and deceit!
—Leo Tolstoy

They were in a green garden near the dormitory, and Westminster Abbey peered at them with its quiet importance. *It is big,* Anna thought. *So big. Don't devour my little brother,* she prayed to herself, because the abbey was also dark. *It's unique, and there will never be another like it.*

Serious and without tears, Anthony was in the courtyard ready to say good-bye to her and to Christopher. With his solemn little face and lack of fear, he seemed more like a professor than a pupil on the first day of school.

"Well, Anthony, here we are," declared her husband in a speech-like tone. "Your sister and I are returning home to tell everyone that you're doing well."

Anthony nodded. *How much has he grown in the last month, this little man?* Anna felt her cheeks getting wet, and she felt stupid because her brother and husband looked at her like she had three arms, seven legs, and more than one hundred eyes, given the amount of tears she was able to shed.

"Anna, you're making a fool of me," Anthony scolded her softly, noticing the looks that other boys in the courtyard were giving them. "I'm not dying, you know."

Oh, Anthony, smile for me, my brother. "I know, I know," she responded, pulling out a handkerchief. "But write us a letter tonight."

"I will."

"Do you have your good-luck charm on you?" This was a family tradition: with a pin they attached a tiny little pouch to the inside of their undershirt, filled with little flowers and fragrant herbs. The day before, Anna had put small pebbles from the road by their house in her brother's pouch.

Christopher took an exaggerated breath—probably to suppress a sarcastic comment—and Anthony seemed uncomfortable. "Shh, Anna, speak softer," he whispered.

"Keep it with you always," she said, ignoring him. *It will protect you, Anthony, and it will give you independence of thought.* "And remember that it takes imagination, and not science, to make a discovery."

"Yes, yes," he replied, and snorted. "Don't worry."

"We can go, or do you want to spend the night here, Anna?" her husband asked her impatiently. He held out his hand to Anthony, who took it. "Good-bye, Anthony."

"Good-bye. And Christopher," he added solemnly, "soon I will be able to pay you back for everything that you're spending on me."

Well said, my little man. Anna didn't say that to him aloud, but Anthony heard her anyway, she was sure of it.

Christopher seemed surprised and shook his head. "That won't be necessary."

"It will be necessary for me," he replied, and Anna was so proud she felt as if she were lifted off the ground an inch or even two.

"Do as you wish," her husband said without emotion. "It makes no difference to me."

Oh, Christopher, how can you? How can you be so cold? "Anthony," she murmured to her brother. "Study all you want, but don't believe everything they tell you."

That was only the third time she had said it; however, her husband couldn't stop making that annoyed face. He snorted and said, "Now, if you have finished making your brother look ridiculous, we must really go."

"Just a minute." She leaned over Anthony, who pulled away.

"Oh, Anna, spare me please."

Could she listen to him? Apparently not, and the kiss that she gave him was bigger and louder than usual. Not happy with that, she ruffled his hair, which he smoothed down right away with frantic hands.

"Come now, Anna," Christopher urged her abruptly. "Let's go."

He took her by the arm just above the elbow and turned, pulling her rather awkwardly.

"Write, Anthony," Anna shouted with her head turned, trying to keep up with the long strides of her husband. "We'll miss you!"

When they were out of sight, they continued to walk at a brisk pace toward the carriage that they would take back home. Rather, Christopher walked briskly; she, dragged by him, was practically flying, and her feet only touched the ground once in a while.

"You didn't even wish my brother good luck, sir," she stated. And she again felt the desire to cry.

"I leave that nonsense to you, since you handle it so well."

Oh, Chris, that child adores you. He adores you, and he doesn't know that you would sell him in a heartbeat. She felt her heart tense up, and she could no longer walk. How important is happiness if it's based on a lie? She stopped on a cobblestone, and her husband, who was holding her arm, almost tripped.

"Anna, what is it?" he asked nervously. "Did you not say good-bye to your brother enough?"

She looked at him silently. Ah, how hard his eyes were, and how arrogant his appearance was, and how cruel his deception was. Too cruel.

"I will not apologize to DeMercy this evening."

She had opened her mouth before even knowing what words would come out, and she was almost dumbfounded to say them. She had said them, however, and with her heart beating madly, she watched her husband with the same helpless expectation that one feels in front of a vase that teeters on the edge of a table before falling.

***

It wasn't a question, it was a statement. Christopher stood beside his wife, trying to grasp the meaning of this rebellion—infuriating and pointless, like all the others that preceded it. And that very day, damn it. That bloody day, with anxiety eating away at him, at the prospect of the decisive step in his plan—to convince his father to invest *everything* into the pyramid—that very day, shit, on which he really needed to stay bloody calm! *And all right, Anna, let's play one more time,* he thought, flexing and stretching his fingers. "Of course you will."

She shook her head. "No. I won't obey you, Christopher," she repeated thoughtfully, looking into space. "And not only this evening," she clarified, turning her eyes toward him, "never again. It's over."

You can't run from me, Anna. You can't. He suddenly had a bad taste in his mouth. Bad and sour, because she could not run from him, though she wanted to. "I don't want to argue with you," he said flatly. "I'll pretend I didn't hear it. Come on." He pulled her by the arm, but his wife didn't move. "Anna, stop it."

She seemed to not hear him or even see him. How long had it been since he felt invisible in his wife's eyes? Quite a long time, and he had hoped that it wouldn't happen ever again—that the damned transparency he had suffered from during his life was finally over.

"This evening I will not come to your party." Anna's tone was indifferent—the same tone she used to tell him what was for supper. The tone of someone who wasn't afraid, and who was no longer controllable.

Christopher breathed deeply. He ignored the nagging stinging that had suddenly grown in his chest and was still growing. He ignored the burning. He ignored the scratches and cuts and the infection.

"What are you trying to do exactly?" he asked her. "You just want to irritate me, or maybe"—he glanced at her sideways ironically—"you fooled yourself into thinking you can actually rebel."

With a tug his wife twisted her arm free, and she faced him on the stony walk. "I am no longer your doll, sir," she said to him with an amplified voice. "From now on."

Of course you are. A blind rage erupted in him with a violent, acid spurt. *You seriously think I'll let you get away?* "As you wish, then," he replied coldly, controlling himself. "But I suggest you think carefully about what you'll be up against."

"I don't care what you do. Not anymore."

(Do you hear her voice, Christopher? Do you hear how distant it is?)

"You know that I won't stop until I have won, and so why . . . ?" he began, but he stopped when she shook her head. She wasn't listening to him. She didn't want to listen to him. "Well, then," he snapped. And the rage in him grew and grew, and he felt it swell in his flesh, contract his muscles, and quicken his blood. And yet . . . and yet it seemed different to him this time. Because he didn't feel a thrill anticipating the battle that was about to begin. Because fatigue had planted its stakes in him. God, he couldn't fight anymore, he realized. With her, with his father, with anyone.

He couldn't anymore.

And, like always, he did. Hardened, he turned his head back. "The first one to pay will be your brother, as you can imagine," he said. "He will come back home with us. Then we'll see."

His wife swallowed hard and blinked. Tears were already there, but she didn't ask him to stop.

(She's not asking you to stop, Christopher. She hates you too much. But you know that, don't you? What are you thinking? What are you thinking, Christopher?)

"You can come with me, Anna, if you *want* to—I'm not ordering you, obviously."

He walked quickly toward the garden in the school.

Anthony was still outside, and he was chatting with a little blond boy who had a stream of freckles on his nose.

"Anthony," Christopher called out loudly from quite a distance away.

Surprised, his brother-in-law turned his head. And in a flash his brown eyes lit up as he saw him again unexpectedly, and a smile replaced the serious look that he had until that moment. And his face showed why that was: he was scared, just the same as any other boy on the first day of school.

"Christopher!" he shouted, running up to him.

Well, Anna, cheer up. Christopher felt his lips sag with a disenchantment that no one could have called a smile. *Look how you sacrifice your brother for the hatred you have for me.*

Anthony reached him. "Is everything all right?" he asked.

"Not exactly," Christopher said, pale. Not at all, in fact.

"Did we forget something?"

Yes, Anthony. I forgot to tell you that you will not be attending this school, and that from now on I will be trying to ruin your future. The little boy in front of him watched him calmly, unaware of the problems Christopher was having getting his words out. *Don't you wonder how bad someone like me can make it for a little chap like you, Anthony?*

"Anthony," he began. *You need this lesson, little chap. You must never trust anyone—never.* Had he told him this, he now wondered? He didn't remember. Maybe not. "Anthony," he repeated, and he looked down, putting a hand on his forehead. He paused a moment, then gave a bitter smile. "Anthony," he said, "I forgot to give you something." He put his hand inside his jacket and pulled out a little sack of black cloth of around three by four inches, which he handed to the boy.

"What is it, Christopher?" Anthony opened the little sack up and smiled. Because he recognized the deck of marked cards with which his brother-in-law had taught him to cheat.

"This will come in handy, I think," murmured Christopher. "But keep it hidden," he added after a moment, clearing his throat, "and do not share our secrets, except with people worthy of trust." *And remember me if you can.*

"All right," the boy answered.

Farewell, Anthony.

***

They climbed quietly into the carriage, and the horses moved laboriously; the coachman was slapping the reins on their backs.

Neither of them spoke for quite a while; then Christopher flashed her a detached smile. "You beat me, Anna," he admitted. "Many have tried, but all it took was you in the end."

Anna said nothing. Christopher was very surprised when he hadn't the courage to disillusion Anthony. On the other hand, she was not; she had already realized it, and a long while before.

"I imagine that now you'll leave me," Christopher continued, as if taking note of something inevitable but fortunately unimportant.

(You will leave him, won't you, Anna?)

She didn't turn her eyes away from the carriage window. The view of streets and shops was soon replaced by the countryside, with colors so familiar and understandable. Time passed without her noticing it as she was cradled by the movement of the carriage, which was sometimes abrupt and sometimes lulling, on the journey to the house.

"You don't love me, do you, Christopher?" she asked him, as if waking up. "You have told me that many times."

Her husband turned his head toward the window. "I don't love you," he repeated, distant.

And so why are we here? she wondered, distressed. She looked at her husband, who in an odd, ironic reversal of roles was now looking at the view outside. *Why are we together? What binds us apart from that stupid glass of lemonade? What? What? What—?*

She stopped breathing suddenly; it was as if lightning had struck her, and she felt burned, blinded—and enlightened in a flash. Her throat became dry, her eyes glazed over. *Nothing, Christopher, nothing binds us,* she understood, and everything came together and became clear in her mind. *Nothing binds us but something has divided us—and very clearly so, causing the worst crisis in our marriage and pushing you to ask me—to order me—to make love with you.* She felt her heart fall with a silent, useless thud, like the sound of a blade of grass being cut. Nausea in her chest, in her stomach, in her head. Nausea and pain in every part of her body. She looked at her husband like she had never done before. *Christopher, do you want to tell me who the baby was that was mentioned in that letter?*

She looked away from him and looked out of the window.

(But your eyes don't see anything, do they, Anna? They see only darkness now.)

She let her mind connect the pieces of a story that was beginning to make more sense while her heart beat in wild jumps, and her head echoed with memories of screams and crying.

Let me tell you a story, Christopher. Oh, I know that the fairy tales I make up seem silly to you, but this one won't be, you'll see. It's about a Martha, seduced by L., and she becomes pregnant with his child. Let's say that she doesn't miscarry and that the baby—who has blue eyes, like yours—is thought by all to be the legitimate son of Mark Davenport.

(Is everything clear now, Anna?)

What happened, Christopher? Something horrible, something that gave you the right to trample on the innocent?

She took several deep breaths so that she could drown the bitter air, the searing heat.

I must not throw up. I must not.

She closed her eyes and swallowed empty gulps over and over again.

You came here for revenge, didn't you, Christopher? That contract—that scam—is for your father, L., the man who discovered what life was when he saw your mother.

Maybe she was wrong; maybe her logic was faulty. And yet why did everything fit together so well, so perfectly?

Who is L., Christopher?

But she already knew. Because if there was something inexplicable—inexplicable until now, at least—it was why Christopher had wanted to marry her. Because nothing bound them together, apart from L.

L. is the reason I came into this story, isn't it, husband of mine?

L. as in Leopold.

And Daniel is your brother.

Her breathing became shallow. She pushed her heaving back down into her soul, but it would return, inevitably.

When did you find out about my engagement with Daniel, Christopher? I assumed that you learned about it after that day in July, and I didn't relate it at all to the rape. But had you found out about it right away? She put her hand over her eyes, which were wide open, and looked at the world through her fingers. But was there really a world to look at? *You said something after you raped me—do you remember? You talked about my imaginary fiancé there in the grass while I could barely stand up, and I—God, how stupid of me—I considered it to be merely an assumption. But that wasn't it, was it, my husband? Someone told you about me and Daniel, and you thought you could take me away from him that day.*

She saw no world, no colors. She closed her eyes.

To top it off, we weren't even engaged, ironically enough. If you had asked me, none of this would have happened. I could tell you this now, she thought, opening her eyes, staring at the side of his face. *You'd be happy, because what is important to you is that I don't go back to him. But do you know what? I won't say anything to you. Go ahead and think that I love him: my pride, humiliated in a thousand ways, will spare me at least this last blow*. She pushed back her tears.

How naive she had been. Naive? Oh, no, idiotic. Mad. Because even the night before, in his arms, she had thought . . .

Oh, but it's all so clear now.

How much was left of this trip? It was so long, so slow, and so unending. And why was this carriage so small and her husband so big, and why did he take up so much room? And why were his knees so close to hers?

I must warn Daniel, she understood. *I must tell him before you destroy him. Poor Christopher, your vendetta will fail; you won't get what you want.* She didn't speak, and she let herself be tossed about, stunned. *What I want is to forget.*

She was sure that she wouldn't remember anything about this trip. Traveling on the roads seemed like a dream until she could see the quiet hills of Coxton looming on the horizon.

"Yes, I will leave you, Christopher."

Her voice was firm and clear, and she said these words without stumbling. Her husband gave her a cold look, imperturbable.

What a fool she had been.

"I want you to get out of my life and my family's life," she said without emotion. "I don't want to see you ever again."

38

The last act is bloody, no matter how pleasant the rest of the play is. Some dirt is thrown on your head at last, and there you are forever.

—Blaise Pascal

"Daniel is out of town," Anna wrote in her diary. *"Lucy told me that he won't be back for four or five days, and that is truly unfortunate. I don't know how to reach him by letter; I will have to wait for his return to tell him what I have discovered—or rather, what I think I have found out. Because what if I am mistaken and everything was just . . ."*

She stopped writing and put her head in her hands. She was still thinking about Christopher, but why? She was free from him, and wasn't this what she had wanted more than anything else?

Christopher, who lied. He was always pretending with all of them. Who called her a queen while he made her a slave, who groaned in his sleep, who calmed down without waking if she rubbed him . . .

What were you dreaming about? Your father?

Christopher never looked down, nor was he ever afraid. Always unassailable and always impregnable. Sometimes, however, such as when he passed by her in the hall, he would pull her close to him and hold her tightly without aggression, without cuddling, without kissing. Then he would leave suddenly, almost embarrassed, almost as if . . .

(Forget it, Anna. Close the door on the damned chapter.)

His whispers, hot and delicate, in the darkness of their room. "Oh, my sweetheart is ashamed," he would giggle. "But let me do it, Anna . . . I just want to adore you . . ." Then he would add, "Obey. Be a good girl."

He said it to make her angry, and it worked.

"Go . . . go to h-hell, Chris."

"No, I'm not going there . . . I'm staying here . . . Here it feels so good, my love."

"Enough. I don't want to think about it anymore," she wrote. *"But I cannot help but wonder: Will he really be happy after he ruins his father?*

"When we came back from London yesterday," Anna wrote, *"he didn't even come back into the house. 'We won't see each other again, as you have requested,' he said in the most polite way possible. 'If you want, I can appoint someone else as guardian of your siblings and your assets.' I made a slight nod of agreement with my head. 'Daniel DeMercy?' he asked me. 'Do you want me to ask him for you?'*

"His question surprised me a lot, and for a few moments I couldn't answer. I was confused, and I still am: Why would he entrust my brothers and sister to someone whom he hates, whom he despises? I don't believe he would, despite everything. For a moment—and I must say, a hopeful moment—I thought I had misunderstood everything, that I had gotten everything wrong. But then I realized in some strange, late, absurd manner he got to know his brother; perhaps he even learned to respect him. Yet—and this is what upsets me and I always notice in him—he won't have any problems ruining Daniel along with his father. 'All right, thanks,' I replied. 'Fine.' He turned on his heels and left without another word."

She heard excited footsteps in the hallway.

"Anna," Nora shouted. She was crying.

"Nora . . . ?"

The door burst open, and a small, disheveled Nora appeared in the doorway. Anna ran to her, with the hope that was impossible to stop, even in the face of that which was beyond repair—the hope of hearing that everything is all right. "Nora, what . . . ?" But she knew. She already knew.

And that was the answer. "Your father. Your father is ill, Anna."

***

"So that's it. Your ugly face is still here?" Matthew snapped at him a few days later. He himself had a grimace that, in terms of ugly faces, could beat them all. "I'll have to find somewhere else to live because I can't put up with you for very long."

Christopher didn't answer. He was standing in front of his liquor table, and he poured himself another finger of whisky. Another couple of fingers, in fact.

"Put down that glass, Chris." Now his cousin's voice sounded nervous as well as annoying. "You know you can't hold your liquor worth a damn."

"Get the hell out."

Matthew didn't leave, of course, and instead responded. "What did you do to Anna to push her to kick you out? Do you want to tell me?"

Nothing, I did nothing. He lowered his head with the smile of someone who knows how the world works. And he agreed. *So, for the first time in my life, I acted in a way you could define as decent.* "Get out," he said flatly. He went to the window and looked at the clear sky that morning.

Staying away from the Champion house was incredibly easy, he realized in amazement. God, what confusion they have there. The children are screaming; Nora is muttering. Anna hates me, and she is constantly complaining. It wasn't that he had ever let himself be distracted, but he recognized that he was more lucid now.

(And when she moaned underneath you, Christopher? Don't you remember that?)

All right, and so what? He did enjoy it, and that's all. Nothing else. There are thousands of women like her, even better than her.

(She never told you "I love you," did she, Chris?)

His cousin was still yelling. "I'm sure you could resolve . . ." he said, then paused. "Christopher," he began again, changing his tone, assuming the same damned tone of a doctor with his patient. "Why not drop everything and call it quits?"

Drop everything. Why not ask me to stop breathing, then? He looked at him. Matthew continued to say stupid things, but luckily he had learned not to listen to him over the years. So many, many years. Matthew had always followed him on every trip, in every way. *But now that's enough, he suddenly decided. That's enough. I must get rid of his deadweight.* Yes, he would move on his own—that was his future. No one telling him what to do, when to jump, and how high. *Enough, enough—they can all go to hell. Always thinking they're perfect, always judging, always breaking my spirit. I'm leaving you here, Matt. You can start your life over, maybe with that Lucy, and it will be better for you, too.*

Drop everything—that was what his cousin had said. He looked at the glass between his fingers, and he thought about the strong-willed girl his mother had been—that girl who had felt the need to leave her opinion indelibly on the pages of a book, but on the day she killed herself she hadn't even written a note. *You didn't even leave two lines, Mummy,* he thought, raising his eyes toward the grass of the park. *You had nothing more to say.*

"Everything is going according to plan, Matt," he said, interrupting the chatter. "My father"—his cousin's eyes grew large—"my father will make his last investment to the pyramid today."

And in a few days it will all be over, and he will realize that he no longer has anything. He will discover that his debts—mostly contracted with Christopher, whether knowingly or not—are of such a magnitude that they will land him in prison. He will discover that his land, already heavily mortgaged, no longer belongs to him. And he will discover that the pyramid in which he has invested all of his hopes and all of his money has collapsed. And him with it. *No one will question his suicide at that point.* He rolled the glass between his fingers, ignoring his cousin's nagging voice. *And then I will disappear. Maybe I will fake my own death, and Anna will be a widow and rich—and free, like she wants.*

"You must be joking," said Matthew. That bloody tone was still there. For Christ's sake, could he leave him alone? "Didn't you move the appointment?"

"I couldn't."

"But you can't go today," Matthew said rationally. "Your father-in-law's funeral is today."

Christopher shrugged. "I have no choice."

"You have no choice?" Matthew gasped out of shock, and for another reason—out of his usual intolerable moralism. "But what kind of a man are you, Christopher? James Champion welcomed you in his house like a son."

Yes, James Champion. That pathetic man—a failure as a father, a failure as a landowner. So dazed that for years he had put everything on Anna's shoulders while he locked himself away in his world of little harvests, his rural world, uninterested in the future of his four children.

He remembered him—his short brown hair becoming gray; his wrinkles and drooping eyelids; his sunken eyes, which had perpetual circles around them; his drawling voice and his crooked mouth, every sentence of his painful, either for him or for anyone unlucky enough to hear him say it. "What do you . . . do you think of these seeds, Christopher?" he had asked him less than a month before while he and Anthony were planting spinach in the vegetable garden behind the house.

"Very good, Mr. Champion," he had replied, sweaty in the hot sun. He had looked up from the ground, where he, with his sleeves rolled up, was filling holes that had been thoroughly dug and perfectly aligned by Anthony.

James was sitting in the shade of a nearby tree, and he had tried to get up to see for himself the work that he cared for so much. He wasn't able to manage, and he sat back down heavily. With sadness and an awareness in his tired eyes, he had watched his son-in-law and his son while they finished the row without a mistake.

Christopher remembered the warmth of the sun on his bare arms. He remembered Anthony's concentration, intensely determined to please his father. He remembered the sweat and his tiredness at the end of this day. He remembered his father-in-law sitting in the fading daylight.

"You'll attend the funeral for me," he said to Matthew. "Come up with some excuse. Now get out or I'll kick you out."

***

Three children dressed in black walked toward the church, odd and unnatural in the midday sun. Anna led them inside the dark building, and the whole family sat in the front pew.

"I am the resurrection and the life, sayeth the Lord," began Reverend Graham. "He that believeth in me, though he were dead, yet shall he live."

Anthony had returned quickly from London three days before. His face was restrained, serious, and he wasn't crying.

"And though after my skin worms destroy this body, yet in my flesh . . ."

Anna thought back to her father, to his last breaths, and to when he had looked at her without recognizing her any longer.

"For we brought nothing into this world, and it is certain we can carry nothing out."

Grace looked very odd with the lack of color; her curls lit up her face, and her expression alternated between sorrow and unawareness, because at four years old, what does one know about death?

"Surely every man walks about like a shadow. Surely they busy themselves in vain. He heaps up riches and does not know who will gather them."

Friends gathered around the Champion family in this difficult moment. Lucy was at their side; even Mrs. Edwards was there. Mr. Gutman was serious, as was Sir Colin. Mr. Clarke, despite the little kindness Anna had always shown him, had come. Rosemary was there—there were also a few friends of her husband—but most people did not come, as if they knew there was no point in smiling at her, this dull and dark girl. Nora was close by, and she was crying with quiet sobs like a child. Matthew's head was hung low, his face tense. A small crowd had gathered in the church to say farewell to this little man, who had lived for almost nothing in the last years of his life. He had big dreams, like everyone else, in his youth; then he settled for a happy family life, and finally he became ill. Anna thought that he had begun to shut himself off from the world before his illness started to affect him, at the moment when he had lost his wife.

"As for man, his days are like grass: it flourishes in morning, is cut down in the evening, and withers. The flower of my days is pain and vanity; the flower falls away and we are gone."

The large church door opened with an inevitable noise. For a moment the daylight exploded into the dark interior, and to Anna it seemed almost like it was a dream—her father's death, and his farewell. Daniel came in—he had probably rushed there, since he had just come back from London—and he silently closed the door behind himself.

"That which you sow does not come to life unless it first dies . . ."

And what about your seeds, Daddy? Your tomatoes, your strawberries? wondered Anna, and a sorrowful awareness made its way into her heart: *I will never again eat anything so good.*

"O death, where is your sting? O hell, where is your victory?"

The journey was long that took them from the church to the cemetery. They finally arrived, and the place was green and wooded, the day was warm, and the countryside was singing. They found themselves in front of the open grave, which awaited the remains of their father.

"Man is born and he comes forth like a flower; like a passing shadow, he quickly disappears."

Anna took a handful of earth and threw it onto the coffin. Anthony did the same, as did Dennis, Grace, and Nora. *You should have done this, too, Christopher.* Anna painfully considered Christopher's absence as a last insult to her father, even now that he was dead, even now that he was far from all that misery, even now that he could not feel. *Oh, Daddy, you deserved to be loved more.* The grave was filled up. Her father's life became just a memory.

"We consign this body to the earth. Earth to earth, ashes to ashes, dust to dust."

***

"Good, Davenport," said Leopold, putting his signature on the contract. "I'm very happy, you know. I believe that you just solved all of my financial problems."

Christopher smiled, and the image of a vegetable garden in the sun came to his mind.

***

Daniel walked up to her with the desolate shyness that comes over one's spirit when witnessing an irrevocable pain. Shy, helpless, and, perhaps underneath, angered for what cannot be changed.

"Anna," he said in a low voice, "my deepest condolences."

Anna smiled at him and put her handkerchief to her eyes. "Thank you, Daniel."

"How are you?"

She grimaced. "So-so."

Daniel's face twitched, and the anger in his eyes became more intense. "Anna, if I knew what to say, to alleviate . . ." he murmured. Words. Words to cover the seas with a handkerchief. Words that did very little good. "If you need anything—for you or your loved ones—know that you can always turn to me."

She nodded, but from far away. Too much pain was confusing her mind.

"I received a message from your husband upon returning from my trip, Anna," he added hesitantly, looking around.

He's not here, Daniel. Christopher didn't come. But no words came out of her mouth; she was too feeble to say them.

"It seems he wants to talk to me about something," he said.

Yes, you'll have to become the guardian for my siblings and for Anthony's inheritance. But she was exhausted, worn out by the sleepless nights and the pain. How could she face such a discussion? "I'm aware of it, Daniel. But let him speak to you about it," she replied in a weak whisper.

He looked down. "I mentioned it only to keep you in the know, Anna," he murmured. "Excuse me, I was tactless."

"No, you were very sweet, as always. It's just that now I am so tired," she whispered. However, she would have to overcome this fatigue, wouldn't she? She would have to ask him to meet—the next day at the latest—to reveal her suspicions to him. On the contrary, she needed to mention something right away, at this moment, even if she was in tears; even if she could barely stand up. An obscure danger threatened this young man. She didn't know when, and she didn't know where—sometimes she wondered even if—but it was her duty, her inescapable duty, to warn him. "Daniel . . ." she began. But an annoying pain kept her from continuing. A pain in her eyes and in her voice.

"What is it?"

Christopher could be your brother.

She breathed deeply and slowly.

He wants revenge on your family.

She clenched her fists and opened her mouth to speak.

You must be careful, Daniel.

"Nothing. Nothing, Daniel."

(Why, Anna?)

The young man standing in front of her—this man who was so wholesome, loyal, congenial, and straightforward—didn't ask her anything else as he suffered for her.

(Why, Anna? Why?)

Of all the truths told, the most distressing are those we discover about ourselves. And Anna, who was upset, understood that. *I hate you, Christopher, but I cannot betray your secret.* This confession left her as bewildered as a child who has lost her way home, and she looked down at her handkerchief. She let out high-pitched sobs that were cowardly and despicable.

Daniel bit his lip and put his hand up to his eyes. He closed them. "Anna . . ." he murmured.

Lucy saw her in despair and raced to her side, embracing her with her irreproachable kindness. "Let it out. Go ahead, let it out," she whispered. And she cried with her, sharing her pain, since she could not make the pain go away. "Let it out . . . Let it go, Anna."

Oh, dear friend; my sweet, sweet friend, she wanted to tell her. *Don't let yourself be contaminated by my rottenness. Don't pity me.* She was facing a terrible ordeal, and she felt overwhelmed: she could see it for what it was, and there was no possible excuse. She raised her head from Lucy's warm chest. Next to them was Daniel—sorrowful, faithful, and undeserving of the backstabbing that she was giving him. Anna, a wolf in sheep's clothing, was choosing to bring down the hand of betrayal on him. *Daniel, please forgive me.* But forgiveness was impossible, and she knew it. She knew it, although she could not do anything else. *I love him, Daniel. I love Christopher. And my soul will burn with his in the end.*

39

Vengeance has no foresight.
—Napoléon Bonaparte

The daylight was still bright, but the red of the sunset covered the whole sky, hiding the blue. Christopher turned toward the room, stopping to look out the window. He had to meet Leopold for his last enjoyable evening—or so his father thought.

In actuality he was about to die.

It's our last evening as father and son, Daddy, he thought. But he wasn't mocking, no. Rather, he was quite solemn. He would not kill him without feeling the importance of this gesture in every moment. I will not laugh, Leopold. Death has its own dignity, even for the likes of you.

Christopher knew that the moment had come, because that morning he had received a note saying, *"Pyramid collapsed. Bob."*

Matthew had rushed to London to help Robert disappear. The news of financial disaster had not yet reached Leopold, of course. Christopher would tell him shortly, and then, finally, he would kill him.

(Hanging, Christopher. You're about to hang him.)

He had planned everything—the place, the method, the words. And when everything was over, he would hang his corpse in a tree on the grounds of Riverstone. With a suicide note if he could convince his father to write one; otherwise, nothing. After all, the reasons for suicide would end up being all too clear after the investigation. "A scam, sir," Christopher would testify before the magistrate. "He was the victim of a scam. In London they were involved in several; maybe you heard of it. I got out just in time, and I advised Mr. DeMercy, but . . ." A contrite sigh, a dark face. Then after a pause: "I can't manage to find peace now. If only I had known . . . when I gave him the news that night . . . but you must believe me. He didn't seem at all upset. He laughed, made a show of being calm . . ."

And even if false, in some absurd way these words would be sincere, because Leopold, had he been able to choose his fate, would have laughed in exactly that way, and he would have pretended to be that calm as he saw things collapse around him. And inevitably he would have killed himself, too. After having spent countless hours with him, and having countless conversations with him, Christopher had no doubt about that.

(Because his eyes look so damned much like Fortescue's, don't they, Christopher?)

Yes, Leopold was a worm, it was true, but he would not accept to crawl. It was a pity, because Christopher's original plan involved letting him suffer for weeks, even months, before killing him. Naturally, these were the pleasant fantasies that had lulled him over the years: moving to Riverstone as soon as it became his; enjoying the sight of his father pleading and lacking all dignity; seeing him beg for help from everyone, even Christopher—*especially* him.

Fantasies.

Reality had compelled him to a much more hurried choice. After throwing his failure in his face—*"Do you see, Dad? The son of Martha*

Askey took everything that was yours. Do you remember Martha, Dad?"—he would kill him, and immediately. Because Leopold would not commit suicide. Oh, the feces would soil his clothes, and his face would be swollen in the same way and in the same squalor as Martha faced, but it would be worse for Leopold. Because he wouldn't have chosen where, when, and how by himself. Oh no. And Christopher would be there to watch him die. And to explain to him why.

He looked at his pocket watch: it was time. He felt calm, almost serene. He was about to finish everything, finally. He would stop in Coxton until things calmed down, and then he would bid adieu to this hell forever. There wasn't much there left for him to do: he had already rushed through the most boring tasks, like transferring legal authority for the Champion heirs to Daniel. And when he had met with his stepbrother the afternoon prior, Christopher could not help but wonder how this dandy would manage once he was left without money, without property, and without a house to live in with that scarecrow mother of his. And without a father, of course.

Matthew, however, would give him a hand. And Anna, obviously. And even he, Christopher. Yes, damn it, even he. Because he wouldn't demand repayment of Leopold's debts from his brother. He would not sink him—not quite—even if the temptation was strong.

"You owe me, DeMercy," he had reminded him. "I have not asked you for anything since I beat you two weeks ago. You will sign. And we'll be even."

Daniel put a hand to his forehead, struggling. His brother was so scrupulous, so damned loyal, even when he was only one step away from getting what he wanted—from getting Anna. He had finally answered "All right, Davenport," and his voiced sounded neither triumphant nor gloating. "If, as you say, your wife also agrees."

Oh yes, she did "agree." Not his wife anymore. Perhaps she had never been his wife. Christopher didn't respond. In silence, they had provided all the necessary signatures. The lawyer with rat eyes in the corner was so silent that they could hardly hear him.

"Now you know where the door is, DeMercy."

Daniel didn't move. He stopped in front of the desk, and he held out his hand. *Here it is,* Christopher had thought. The inevitable, sickening outstretched hand. He didn't shake it, and Daniel finally turned and left.

(He will make her happy, Christopher.)

You will make her happy, Daniel.

As far as he was concerned, he had already decided his next destination. With a little bit of money in his pocket and a new identity, he would move to Manchester to start off. Then maybe to America. He would fake his own death with some corpse that he would get off the street—he would only have to spread the word among the beggars. How many people died and no one knew who they were? Brutalized, abandoned, forgotten, and practically nonexistent corpses? The fate of men who lived on their own; perhaps ironically, it would be his fate as well in the end.

He prepared to leave. He took the documents for the pyramid and his mother's letters. He opened the drawer and took out the pistol; then he put his overcoat on to protect him from the damp night, and he went out to the stables.

Joseph greeted him when he saw him coming near his domain. "You're going out at this time of night, sir? Soon it will be dark. Should I call Garret for the carriage?"

"No. I'll take the phaeton and I'll lead it myself, Joseph."

"I'll have it for you in the blink of an eye, then."

Christopher nodded and went into the stables. Basil raised his muzzle to greet him, and Christopher stroked him. "You won't be coming with me this evening," he said. "But it won't be the same without you."

"It's ready, sir," Joseph informed him after a few minutes. "The lamp is full, even if . . . even if it won't light the road up much." He paused, frowning. Like everyone at sixteen, he vaguely resembled a raisin when he thought things over. "But tonight the moon's almost full, isn't it? It will seem like daylight."

"Yes, good. Thanks, Joseph."

He took his place in the phaeton and spurred the white and brown bay—unnamed—toward Riverstone Manor. He stopped not far away, on a small hill that for the last two months had given him a view of the dwelling he hated so much. He took in the view again that night, then drove off and quickly arrived there. While he was entrusting his carriage to a servant, he considered the house as if for the first time. He looked at the garden. The front door. The long corridors, the shiny floors, the decorations, the paintings. He wanted to remember every detail of that day. He had been waiting for twenty years.

"Davenport," Leopold greeted him when he was shown into his office. He got up and met him. "Do you want something to drink?"

He looked carefully at his father. His hair, his features. His eyes, which resembled his most.

(He's about to die, Christopher.)

"No, thank you, sir," he replied. "In fact, I'm in a bit of a hurry. I stopped by to tell you that unfortunately this evening I won't be able to keep you company. Something has come up that . . ." He bit his lower lip, looking over at his father with a look of regret. "I don't have permission to talk about this with you, but . . ." He hesitated again, and again looked at him sideways, then said, "This could be of interest to you as well, DeMercy."

Quiet and calm. But on the inside there was a fire. *He must say yes. He must.*

"Ah, something secret? Gambling, Davenport?" His father gave an amused grin that chipped away at his heart one last time. "I hope not for you. As inept as you are, you would lose everything."

Christopher laughed—tensely but with enthusiasm—for the first time. "No, fortunately it's not gambling. As I told you, it's something . . . private. Oh, to hell with it! You have been so understanding with me. When I arrived in this town, you introduced me to the place that otherwise I could have only dreamed of—and just once I would like to repay you the favor."

"You've piqued my curiosity a great deal! Spit it out, Davenport."

"Listen, this is the first time that I'm participating, and so I'm not sure what to expect. Have you ever heard of the Hellfire Club?"

His father's eyes glowed with envy and surprise. "Of course. Who hasn't heard of it? But it hasn't been there for a long time."

"That's true, but some friends of mine have used it as an inspiration, and tonight they're putting on . . . let's call it a special kind of entertainment . . . a few miles from here."

"A secret meeting that's very special, you say?"

"Quite. I missed the first meeting that they had in London, damn it, and from what they told me, missing it was a mistake on my part. A very big mistake. It seems that they do . . . special things. And they never do the same things twice—that's one of the rules of the club."

"It sounds very stimulating."

Oh, it is. You'll see. "It is," he confirmed. "The only problem . . ." He gave him a doubtful look. "The only problem is the secrecy. My friends don't want to risk being seen by people who aren't trustworthy, because . . . because sometimes things can get out of hand, as they say. We are men, after all, and we're hot-blooded—isn't that what you always say? And no one would want witnesses if someone . . . if some woman . . . complained or got hurt."

Leopold narrowed his eyes and looked at him with the attention of someone who knew what he was talking about. "I understand."

(It's almost over, Christopher.)

"I took the phaeton," he said. "If you'll come with me, I'll lead it myself. It's bright out tonight, and I shouldn't have any problems finding the road. I'm not worried about the way back," he said, smiling to his father with the look of an accomplice before a robbery, "because it will already be the crack of dawn by then."

"You said that it would be unique entertainment, Davenport."

Unique. "So it seems," he replied. "If you don't see it, I'll have to report back to you on whether or not it was worth it, sir."

"It's intriguing, damn it, even if it will be nothing new for me, I imagine." He scratched his nose, a habit of his when he was particularly excited, Christopher had noticed. "You don't have much experience in these types of things—not yet, at least—but me, Christopher . . . Oh, sorry." He paused as a smile spread across his face. "I used your first name. I hope you're not offended. You're so much younger than me that it came out spontaneously."

A moment of silence and of confused bewilderment. And then a different emotion, too: pain. "Davenport" didn't belong to him, but "Christopher" was his name—his fucking name—and he didn't want his father to use it. He didn't want it, damn it.

"You can call me whatever you'd like, DeMercy." *And say yes. Come with me, Dad.*

"Thank you, Christopher." He looked at him with kindness. Or with what could be considered kindness for him, meaning he was probably more patronizing than kind. "It seems to me that you are very impatient to get to tonight's entertainment, or am I wrong? It's obvious that you must be feeling very lonely now that you and your wife . . . are living apart."

(You see how he enjoys himself? Go ahead, Christopher. Make him have more fun.)

Whether this surprised or irritated Christopher, it made no sense. It was common knowledge in town, and his father could not have avoided bringing up these troubles, not even if he wanted to. It was an essential part of his nature, after all. "I don't deny it, sir."

Leopold went to the liquor table and filled up two glasses with whisky.

"Thank you, sir, but . . ." Christopher said, trying to stop him.

"Come on, you don't want me to drink alone."

"No, of course not."

(Only a sip, Christopher. Then when this is over, you can drink an entire bottle. Two. One hundred.)

His father approached him, holding out the glass. Christopher accepted it with a smile and barely wet his lips with it. The liquor excited him.

"I would like to toast to you, Christopher." Leopold raised his glass. "And now that I think of it, going with you this evening could be the best way to celebrate the profits that you've made for me."

That's it. That's the only way, Dad. Tell me yes. "The profits you're about to make," he corrected him mechanically.

"No." Leopold gave him a gentle smile. "The profit that I made. Just this afternoon."

Christopher said nothing. Nothing. Nor did he waver, but his heart . . . Ah, his heart. *Hadn't his heart already figured it out?*

"Didn't your cousin come back from London?" Leopold asked.

Even his blood raced madly, but to no end—there was no way out, no possible hope.

"Didn't he tell you anything?" Leopold laughed. "He's nice, that friend of yours. Robert Barrett."

Christopher continued to look at Leopold without speaking. His vision had become blurry from the pressure that he felt in his temples, or maybe from the collapse of an illusion that had lasted a lifetime. The collapse of the only truly important thing.

He blinked. The world around him came back into focus.

Leopold took a sip of whisky. "You're not saying anything, Christopher, my boy. Usually you are so ready to endorse any statement of mine."

Silence.

"No?" Leopold smiled mockingly. "All right, that means that I will do the talking, then." He sat on the edge of the desk, stretching his legs out in front of him, relaxed. Such a casual pose; so sure of himself. So typical of Christopher. "Your friend was very happy when I contacted him a few weeks ago to explain to him that he could get much more out of a deal with me compared to what you had promised him."

. . . get much more compared to . . .

The words danced in Christopher's mind, and the meaning escaped him. In his mouth he seemed to sense a sweet taste, like almonds and caramel—the sweet, unforgettable taste of betrayal. Was he really surprised? Years ago, hadn't a girl said to him, "You're such a good little boy" and given him a kiss on the forehead—and then sold him to Bernard Jones?

"It's likely that your cousin hasn't found Barrett in London, Christopher. It's indeed certain, unless Bobby could manage to be in two places at once—which I doubt, considering that he's such an insignificant little man that he's barely able to be in one. He was here in person this afternoon to cash in a few new shares."

Christopher emptied his glass and felt the alcohol burning his throat like the pain that burned his guts. He walked up to the table and put down the glass, then went halfway back across the room.

"They wanted to invest a lot today," said the smooth voice coming from his father's lips, which arched into the smile of someone who has won. "Your friend Gutman, for example. And a dozen small local farmers who jumped at the chance to invest in your . . . What do you call it, Christopher? 'Pyramid'?" His face looked angelic in spite of everything. A perfect deception of nature. *You had no hope, Mummy. Not with this man.*

"Maybe I forgot to inform you of these new members," Leopold continued, "but I hope that I haven't offended you. You should be happy, you know. The laws on fences have greatly reduced the numbers of small farmers—even if they made me most of my fortune—and those few remaining have countless problems getting by. For them this deal represented a ray of light in the very darkest of days." He gulped down his glass in one draft and placed it on the desk. "Yes," he continued in a tone of regret, "it's a pity that tomorrow they will all wake up with nothing in their hands. I believe that this friend of yours is a scoundrel, Christopher, and he probably will make off with all of their money tonight. For me, however, I've been paid back everything that I invested, including the profit that I expected—indeed, with even a little something extra, I'll tell you. Isn't that great for you, too? If I'm not mistaken, you're one of my biggest creditors. Just think: now I will be able to pay you back for everything that I owe you, and much sooner than expected."

For several long moments the only sound in the room was the ticking of the clock.

Tick, tock, tick.

(Do you hear it, Christopher? That's all you have to say?)

Tock.

Then Leopold's voice again filled the room. "You don't seem very happy to me, Christopher, my boy." His father had the soul of a comic actor, a real natural disposition. "You're worried about these farmers? You shouldn't be. They were happy—at least for today. And what's a moment of joy worth, even if it will be swept away by a rude awakening?" He laughed, shaking his head. "My God, I'm becoming like my idiotic son, aren't I? A bloody poet." He paused, looking at him with half-closed eyes. "I see you still have nothing to say, Christopher. Well, allow me to go on, then, and don't be afraid to interrupt me if I become too emotional."

Christopher held his head high, and he fixed his eyes on his father's, ignoring his dangerously shaky legs.

He had to think—and quickly.

"Do you know the funny thing? For me, the failure of these farmers is even better than the profit I made." He paused to emphasize the words he was about to say. "I didn't pick them by chance—not all of them, at least. I particularly picked the ones who bordered my lands. Some of them asked me for a loan to participate in the pyramid. Isn't that amusing? Now, with just a few coins I will own their possessions." An irrepressible triumph showed in his smile. "As I mentioned to you a few days ago, I am very happy that you moved here, Davenport. I would have probably been ruined without you."

Slowly Christopher put his hand inside his overcoat, which he had not taken off at the entrance. He drew out his pistol and pointed it at his father. Stepping backward, he went to the door.

He locked it.

Leopold did not seem impressed. His pupils didn't widen, and his face didn't flash with terror. Christopher had pointed a pistol many times at other people, and he expected a different reaction than the one his father was giving him.

(But he's not like "other people," is he? He's your father.)

"Was this the special entertainment you had prepared for me, Christopher?"

Christopher's damned mouth. He couldn't manage to smile. Then, in a parody of a smile, his lips defied gravity and curved up. "Yes, essentially that's it," he replied calmly. "If we don't want to split hairs, like poets do."

"This hatred you have for me is quite flattering, I must admit. But not even Barrett knew the reason. Would you be so kind as to explain it to me before killing me?"

"No." It was true. He didn't want to explain anything anymore—no bombastic sentences, no epitaph. No good-bye. He was tired, and he just wanted to murder him. Immediately. With this pistol. It was hardly poetic, but that didn't matter. Neither did it matter that no one would think it was a suicide. He would have to flee that very night, and now, after the deed was done, there would be nothing to keep him here. He looked out the open window of the ground-floor office: he just had to get out of Riverstone Manor alive, and in Coxton they would never hear from him again.

"Don't you think that I could scream?"

"Go ahead." He raised the pistol with a steady hand. "I will kill you before anyone can come."

"They will arrest you."

"I don't care."

Leopold sighed, as if annoyed. Then he stood up and stepped away from the desk.

"Don't move, DeMercy," Christopher ordered him.

Leopold paid no attention to him and walked to the liquor table with his back to him. "Oh, I'm sure you'll let me drink something before killing me." He poured a couple of fingers of whisky into a glass. He was in no hurry. The sound of the liquor falling into the glass seemed like it would never end. Then he turned toward him. "Isn't that so, Christopher . . . my son?"

(Isn't that so, Christopher?)

He couldn't answer, because for several moments his mind went completely blank. He tried to collect his thoughts—but only *one* thought, just one, came back obsessively again and again: *He knows. He has always known.*

40

All happy families resemble one another; each unhappy family is unhappy in its own way.

—Leo Tolstoy

Leopold smiled, and Christopher was sure he would never forget the sweetness of that smile. "Did you really think that I didn't know, son? I hoped that at least you had gotten a bit of my intelligence."

"How long?" he managed to ask him, in a voice that was steady, all things considered. "For how long?"

"Oh, for many years," his father responded. There was amusement in his voice and endearing irony. And frighteningly, beneath that was pride. He was proud of Christopher. "I followed your entire rise, in truth. And I must admit, it seems that one of my children isn't a weakling, after all." Leopold took a sip from his glass. He was not joking now: his compliments were sincere. Fearfully sincere. "You've come a long way, and you haven't been afraid to get your hands dirty. Bravo. Of course, on a couple of occasions I helped you—that time when they were almost about to arrest you. Do you remember? In that gambling house—but greasing the right wheels saved your arse. You really should thank me."

"Yes, I should thank *you*." In spite of it all, Christopher laughed, because his father had a damned good sense of humor. "If you know who I am, you know why you're about to die."

"You want to avenge your mother, don't you? Martha Askey. That whore."

(That whore, Christopher. Your mother.)

Leopold was obviously hoping to be murdered. Maybe he was tired of living, Christopher thought. Maybe waking up every day in this existence had worn him out in the long run. Who could blame him? In any case, he would soon find relief. Christopher took the gun and pointed it at his heart without shaking. "Exactly."

"You know, son, I don't understand why you are going to so much trouble for her. She was only a bitch."

Christopher said nothing, and he was amazed that he felt no anger come over him. He kept looking at Leopold, examining his fine clothing, his determined posture, his icy green eyes shining brightly.

Leopold took a step toward him, and there were only a few feet between them. "Do you want to acknowledge your mother like she deserves to be, Christopher?" he asked with an amiable smile. And he took another step closer. "You must know that even she had her good qualities, in her own way. For example, when she took me all in her mouth, I could see paradise. She sucked me like she was swallowing my soul." He had a dreamy look on his face, as if reliving the memory. "Really, my son, you should be proud. And when I put it up her arse . . . Oh God, how she loved it when I put it up her arse. She enjoyed it so much that I had to cover her mouth to keep her from screaming too loudly."

Christopher smiled. "You want to die, then."

"It doesn't matter what I want, Christopher, my son." He took another step closer. The pistol was touching his jacket, directly over his heart. Fascinated, Christopher stared into his eyes. The eyes of a man who was about to die. "You've come this far. You've chased me all these years. Kill me now."

Christopher realized his father would die with a smile on his lips. And it didn't surprise him at all; perhaps he had always known that this would be his last memory of him. "As you wish, Dad," he responded. And yet he stood motionless, with his arm raised.

"Come on. Don't you want to avenge the memory of that whore you had for a mother?"

(Shoot, Christopher. Shoot at that smile.)

Yes. And finally I will be free. But he didn't shoot, not yet; he kept his finger on the trigger and waited some more.

"Your mother never stopped loving me. Do you know that?" His father's tone was lighthearted, as if he were talking amongst friends. "Not even after I dumped her, after I used her all I wanted." He laughed, and his face was so close to Christopher's that he could smell the whisky on his breath. "Are you wondering why I'm so sure?"

(Why is he so sure, Christopher?)

"It's because I saw her again, son, a few years after, and she was still madly, ridiculously in love with me. Ah, your mother was an idiot, let me tell you."

Christopher didn't speak. He didn't ask. But his internal organs were completely shuffled around, like he had been thrown from a speeding carriage.

"You really didn't know, my son?"

Silence.

"No, I guess you didn't know." Leopold smiled in anticipation. "But I think you can imagine where I met her." Yes. He could. But he didn't answer. His hand held the pistol steady. He was motionless and stopped breathing. Leopold continued calmly: "In that Covent Garden brothel, son, that very same one. You remember it, don't you? A rather quaint spot, before you set fire to it. You were quite a sentimental fool on that occasion, Christopher, and excuse me if I point it out to you." A good-natured rebuke, with the indulgence of maturity toward youth—or the indulgence of a father for his own son. "Anyway, one day I went by there to empty my balls a bit, and who do I find there? Your mother. I recognized her immediately, even if she was worn down by all the men who had fucked her over the years." Leopold's tone was absolutely calm, as if there wasn't a pistol pointing at his heart; as if he wasn't deliberately provoking the person wielding that pistol. "I didn't want to be rude, and I chose her that night."

(Really, Christopher? Do you really want to know?)

"But I wanted to make our encounter a bit more . . . you know . . . lively. Shall I tell you how?"

Christopher's eyes were accustomed to his father's office. He had been there often in the last two months. He could remember every word he had told him, every smile. But now he felt as if he wasn't there. No, he was back in that room with the ochre and beige wallpaper.

"I had her, along with some friends who were with me."

A room that Christopher had seen many years before. He had awakened in a bed in that room, and there was a girl with a feather. A feather . . .

"Don't look at me like that, Christopher. I didn't do much that night. I mostly just observed the other two, who were taking turns with her, and I gave them a few suggestions."

The flower on her dress rocked along with her body.

"It was quite fun, son. But not for your mother, I think. She cried the whole time."

(Not for your mother, Christopher.)

"I truly enjoyed that evening so much." His father smiled, and again that sweetness . . . Ah, that sweetness. "So much so that two days later I went back to look for her, because I wanted, you know, an encore. But when I asked for her, they told me that she didn't work there anymore, and no one could explain to me how to find her." He narrowed his eyes, looked at him, and tried to read his thoughts. A naked child in front of his father. "But whores don't stop working, do they, my son? What happened to her?"

(What happened to her, Christopher?)

"Did she die?"

He said nothing. His grip tightened on the pistol. He shoved the barrel as deep as he could into his father's chest.

"Let me guess . . . she committed suicide."

(Do you remember what happened to your mother, Christopher?)

He didn't react at all. He didn't even blink. He wouldn't have moved a muscle even if the entire earth began to shake. And yet Leopold nodded, as if he had responded. "But of course," he murmured. "I imagined so. After all, she always was a failure."

Christopher cleared his throat, and this simple act seemed the most difficult of his whole life. Perhaps it was. "I would say that we've really said it all . . . *Dad*," he stated, lifeless and exhausted but finally determined to end this story. "Now I will kill you."

He stared into Leopold's eyes, and they drew imperceptibly closer. The barrel of the pistol pressed deeper into his flesh.

"Go on, shoot, son."

Christopher swallowed saliva from his empty mouth, as dry and rough as the ground in August. He thought again about his mother, who hadn't even been Leopold's second love, but the thousandth, or the millionth. His mother—she was nothing in the eyes of the world.

"Come on, boy. You don't want to wait, do you?"

Christopher's hand trembled, and he looked at it as if it didn't belong to him. *Mother, my mother, my hurt mother, my killed mother, I'm going to get revenge for you.*

"Pull the trigger, you son of a whore."

This man didn't look down. He and he alone had annihilated and killed Christopher's mother. When she climbed up on that chair and put her head in that noose, Martha knew that no one would miss her; she knew no one would avenge her. *But you were wrong, Mummy.* Christopher bit down hard on his lip to distract himself from the pain stabbing him in the chest, the stomach, the head, and in every fiber of his being. *You wanted to take me away with you, but my life will be useful for something in the end.*

"Shoot, my son. Avenge your mother."

Yes, it was time. Killing him was right. What was more, it was necessary. "Spring is coming, ducky," Martha had said to him a few days before committing suicide. "Things will be better in no time."

He prepared to fire. His father's eyes hadn't flinched, nor had his chest heaved. He stood still and attentive with this slight smile on his face, incomprehensible and distant.

Christopher closed his eyes, exhaled softly, and slowly moved his finger on the trigger. He touched it, feeling the cold metal under his finger. There it was, ready, and justice had waited for so many years—too many years. His mother had been thrown into the river to rot in a tomb without a name, massacred in life and in death. He could not kill her a second time: he had to shoot.

A cold sweat broke out on his forehead and on his skin. Leopold was silent. In his eyes there was the inexplicable glow that had killed Martha.

(You must do this, Christopher.)

He loosened his grip on the weapon, and his arm seemed very heavy. What was he doing? Why wasn't he pulling the fucking trigger?

My God.

His heart was beating madly, but why? And his finger—justice—had less and less strength.

My God.

Sweat in his eyes, cold on his skin. And in his heart, and in his breathing. And his slippery emotions, eroding and aggressive, coursing through his blood—the blood of a son of a whore.

(Shoot, Christopher. Shoot. Shoot! *Shoot!*)

I can't do it.

He was still looking at his father, and his father was still looking at him. And he admitted silently that he couldn't shoot this man. He was desperate, but more than anything he was astonished—astonished by finding a monster under his bed. He didn't believe it; then he encountered it. He felt fear, of course, and anguish. But most of all, astonishment, because this monster existed and he had caught up to him.

I can't do it.

Four little words, so short they barely even existed. And yet here they were—wasn't that funny?—four little words and it was all over.

Forgive me, Mummy.

He lowered his arm. Heavy, devoid of anger and life. With its useless weight, his hand fell to his side without making a sound, and the pistol was heavy in his hand. His shoulders collapsed. He became shorter, more slender, smaller than he had felt for decades.

(Rest, Christopher. It's over now.)

He bowed his head, and a wet heat filled his eyes. He didn't realize it immediately, not even when the tears started to roll down his cheeks. Still, it was an unforgettable rite, although it had almost been forgotten by him. An ancient and eternal rite.

A minute went by, then two.

Then Leopold put his hand on Christopher's head, and he pulled him closer. Their temples touched. "Did you think it would be easy, my son?" he asked him in a gentle whisper. "Did you think it would be easy to look a man in the face and kill him?" His fingers moved lightly on Christopher's lowered head with the hint of a caress that a father gives a five-year-old child.

Christopher did not answer, and he put his hand up to his eyes. The pistol fell out of his other hand, landing with a thud on the carpet of the office floor. He cried without making a sound.

A few moments later Leopold finally removed his hand and took a step back. "Well," he said without emotion. In his voice there was only coldness now. The game was over once and for all. "If there's nothing else, Christopher, I have a few things to do now." He turned away from him and went to the door. His steps had the calm gait of victory. He turned the key calmly and opened the door. His footsteps faded as his walked farther away from him down the empty hallway.

Christopher didn't look up. For the first time in many years his eyes burned with invasive tears, which rolled down his face and caressed his skin. It took him back to the inevitable moment he dreaded the most.

The moment when he had to face himself.

He held his hand over his eyes, sobbing and sucking air down to the depths of his soul. The seconds ticked away on the clock in the office—it hadn't stopped; nothing around him had stopped—but Christopher wasn't able to move, suspended in time that seemed never ending.

Oh, Mummy. I should have died then. He lifted his face up to the sky—to the ceiling—in a pose that was typical for him on sunny days, when the rays of sunshine made him feel strong. Now only tears came down slowly, and they wet his skin, his neck, his neck scarf. *You were right, Mummy. You were always right. And today . . . today I killed you . . . once again.*

He wiped his face with his hand, rubbing the back of it against his nose, like the child in him who had returned. How many minutes had gone by? Ten? One hundred? But what did that matter to him now? There was no longer any hurry, no longer any goal. He looked around and looked at that office so similar to his own, down to the smell—a mixture of alcohol, ink, and old documents, and maybe even the vague scent of a pipe. The pistol was at his feet, but he did not pick it up. He raised his hands and stared at his palms. Still astonished, still disbelieving. Those hands of his weren't shaking, but even they had betrayed him.

He lowered his head. Bending down, he headed for the door. He went out down the long hallways and found himself outside, almost in a dream, and then sat in his carriage, without even knowing how he had gotten in. He moved the reins and the horse took off, carrying his soul like a pathetic Charon. He couldn't feel his hands, his feet, his arms, his legs. His senses were no longer his own. The shock to his body was physical before it was mental, and his irregular breathing put him into a stupor as his heart pumped a steady flow of unreasonable, mad blood.

In his agitated state, he did not calm down immediately, but only very slowly, little by little, in the fresh evening air. He went down the deserted roads without recognizing them, back and forth, in a circle, without logic. He would have liked to have had Basil with him; he would have liked to gallop under the moon, clutching on to Basil, racing against the night—and losing perhaps, but with him.

Now what?

The moonlight gave the world a cold, gloomy paleness, and the distant sounds were incomprehensible and unfamiliar. A child would have been frightened and would have searched for a place to hide—a small, secret place where he could wait for the soothing light of day.

I will leave, as planned.

What a disaster he had created. Not only had he not killed his father but he had ruined most of the farmers in the area.

Patience. I certainly can't pay all of them back myself.

Could he?

Maybe so. Maybe I could pay them back, but not from here. I have to go away. If Matthew gets involved, and Daniel helps him, and I . . .

He realized he was on the way to the redbrick house. He was almost there—perhaps less than a half mile away.

It's only right, he told himself. *Anna deserves a farewell from me. Ironically, the only one to pay for my ridiculous vendetta was her.*

He passed by the haunted house and reached the lane with linden trees. He went up it slowly, stopping the carriage a little way off. It was very late; Anna and the children were surely sleeping.

He got out of the carriage and approached the house. Someone must be awake; there was a light in the kitchen window. He walked to the window, stopping to the side of it, resting his back against the wall like a thief or a child playing hide-and-seek. He peeked inside and his heart hurt.

His wife. It was his wife.

She was sitting at the table, leaning over a doll—the doll that he himself had broken, and he admitted that painfully. Anna was holding a pair of tweezers in her hand and she was carefully gluing back together the pieces that had fallen from that porcelain face. In a box on the table were the dissimilar fragments of what once was whole. The bulk of the work seemed finished; only the smallest pieces were left, and Anna assembled them with an affectionate precision. She was serious and careful, and she was muttering something while barely moving her lips. *She is talking to the doll,* Christopher understood, and a slight smile appeared on his lips.

41

Enjoy life with the wife whom you love, all the days of your vain life that He has given you under the sun, because that is your portion in life and in your toil at which you toil under the sun.

—Ecclesiastes

He walked back to the rear and entered the house through the window with the crooked lock. He didn't try to walk quietly while he went toward the kitchen; he made his footsteps deliberately heavy, booming in the house with everyone asleep. He wanted his wife to know what was coming.

From the hallway he saw the lit doorway, and he was drawn to it like a moth. He came into the light without stopping for even a moment; if he was going to get burned, he might as well get it over with.

"You'll never be able to get her back the way she was before, Anna," he said abruptly, pausing in the doorway.

She didn't look up from the doll on the table or respond. She was wearing black, her eyes tired, with dark circles around them. She seemed very beautiful to him.

He approached her, staying a few steps away.

Anna took another tiny piece of porcelain, but her hand was shaking. "Did you come to break her again, sir?" she asked softly.

Christopher walked up to her, stopping at her side. He looked at the doll, her glued fragments against one another forming faint lines on her lifeless face, like scars. "It's ruined and ugly, Anna," he pointed out harshly. "Throw it away."

"No."

Christopher looked at her sideways. "Don't tell me that you like it more now that it's imperfect?"

His wife was silent and didn't look up, but he knew the answer. "So that's it, is it?" He leaned his side against the table and sat on the edge. "You see? Maybe not everything I did was bad for you."

Anna sighed and lowered her tweezers without raising her head. "Maybe my memory isn't what it once was," she admitted, "but it seems to me you said I'd never see you again."

"Yes," he agreed, getting up. "That's so. I just came by to inform you of something."

He paused and looked again at the doll on the table—it wasn't so ugly, to tell the truth.

"What do you have to say to me, Christopher?"

He fidgeted. "I'm leaving, Anna."

No reaction from her, not even a tremor. "I understand."

"It's possible that I may have some financial problems in the coming months," he informed her. She didn't look at him. "But don't worry about it; I will continue to cover all the expenses for you and your family."

"Oh."

"Good." He swallowed saliva that seemed like dust in his throat. "Farewell, then."

"Farewell."

(It hurts to breathe, doesn't it, Christopher? But it's almost over now. Go. Forget.)

He walked to the door and soon would be gone, out of the life of this young woman who he was unable to destroy. And who, in the light of the full moon, had at least spared him this regret. He went to the doorway and put his left hand on the doorjamb.

"Anna . . ." He didn't turn toward her.

"What?"

One final good-bye, Anna. I only want to tell you farewell again.

"I love you, Anna."

There it was—an excellent ending to a spectacular day.

Why the hell would he say such a thing?

Because I love her, by God. I love her. Love. Knowing without turning around, as cowardly as a wretch, goddamn, fucking love. It was so clear now, so damned clear. He turned. Anna hadn't responded to his comment and instead was polishing the face of the stupid doll with a cloth.

Christopher had forgotten how insufferable his wife could be when she wanted. "Well, no response?" he asked her bitterly. "I wasn't expecting you to jump for joy or dance on the table, to tell the truth, but certainly at least an arrogant little sentence or a smug giggle. Don't you feel the slightest bit happy now?"

Silence.

"Doesn't it surprise you at all?" he insisted, irritated. "I thought you would be proud."

"Yes, it surprises me." Her distant and indifferent tone seemed to belie her words. "I was convinced that you would never resort to lying about that."

(She thinks you're lying, Christopher. Even though you're not—not this time, are you? But let her believe it, Christopher. Don't beg; don't hurt yourself anymore.)

He put his hand on his forehead and rubbed it slowly. "I'm not lying," he murmured.

His wife looked up toward him with a look of anguish and pain, and Christopher felt lost after not seeing her eyes for so long—ten days. He leaned his shoulder against the doorjamb, trying to hold himself up.

"No, really, you don't have to," she repeated, shaking her head and smiling faintly. A smile that she never had on her face before she had met him. "I won't go back to Daniel in any case, if that's what you're afraid of." She paused and looked back down. "Your vendetta is safe," she stated in a whisper.

"My . . . ?" Christopher felt the ground giving way under his feet. The floor was caving in and he could barely stand. *Good God in heaven, what exactly did Anna know? Not that . . .*

"I am not sure," she said. "But I believe you may be the son of Leopold, and Daniel's brother. Is that it?"

Christopher gasped for a moment. "You . . . ? But how?" If his wife knew that he was Daniel's brother, then . . .

"I'm right, then."

"How . . . how did you find out? Matthew . . ." *No, not even that. No.* He closed his eyes. "Matthew told you?"

"Oh, Christopher." Her voice was distressed but tired, as if she was resigned to expect the worst. "Don't you even trust your cousin? You should. No, he didn't tell me, obviously. I found the letters and the documents in your office."

"In my . . ." murmured Christopher. He had underestimated his wife, and greatly so. Or perhaps, he came to realize, he had overestimated himself. "In my office . . . but of course. That day, before the trip to London, when you disappeared for three hours in my house . . ." He paused. *What's it called, that thing that is born among the ruins? That flowers in the middle of a fire that lasts so long as there is life?* "You knew the truth, Anna, when you asked me to leave this house."

She ignored these words. "What happened to your mother, Christopher, to make you hate the DeMercy family so much? Tell me. I . . . I believe you owe me that."

He did owe that to her. "She died," he replied. Two words, inadequate and pale, but in the larger sense it was all there, right there. "My mother died because of Leopold DeMercy." He lowered his head, smiling. A bitter smile, of course, while he still heard the voice of his father inside his head. "She was a failure," he explained in that voice. "And so am I." He watched his wife, so far away from all that misery, so innocently dragged into the mud. "Anna, why didn't you tell Daniel what you had discovered?" he asked her softly as his heart again filled with stupid illusions.

His wife didn't answer or raise her head to look at him. Perhaps he hadn't said anything at all.

"Anna, I wasn't lying to you before. If you want to know, my vendetta no longer exists . . . and . . . I just failed. Miserably."

"Oh."

She isn't taking me seriously, damn it. "For once, when I'm humbling myself, it would be nice if you paid attention to me, by God." He left the doorway and walked to the table. He stood over her with his height. She kept her head bowed. *Oh damn it!* he thought. *To hell with it.* He got on his knees near her to be able to look her in the eyes. "And . . . Anna . . . what I did to you that afternoon . . ." he said hesitantly. "It was not premeditated, I swear."

"Stop it, Christopher." Her eyes darkened, and she jumped up suddenly, angry, making her chair fall over with a loud noise in the quiet house. She went to the window and stood with her back to him. "I never loved Daniel, and you are a fool," she snapped, exasperated and tired. In her voice there was no desire except the desire to rest—to stop fighting, and to rest. She turned toward him, her face tense. "You married me for that reason, but you should have known better. Be assured of this, however: Daniel will never have me. I don't love him. The day when you . . . you know . . . I had already rejected him. As I told you a while ago—it seems to me that you don't know how to listen, Christopher—our engagement barely lasted six hours."

Christopher was silent for a few minutes, unable to understand. *Six hours?* That was what everyone had been repeating—but he had not listened, in fact.

"You had already rejected him when I . . ." he repeated to himself. *Dear God. Anna wasn't engaged when I surprised her in the grass. Anna didn't love my brother. And I hurt her immensely when I could have attempted to gain entrance into her heart slowly and sweetly.* "Oh, Anna," he murmured. He walked a bit closer to her. But slowly. Hesitantly. *Don't run away, Anna. Please.* "Have I hurt you badly?"

She looked away. Christopher took another step closer. They were only a few feet apart. Anna didn't try to run from him.

His heart was beating wildly in his chest. "Anna, I . . . what I did to you . . ."

"To take me from your brother, I know."

"No, I think . . ." He paused. "Anna, I think that . . . maybe . . ." He forced air down in his lungs, but he couldn't keep his hands still at his sides. "I wanted you for myself, Anna. And that's why . . ." He stopped and nervously ran his hand through his hair. "I didn't want him to marry you, it's true, but it was not to get back at him." He admitted it for the first time, even to himself. "It's possible that I loved you even then."

He took another step toward her; they were now very close.

"It's possible, you say?" she asked him, her eyes lowered.

Christopher put a hand on her side. Anna did not push him away, provoking an emotion in him so strong that he was almost afraid of falling. But if he fell on her, it would be fine. "I loved you then," he clarified. "And I love you now."

Anna looked up just for a moment. *Are there possibly tears in those eyes of hers?* Christopher couldn't tell for sure because she lowered them quickly.

"It's not an excuse, you know," she whispered, and she sounded as wounded as she was two months before, in the grass.

Christopher cleared his throat and approached her a bit more. "I'm not asking you to forgive me, Anna. I'm asking you . . ." *I'm asking you to love me.* He paused, biting his lip. Their bodies were less than five inches apart, and he felt the warmth of his wife and smelled her scent. It was intoxicating. "And you, Anna?" he asked in a whisper. He put his other hand on her hip as well. "Is it possible that . . . that you feel some kind of, you know . . . love, maybe . . . for me?"

She kept her head down and didn't answer.

"If not love, then perhaps a warm friendship. I would be happy with even a light indifference, you know."

He put a finger on her mouth and realized she was faintly smiling. He embraced her, pulling her toward him, and he gave her a kiss on her head. What was that scent, he wondered? Bread, apples, and what else? He would figure it out sooner or later, he was sure of it. He leaned his face over to look at her sweet profile. "A moderate dislike?" he attempted again. "Or even an excessive hatred?"

Anna grinned. "Maybe," she murmured.

"An excessive hatred? Is that your answer?" He smiled as well, an annoying hoarseness settling in his throat. He kissed her lightly on the cheek. "That seems to me to be the perfect grounds for a marriage, wouldn't you say?"

Anna moved her head up and down once, very slowly.

"Was that a yes, then?" His voice cracked, and he cursed—a bit of dignity, by God! He held her close, pushing her against the wall. "Does that mean that I get to return here to this house with you?" he asked, moving his lips on her soft, warm cheek. On her soft, warm body.

"Yes."

He couldn't manage to look up, because for a few moments—a brief moment, which was worth all the years he had lived perhaps—he savored a new sensation, and it was too enormous, so big that it might hurt him.

"You can come back if you want."

If you want. Christopher raised his head and stared at her red, full mouth. Oh, he wanted to. And he wanted to kiss that mouth. And experience her taste, adore her, and devour her. He bowed his head down to meet hers. Anna turned her head to the side, denying him a kiss on the lips.

Oh God, no. With a groan he dropped his forehead to touch her face and closed his eyes. *Please don't reject me, my love.*

"You can come back, Chris," she repeated, and she ran her fingers through his hair, which was a bit too long, tousling it. "First, of course," she added in a whisper, "you will have to offer me your apology."

For several minutes Christopher said nothing, lulled by her gentle touch. "I've had a really, *really* bad day, Anna," he murmured finally. "Couldn't we let it go?"

She shook her head. "No, I'm sorry," she said sadly. She put her other hand up to his head, taking his hair in her closed fists. She gently raised his head until their eyes met. "But you shouldn't worry, Christopher," she whispered with a smile that was both loving and fierce at the same time. "There will be just a few words."

About the Author

Nina Pennacchi lives in a city near the sea. She enjoys walking on the beach and imagining stories of nineteenth-century England.

About the Translator

A native of Nebraska, Scott P. Sheridan holds an MA in modern languages from the University of Nebraska at Lincoln, and a PhD in French literature from the University of Iowa. While at the University of Iowa, he worked as a research assistant at the Translation Laboratory. In addition to being a scholar of nineteenth- and twentieth-century literature, he is a translator of both literary works and scholarly articles from French and Italian into English.

Sheridan is a professor of French and Italian at Illinois Wesleyan University in Bloomington, Illinois, where he has offered courses in French and Italian language, culture, and literature; world literature in English translation; Western humanities traditions; international studies; and women's and gender studies. He has led students on course outings to Chicago, as well as on travel courses to France, Italy, Canada, and the UK. Students have studied with him in museums such as the Musée D'Orsay in Paris, the Tate Britain in London, and the Uffizi Galleries in Florence. He has shared cultural experiences with them as varied as a *cabane à sucre* (sugar shack) in Québec, Canada, and the incredible Scrovegni Chapel in Padua, Italy.

Made in the USA
Middletown, DE
17 January 2024